Dear Reader,

This month we're delighted to welcome best selling author Patricia Wilson to the *Scarlet* list. With over 40 romance novels to her credit, we are sure that Patricia's new book will delight her existing fans and win her many new readers. You can also read *Resolutions*, the conclusion of Maxine Barry's enthralling 'All His Prey' duet. And we are proud to bring you books by two talented new authors: Judy Jackson who hails from Canada and Tiffany Bond who is based in England.

You will possibly have noticed that some of the *Scarlet* novels we publish are quite sexy, while others are warmer and more family oriented. Do you like this mix of styles and the different levels of sensuality? And how about locations: is it important to you *where* an author sets her *Scarlet* book?

If you have written to me about *Scarlet*, please accept my thanks. I read each and every one of your letters and I certainly refer to your comments and suggestions when I am thinking about our schedules.

Till next month,

Sally Cooper

SALLY COOPER,
Editor-in-Chief – *Scarlet*

PATRICIA WILSON

A DARK AND DANGEROUS MAN

Enquiries to:
Robinson Publishing Ltd
7 Kensington Church Court
London W8 4SP

First published in the UK by Scarlet, 1997

A copy of the British Library Cataloguing in
Publication data is available from the British Library

ISBN 1-85487-909-X

Printed and bound in the EC

10 9 8 7 6 5 4 3 2 1

CHAPTER 1

This was not the rugged, wild coastline that usually came to mind when Cornwall was mentioned. Here, there was rarely the sound of violent seas crashing onto rocks. This was a land of beautiful wooded creeks that ran to the shelter of a hundred small bays, a land of dreams and legends, blue water and glittering sunlight. The wild moorland seemed to be miles away from this soft paradise. The whole area was hidden, secret, stealthily welcoming, a sanctuary. But it was not like that today.

Kathryn stared out of the window at the swirling mist that had covered the coastline since early morning. It had swept in unexpectedly, seeping up from the bay like an invading army of furtive ghosts, creeping through the trees that clothed the sharp, falling sides of the wide creek, permeating the high bracken and turning the summer day into misty autumn.

She had been trapped inside all day, knowing that any venture outside to the top of the cliff would be a waste of time and energy. The light was poor and any self-respecting insect would be hidden. It had been a wasted day, and she hated to waste any day at all. There was so much to do, so much to catch up with. She had almost lost her life and she would never again waste time. Each day seemed to be a race to do more and she forced herself along without mercy.

She was under no pressure except for the pressure she put on herself, but she had taken a decision, committed herself to an attitude, and it was impossible to shake it off simply because the weather was uncooperative.

The frustration she felt at the eerie fog was all the more intense because she had no one at all to battle with. The light outside was fading in any case, and she would have been back at the cottage long before now, but even knowing that Kathryn still lingered at the window, watching the mist resentfully, a vague feeling of depression filling her when the night began to take over and the misty landscape began to give way to darkness. A lost day, just like the many days she had spent in hospital. It was inescapable but infuriating.

'Goodness, Kathryn! How much longer are you intending to stand there? Are you never going to leave that window and sit down?' Clare Holden bustled in with a laden tray and glanced across at her niece with wry amusement. 'I know I'm not supposed to mention it but you should be resting that leg every chance you get. Staring out of the window isn't going to drive the fog away. It comes and it goes. There's always tomorrow.'

Kathryn turned to look at her aunt, ruefully admitting that, at fifty, her Aunt Clare seemed to have about twice the energy she had herself at the moment. There was vitality in the springy white hair, vigour in the smooth rosiness of her cheeks. Everything that Clare Holden did was done with speed and efficiency. Sometimes it made Kathryn feel doubly tired, but in many ways it was an inspiration. Clare was wearing a blue skirt and blouse that did nothing to hide her figure, which was candidly plump. And she was wearing pearls; Clare always wore pearls like a trademark.

'It's frustration,' Kathryn murmured, her eyes turning back to the darkening landscape. 'I've been in here all day when I wanted to be out there. Yesterday I had those beetles exactly where I wanted them and today has been a write-off.'

'Well, I don't expect they'll have changed their place of abode by tomorrow. The sea fog doesn't last long at this time of the year. In any case, you could easily have brought some beetles back home in one of your little pots. You would still have had them then.'

'I can't leave them in pots. I want them lively, not stone dead with their feet up in the air. They have to perform naturally or they're quite useless to me.'

'Yuk! I really don't know how you can,' Clare muttered, setting out the things for high tea in her usual brisk manner. 'I don't care for creepy crawlies. All those legs. My natural inclination is to step on the horrid things.'

'That's the prejudice of fear. You don't see them as I do.' Kathryn glanced across as her aunt pulled a face.

'Who does, dear? To me they're hideous, although I suppose if I saw a beetle in a spotted waistcoat and a bowler hat it would give me pause.'

'Children see things like that.'

'They do when they've read your books and pored over the pictures,' Clare pointed out drily. 'Until they've been introduced to the gentle touch, children can be quite cruel, believe me. Come along now, Kathryn. Close the curtains and sit at the table. Give the weather best. It will probably be bright and hot again tomorrow, and you'll be out there again. You just have to expect this sort of day occasionally when you live in Cornwall.'

Kathryn reached up to shut the thick blue and white curtains her aunt favoured. She hated closing out the day, even when it was almost gone. It was admitting defeat.

She stopped with her hands on the drawstrings and stared, concentrating on the darkening landscape. There was a light – bright, strong and steady. It came from behind the woods across the creek, the private acres of high, tree-covered land that looked down on the bay. There was a house there, but it was always in darkness at night, almost hidden by trees during the day. Now there was a light, as if a small new world had suddenly sprung into being.

'There's a light at that old house.' Kathryn spoke without taking her eyes from it and Clare was immediately intrigued.

'Pengarron Manor? Is there really? I must see.' She rounded the table and came over quickly to stand

4

by Kathryn, her face filled with excited interest. 'You're right. There certainly is a light at Pengarron. So he's come back, then, has he? I never thought he would, not after what happened. I wonder why he's here? It's either to lick his wounds or to hide.' She turned away, shaking her head thoughtfully. 'No. He wouldn't hide. He doesn't give a damn what people think. He never did. I don't expect he's changed much as he's grown older.'

'Who?' Kathryn drew the curtains and followed her aunt to the table. Her leg was aching and she rubbed at it unconsciously. She always forgot about the leg until it forced itself to the top of her mind by aching badly or letting her down. 'It would help if I knew who you were talking about.'

'Jake Trelawny, dear. Obviously he must be back at the old manor if there's a light on at this time of night. It must be years since he was here last, except for that brief, unfortunate visit. I'd love to know why he's chosen to come back now, in view of what happened.'

As Kathryn had never heard of Jake Trelawny, and as she had never even seen the house except in the extreme distance, her interest waned. She watched with dismay as her aunt cut a large piece of quiche and handed in to her on a plate. She pushed the salad across too, and Kathryn wondered how much she could leave without a well-meaning lecture. She was not hungry. She had not been really hungry since she left hospital.

'Why should he be wanting to hide?'

5

Clare loved gossiping, and urging her on was one sure way to keep her aunt's mind off the fact that her beautifully prepared high tea was merely being nibbled at.

'Oh, I doubt if he's hiding,' Clare said in an earnest voice, selecting a hot roll and buttering it vigorously. 'In fact I'm sure he isn't. Jake Trelawny is tough, strong, fearless. He always was, even when he was a boy. He was wild as a gypsy. He would never hide; he's not the type.'

'You said that he's either hiding or licking his wounds,' Kathryn persisted, when Clare's eyes skimmed across her plate in polite inspection.

'Well, with anyone else I would say both of those. But this is Jake Trelawny, so I doubt it. In fact I refuse to believe it at all.'

'You know, you're capable of being quite maddening,' Kathryn declared, intrigued now merely because of her aunt's refusal to give her a straight answer. 'Why would this mythological "anyone else" hide when Jake Trelawny will not?'

'Because they say he murdered his wife, dear. He's been in the most terrible trouble.'

It was typical of her aunt to work up the story and then drop the answer into the ring like a swordsman delivering the *coup de grâce*, but all the same it shocked Kathryn into stillness. It was a long time since French pirates had put fear into the people who lived along this coast, over a hundred years since smugglers had landed their contraband in the small secluded bays at dead of night. This was a sleepy corner of Cornwall, not some violent inner city region. The word 'murder' didn't seem to fit into this place in any way at all.

'Why isn't he in prison?' she asked blankly, surprised into real interest, and her aunt fixed her with startled eyes.

'Jake Trelawny? In *prison*? What a thing to say, Kathryn! He's not in prison because he's innocent. Well, perhaps innocent is not exactly a good word to use when describing Jake Trelawny, but in this particular case he's done nothing wrong at all. They never found the body and all the evidence against him was circumstantial. In any case,' she added firmly, 'even if they had found the body, he didn't do it, I can assure you.'

'How do you know?' Kathryn asked quietly, astounded to realize she had become vaguely interested. Nothing except her work had interested her for a long time, but now she felt as if she was gingerly testing the water, cautiously admitting that life went on.

'Quite impossible!' Clare Holden exclaimed in her best schoolmarm voice. 'I knew him when he was a boy. He was always in trouble, and as he grew up the troubles got bigger – girls and things. They say he was quite ruthless in that direction, and just dropped them when they bored him. He's not capable of anything like murder, though.'

'You said he was wild,' Kathryn pointed out, beginning to feel a little wild herself, and already regretting being drawn into this oddly disjointed

7

discussion. Her aunt made sweeping statements with no good basis of fact. This type of discussion was nothing unusual, although the subject matter was out of the ordinary.

'Wild, strong and very clever indeed. Handsome as the devil too. The girls used to flock after him and I haven't the faintest doubt that he grew up to be dangerous. But to kill his wife? Definitely not, Kathryn. A man like that would never harm a woman.'

'Unless she got on his nerves,' Kathryn murmured wryly, a little smile touching her lips at her aunt's utter faith in someone who sounded quite alarming. Wild, strong, handsome, dangerous and clever. Jake Trelawny didn't seem to have a lot to recommend him as far as Kathryn could see.

'He doesn't have nerves, dear,' Clare explained seriously. 'He's big and powerful, as I told you. People like that just don't have nerves. They're very different from ordinary people.'

'Well, I wouldn't like to meet him, nerves or not,' Kathryn murmured. 'He sounds quite alarming.'

'Oh, I'm sure he is, now that he's grown up. I haven't seen him to speak to since he was a boy, but he had all the signs then of being a force to be reckoned with. Not that you're likely to meet him. The Trelawnys were never fond of strangers.'

'Did you know his wife?'

'No.' Her aunt shook her head gravely. 'None of us knew her because she never came here – well, only that one time. They lived in London. It's a pity she came at all because her visit certainly made trouble for Jake. I mean, if she was intent on disappearing, why couldn't she be considerate and do it in London? Plenty of people disappear in London, I expect. It would probably have gone unnoticed there.'

Kathryn gave up. Aunt Clare was a fount of knowledge, even though she had rarely left this part of Cornwall in her whole life. She had a way of twisting facts to suit her own convictions, however, and as she clearly knew nothing, any other information would be severely prejudiced. Not that Kathryn was interested really. She told herself that very firmly. She had things to do. The mysterious and probably sinister Jake Trelawny was no concern of hers.

The light was still there when she went to bed, and Kathryn found herself staring at it almost morbidly, curiously unwilling to draw the curtains. There was something defiant about it, and even though it was bright it looked strangely threatening.

She had pictures of the old, dark house in her mind, even though she had merely glimpsed it from the distance, and the light seemed to be ominous. It almost appeared to be beckoning to her.

Of course, Aunt Clare's description had coloured her own thoughts on the man who was probably in the house at this moment. In her mind she could almost see him, and she did not like what she saw. Kathryn went to bed with a distinct feeling of uneasiness, and for no good reason – except perhaps a vivid imagination and her own lingering weakness.

The weakness had been there since the accident, and the illness that followed it. Recovery had been slow and painful, and the doctor had told her it would take time. Sometimes she had the feeling that she would never feel strong again, but she knew this was just one step on from her black days. It would pass. She would make it pass. Nothing defeated her for long.

When she got up in the night, after one of her disturbing dreams, the light was still shining, strongly and clearly – more clearly still, now that the fog had gone. The hazy, swirling mist had withdrawn silently over the sea, going back to some distant, unlikely beginning, like phantoms who had left in order to haunt another place, and the chill of its passing lingered in the air.

Kathryn shivered and went back to bed. At least she would be able to get out tomorrow, to let her mind concentrate on something other than her own personal woes. She was lucky to have her aunt. She was not sure that this remote and sometimes melancholy area was the right place to be, feeling as she did at the moment, but she was slowly getting better, and the choice had been either come to her aunt or stay in London and attempt to cope there. She had not been really capable of that. She was only just beginning to manage now.

When the sun was shining it was very different. She could get on with her work. But the swirling mists and the lowering sky had seemed to trap her today. She had been enclosed with her own lingering weakness and that was not good.

At least the irritatingly fragmented story about Jake Trelawny had taken her mind away from her own problems for a while. Aunt Clare's words had left a vague picture of the man in her highly imaginative artist's mind. Dark, dangerous, sinister, cruel. She was already painting his form in her head. She muttered in exasperation and made a determined effort to go back to sleep. It was more important that the weather stayed bright until her work was finished. She was not about to be sidetracked by a man she would never see.

The next morning dawned bright and beautiful, and Kathryn managed to eat enough breakfast to satisfy her aunt's sharp surveillance. When she was gathering her things together, though, Clare Holden offered a word of warning.

'It might be a bit tricky working where you have been, along the old cliff top, Kathryn. Strictly speaking, it's Trelawny land, and if Jake's back . . .'

'I'm not doing any damage,' Kathryn protested. 'I'm only sitting there painting. Anyway, I thought you said he would never harm a woman?'

'Well, of course he wouldn't! I'm not expecting that he'll appear and throw you over the cliff, but it's Trelawny land and they've never welcomed either strangers or trespassers.'

'Is the whole family there? I gained the impression that he was alone at the house?'

'Unless he's brought someone with him, he is alone. He's not likely to have brought anyone with

11

him, not after what occurred with his wife,' Clare assured her. She began to remove the breakfast dishes. 'There is no family, not now.'

'What happened to them?' The thought of the man she had painted in her mind prowling around that big old house alone made Kathryn uneasy, even though she was most unlikely to see him.

'Oh, they died ages ago,' her aunt informed her vaguely. 'Jake was the only son. It seemed at one time that the line would die out, but it didn't. Of course, now that his wife has disappeared . . .'

Kathryn had heard enough. She hastily put her things into the big basket that Clare had found for her. She had a lot of things to take and it was easier to have them all together. She made for the door fast. She most definitely did not wish to hear another word about the dark old house and the fierce Trelawnys. She didn't know if their story would be tragic or frightening. She didn't want to know. The house was a long way from the place she had chosen to work. He would never know she was there. He might not even be back anyway. There could be another explanation for that light, somebody in doing jobs, or even burglars – if they had the nerve.

Kathryn made her way through the leafy lane that led to the cliff. It was one of those deep Cornish lanes, edged with wild flowers, that lay so low and secluded that it was difficult to hear the sea. It was hot, such a relief after the day of melancholy mist. The sun was brilliant, and Kathryn's flagging spirits lifted with every step she took.

It was easy walking in the lane. Countless down-pours in the winter months had washed away any small stones and left the path smooth and sandy beneath her feet. All the same, she took care. She was quite used to taking care by now. It had been over eight months but there was not much sign of any improvement in her ability to walk normally. Her slight limp was no real disadvantage, but the feeling of uneasiness it gave her made her wary of any uneven ground.

On the cliff top the path was not so smooth, and she took greater care, but the slight breeze blew her hair and the soothing sound of a quiet sea brought a smile to her lips. Last night's gloom had vanished. All she wanted now was to get to her chosen place and begin work.

This was no barren cliff top. A field ran almost to the edge. Not that anyone would have thought of taking a tractor close to the crumbling, uneven perimeter of the towering cliff face. At some long past time the sea had eaten away the farmland here, and the fallen rocks that edged the sea down below showed just how much had been lost.

Land was always on the move, especially by the sea. It lived and died like everything else, and Kathryn had always been very much aware of it. Everything she did was in some way attached to the land. The tiny creatures she drew and painted, the flowers, the trees, the bracken and the hedgerows – all were a part of the land and the land soothed her

The path was safe enough when it was well clear of any dangerous drop, and she avoided those places.

There were poppies growing and the lingering blue of forget-me-nots. It was an ideal place for her task. In the thick, coarse grasses further along, insect life abounded. Her glowing watercolours brought everything to vivid life and made her books into children's classics that would never lose their appeal.

She glanced across towards the house. Pengarron Manor her aunt had called it. She could see it fairly well from here on the cliff top. It was an old manor house with what would be a striking view of the sea. The woods between the cliff and the house looked intriguing, but after her aunt's warning she felt that they were definitely out of bounds. She had no desire to put Jake Trelawny's consideration for women to the test.

Kathryn reached her place and settled down into the little hollow. She had brought her lunch today. Walking back for lunch was too tiring. Besides, out here by herself she could eat whatever she wished and, more importantly, leave anything she did not want.

She took out her working tools, her pencils, paints, water and thick sketching pad, and then she unscrewed her tiny jars. These were to capture the unwary beetles, perhaps even a tiny field mouse, but they would all be returned to their habitat as quickly as possible.

She settled to draw, her mind sinking thankfully into the depth of the thick grasses, the golden-stalked remains of past crops and the bright scarlet of the poppies. In her little hollow overlooking the sea she was in another world.

It was a remarkably safe world. With her mind adjusted to the miniature, Kathryn could allow her thoughts to skim over the past, searching it without fear. Her fingers were well trained, her imagination already taking control, and part of her mind was free to look back and soar over the past like the gulls that soared over the sea, untouched by anything.

She could hear Colin's voice without flinching now.

'I met her while you were in hospital, Kath. It was just one of those things. I know you and I . . . but you always understand.'

One of those things! Words so easily said. It had meant the end of any possible engagement, and in the weeks it took her to fight back to health Colin had not visited her again. She certainly understood. He had not had the nerve to face her. It had all been his fault and he had not had the courage to confront the fact that his actions had left her lame, possibly for the rest of her life, had almost killed her. His reckless driving had caused the accident, and he had left her lying there for a long time. She remembered the snow, the cold, the pain.

Just before the crash, when she had seen the road coming up to meet her, he had screamed. It seemed that the sound would always stay in her mind. He had grabbed her, not to protect her but because he was afraid and needed support. In that split second she had known how little he really cared.

They had been going too fast. Kathryn had been chewing at her lip, wondering if she should say something but knowing that if she did Colin was likely to pour scorn on her and tell her yet again that she had no spirit of adventure. He had been drinking again, and she had not realized quite how much until she was in the car and he had set off as if they were on a race track.

One more party that she had not wanted to attend, one more argument looming up if she remonstrated with him now.

'Please slow down, Colin!' The words were almost jerked out of her as he took a bend too fast.

'Everything's fine, under control. Stop worrying. This car can practically drive itself.'

She would have felt safer if the car *had* been driving itself. Kathryn gripped the seat with both hands and told herself that in all probability she would make it home in one piece. It wasn't far. Many people drove too fast and avoided an accident. Most of them hadn't been drinking though and the roads were icy in places.

It was the night after Boxing Day, and she wondered if they would meet another fool coming in the opposite direction, doing the same thing. She knew that Colin did not have his wits about him. His reaction time would be too slow.

'Can I drive?' she enquired desperately, too scared to take her eyes from the road even though she had no control of events.

'No way! Nobody lays a hand on this car except me. You don't seem to realize that this car is a collector's item. I pamper it.'

'You're going to smash it into a tree and then it will be a scrapyard item.'

'There you go again,' he snapped, 'reprimanding me as if I were a child. You've been looking at me all evening with disapproval. You're always doing it. You're heavy going sometimes, Kath.'

Kathryn's hands tightened still more on the soft upholstery of the seat. Maybe she had looked disapproving because she had not approved at all. She hated it when Colin started to drink and became loud and foolish. Her own nature was too quiet to be able to cope with uproarious behaviour. And she hated being called Kath! Colin knew that perfectly well.

She watched the streets go by, the roundabout, the edge of the park, under the bridge and then the long ill-lit road by the docks that led to her own part of town.

Nearly there! There were few people about and thankfully no cars at all. Still, it was very late, anyone still celebrating Christmas would be indoors by now. Colin had insisted on staying at the party until they became that nuisance of a couple who lingered unforgivably. Colin never seemed to notice things like that. It was left to Kathryn to notice. Little good it did. He usually ignored her quiet advice about leaving or he moaned at her.

Nearly there. Kathryn made her hands relax, and she had to do it one finger at a time. Colin's driving had scared her many times in the past but never as much as this. In future she would take her own car, even though it was not a collector's item. There was

17

no more than half a mile left now. She let her hands sink into her lap and forced her mind from the road.

'Nobody drives this car except me.' Kathryn noted that she was relegated to being just anybody, even though they were supposed to be getting engaged soon. Sometimes she was well aware of why she resisted the idea and sometimes she asked herself what was wrong with her.

Under normal circumstances, Colin was pleasant and kind. She wasn't sure, though, that she wanted to marry a man who was pleasant and kind but who had bouts of drinking that left him totally stupid. And she most certainly did not appreciate being blamed for Colin's faults. That was what usually happened.

When he hit a patch of ice under the dark trees, Kathryn didn't even think of screaming because somehow it had been inevitable, completely expected. The car went out of control, skidding from one side of the road to the other, and it seemed like fate when it turned over.

Kathryn's world went into slow motion, and all she could think of was her work. I'll never draw again, never see another sunrise, never walk through the long grasses.

She heard the horrendous crash, the sound of tearing, grinding metal, and she heard Colin scream.

He's afraid, she thought calmly. He never imagined that anything like this could happen to him. He's always sure that he's right. The total confidence of ignorance.

She felt far away from things, outside the crash, clutched by the bitter hand of fate. She was tossed about like a rag doll and then the whole world went black.

When she came round it was cold, terribly cold, but she could not move away from the cold at all. One leg was trapped and Kathryn knew she was lying on ice, possibly the same area of ice they had hit at speed. The car seemed to be hovering over her and she could smell petrol. The fear that had left her in the crash came rushing back as she thought of fire. She would not be able to move away.

'Colin!' She called his name but even to her own ears her voice was little more than a whisper. He was not in the car. She could see right through it from the passenger door to the driver's seat. He must have been thrown clear. Kathryn had the dreadful feeling that he was dead, lying somewhere in the trees at the side of the road.

'Colin!' She managed to make her voice louder, and almost at once she heard a groan and the sound of movement. It was almost directly behind her but she could not turn her head.

'I'm hurt, Kath.'

He moaned and came closer and she could see him now. Relief rushed through her. He could move. He was not standing yet but he could move. He came into the light and she realized then that the car headlights were still on. Electric power, petrol, fire!

'I'm trapped!' she told him urgently, but he didn't seem to be taking it in. He was sitting beside her, his head in his hands, and she wondered if he could possibly still be drunk. She thought wildly of tales she had heard of people being sobered instantly by shock or fear. She just hoped it had happened to Colin like that.

'Colin!' She spoke his name sharply and he looked at her in such a vague manner that all hopes failed. 'I'm trapped,' she said as loudly as possible. 'You have to get me out of this.'

'I hurt all over.' He was groaning, thinking only of himself, and right at that moment she knew he was not even going to try to help her.

'Colin, I'm trapped. Help me!'

There was blood on his face. A thin line of it trickled slowly down to his chin and he wiped it away, still in that vague manner. Maybe it was his own action that roused him because he stood up, swaying giddily, and, to her horror, rested his arm on the car that seemed to be balanced precariously over her.

'Got to get help,' he muttered. 'I'll go off up the road.'

'Try to get me free,' Kathryn urged. 'One of my legs is trapped. There could be a fire.'

He stood looking down at her and then shook his head as if he was clearing it.

'You'll be fine, Kath. There's no chance of fire. Everything is under control.'

He started to move away and she had one last desperate try.

'I'm lying on ice, freezing. Can you get a coat or something under me?'

'Best not to move you. I'll get help.' His voice was slurred and she just let him go. He was incapable of thinking and she knew it was more than the accident. He seemed to have got off very lightly. Maybe a few steps along the road and he would come to his senses, return and try to help her. She waited but he never came, and by now she was too numb with cold even to shiver.

I'm going to die here, she thought helplessly. I've come through that spectacular crash and now I'm just going to die of cold. She felt the first snowflakes touch her face and then she closed her eyes. There was one good thing about being numb; she couldn't feel pain.

After he had walked away to get help, somebody had come. She found out later that a car had stopped and they had called the police, the ambulance. She also found out later that Colin had gone to the small nearby pub and had several brandies. He had been wanting to make sure that when he reported the accident he had a good excuse for alcohol in his bloodstream. He had ignored the fact that she was trapped and injured.

And apart from that one, uneasy, shamefaced visit, she had never seen him again. The police had wanted her to testify that he had been drinking before the accident but she had refused. It was all over, and she had not wanted either to face Colin again or pursue a vindictive course. There had seemed to be no point – not much point, in fact, to anything – but that feeling had been because of her illness.

Kathryn shivered in the bright sunlight and drew her mind back to the present and her task. Reminiscing was pointless. She had decided that a long time ago. The pain was gone, unless she put too much strain on her leg. The fight to get well was not entirely won but she was getting there. She had let the past go and she was not quite sure why it had slipped back. Perhaps it had been the misty gloom of yesterday, or perhaps it had been the unwelcome dreams of the accident that never seemed to go away.

She concentrated on the beetle that was running in irritated circles in the bottom of the jar and her swift fingers sketched him in every pose he attained. Later he would be altered but for now she worked fast, not wanting to keep any creature captive for too long. Being trapped under the car still brought a chill to her skin and anxiety to her mind. She would never trap anything.

Kathryn paused only for lunch, the sandwiches and coffee her aunt had made. She worked on, feeling really lucky when she managed to catch a green hairstreak butterfly. Normally they stayed in the woodland, but this one had ventured out and nestled with every appearance of calm in her jar while she quickly drew it in detail. In her head, she wove the delicate creature into her story, dressed it in gauzy finery, put a small glittering crown on its head.

By mid-afternoon she had done as much as possible out of doors and Kathryn stood up, moving out of the cosy hollow where she had been working and standing to watch the sea before she left. The tide had turned, and down below she could see it splashing against the rocks. Even the cliff face was clothed in greenery for part of the way down. This place was a luxurious, verdant haven, a place to finish off her recovery.

She gathered her things and started back, picking her way with care along the path. In a few places the path ran just a little too close to the edge of the cliff and nobody had ever put a fence there. Or if they had, the sea and wind had long since claimed it. Kathryn kept clear of places like that. Heights had never bothered her, but now that she was afraid of falling she had to take extra care.

She was just past one particularly bad spot when she became aware of the sound of movement behind her. She tensed. She was always unwilling to step aside and move to rough land. Most people gave way for her but some ignored the fact that she was unsteady on her feet. This was not exactly like walking on the pavement and she looked at the land at the side, knowing that to step into the coarse grasses there would unsettle her balance. She held her ground. Whoever was coming up behind would just have to walk round her.

Curiosity and uneasiness made her turn to look back after a second or two. She didn't like to think of anyone behind her in this secluded place. She had never encountered anyone here before and she had been working here for a long time. It had almost become her private haven and a faint resentment mingled with her uneasiness.

It was a horse and rider, and as she turned Kathryn felt a sharp stab of fear. The rider was a man, tall, dark and still, as if he had come in with the chill mists from the sea last night and decided not to leave. He almost seemed to be part of the horse. He was coming slowly and everything about him was silent, cold, hostile.

There was an inevitability about him that scared her like some dreaded dream coming to life. He just didn't belong in this sunny place, with the waves slapping gently on the rocks below. It made him unreal, alarming, a lingering threat from the drifting fog of the night before.

She had never thought about being attacked out here. This was Cornwall, her aunt's home, safety and peace. The peace was gone, though, in one flash of anxiety. Danger was riding towards her and she was totally unprepared for it.

CHAPTER 2

Kathryn turned away quickly, not at all anxious to glance back. One look had been enough. There were plenty of legends in Cornwall and she had the awful feeling that the man might not be real, that if she looked round again he would be gone.

The overall impression left with her was one of blackness – black hair, black sweater, black horse. His eyes had been fixed on her with a sort of menacing intent that made her heartbeats quicken with dread. She found herself picturing him in the swirling mists that had covered the coast yesterday, riding on in that inevitable way, coming through the sea fog. He was like a phantom who had been left behind, a being completely alien to her world.

Kathryn was irritated when she realized that she would very much have liked to run. There was a sort of welling up of panic that threatened to grip her. It was lonely here, silent except for the sea. It would not be a good idea to run, though, because it was a long way to the end of this path, and even then the low, silent lane was her next destination. There was nobody around for miles.

Kathryn's lips drew together in annoyance. This was absolutely ridiculous! She had faced dreadful fear in her life just eight months ago, real fear, not something she had conjured up out of her nightmares. This was nothing. Her imagination was working overtime and that was all. It was just somebody on a horse and he definitely was there. She had not imagined him. In all probability he would say 'Good evening' and ride past.

Anyway, according to Aunt Clare, this was Trelawny land. If it was, then this man was trespassing too. She would point that out sharply if he spoke to her in anything other than pleasantly polite words. He had no more right to be here than she had herself, and she would not be intimidated.

He forestalled all that. Kathryn heard the horse more clearly as it came closer. She didn't look round or acknowledge another presence in any way, but she was well aware of the bulk and power of the beast. As it drew alongside the man spoke.

'Are you aware that you're trespassing?'

He had a voice like soft gravel, harsh, dark, washed by the sea. He was speaking quietly but the sound of his voice was instantly forbidding.

A shiver ran helplessly down her spine but Kathryn stopped and turned to face him. It was face him or run, and she could not run. Her leg would give way – and in any case where would she run to? She would look like a fool too, and she strongly objected to that.

She had come to Cornwall to get better but she had also come to face her fears. This was nothing. He was only a man and at the moment her opinion of men was very low indeed.

She had to look up a very long way to face him, and at the sight of him so close her heart gave an extra bound of unease. She could tell that in the normal course of events he would tower over her, but sitting astride the huge black horse he was like a giant, much bigger than she had expected.

His hair was black as jet, and from above his eyes looked too dark to be called brown. He was wearing black jeans and a black roll neck sweater and she had the feeling that none of this was deliberate. He was not in any way dressing for effect. He was comfortable with his appearance, regardless of the impression he made on anyone else.

The rising breeze from the sea was tossing his hair, hair that was straight, shining and beautifully cut but longer than she would have expected in a man like this. It was below his ears at the back, heavy, framing his face. It suited him and he probably knew it. He looked arrogantly sure of himself, distant, cold, and as the thought came into her mind Kathryn suddenly knew who he was. Her aunt's words rang in her mind, 'wild as a gypsy'. He almost looked like one.

She knew she was looking at Jake Trelawny, and any defiant challenge she had been contemplating faded away. She had painted him in her head last night. The reality was much more alarming. She could understand why her aunt had said that girls used to flock after him – girls who didn't recognize danger. Kathryn recognized it instantly.

All the same, he was only a man and not some phantom. Also, his attitude annoyed her. It seemed to be particularly small-minded. This path was useless. It wasn't even quite safe. If everything was as it should have been, this would have been a right of way.

As far as Kathryn could see, the cliffs and the sea belonged to everyone, and nobody had any right to keep them for themselves. The house might be his, the woods and grounds, but this was a bit of the coast, a part of Cornwall that should be accessible to all.

'Theoretically, I suppose I am trespassing,' she said haughtily, pushing down the feeling of fear that was still trying to clamour inside. 'But what is trespass, after all? I haven't taken anything, moved anything or left anything behind. To sue me for trespass would be rather tricky. I believe you would have to prove damage. You'll be hard-pressed to find any.'

'Theory is abstract. You, however, are extremely tangible. You are on my path, on my land – trespassing.'

He frowned down at her and Kathryn didn't like the sound of 'tangible'. It had always meant 'touchable' to her, and if he reached down and touched her she would either scream or run, in spite of her defiant thoughts. She was not particularly timid, but in this case she was prepared to make an exception. He was an overwhelming presence. She had never seen anyone like him before in the whole of her life.

There was an uncomfortable tingling inside her that was mixing with the fear like a volatile cocktail that made her head spin.

'My aunt warned me I would be trespassing,' she managed breezily. 'I never thought, though, that someone would be so utterly mean as to object to my presence on a cliff path. I could not easily be mistaken for a gang of rowdy youths bent on mischief and it's years since I threw stones at windows.'

For a second he stared down at her with raised brows and Kathryn gathered all her courage to stare right back. She saw the night-black eyes start to gleam, a pinpoint of silver light in their depths, and a wave of near-relief washed over her when his hard lips quirked with amusement. It was not total relief, however. The amusement was not actually shown in a kindly manner. If it was humour it was icy. It was also extremely calculating. The dark eyes narrowed thoughtfully

'Well?' She raised her chin aggressively when he said nothing. 'Are you going to give permission for further trespassing or are you going to escort me off your property with due ceremony?'

'What are you doing here?'

'I'm an artist. I paint wildlife. This cliff has exactly what I want at the moment.'

'Really?' he enquired in a cold, bored voice. He turned his head and looked back the way she had come. 'The seagulls?' It seemed to Kathryn that he was sneering and her temper flared. She snapped at him.

'No. I could paint seagulls from my aunt's cottage with no trouble at all. I need to be here. I need to be by myself, to sink into the grass, to be small . . .' Kathryn glared up at him, irritated that she had been driven to explaining herself. '*Look*! Can I or can't I continue painting here tomorrow and any other day until I've finished my work? Please answer before the bell sounds or you're out of the contest.'

The black eyebrows rose further at her snapped-out words and he stared down at her for a minute, his dark eyes unwavering. Kathryn had a nasty feeling that he was sneaking into her head but she held her ground.

'If you like,' he murmured finally, with so little interest that she almost felt he had never challenged her at all. After scaring her with his appearance and his tone of voice he was now totally indifferent.

The rest of Kathryn's lingering fear vanished. He wasn't a ghost or a legend. He was just a goddamn man! She gave him one last furious glare and started on her way. What had been the point in challenging her when he had so readily given up? Had he merely wanted to frighten her? Well, she didn't scare that easily, as it happened, and *he* certainly didn't know she had been scared by the sight of him initially.

All the same, she was almost holding her breath, waiting for him to turn away and go elsewhere. It was no use pretending that he had left her feeling simply annoyed. He was giving off vibes and she was collecting them.

But the huge horse kept pace with her, making it difficult to walk on the smoother parts of the path, even though her tormentor was riding on the rough grass at the field edge.

The animal's sheer size was in danger of moving her off the middle of the path. Even if it didn't step on her, she was well aware of its capabilities. One small nudge and she would be flat on her face. There was another dangerous place coming up too, a place where the path was much too close to a drop. It was by far the worst place.

'Who is your aunt?' Jake Trelawny asked after a time of unnerving silence.

'Clare Holden.' Kathryn curbed her annoyance and glanced at him politely. 'She lives at Jasmine Cottage down the lane and . . .'

'I know where Jasmine Cottage is. I also know Miss Holden. A very vigorous lady. When I was a boy, she boxed my ears on one occasion.'

'Richly deserved, I'm sure,' Kathryn muttered, remembering that her aunt had once been the head and only teacher at the tiny village school. 'Did she teach you at the school?'

'No, she did not. I escaped that fate. I simply took some of her apples.'

'Trespassing!' Kathryn pronounced loudly, noticing that he prefixed his crime with 'simply' when he was in the wrong. She looked up at him again to show her triumph and almost lost her balance on an uneven part of the path.

'Take care!' His hand was on her arm almost before she had stumbled, and Kathryn felt a renewed shock of anxiety.

31

'I wouldn't be at any risk if I could walk alone,' she snapped, pulling away irritably.

In leaning over to catch her he had come close, and now she found herself looking into his eyes in almost choking proximity.

She had always thought of near-black eyes as being cold, blank, expressionless, like a snake's. But the eyes that looked at her now were almost beautiful, compelling, edged with thick lashes. She felt driven to rage on, uneasiness fuelling her annoyance and a renewed flare of the tingling starting up in her arms.

'I'm trying to avoid that great beast and to answer your questions. I'm watching the path and then turning to speak to you. I can't look at two places at once!'

'The perhaps you should concentrate on the path?' he suggested sardonically.

'Then perhaps you should ride off and leave me alone. I was taught to look at people when they speak to me. It's called good manners.' He was amused. She just knew he was. And he was making her feel that she was anxious to look at him like a simpering idiot.

He had straightened up and let her go, but as she drew breath for a further attack he suddenly reached down and lifted her lightly onto the saddle in front of him. It was utterly unexpected and for a second it took her breath away completely. She was pressed back against his hard body; his arm was round her waist like an iron band

'That seems to have solved the problem,' he said silkily. 'I can now escort you off my property without risking your health.'

'Put me down!' Kathryn snapped, clutching at his arm with tight fingers. 'This is assault.' She was terrified again, ready to scream.

'This is common sense,' he informed her quietly, his voice back to gravelly darkness. 'You need help. You're tired and the cliff path is dangerous.'

'You made it dangerous!' Kathryn protested hotly. 'I was doing all right before you came.'

She was frightened by his nearness, frightened at being so far up and away from the ground, suspicious of him. Soon they would be at the deep, lonely lane. If he could behave in this unpredictable manner, what would he do then? Why was he doing this anyway? It was outrageous, unbelievable!

'Have you been ill?' The unexpected question, right out of the blue, made her tighten up inside even more. It was a peculiar way to speak to a stranger. She wanted to struggle and kick, but she was afraid of startling the horse into precipitous action.

'No!' Kathryn lied vigorously, and set her lips tightly closed.

'You're very pale.'

'It's shock and – and outrage.' She decided that he might just be mad. He was behaving in a bizarre manner. Nobody did this sort of thing at the sight of a stranger, and he was asking her questions as if she had never shouted at him in annoyance, as if they were at some sort of polite garden party. The thought that he had murdered his wife took strong hold, in spite of Aunt Clare's touching faith in him.

'You've been painting. What are those little pots for?'

That settled it as far as Kathryn was concerned. She was in danger, riding on a great beast of a horse with a madman who started one chain of questioning and then switched to another with no connection.

And he had definitely murdered that poor woman. It was really obvious. The police surely knew. They must be waiting for further evidence. She just hoped they were watching now. She decided to humour him. He was a lot bigger than she was.

'I draw beetles, fieldmice, butterflies – anything that runs in the grass and hedges. I draw the flowers and put the little creatures into their natural habitat.'

'You illustrate wildlife books?'

'Er – not exactly.' If she told him that she then went home and drew the beetles in yellow sweaters and flat caps, top hats and bow ties, let them ride bicycles or proceed on their way using roller skates, he might just think she was mad too.

She didn't want to give him any feeling that her attitude of mind was in any way compatible with his. She was quite sure that his sense of humour was limited, and he had an odd way of asking intense questions in a sort of detached manner. Nothing about him was normal.

She tensed up inside when they came to the quiet lane. Out on the cliff top she could have screamed if things got too bad. There had been nobody in sight but someone might just have heard her. At the very least it would perhaps have put him off. Here, there was no chance at all. And it was no use pretending that she was calm and disgusted. She was terrified and he probably knew it.

'I'd like to get down now, please,' she murmured faintly.

'Why?' He didn't turn his head. He just looked straight ahead as he asked the question, and all Kathryn could see was his hard profile. She did some quick thinking.

'Well, I'm nearly home and this is a safe path. It – it will look peculiar if you ride up to the cottage with me. You must admit that this is strange. Besides, you could go back now – er – before you get too far away from where you're going . . .' Her voice trailed away uneasily.

'I'll take you down the lane. I'll drop you at the end of it, if you're worried about being seen with me.'

His voice had iced over considerably, and Kathryn felt a renewed burst of fear, wondering if she had alerted some savage instinct in him. Maybe murderers were born like that? Maybe they simply needed a trigger to set them off, some small key word or deed, like being embarrassed about being seen with them.

'It's not that I'm worried about being seen with you,' she said hastily. 'It's just that it would look odd if – '

'Don't bother,' he cut in harshly. 'You know who I am, don't you?'

'I fathomed it out,' Kathryn confessed, in a voice that trembled slightly as she gave up any attempt at psychological manoeuvring. She was watching frantically for the end of the lane and she had a feeling he knew that perfectly well. He still had plenty of time to do almost anything.

'What's your name,' he asked when he heard her carefully suppressed sigh of relief at the sight of the lane end

'Kathryn Holden.'

'Ah, yes. Clare Holden's niece.' He glanced at her ringless fingers. 'Another Miss Holden with an equally strong desire to box my ears. Care to try it now, Miss Holden? You've almost reached safety.'

'I would like to get down,' Kathryn said quietly. To seem to be dignified was the only thing she could think of to protect herself. She felt he had frightened her deliberately. There had been no need whatever for him to behave as he had done.

The cottage was right there, across the road, but even now he could turn the horse quickly and go back down the lane. He might do anything. If he had murdered his wife, what did he have to lose? He was obviously some sort of maniac in any case, and she did not have her aunt's touching faith in him.

He looked at her steadily. He was so close that she could see the flicker of silver light at the back of his eyes. The lashes were thick and silky, much too good for a man, and he suddenly lowered them slightly, shutting her out without actually looking away. It was like a curtain falling.

His arm slid round her again and Kathryn felt herself being lowered to the ground with great care.

He did not let her go until he was quite sure that she had her balance. He handed her the basket and said nothing at all. He just looked at her steadily and Kathryn turned away and walked across the road to the cottage.

She absolutely refused to say thank you. She had not asked for that frightening ride. In any case, she was not sure that any words would come out if she tried to speak. She was trembling, and her eyes were fixed on the door of the cottage with urgency.

She was aware that he was watching her still, self-consciously aware of her limp and perfectly sure that for the past few minutes she had been in grave danger. Even now he could gallop across and get her. There wasn't a soul in sight.

Her hand fumbled with the catch on the door. In her anxiety she thought for a moment it was locked, and just as she had it opened he spoke.

'You may trespass whenever you wish, Miss Holden,' he assured her icily.

He turned his horse and disappeared down the lane and Kathryn almost fell into the cottage. She was safe! It had been a long time since she had felt such fear. Months. Even then, it had been a different fear. She had known, in the car with Colin, exactly where the danger lay. This fear had almost been superstitious, because most of it had come from her earlier thoughts of him. His behaviour had simply fitted into the picture she had already painted in her head

Kathryn sat down, glad for the moment that her aunt was not there with her inquisitive nature and her motherly ways. She did not want to have to explain that she had met Jake Trelawny and had been forcibly carried home. She did not want to have to tell her aunt that he was a lot more than wild and that in her opinion he had definitely murdered his wife.

The trembling stopped and she went to make herself a cup of tea. It would take a lot of nerve to go back to the headland and finish her sketches. She was not at all sure that she dared. He might see her again and decide to follow her.

She caught sight of herself in the mirror and grimaced. If he did, it would really mean that he was mad. She was pale, thin, her green eyes too big for her face, her hair a windswept mess. If he had killed his wife it would have been for a good reason. He looked too clever to simply go around killing people haphazardly when the mood took him. Any interest he had shown in her had been purely to make her afraid. He wanted her to be too afraid to go there again.

Her eyes narrowed at the thought. Perhaps Jake Trelawny was not mad after all. Perhaps his sole aim had been to frighten her off his land. Perhaps he was making sure that nobody got too close to that house. Perhaps he had too much to hide.

Kathryn shuddered and sat down to drink her tea. A dark, dangerous man. Colin had been dangerous, as it turned out, but not for any other reason than that he had never quite grown up, could not face any responsibility, thought only of himself. Colin had placed her in danger and then walked out of her life.

Jake Trelawny was dangerous inside. There was danger in the near-black eyes, danger in the alarming strength, danger in the waves of powerful masculinity that seemed to reach out from him like electricity. He had lowered her to the ground with one arm, lowered her slowly as if she weighed nothing. He would be capable of anything. The danger was silent and deep but it was there. His wife must have been a very brave woman to live with him, especially if it had been for any time at that lonely house in the woods above the sea.

Jake paced about the study and finally went to stare out of the window. There was a wonderful panoramic view from here but he was not looking at it. He was irritated, restless and bordering on savage anger. He was not normally puzzled by things. His thoughts were always clear, concise, based on fact, but at the moment nothing added up. Somehow, somewhere he had walked into a trap, and the only reason he was not still ensnared was due entirely to the fact that the trap had been carelessly set.

Who and why were the thoughts that had occupied his mind for weeks. He had mentally gone over all the ground many times. It had even seemed possible at one stage that he would be arrested but the trap had not been good enough. His unseen enemy was careless, or perhaps a little too sure of success. The stigma remained, though. Under suspicion! He had never really known the depth of that phrase until now.

Gillian was gone, and although he had never wished her dead honesty made him admit that life was a good deal less complicated without her. She had made his life hell, had almost brought a stop to his work, and for the first time in his existence she had made him confront humiliation.

He could only thank any gods who watched over him that he had brought her down here to Cornwall on a sudden impulse. That fact alone had saved him, because after a blazing row he had gone back to London *and* he had been seen. He had witnesses. All fortuitous.

He might very well have simply gone back to his flat and stayed there alone. Only anger and frustration had driven him out to his club. Gillian had been seen in the village when he was already in the company of others, talking to people, trying to swallow his anger.

'Where are you, you bitch?' he asked through clenched teeth. 'Where did you go when I left you? Who came here to meet you?'

There had been no telephone call. That had been checked. This house was rarely occupied and any call would have stood out clearly.

He turned away from the window and surveyed the room sourly. It had never been changed or refurbished in any way since his parents had died. It looked old-fashioned, gloomy, in perfect harmony with the rest of the house. He had never particularly liked Pengarron Manor. He had always been lonely here. That was why he had fallen for Gillian's charms.

None of it would have happened if he had not decided to write. Making the transition from journalism to writing fiction had not been easy at first. Jake was a loner. The few friends he had made in the world of the Press were staunch but his own attitude had always been against him. He was silent, watchful and clever, and he had very little trust in anyone.

To his astonishment his books had been a roaring success from the first, and he had been catapulted into the limelight. He was expected to attend dinners, book-signings, make speeches and appear at receptions. He hated it. All he wanted to do was write. To him the glitter was so much nonsense, a reminder of the days of his childhood when the house had rung with laughter and music and he had been expected to be invisible.

He remembered the reception where he had met Gillian Cauldwell. There was no denying her beauty but it was her vivacity that had intrigued him. She was like a brightly coloured moth, her smile shimmering with sincerity. She had been so interested in him, and after a few drinks and a quiet conversation about nothing in particular she had contrived to stay close all evening.

Jake had been grateful. She was easy to talk to and she'd agreed with him that the whole event was a bore. She'd also managed with a good deal of charm to fend off most of the people who tried to buttonhole him. She was with him to the very end of the affair and it was Gillian who stayed in his mind after it was all over, not the toe-curling stupidity of the evening.

After that, she seemed to be at every function he attended. His publishers had always found it necessary to almost drag him there in the past, but it soon became obvious that Gillian was on the tight circle of people to be invited. She took him under her glittering wing and life became easier.

Spending the night with her after a couple of such events was almost inevitable, and, from being alone and self-sufficient, Jake found himself carefully managed and leaning on Gillian at any social gathering. Marriage was the obvious thing, and he simply drifted into it.

It was not long before he discovered her true worth. When he was writing, Gillian was out on the town. Any question was answered with a cool smile.

'Mind your own damned business, darling,' was Gillian's favourite expression. There were other men. There had always been other men. Jake retreated to his club with much more frequency and people started to talk.

'Look, Jake. It's none of my business,' Mike Ellis began one evening, and Jake gave him a wry glance.

'But you're going to make it your business?'

'It's about Gillian.'

'And her army of admirers? I know,' Jake murmured with little interest. He knew he had never loved her. Love had not come into it. He wasn't exactly sure what love was anyway. But he had been faithful and he had expected Gillian to be faithful too.

'Aren't you bothered?' Mike Ellis looked at him in astonishment and Jake sat back and surveyed the deep ruby of the wine in his glass.

'Bothered? It depends what you mean. Sick, weary and heartbroken? No. Wildly irritated? Yes.'

'She's making a fool of you, Jake.'

'What's the saying about not being capable of improving on nature?' Jake muttered. 'I was a fool to marry her. Now I'm stuck with her.'

'Get rid of her!'

'If only it were that simple,' Jake sighed. 'According to Gillian, these people are friends – friends she had long before she met me. A modern woman does not give up her friends. She has always moved in that glittering circle, and as I'm a social dwarf she retains the right to amuse herself, or so she says.'

'She's doing more than amuse herself,' Mike pointed out furiously. He had known Jake for years, since their early journalist days, and he was a staunch ally.

'I assumed as much. I suggested a divorce but she laughed wildly. She's not about to give up the bright lights and, even more than that, she's not about to give up the sound of money in the till.'

'You're earning it and she's spending it.'

'Apparently, that's the way the world turns.' Jake looked across at his friend and shook his head. 'Give it a rest, Mike. I came here to escape the mindless chatter that now permeates my life.'

'She doesn't give a toss about you, and if you don't love her . . .'

'I've never suffered from that particular affliction,' Jake grunted, 'and I shall shun it like a new form of the plague – if Gillian ever decides to leave me in peace.'

'Why should she?' Mike asked angrily. 'She's got it all ways.'

'Precisely what she said,' Jake told him drily. 'If I sue for divorce, she will contest it and make a counter claim. I'll be branded as a pervert or some other outcast. She assures me that she'll "come up with something" and get her cronies to back her.'

'Bloody hell!'

'My thoughts at the time exactly.' Jake stated, downing his wine at one go.

Well, he had got rid of her months ago, and even in disappearing she had left him with a life in turmoil. He had insisted on coming down to Cornwall so that they could thrash things out in the silence of Pengarron Manor, without Gillian being able to storm off to one of her friends. All that had happened was a furious and bitter quarrel, one of many but this time worse. Jake had walked out and driven back to London leaving her to find her own way back or stay where she was and contemplate her twisted character. She had simply disappeared.

Had he not had witnesses to his lack of involvement it would have gone very hard for him. Gillian had actually walked to the village to call someone, although the telephone at Pengarron was in full working order. Jake had been at his club talking to Mike Ellis and other acquaintances. But, all the same, the police had pounced on him like a sack of rocks.

It had turned his life upside down and it was still going on. He knew they had not given up. After all, it was barely five months since she had vanished. They had brought Jake back to Cornwall, made him almost pace out his movements, and the whole village where he had spent his childhood had been agog.

'It seems, Mr Trelawny, that they remember your "black" youth,' Inspector Harrison had informed him in his curiously monotonous voice, and Jake had not know whether he was joking or not. He still didn't know. What he did know was that they were suspicious. Everyone was suspicious. They had nothing to charge him with but they suspected him of the worst kind of villainy.

Apparently, the village was split in half about the matter.

'Some remember you with amusement, Mr Trelawny,' the inspector had droned on. 'Some of them, though, seem to think you capable of anything.'

Jake had searched the man's expression but had been unable to see beneath the bland exterior. Inspector Harrison looked like a sleepy bloodhound, but Jake knew it was a mask to fool the unwary.

Gillian had left him under suspicion. The people in the village either glanced at him anxiously or turned their backs. In London, those who knew him were also split into two camps. Mike was staunch and vociferous on the subject of the bitch of a wife that Jake had been landed with, but Jake wished he would hold his tongue more often. The steady stream of unpalatable facts that Mike poured forth about Gillian only led others to glance at him with more uneasiness.

Pretty soon it seemed that the only person on his side at all was Mike Ellis, and Jake had retreated to his old ways and finally come back to his childhood haunts. He didn't have to go into the village if he didn't want to and nobody ever came here. They never had done, but now he suspected they would not dare.

And all because he had been taken in by a glittering female who was more tarantula than moth when her true face appeared.

Well, he rarely made mistakes and certainly he would not make the same mistake again. If he wanted a woman, there were plenty about without the need to saddle himself with a glamorous bitch who would take everything she could and then turn on him.

Maybe he should stay here permanently and work from the house? It would be easy enough to travel to London whenever it was necessary. He could do any extra research and then come back here. The elderly couple who had worked here for years would be good enough for him. They were used to the Trelawny ways. The house would do also. If nothing else, it was atmospheric.

There was also the scenery. He turned back to look. The trees had been planted years ago with the house in mind. There was an unrestricted view of the sea, the end of the cliff and the deep, falling sides of the wooded creek. He had canoed on the creek when he was a boy. Maybe he would take that up again.

His lips twisted wryly at the unlikely thought, and then the beginnings of the smile died on his face when he saw movement on the cliff top.

Damnation! That odd girl was there again. He could not mistake that dark red hair; even from so far away it was shining like a beacon. He could have sworn he had frightened her out of her wits yesterday. She'd been trembling when he had set her on her feet and he had watched her to the door of the cottage with some anxiety, sure that she would never make it.

But she was back, making her way towards the end of the cliff, carrying that ridiculously big basket. He cursed himself for his final words to her. He should never have said she could go back to the cliff. Only anxiety about her condition had made him do it. She had made him feel like a villain and she had stood up to him bravely for a good deal of the time.

He watched her through narrowed eyes and saw her sink down into some little hollow. After that he could only see the top of her head. What had she said? That she had to make herself small? That shouldn't take a lot of doing. She was hardly an Amazon when she was upright.

He would simply have ignored her and ridden off in another direction, but he had seen that slight limp she had and after a close look at her he had really begun to wonder if she would make it back to the village. She was pale, thin and had obviously been very ill at some recent time. He had expected her to sink down in a faint at any moment.

Her sharp rejoinder to his challenge had surprised him. However she felt physically, there was nothing wrong with her spirit. She had lashed out at him with her tongue when she should have been too scared to speak. He had only caught up with her to assure himself that she was all right. Then, of course, he had needed an excuse to take a close look at her. To inform her that she was trespassing had seemed like a good idea, and as it was the only idea he had he had used it.

The pallor of her beautiful face had not really surprised him. Even from a distance she had looked breakable. Her swift retaliation had stunned him, however, and he had almost laughed. The fact that he had very little to laugh about nowadays was definitely a point in her favour.

When she had stumbled, though, his own instinct for self-preservation had surfaced rapidly. If she had fallen over the cliff he would not have been merely under suspicion, he would have been arrested with some speed. Two women disappearing in the proximity of Pengarron Manor would have been too much for anyone to swallow, especially if one had been found at the bottom of the cliff.

When he had grasped her arm his action had been purely automatic, but when she had raged up at him he'd been able to see that she was quite likely to walk off in annoyance and proceed to her own destruction. Just ahead the path was to the very edge of the cliff, definitely dangerous. He had swept her up in front of him with very little thought of how this would appear to her. With hindsight he could see that she would probably have panicked, although she had tried very hard to control her fear.

She undoubtedly had him labelled as insane, and it had dawned on him very quickly that she was scared not only by his rather bizarre actions but also by the fact that she knew who he was. Clare Holden, of course, the rather gossipy aunt.

Normally the girl would have intrigued him. She had been feather-light, pale, beautiful, with that long dark red hair and brilliant green eyes. The Lady of the Lake. In spite of her swift, uncompromising lie he was certain she had been ill, very ill. His arms had enclosed her fragility and he had felt her trembling anxiety.

He did not write about legends, however, and his only thoughts had been to get her well away from his land and scare her from any further excursions there. At the last minute he had relented, and he knew now that it was because he had felt sorry for her and rather ashamed of himself.

Well, it served him right. She was now back on the cliff, no doubt just as pale and strained this morning as she had been yesterday. If he went near her he would feel like taking a chaperon, a witness who could testify that she had been safely at home and locked in and that the master of Pengarron Manor had been well out of the way.

She seemed the wrong sort of person to be crouching in long grass and watching insects. He glanced at her again, his near-black eyes sparking with annoyance. He had problems of his own, and a delicate, intriguing girl was the last thing he wanted to be considering. Whoever had attempted to bring about his downfall had not finished yet. He was sure of that. But why? Why? Why?

Which one of Gillian's dubious friends had reported her missing so quickly?

Jake had had weeks to think about this, weeks when he had expected to be arrested each day. The papers had had a field day. 'WRITER'S WIFE DISAPPEARS. Jake Trelawny, writer of many best-selling political thrillers, is now involved in a mystery of his own . . .'

They had blown things up out of all proportion. If anything else happened he would be back in the limelight, and that was why the girl had scared him into taking drastic action – action that was quite out of character.

He was not in the habit of rescuing damsels in distress. Gillian had cured him of any chivalry. His opinion of women had sunk to an all-time low. The rescue had been pure self-preservation, and he had not felt the need to acquaint the girl with that fact.

He went to his desk and took out the beginnings of the manuscript. He hadn't worked on it for weeks. Part of the reason for coming down here had been to get back to work without interruption. Much of the research had been done. It was now merely a matter of getting the rest and writing the story.

Before that, though, he had to go through the whole thing again and sort out the research he had

– the amount he had done himself and the hefty quantity that his researcher, Bob Carter, had sent on to him.

His books were fiction but there was always the hard core of fact in them. Facts had to be accurate. He would have to get down to some serious reading and sorting out. He had no time at all to be keeping an eye on Kathryn Holden. She would have to take her chances with the cliff top and her limp.

In any case, she was a woman. He glared down at the papers stacked on his desk. Papers were easy to deal with. If the worst came to the worst you could always throw them away and begin again. Women were a good deal more complicated, and any mistake with a woman tended to be permanent.

CHAPTER 3

Two days later, Kathryn decided to change her
location. She had exhausted all the possibilities of
the cliff top and she needed a field mouse. There was
obviously no chance of finding one where she was, so
after some consideration she turned her gaze on the
grass and woods bordering the creek.

There had been no sign during the week of Jake
Trelawny, and although she had surreptitiously
watched for the light from her bedroom window
she had studiously ignored the windows downstairs.

She had said nothing to her aunt about her peculiar
encounter with the seemingly notorious owner of
Pengarron Manor, and to her surprise Aunt Clare
hadn't mentioned him either. Whatever she and her
cronies in the little village thought, they were obviously keeping it to themselves. In any case, they
might have decided that it was not something to
discuss with an outsider, and Kathryn readily admitted to being one of those.

Her parents had died when she was only ten years
old and she had been raised lovingly by her grand-

52

parents. Sadly, they were no longer alive, and when she had been in hospital the only person she had been able to summon to help her had been Clare Holden.

Not that Aunt Clare had been a stranger to her. She had known her aunt for a long time, but her grandparents had never really approved of the fact that Clare was unmarried. To them it had been a sign of a bossy spinster, and in many ways that was exactly what Clare Holden was.

She was kind, though, and she had taken Kathryn in hand and brought her to Cornwall without any hesitation. Kathryn had tried to live in London again after coming out of hospital but she could not manage at first, and Cornwall was an ideal setting for her books. It had meant a new way of life, an escape from the past and any chance encounter with Colin. Sooner or later, though, she would have to go back.

On the morning of her change of venue, Kathryn started along the deep lane and then, instead of taking the path to the top of the cliff, turned towards the woods. She was well aware that this might not have entered Jake Trelawny's mind when he had given her his grudging permission to continue to come on his land. This time she would be somewhat closer to the manor house, and if he saw her he might very well object strongly.

Kathryn had survived the bout of fear. She had reasoned it out that he had been simply trying to get rid of her in case she found something to incriminate him. Well, she was not looking for anything other than a mouse. Police work did not interest her. She knew she was taking a risk but she decided that the risk was worth it. The book was finished, only a few illustrations were needed now, and she would like to get the whole thing off to London and her publisher before too long.

The fact that there were trees here made no difference to her sketches. She worked in the grasses, worked small, and the grasses and flowers in the woods would do well for the setting of the field mouse – if she could find one.

It was silent and cool in the woods and she stepped carefully over a little stream, crossing on rounded stones, trying to find the exact place, trying to keep her balance. The trees were tall, gnarled at the roots, moss-covered in places. There were a few bulrushes by the water and Kathryn's eyes were wide open, searching. She could scarcely believe her good luck when she actually saw a field mouse.

Kathryn sprang forward with one of her little pots open and pounced on it, almost overbalancing, and when she had it in her jar she looked for a good place to settle. She had brought a small rug to sit on today, knowing that the woods would be damp in places, and when she found her spot, she took the rug from her basket and folded it small to make a cushion.

There was bracken, lush, bending grass, and a little way down the stream she could see the clear yellow of a flag iris. She would need her colours today. It was wonderful here, like a sort of dream world, so different from the bright world at the top of the cliff. The colours were subdued, secret, another little universe.

The field mouse was afraid, sitting staring at her from the jar, and she handled it with care.

'I'll be quick. I really will,' she promised. 'I know you're scared. A few minutes and I'll let you go. Just behave yourself and you'll be free before you know it.'

Kathryn settled back to draw, and then stopped abruptly when she became aware that she was not exactly alone. There were two strong legs just in her vision, and when she looked up it was to meet night-black eyes below black, winged brows as Jake Trelawny stood over her and regarded her with a sort of furious resignation.

Kathryn suddenly realized too that the hem of her dress was wet. In her awkward journey over the little stream she had been very precariously balanced, and the hem had obviously trailed in the water. She looked at it blankly, touched it and then looked back up at Jake. She wasn't quite sure how annoyed he was and she wasn't quite sure how scared she was either, but he was there, inevitable.

It had to be fate, and if he attacked her then she would just have to scream. He looked annoyed enough to do just about anything. She was trapped anyway, so she decided to take matters philosophically. He didn't look quite so terrifying on foot as he had done on horseback And even if he was, there was nothing she could do about it.

'Oh, dear. I suppose I'm in trouble again?' She shrugged her slender shoulders helplessly, resigning herself to the irrevocability of it all. 'There was no field mouse on the cliff top.' She looked up at him again. 'I was hoping you wouldn't notice me.'

He still said nothing. He just pointed through the trees. And when she followed his direction, Kathryn could see that she was, in fact, almost in the garden of Pengarron Manor. It was a shock. She had been too scared even to think of going so close to his house and here she was almost in his lair. She had blundered into his domain like a fool.

'A Christian to the lions' den,' she muttered, and he suddenly looked thoroughly amused – the first time he had shown any sign of being really human.

In fact, he was very human, as he admitted ruefully to himself. He had struggled to work each day with his mind only half on what he did. His own private mystery was much more pressing than the manuscript. A good deal of the time today he had been simply wandering about the house, thinking deeply, staring out of the window and seeing nothing.

But he had seen Kathryn Holden, and his burst of annoyed disbelief when he saw the direction she was taking had faded into astonishment at her antics. She had almost had him holding his breath as she had gone over the stream, her balance greatly tested by the slippery stones. At one time he had thought she would fall in completely. She had managed to right herself, but not before the oddly coloured dress she was wearing had trailed in the water.

He had heard himself sighing with irritated resignation. She was an eccentric menace. He would have to go out and get rid of her. He could not afford to have her wandering around here. He would never willingly allow a woman here again, and even if he had been contemplating such a thing, it would never have been a woman like Kathryn Holden. He wasn't even sure if she was a woman. He wasn't sure what she was.

That was when she had started to dart about with one of those pots and pounce into the grass like a demented pixie. It had taken him some seconds to realize that she was catching something. One black eyebrow had risen sardonically. A beetle, no doubt. He saw her put it in one of those minute jars and then there was the rather complicated process of the blanket.

By the time she had finished and was prepared to settle down, Jake found himself out in the garden, heading purposefully towards her, and in spite of his inner irritation his lips were quirking with amusement. There were fairies at the bottom of his garden, or at the very least a disturbing water sprite. She hadn't exactly fallen into the stream, but her dress had been soaking up water as far as he could see. She had paid no attention to that at all.

As he looked down at her now the reluctant amusement faded and his eyes skimmed over her with a good deal of curiosity. He had never seen anyone quite like her before. He had always lived in a hard world which had not countenanced eccentricity. Women who had been interested in him had always been out for what they could get, and it had been there in their eyes, easily recognizable. He had always discarded them without a backward glance until Gillian had ensnared him.

This odd creature was different. She was almost too much for his mind to grasp. There was something about her that defied description. She did not fit into any category that he could recognize and he liked categories; they were safe, recognizable.

Kathryn looked up at him glumly.

'I've just this minute caught the mouse,' she told him dolefully. 'I suppose I'll have to let it go now. I can't take it away from here.' She looked at the little pot and its occupant in a dejected manner. 'Anyway, I should be drawing it already. It doesn't like it in there.'

'Can't you just ignore its finer feelings?' Jake enquired vaguely, feeling almost at a loss for something to say. The idea of speaking to her sharply and ordering her off his land now seemed to be altogether too harsh. One blast of his temper and she would simply blow away.

'It will die!' She glared up at him. 'Things as small as that go into a sort of panic attack and they die. Look at it! It's not moving, not even trying to find a way out.'

There was that quick flash of temper again that made her witch-green eyes glitter, and Jake's own eyes narrowed with irritation.

'Then get on with your sketching. The quicker you draw it, the sooner it can dart off and tell the terrifying story to its cronies,' he snapped. He could hardly believe he had actually said that. He was *encouraging* her. To his surprise she gave him a very approving look.

'Not many people can see that,' she murmured obscurely.

He was somewhat taken aback by the praise, especially as he could not follow her chain of thought, but she was now ignoring him, her pencil flying over the thick pad on her knee. However scared she was of him, she was more intent on doing what she had come here to do, and he realized with a sinking feeling that he would not have the heart to tell her not to come back again.

In any case, she looked uncannily at home here in the woods, as if she belonged here more than he did. If he hadn't seen her arrive he would have thought she had simply materialized in exactly the position she occupied now. It was the same when he had seen her on the cliff top. She had just seemed to appear. He knew where she was staying, but that made no difference at all to this uncanny feeling he had about her.

He sank down, sitting on a fallen log to watch her, and he assumed by her rapt expression that she had simply forgotten he was there. Any fear she had was being overridden by the task in hand. Her eyes kept flicking to the mouse in the pot and then back to her sketch.

It grew lifelike on the page and Jake didn't know what intrigued him most, the girl or her skill. She turned the pot to another side and the mouse didn't move. It gave her the chance to sketch another angle, and Jake found his eyes roaming over her with growing interest, his irritation fading.

There was something almost carelessly beautiful about her. Nobody had trimmed that magnificent hair for months by the look of it. It was a deep, glowing red, falling well over her shoulders, slightly wavy, enough to give it an odd look of untidiness that was strangely attractive. He knew a few women who would pay a fortune to have their hair arranged like that. Kathryn Holden's hair had just arranged itself.

There were the eyes too, brilliantly green, looking enormous in her pale face. And she *had* been ill, no matter what she said. Her arms and hands were much too slender. He wondered what had been wrong with her. She kept restlessly moving her leg, as if it troubled her.

He couldn't see her leg. The dress was too long. No wonder it had dipped in the water. It was gauzy, too light for the cool temperature of the woods. It looked as if she might have dyed it herself in a bucket at the sink. It was a strange jumble of odd colours. Well, she was an artist. They were usually a peculiar lot.

His eyes came back to her face when she sighed and looked across at him.

'That's it, then,' she told him in a resigned voice. 'I may as well let it go. Obviously it's not going to perform.'

'What do you want it to do?' The words were out before he gave them any thought. He was stunned at his interest in her. She had taken his mind completely off his problems.

'Run about, act naturally.' She frowned and stared at the mouse in deep concentration. 'I suppose it's too much to expect. If anyone put me into a jar, I wouldn't act naturally.'

When he found himself staring at her in fascination, Jake got to his feet and looked round quickly. The best thing to do was help her and then get her on her way. Clearly she had forgotten to be scared of him, so that was no further use as a ploy. Brisk assistance was needed and then she would go.

'You can release it into a barrier,' he said firmly. 'It will run around then.'

'You don't know a lot about small creatures, do you?' She squinted up at him seriously. 'It will either make off rapidly, before I can put pencil to paper, or it will sit absolutely still and go all catatonic, or it will keel over and die.'

Jake was extremely irked that his brilliant suggestion was being scorned.

'It's either try my idea or give up the whole thing,' he pointed out irascibly.

He was used to being in control, sure of himself, and this nymph-like oddity was regarding him with a somewhat scathing gloom, as if his education was lacking in important points.

He arranged a high barrier of sticks, ignoring the fact that he felt ridiculous doing it, and after watching him with wide, speculating eyes for a minute, Kathryn moved forward and let the mouse out of the pot. It didn't do anything at all and Jake was furious with it. He glared at the inoffensive creature and then glared at her. What was he doing here, playing like a child in the woods?

Kathryn shrugged her shoulders, 'what did I tell you?' written clearly on her face, and he sat back down on the log and stared at her coldly. He was very pleased with himself when she began to look uncomfortable. It restored his good humour because there was a definite feeling of a silent battle of wills with this irritating female.

'Why do you want it to run about if it's just to illustrate a book?' he snapped. He spoke to her because her look of discomfort had subtly changed, and she was beginning to look scared again. He found, to his vast annoyance, that he didn't really want that either.

'It's not just to illustrate a book! It's to illustrate one of *my* books. The illustrations are for children. I – er – I turn the creatures into a sort of small human world of strange things.'

'Insects? Beetles?' Jake tried to sound scathing but he was intrigued again. He leaned forward and rested his elbows on his knees, his hands hanging loosely between his legs.

'Oh, beetles are a good subject. This one for instance.' She turned the pages of the pad back and he saw a wonderfully accurate drawing of a beetle. 'Look,' she muttered enthusiastically. She executed the drawing again at lightning speed, but this time the irritated-looking beetle was dressed in a waistcoat and flat cap. She dived into her colours and the waistcoat became a brilliant red, the cap a dark tweed. Binoculars appeared and a flower in the buttonhole. A race track grew around him and she grinned up at Jake.

'A day at the races.'

He was just beginning to let himself relax when she suddenly muttered excitedly, 'He's off! I must get him fast.'

It was the mouse, and Jake was ignored totally while she sketched away. There were only a few minutes before the mouse made it through the fence Jake had created and then it was gone. Kathryn was smiling, and when he looked down Jake could see that she had spent the time well. He wondered exactly how she would dress the mouse.

He frowned at the thought. What was he thinking? This bizarre girl was growing on him, making him feel slightly disorientated. It was high time he got rid of her. He stood up and glared down at her.

'It's time to go now, Miss Holden,' he announced coldly.

'I wanted to get that flag iris.' She pointed down the stream and Jake felt his hold on his temper slipping. She just didn't know when to stop, did she?

'No,' he said uncompromisingly. 'Trespassing is over for today.'

'All right,' she agreed with quiet resignation. 'I suppose you've behaved as well as could be expected under the circumstances.'

'What circumstances?' Jake glowered at her more than ever. If she was meaning he had behaved reasonably well for someone suspected of dark deeds . . .

'Well, I was trespassing. Almost trespassing into your garden this time. Most people would have been annoyed.'

He forbore to point out that he was annoyed, instead he decided to remind her that she was scared of him. It seemed, after all, to be the only way he was going to get rid of her. He did not want her hanging around here and he had to make sure that she never came again.

'If I recall, the last time we met you expected to be attacked, Miss Holden,' he said grimly.

She nodded, bending forward to collect her things.

'I know, but if you'd been that way inclined you would have done it then and there. Nobody could have stopped you. I decided you were most unlikely to murder me.'

'I have not murdered *anybody!*' Jake raised his voice to an actual roar but she glanced up at him without any sign of fear at all, just complete astonishment at the power of his voice.

'I didn't say you had.' she pointed out gently. She gave it a moment's serious thought. 'I suppose you haven't anyway, and Aunt Clare says it's impossible. She says you're wild and probably dangerous but you would never hurt a woman under any circumstances.'

Wild and dangerous! Jake held his temper in check by a very thin thread and looked down at her icily.

'My thanks to your aunt.'

Kathryn didn't even look up. She was busy collecting her things, stuffing them into the basket, behaving as if he wasn't there, and then she stood up ready to go.

He could see immediately that she was a little unsteady on her feet. The leg again, he supposed. She had been sitting for quite a time and now it was hurting. All the same she didn't say a thing. Not one word of complaint. Once again he felt ashamed of himself.

She was a nuisance but she had courage, and she had never tried to use her problem to gain his sympathy and get what she wanted. Most of the women he knew would have played on it, but not this one.

She shivered and that was it. If she was going to die it was most certainly not going to be on his land. Not everyone had her aunt's faith in his integrity. If anything happened to her he would be blamed instantly – if not by the police then by the general populace.

'I'll take you back to the cottage,' he said sharply.

'No, thank you. I don't like the horse.' She looked up at him very firmly indeed, and Jake blinked before his mind righted itself. He seemed to keep stepping into an oddly slanted world with this strange girl, losing the drift of things.

'I am not riding a horse, Miss Holden,' he pointed out sarcastically, but instead of looking embarrassed, she gave him a small, potent glare.

'I'm perfectly capable of seeing that, Mr Trelawny! Your offer to take me back to the cottage suggested a form of transport, and as I know you possess a horse, and have forcibly made me accept a ride on it already, my mind naturally went in that direction. I don't like riding so high up. I prefer to walk. In any case, there is absolutely no reason why you should think of escorting me. I can go back to Aunt Clare's cottage all by myself.'

'Your dress is wet, the basket is heavy and your leg hurts,' he snapped, no longer caring if he hurt her feelings by pointing out that he had noticed her limp. She was weird, irritating. He would bring her down to earth if it killed her.

'Apart from the wet dress, I had all the other handicaps when I arrived. Taking them back with me is no great problem.'

She looked slightly amused, gently condescending, and Jake's ready temper rose again very swiftly, simmering at the edge of boiling.

'You're shivering with cold. Would you like to have pneumonia?' he rasped.

She turned away and moved off, not even glancing back at him.

'No, thank you. I've already had it quite recently,' she informed him softly. 'But it was nice of you to ask.'

She went over to the stream and managed to get across without falling, although her dress trailed in the water again, and Jake watched her in stunned silence. He wasn't even sure if she was real. For a second it actually came into his head that on the two occasions when he had seen her, there had not been anyone else there at all.

He shook his head angrily, and as she passed out of sight he turned back to the garden and the house. Of

66

course she was real! He had touched her. She was as light as gossamer, breakable, and she smelled of some delicate perfume. She was no trick of his imagination and she was a damned nuisance. He didn't want her here.

Next time she came he would show her what he was really like. He would storm out and order her off his property. She had to stop coming because it was dangerous – dangerous for him. She didn't look at all capable of seeing to her own safety and he already had problems in good supply. He did not need any more. And every instinct told him that Kathryn Holden would be a problem that would grow alarmingly if he didn't get rid of her.

Pneumonia. No wonder she looked so pale. And she had joked about it in her peculiar way. Everything about her was unusual, and he had a strange feeling that she represented an on-going threat. It was like an omen. If anything happened to her, all hell would break loose.

He grunted angrily. He should have taken hold of her arm, marched her to the house and got the car out. He should have driven her to the cottage and informed Clare Holden that she was not to allow her niece to trespass on his land ever again.

As to the damned horse, he didn't even own one now. He was never here. He had borrowed the great black brute for a day from a neighbouring farm with some idiotic idea of going back to the past. But he had no desire to go back to the past. He had never been happy at home. Clare Holden was right, as usual. He had been wild because nobody had really cared at all what he did.

By the time he got back to the house he was furious with himself. He felt as if he had been playing in the woods. God! He'd even enjoyed it for a time, and he had never once thought about his problems. If he had not borrowed that horse he would never have seen Kathryn Holden. Tomorrow, if he saw her, he would let her know without any doubt that she was not to come here again.

Very early next day he showered and dressed and prepared to put in a good day's work on the manuscript. He knew he was neglecting important things because of the mystery of Gillian's disappearance. She might never be found. It might all be true – she might be dead. Work was the solution, and in any case his editor would soon start prodding him, asking where the manuscript was.

He opened the curtains downstairs and looked out at the day. It was not too good. That damned fog was creeping back. Not that it mattered. He intended to stay inside the house and work all day. As he turned away from the window movement caught his eye and he stopped, sheer, disbelieving annoyance flooding through him when he saw that it was Kathryn Holden.

She was standing up, sketching in that fast and furious way of hers, and he knew what she had come after – the flag iris. As he watched she closed her sketchpad and moved off to leave the wood. She had came and done what she wanted to do even before he was about. He looked at his watch. It was only just seven.

One thing about her: she was determined. It irritated him to acknowledge that he had been relieved to see that she was warmly dressed.

And that made his mind up. He was rapidly turning her into a responsibility. Next time she came he would order her off his land and he would ignore the huge green eyes, the pale, smooth skin and the delicately curved mouth. She could go and haunt somewhere else. Tomorrow he would watch for her and do a little pouncing of his own. He would pounce so ferociously that he would scare her off permanently.

But she never came. He watched for her when he should have been doing plenty of other things. He even found himself walking along the edge of the cliff, going down the steep, rocky path that led from the end of his garden down to the sea.

His relief that she had not fallen after all was tinged with unreasonable annoyance. She had drifted into his life and now she had drifted away without giving him the chance to put a stop to her himself. She had left him with the feeling that he was not quite in charge of things.

Who the hell was she anyway? Where had she come from? Did she always live with Clare Holden? She had taken his mind off work, and he had the feeling he would spend a lot of time peering through the windows, expecting to see her again. He did not need such irritating distractions. He had work and he had problems. He could do without any more.

Kathryn did not send her book to London; she decided to take it instead. And she did not look at her reasons too closely. In the first place, she was beginning to feel guilty about staying with her aunt for so long. Clare Holden had a busy social life even in this small place, and Kathryn sometimes felt in the way.

She also felt that she was somehow dodging life by hiding in Cornwall – because that was what she had really been doing, hiding away in a little paradise, refusing to think about Colin and the accident and determined not to acknowledge that there was now a small gap in her life where he had been.

Kathryn knew how weak he was, how selfish, and it had come as no surprise. Deep down she had always known his faults. She had simply accepted them. When he had come to her in hospital with his flimsy excuses he had been expecting her to exonerate him, to absolve him of any guilt.

Normally she would have done exactly that, but she had been too ill and so the cover story had sprung to his lips – another girl, someone he had met, one of those things. He might very well have been speaking the truth, but she knew it would not last long. His true colours would emerge and he would be looking around again.

There was no reason to hide from him at all. Kathryn had no real idea of how she would feel if he came back and wanted to take up where they had left off. Normally she would have just smiled and accepted it, but her attitude had changed while she had been down here and that was another reason for leaving.

She was becoming much too enthralled with Jake Trelawny. He was unusual, unpredictable and mysterious. He appealed to her artist's mind and instincts. Kathryn was not quite sure whether she was afraid or fascinated, but she was not about to try and find out.

That he was dangerous was a fact, obvious. Even if he had not murdered his wife, it was only necessary to look at him to see the danger. Those winged black brows, the penetrating dark eyes and the feeling she had that he was barely holding down a violent rage for most of the time. He was savage, untamed, untameable, and she was becoming enthralled by the land he owned, the cliffs, the woods and the old manor house. It was time to return to reality.

'You're not fit!' Aunt Clare had stated strenuously. 'Once back in the city all your old problems will resurface. Besides, you still need looking after. You have no appetite, you're too thin and London is full of traffic fumes – not good for anyone recovering from pneumonia.'

'I'm going to take care of myself and go very easy,' Kathryn had promised. 'I must face life again. In any case, I have to have physiotherapy for this leg.'

'Anything you need can be found in Cornwall There's life here, you know!'

'My doctor at the hospital has arranged everything. I wouldn't feel too happy about ignoring his advice.'

Kathryn had felt very guilty when her aunt had looked at her intently, reminding Kathryn without words that she was ignoring *her* advice.

Still, they had parted amicably, as usual, Kathryn mused as a taxi deposited her by her studio flat, and she realized that she was happy to be here, back in her own place, surrounded by her own things. For a while she had seemed to be living in a dream, and meeting Jake Trelawny had merely deepened the feeling. Reality was a safer bet and this place was certainly real.

Kathryn grinned to herself as she dismissed the taxi and stood with her luggage outside the old market that took up the bottom of the building that she called home. She lived in a bizarre place. Her aunt had pointed that out a little grimly when she had arrived to take Kathryn back to Cornwall months ago.

The market was old, and brightly lit even in the summer – Kathryn had never discovered any windows down on the bottom floor. It was old, Victorian, with a concrete floor that had been added at some time when building regulations had demanded it. The stalls were fixed, brimming over with vegetables, fruit, meat and fish.

You could buy anything here from bread to rather gaudy lampshades, from reels of thread and yards of material to cheap shoes and umbrellas. The whole

72

place smelled of everything from fruit to spices, and the stallholders seemed to be as fixed as the stalls they owned.

'Yer back, Katie!' One burly man in a green apron, his sleeves rolled up over muscular arms adorned with bright tattoos, beamed at her. 'Missed the sight of you!' He pushed a boy out into the narrow aisle. 'Help Miss Holden to the lift with her things, Teddy. She still looks like a ghost. Didn't I tell her not to go off to Cornwall? Well, didn't I?'

There was a round of grinning agreement from several of Bert Lewis's fellow stallkeepers, and Kathryn found herself escorted by a boy as burly as his father, who picked up her things and led the way, leaving her to walk through good-humoured teasing to the lift at the back of the market.

'There yer go, Miss Katie.' Teddy deposited her luggage in the old lift and when Kathryn was inside pulled the huge doors closed, and she was in silence that was only broken by the whirring of machinery.

The huge service lift that had been used when the whole building was market and warehouse was now her way to her flat. She grinned to herself again. Not a flat, an apartment – an artist's lair at the top of an old warehouse. She was longing to see it again and she would get Snowy back as soon as she could contact Ralph. She hoped Ralph had watered her plants.

She peered through the iron grilles of the old lift as it creaked its way upward. Ralph was on the floor below her, and both of them never ceased to exclaim about their good fortune in finding this place.

There were just the two of them here in the building. When the market closed at night there was silence, and it was just what they both wanted. Ralph had been with Kathryn at art school and he had found this old place originally. In his spare time he had wandered all over the riverside, and it had been the market men who had told him that the top two floors of the building were empty and dilapidated.

It had taken a lot of searching to find out who owned the place, and a lot of arguing to get permission to have the two floors altered, but finally they had succeeded. Kathryn had had a little money left by her grandparents and Ralph had borrowed from his father. What they had turned the two floors into was a credit to ingenuity and artistic flair.

The lift passed Ralph's floor, and as he didn't come out to look Kathryn knew he was not in at the moment. When it stopped at the top of the building she breathed a great sigh of relief. Home! The best home she had ever had. The little square landing was still undecorated, that was her next project, but as she put her keys in the door to her apartment Kathryn's heart gave a great leap of pleasure. This was hers; she owned it. Nobody could intrude unless she invited them here. Even Aunt Clare's frowns had faded when she had seen Kathryn's lair.

As she opened her door the dark little landing faded from the mind. She shut it out and just stood looking round with pleasure. Everything was light, bright and airy, almost dazzling. There were great floor-to-ceiling windows that looked out over the river, and the fact that the view was of other warehouses, barges and run-down streets did nothing to distract from the view really.

It was interesting – bustling in the daylight, silent at night – and often Kathryn wished that her skill was in painting busy people, unusual and amusing people, because she could sit all day and watch them.

Her main room was huge – living room, sitting room, dining room and studio all rolled into one. The white walls were covered with bright pictures. Some of them she had painted herself, others had been her grandparents'. There were a couple that Ralph had generously donated and the rest she had bought at sales and cleaned up with loving care.

There were two long settees and two deep armchairs, all upholstered in pale oatmeal and brightened by soft cushions. The old oak tables had also come from sales and had been polished until they gleamed. There were brass pots with plants in them, and Kathryn hurried across to look at them carefully, her smiles growing when she saw that Ralph had not forgotten to water and feed them.

She took her cases into the one bedroom and thankfully kicked off her shoes. She had a bathroom and kitchen and that comprised the whole of her little paradise. Ralph's place was pretty much the same. Both of them had sacrificed another bedroom for the luxury of the huge room that served as their place of work and their living quarters. Each apartment was an artist's dream and the light was wonderful.

Kathryn had just showered and changed into jeans and sweater when her doorbell rang. She hurried to answer it, and when she opened the door a great, furry ball of white sprang at her as Snowy leapt for her shoulder, leaving Ralph's arms in a flurry of feline claws and open-mouthed pleasure at seeing Kathryn again.

'I thought I might get to say hello before he hit you like a rocket,' Ralph Preston muttered, rubbing his arms where Snowy had dug in strong claws to get his purchase for a launch. 'I need a coffee and medical attention.'

'I'll make the coffee; you can see to your own wounds,' Kathryn laughed as she turned back to the little kitchen with Snowy on her shoulder. 'You've been over-feeding him again. I can feel my legs buckling.' She rubbed at her shoulder when the big cat sprang lightly to the back of the settee. 'He's going to have to let that old habit go.'

'You'll get your strength back,' Ralph promised, coming in and closing the door behind him. His eyes ran thoughtfully over her. 'How do you feel?'

'Much better. I can now cope.' She glanced at him with a smile, turning it into a wry face when he looked doubtful.

'So how did things go down in Cornwall?' he asked, perching at the edge of the kitchen table.

'Very well. The book's finished. I'll show you when we've had the coffee.'

'Did you have any adventures?'

'In Cornwall? You've got to be joking.' Kathryn supposed that Jake Trelawny could have been classed as an adventure, but she was not about to tell Ralph about that. She had not even mentioned it to Aunt Clare because it had all been so improbable.

What would she have said to anyone, come to think of it? Well, I met this man and he scared me because I thought he just might have murdered his wife. All the same, I went on his land, and he built a barrier for a field mouse and then he wanted to take me back to the cottage because he was worried about me, even though he was furious.

He *had* looked worried. He had also looked at the edge of violence, but it hadn't really scared her. Kathryn wondered why. She felt a bit wistful about not being able to go in the woods round Pengarron Manor ever again. There was something very special about the place. She had only just left and yet it was calling her back, almost spoiling her pleasure at being in her own place.

She could not get Jake Trelawny's face out of her mind either. Nobody had ever made such an impression on her before. Dark, dangerous and unpredictable, he had fascinated her.

CHAPTER 4

'So what are you pondering about?' Ralph asked astutely when she methodically made coffee without her usual chattering.

'I'm thinking about the physiotherapy I have to have this week. I might just combine my two journeys. The book to my editor and a swift visit to the hospital.'

'An exciting prospect.' Ralph sat down with his drink and squinted up at her. 'It all sounds very mundane. Therefore, you're hiding something.'

'I wish I was,' Kathryn laughed. She came into the bright room and sat facing him. 'How is the masterpiece progressing?'

'Not bad. After two false starts, I now have the hang of it.' He grinned at her concerned expression. 'Seriously, it's good. You'll be the first to see it when it's finished.'

Kathryn nodded, smiling across at him, thinking once again how comfortable Ralph was to be with. He was just a year older than her, but his crisply curling fair hair made him look much younger. He was not really anybody's idea of an artist. Boyish, bright, friendly, there was nothing of the brooding quality about Ralph.

'While you've been away I've been thinking,' he remarked as she saw him out of her door later. 'If you and I had been sensible, we would have fallen in love. Under those circumstances you could have stayed here without any necessity to go to Cornwall. I could have looked after you. It would have been my duty.'

'No, thanks,' Kathryn laughed, pushing him into the hall. 'You even over-fed the cat.'

'That was deliberate. Snowy is ungrateful. He only likes you. I had to feed him regularly to keep him even reasonably tame. I figured that if he was too heavy he wouldn't be able to leap for my throat.'

Kathryn looked at the cat as she finally got the door closed.

'Slimming begins right now,' she warned, but Snowy simply stared at her and went to sleep. He was contented, back in his own world, and so was she.

Kathryn walked across to look out over the river. The lights would be coming on soon and she would settle to a quiet evening alone without any inclination to sneak to the windows and surreptitiously watch. She knew the lights of Pengarron Manor were a long way off, a safe way off, and it was better like that.

Jake sat in the taxi and frowned at the passing traffic without really seeing it. He didn't know why he was back in London. He had never intended to leave Pengarron and come back here. It was noisy, too busy, not the best place to work under any circumstances. He had planned to stay in Cornwall and really get down to work. Instead, he had come back. Illogical actions always annoyed him, especially when he was the one being illogical.

He looked at the park beyond the railings as the taxi sped past. A little area of tranquillity and not a soul stepping onto the grass. They were all hurrying past on the pavement, getting out of taxis, stepping off buses, heads down and busy – people he didn't know, would never know and didn't want to know.

What was wrong with him? He had never had any difficulty in working in London before. He had *always* worked here. He lived here! Now he felt too restless to settle to anything.

It was the damned mystery. And he knew perfectly well why he had come back. He had been bored, too bored to concentrate. There had been so much silence for the past two weeks that it had threatened to deafen him. He had wanted to be back in the traffic, back with the bright lights, the bustle. And now he was regretting it.

He glanced sourly through the window, his mind far away. Who? And why? Somebody had set him up, but for what reason? After being a political journalist for some years he had probably made a few enemies, but none he could think of off-hand.

It must have been something that had happened quite recently, happened while he was researching this book. He had gone over each day painstakingly, gone through his notes, questioned Bob Carter, and neither of them had been able to come up with anything.

He was left with only one conclusion. Either Gillian had decided to hide herself away for some obscure reason or one of her dubious lovers had killed her. The latter wouldn't surprise him. He had felt like killing her himself on more than on occasion.

The idea of her running off was not really likely. Gillian liked money too much – *had* liked it too much. He had plenty of money, his books earned it, and the thought of her leaving it willingly was hard to swallow – unless she'd had a better offer.

Somehow he couldn't picture her being alive, and that worried him. He was not at all psychic but he had this feeling about it. And he was sure she was still somewhere in Cornwall, alive or dead. Perhaps that was why he had wanted to get away? Perhaps he didn't really want to know what had happened?

He scowled out at the traffic. That had not been the only reason for his coming back and he knew it. He had spent a lot of time looking for Kathryn Holden – more time than he could spare. But, like Gillian, she seemed to have disappeared – somebody else who had whisked away out of his life with no warning. He was really concerned that something had happened to her, but he could hardly call on her aunt and ask if she was all right. He had enough to worry about without taking that on board. If she had actually disappeared, though . . .

Jake suddenly sat up straight and banged on the glass partition behind the driver.

'Stop here!'

'We're nowhere near Kensington . . .'

'Never mind. Stop here and wait.'

He had seen her well before they got to the place where she was standing. There was no mistaking that red hair, that slender figure. Even if he hadn't been able to see her face he would have known it was Kathryn Holden after just a glimpse of her. And she was in trouble, leaning against the railings of the park, her face whiter than ever with pain. Well, at least she wasn't lying dead in some sea-washed cave. He was astonished at the feeling of relief that knowledge gave him.

Jake actually had one leg out of the taxi when she moved and threw up her hand, and he swore under his breath as a taxi skimmed in skilfully and picked her up.

He almost fell back into his seat, slamming the door.

'Follow that taxi!'

'You joking?' A grinning face looked at him through the mirror and Jake glared back.

'I am not joking. Keep it in sight and I'll double the fare.'

'Right. You're not joking. Just the fare on the meter, guv. I don't get to do this crime stuff often.' He signalled and swung round in the road when it became obvious that the other taxi was doing the same, and Jake felt his hands clench at the idiotic thing he was doing.

He was out of his mind. He didn't know this odd girl. He didn't want to know her. She was safely in

London and not posing any threat to him by being dead in Cornwall. He had mountains of work to do. She hadn't collapsed on the pavement; she had signalled for a taxi and got one. She had damn all to do with him. He knew the local milkman better. There was nothing wrong with her. She had even been dressed properly, in a cream linen suit and flat yellow shoes.

His jaw tightened. Why had he noticed all that in the few seconds before she had disappeared into the taxi? And what was 'dressed properly'? He knew deep down. He had expected to see her in some flimsy, gauzy, extraordinary dress, wet at the hem, her huge green eyes staring up at him. He had got used to thinking of her as some sort of strange nymph, part of his other environment.

She was normal, ordinary, and he didn't know her from Adam. He leaned forward to tell the driver he had changed his mind and then leaned back grimly. He hadn't changed his mind. He wanted to follow her, find out where she lived, speak to her.

It really was like being haunted, and he had to put a stop to it. He had to run her to earth and then forget about her. He could not do with thoughts of her floating around at the back of his mind like something he had imagined.

Anyway, the driver was enjoying himself, skimming round cars and buses, after the taxi in front like a ferret, grinning and whistling through his teeth. Jake was sliding across the back seat each time they made a bend. It did nothing to improve his temper.

They turned down by the old docks. So far this place had escaped the developers and it did not look too salubrious. Jake frowned out of the window at the warehouses and the few mean-looking houses that had survived. Where the hell was she going? She couldn't possibly live in a place like this. It just didn't suit his picture of her. She was light, airy, an illusion, something at the edge of a dream.

'There she goes, guv.' The taxi drew up well behind the one in front as the driver played his part to the end and hid his vehicle round the corner of the wall. He nosed out a little way and Jake saw Kathryn getting out and paying off her own taxi.

He could have hit his own film-struck driver. She would be out of sight before he could get to her. He jumped out and thrust some notes into the man's hand.

'Keep the change.'

'Thanks, mate. It's been a pleasure. If you want to do this sort of thing again, I'm game. Take the cab number.'

Jake glared at him. He strode out quickly, telling himself that he didn't give a damn whether she was an illusion or not. He was doing this because he was bored, too bored to write, too bored to settle to anything. He was going to see her in her own environment and get her out of his head.

When he got to the entrance to a very peculiar market she had disappeared, and he felt like a fish out of water. About fifty eyes seemed to be staring at him as he walked into the place, and looking round he could see no sign at all of Kathryn. That red hair was no longer visible. She seemed to have vanished and Jake wasn't really surprised. He was getting used to being haunted. The fact that she had disappeared as usual was only to be expected

'Can I help you with anything?' A burly man appeared in front of him, looking very suspicious, and Jake decided that the truth would probably serve him as well as anything.

'I saw a friend come in here, a young lady with red hair.' He got another suspicious glare and added quickly, 'We met in Cornwall. I lost touch.'

'That'll be Katie, then.' The man relaxed into smiles. 'She's got the top floor – the one above Ralph. She's just gone up in the lift.' He turned round and bawled at the top of his voice. 'Teddy! Take this gentleman to the lift. A friend of Miss Katie.'

Jake found himself being escorted across the market, all eyes following his progress, and then he was in the old lift. As it groaned upwards he was wondering what he was going to say to her when he got there.

It was a long time since he had done anything idiotic, unplanned and impulsive. He glared at the iron grid of the lift when he remembered that it had not actually been all that long ago at all. He had acted like a fool when he had first seen her, and even more so that day in the woods.

The lift came to a shuddering halt at the top of the building and he stepped out onto a small, square landing, his frown growing at the sight of it. God! What a place. She would be embarrassed if she knew he was here and had seen where she lived. There were peeling walls, old paintwork. Her flat would be cheap, sordid. He had no right to run her to earth.

He was just about to leave without her knowing when the door opposite opened and she was there, staring at him with nothing but shock in her eyes, and it was all too late.

Jake couldn't think of anything to say. For once in his life he was speechless, because now that she was close he got the feeling again that she was unreal, and the fact that she was still wearing the skirt of that cream suit and a pale blouse under it didn't seem to make much difference at all.

'Mr Trelawny!' She stared at him with those incredible eyes and Jake just stared back, trying to think of a way to explain his unforgivable behaviour.

'I saw you,' he said finally. 'I thought you looked ill.'

Kathryn nodded, running the tip of her tongue round her bottom lip nervously. She seemed to simply take his lame excuse at face value.

'I was going to get Ralph, but I wasn't sure I could make it to the lift. It's my leg, you see. I went to physiotherapy and then I slipped. I really hurt myself. There was this man – he bumped into me. Otherwise it would have been all right – I mean, I could have managed. But then it hurt . . .'

Her voice faded away and Jake felt an odd wave of feeling sweep over him. It was something that grew deep inside, something he had never felt before. It was like the swell of the ocean before it crashed on the sand, a peculiar bitter-sweet sensation. Suddenly she was his responsibility, and he automatically grasped the awareness. He took a step forward and she bit into her lip.

'I could have given you a coffee, but now I don't think . . . Will you get Ralph, please? He's one floor down. He said he would have looked after me, and I need . . .'

She pitched forward just as Jake stepped towards her, and he caught her easily. She seemed to weight nothing at all and he swung her up into his arms, using his foot to push the door open wider. He was fiercely glad now that he had followed her. She would have been lying out there on the cold, miserable landing, and if she had been, somehow or other it would have been his fault. He accepted it.

Jake kicked the door closed behind him and then stopped as he looked round in surprise. He might have known. The water nymph had always looked fastidious. This room was refined, sensitively and charmingly arranged. All the colours were pleasing, calming. It was an artist's room, light, airy and attractive with quite the biggest damned cat that Jake had ever seen.

Kathryn opened her eyes to find herself lying on one of the settees. Jake was just moving away from her and she felt such a fool. He turned round as she moved and Kathryn looked up at him a trifle sheepishly.

'I'm sorry,' she whispered. 'I've never actually done that before. I expect it was the pain.'

'I'm sure it was. All the same, you should see a doctor.' He came back to crouch down beside her and look at her seriously. 'Give me the number and I'll ring for someone to come and take a look at you.'

That was enough to have her struggling to sit up, and Jake stood and moved back. Suddenly he felt as if he was intruding unforgivably. The feeling of being responsible for her was, after all, no more than a passing quirk of imagination. She didn't know him, he didn't really know her, and yet here he was, in her flat without permission, crowding her.

'I'm all right now,' Kathryn said more firmly. 'I don't normally faint. It's just that I went for physiotherapy and it was a bit rough. When I was coming back a man bumped into me and I slipped and twisted my leg.' She looked away from him and rubbed at her leg. 'I expect I was being clumsy, not looking where I was going.'

Jake glowered down at her bent head, flaring with annoyance. Who could possibly be so churlishly careless as to knock her over? She looked so vulnerable. Maybe the man hadn't been looking where he was going. Maybe the man should have been knocked over forcefully himself. Kathryn glanced up and caught his ferocious expression and her face flushed.

'I'm sorry,' she repeated. 'I never actually got around to asking you why you came.'

It was Jake's turn to look embarrassed, and he walked over to look out of the window at the river and the warehouses that lined the nearer banks.

'I saw you,' he confessed stiffly. 'You looked as if you were going to collapse. You got a taxi and – well, I followed.'

She astonished him by saying, 'Thank you. That was very nice of you.'

'Nice? I don't even know you.' He swung round to look at her and she smiled.

'Of course you do. I trespassed on your property. You know me quite well because I was making a nuisance of myself. Somehow, one always remembers nuisances because of the irritation. Sensible people never linger in the mind. It was good of you to think of helping me.'

Jake looked at her almost blankly. She constantly took him by surprise. He had a great urge to shock her by saying that he had not followed her to help, that he had simply followed her. He had not expected her to live in a place like this, alone. Maybe she didn't live alone. There was Ralph, whoever he was.

'You asked me to get Ralph for you,' he reminded her rather grimly, and she nodded.

'Oh, I remember. It doesn't matter now, though. I'm fine. I'll make some coffee.'

'Don't bother,' Jake said tightly. 'I don't want to intrude.'

'You're not intruding.' The clear green eyes looked up at him curiously. 'You were being kind. Anyway,' she added, 'I want a cup of coffee myself.'

'I'll make it.' When she started to get up he waved her back to the settee and moved towards the kitchen, glad of the chance to have her away from him for a

89

minute. He had a tremendous urge to start ordering her about, to take charge of her and firmly turn away all other people who called. She needed looking after and he wanted to do it.

He could see where the kitchen was; the door was open. He brushed past the cat and it opened rather baleful eyes and glared at him.

'That's funny,' Kathryn said in a thoughtful voice.

'What is?' He turned to look at her and found her eyes on the cat.

'You touched Snowy. Normally he would be unreasonably annoyed by that. He hates it if anyone invades his space and usually he takes immediate action. He growls, you know. Just like a dog.'

'He looks like a monster. How much does he weigh?'

'I don't know, actually. Anyway, he's slimming at the moment. Ralph over-fed him when I was in Cornwall. He was trying to bribe him. Snowy doesn't like anyone but me.'

'Who's Ralph?' Jake called from the kitchen. It was none of his business but he had to know. He felt strangely irritated that she lived here, knew somebody called Ralph, went out, caught taxis and had a great monster of a cat. She should stay in the woods where she belonged. She should be sitting with her sketchpad, with the sunlight catching that red hair. She should be talking to him in that weird way she had. How did she talk to Ralph?

Jake scowled his annoyance at the coffee jar. It was easy enough to find things because they were all out

90

on the immaculate surfaces, everything labelled. That was wrong too. She should have been disorganized, helpless, but he had the feeling that if she had not been ill and temporarily lame she would be forceful and irritating, arguing all the time.

'Ralph? He's my friend. He lives below. There are just the two of us in this building. Ralph found it and we bought the two floors. When the market closes at night it's wonderfully quiet.' There was a little pause, and when Jake said nothing and got on with making coffee she added quickly, 'We went to art school together. Ralph is a very fine artist – a real artist.'

'So are you.' He came out carrying two mugs of coffee and frowned at the cat as he carefully avoided it. He had the feeling that she would not be too thrilled if he scalded the great beast with hot coffee. And he was damned if he was going to let her get away with praising this Ralph person as if she was no sort of artist herself.

'Ralph paints people,' she pointed out softly.

'And you paint mad-cap beetles, but you do it wonderfully.'

She smiled up at him. 'Landscapes are actually my forte, but there's really no money in it, and the idea of writing children's books and illustrating them took my fancy. I get well paid.'

Jake gave her her coffee and then sat facing her, staring at her in fact, unable to take his eyes off her fascinating face. She gulped down some of the hot liquid and then looked at him levelly, showing no sign of her previous embarrassment.

'What do you do for a living, Mr Trelawny?'

'Jake,' he corrected her. 'I write. Political thrillers.'

'I've never read one.'

'You're not missing much. Your education won't suffer if you avoid my books.'

Kathryn put her head on one side and stared back at him for a minute. He looked angry, and now that he was in ordinary clothes, city clothes – a dark grey suit, white shirt and grey tie – he looked different. He was no longer the dark master of Pengarron. He was somebody else entirely. She couldn't make her mind up what he looked like now.

He still looked forbidding, though, and in ordinary clothes he looked perhaps more dangerous than ever, like a strong, fierce, beast torn from its natural surroundings, waiting to defend itself in a hated world. Those incredibly dark eyes could still fill her with unease but she was also intrigued. He had a funny way of looking at her, as if she weren't there, although he seemed to be studying her minutely.

'I belong here, you know,' she pointed out softly.

'Meaning what?' he asked crisply. The night-black eyes snapped to hers, the winged brows arrogantly raised.

'You're looking at me as if I sort of landed here accidentally, as if I might just disappear for no reason.'

And that was not a bad bit of mind-reading, Jake thought disgruntledly. He was having trouble keeping her here in this atmosphere. He knew damned well that she was an artist, and this was the best artist's lair he had ever seen, but he couldn't get it out of his mind that she should be in the woods, looking ethereal.

He almost wished he hadn't seen her here, like this. When he was back in Cornwall her other image would have vanished.

'You left Cornwall,' he stated flatly, and Kathryn felt a small shudder of feeling. His voice was almost accusing, as if he had the right to question her movements, as if she should have stayed where he had found her. For a moment she actually felt guilty about leaving his land.

'Yes. I considered that I had put on my aunt's good nature for quite long enough. She's quite a busy person and sometimes I knew she was staying in and missing something just to be with me. In any case, I live here. My book was finished too. I decided to bring it instead of sending it.'

She had no intention of adding that she might well have stayed if he hadn't been there. She could hardly tell him that in some peculiar way he was interfering with her thoughts, drawing her into his life.

Jake stood abruptly and put his cup down, annoyed with himself for being here at all. He didn't want to have an image of her in Cornwall. He had come here to set his mind at rest that she was normal and now he was right back where he had started, staring at her with a sort of annoyed compulsion, fighting the urge to take over her life.

The tables were polished like glass. She would really raise her eyebrows if she had a good look at

Pengarron. The two old bodies who looked after it had probably run out of polish years ago. He had expected her to live in some sort of hovel when he had followed her through the market and seen the little landing outside her flat. Instead everything was immaculate, tasteful. Nothing made sense with her.

'I'd better be on my way,' he said coldly. 'If you like I can get your friend up here first.'

'Ralph? No, don't bother, thank you. In any case he'll call in later; he always does. I feel fine now.'

She didn't, and he knew it, but at least there was a little more colour in her face – and it was nothing to do with him in any case.

'How's the pneumonia?' he asked sourly, because he couldn't give her a shaking which for some obscure reason he wanted to do. He wanted to snap her into being another character that he could dismiss scathingly, as he usually did. He wanted to bring her to her senses, and yet she probably had more sense than he had himself. She grinned at him, taking him by surprise.

'The pneumonia is quite gone, thank you. It was nearly eight months ago since I had that. The complications lingered for ages, but I'm better now.' When he went on staring at her in silence she looked away and then said, 'I was in an accident, a car accident. I was lying in the snow for quite a long time, lying on ice. With the shock and the cold . . .'

'Is that where you hurt your leg?'

'Yes.'

'And is it improving?'

'So they tell me, although today I have my doubts. As soon as the pain stops I'll believe them again.' She stood carefully and went with him to the door. The cat got up too and Jake eyed it warily, but it rubbed against his leg and Kathryn laughed delightedly.

'I wish Ralph could have seen that. Snowy sneers at Ralph and looks threatening. Obviously he likes you. It really is odd.'

'Maybe I frighten the cat too,' Jake muttered, and she looked at him seriously.

'I don't think you're frightening now, and Snowy fears nothing. He chases dogs.'

'I can believe it.' Jake suddenly found himself smiling. Of course, she would have to have a monster of a cat who thought it was a big dog. He turned at the door, reluctant to leave. He felt curiously at home with her, peaceful. Something about her drained his temper and his restlessness. He had never actually felt like that before in his whole life. Everything had been a fight, always.

'Have dinner with me?' he asked quietly, and she looked back at him in that level way she had.

'I don't think so.' She shook her head and gave him one of her strange little smiles.

'Why?' He couldn't seem to let it go so he was crowding her again, unreasonably annoyed that she hadn't simply said yes. He wanted to prolong this meeting, see her again. He hadn't got her sorted out in his mind and he liked to have people classified and dismissed. Sooner or later she would do or say something that would fill him with contempt, then he would be rid of her, back to normal, by himself.

'I don't think you would be comfortable to be with. You would overwhelm me. I can't do with people like that at the moment. I have to get really well before I tackle anything powerful. I like very simple things.'

'Like Ralph.' He couldn't stop himself from saying it.

'Like Ralph,' she agreed with another smile. 'Ralph doesn't try to read my mind. He doesn't look at me as if I'm not here either. He *knows* I'm here. He's safe.'

'So am I,' Jake assured her, knowing it just wasn't true. He was pushing her and he knew it. He wanted to overwhelm her, to take charge of her. He had the feeling that *she* was the reason he had suddenly found the silence at Pengarron ear-shattering and he had to get rid of that feeling. 'I only asked you out to dinner. I'm not inviting you to fight me.'

'I know. I don't think I'm up to it, though. Not yet.'

'You'll think about it when you're fit and able to take me on?' He was being sarcastic but she chose to ignore his tone.

'Something like that. In any case, I like simple things.'

'And what makes you think I don't?'

'You're different. You're powerful, strong and a little dangerous.'

'And I murdered my wife?' Jake asked harshly.

'Did you?' The clear green eyes looked directly into his and he frowned blackly at her.

'No!' He turned and went to the lift and as it went down he looked at her through the grille. She was still standing there; the cat had jumped on her shoulder. It was a huge, white monster but it somehow looked tame sitting there, and she didn't look strong enough to take the weight.

There was a fair-haired man standing on the next floor waiting for the lift to come back up, and Jake glared at him too. Ralph, no doubt. Another artist. They were probably lovers. He stalked out of the market without looking at anybody. He was used to getting what he wanted and she had simply said no in her quiet way.

He hailed a taxi and slumped in the back seat, glowering at the darkening day. It would have been a good thing if he had not seen her, because he wouldn't be seeing her again. Today had been that chance in a million, and he could well have done without it. Kathryn Holden unsettled him. He told himself that he didn't want her in his life at all. Powerful and dangerous! If she thought that then why the hell had she taken the risk of going into the woods at Pengarron?

Jake had a flat in a great, curving development fairly close to the West End. The rents were prohibitive but he had never had the slightest desire to own a house or flat. Renting one suited him fine. In any case, he had Pengarron.

The flat was big, looking out over the park, and was sufficiently high up to give him a good view, should he ever need one. He rarely needed a view. Mostly he worked and never even glanced out of the window.

Since Gillian had disappeared he had had the whole place redecorated, and had even got rid of some of the furniture. He had not wanted anything that reminded him of Gillian and the turmoil she had brought to his life.

He spent the next two weeks working almost constantly. Gradually he was getting all his notes in order, and making more as he waded through the research. The problems that had plagued him since Gillian had disappeared were pushed to the very back of his mind as work took hold and the plot of the book grew.

He made his own lunch each day, walking around the flat as he ate, dictating into his machine or reading. Most evenings he went out for a meal, usually by himself. He was not good company when he was working at the best of times, and now he was more than ever hard and unapproachable. He had grown a tough shell around him a long time ago, and since Gillian had disappeared he had deliberately let it harden more.

The real mystery was working its way around his mind and becoming mixed up with the plot of the book he was attempting to write. Normally he wrote fast, with few distractions. Once he had sorted out his notes and research, any book just came together without pause. Now, though, he seemed to be working with no real end in sight, making only half his usual progress.

Jake let himself into his flat one evening two weeks after his meeting with Kathryn and did what he did every night. He took off his jacket, dropped it on a chair in the hall and went to turn on the shower in the bathroom.

As he was coming back into the hall there was a rush of flame, and a bundle of rags dropped through the letter box and fell to the parquet floor, burning furiously. There was the smell of petrol and Jake acted on sheer instinct.

He swept up the burning mass and threw it into the shower cabinet. He could feel it scorching his hand, but luckily one portion of the bundle had not caught the flames yet and he got away with little more than an angry red mark.

He opened the door and raced into the passage. There was nobody there and the lift was not moving. He took the stairs two at a time and was in the foyer in seconds.

'Who came in just after me?' he snapped out at the doorman.

'Nobody, Mr Trelawny. I locked up as you came in, as usual. You always seem to be the last in at night. I generally make myself some coffee when you're safely home.'

'Any new tenants?' Jake wanted to know, but even as he asked it he knew he was wasting his time.

'Definitely not, sir. People tend to rest content when they've managed to get a flat here. We haven't had anyone new for at least three years.' He looked concerned. 'Is something wrong?'

'No, nothing.'

Jake managed a rather grim smile because he was cursing himself for a fool. Of course nobody would have run down here after trying to burn him out. They had not come down the stairs. They had gone up. There were three floors above his own and then a perfectly flat roof. Anybody trying to escape would have had that move planned beforehand. By now they would be down the fire escape and well away. They would have come in that way too.

He took the lift back up, suddenly realizing that he had left his door wide open and the shower running. If the rags had fallen over the outlet the shower would be running all over the floor of his bedroom by now.

It was not, and he closed and locked the door, switched off the shower and began a thorough search of his flat. Nobody was hiding there, and as far as he could see nothing had been stolen while he was downstairs.

So what had it been about? Somebody had taken a great risk, placed the other residents in danger, and for what? Who hated him so much?

Jake poured himself a drink and walked about thinking, and it was so obvious after a second that he felt idiotic for not seeing it right away. Nobody had meant to set fire to the flat and this building.

Whoever had pushed petrol-soaked rags through his letter box had been watching for him to come in, had seen him come in and had acted immediately. They had probably been on the stairs above, knowing exactly when he would come back home. He had been meant to see the flames and put them out.

So it was a warning. And if it was a warning then it must be tied in to Gillian's disappearance. For the first time ever he began to wonder if she was a prisoner somewhere, a hostage to his good behaviour. The trouble was that he had no idea what he was supposed to do.

It told him something else too. He was being watched, probably followed. He asked himself if Gillian would have this done but immediately dismissed it. She had nothing to gain. She could walk back in at any time, divorce him and take a great deal of his assets. Gillian would be much more interested in that. And she certainly would not pay to have someone follow him. Money was for clothes, jewellery, expensive restaurants and tropical holidays. It was not Gillian. Two mysteries in his life were too much, though. In some way this had to be connected to her disappearance.

He called the police but it was not the lugubrious Inspector Harrison. Two young policemen arrived and looked over the flat. They were totally unimpressed.

'No real damage seems to have been done, Mr Trelawny. We get a lot of this sort of thing,' one of them assured him.

'You mean it's not unusual for somebody to enter a building, pick out any flat and try to set fire to it?' Jake asked scathingly. 'People do things for profit. What are you suggesting? That some mindless youth took the risk of stealing up here via the fire escape, just happened to pick on my flat and then shot off without another thought?'

'Oh, I would imagine the thought was there, Mr Trelawny,' a gloomy voice predicted, and when Jake looked round Inspector Harrison was standing in the open doorway, squinting across the hall, his mouth twisted unevenly as if he had been sucking a lemon. 'I'm inclined to agree with you. People do things for a purpose. The trick is to discover what the purpose is.'

He nodded his dismissal at the two young officers and they seemed to Jake to be thankful to leave. He felt a twinge of sympathy for them both. Inspector Harrison was not the sort of man to inspire gushing confidence and undying devotion. He looked as if he would keep his own counsel at all times and offer no assistance to the young and floundering. He also had a nasty habit of appearing when least expected.

Jake gave him a baleful stare.

'I suppose you have ideas about the purpose?'

'Possibly.' The inspector put his hands in his pockets and rocked back and forth on his heels. 'Given that it's extremely unlikely that some odd-ball is going to climb up here and pick you out by sheer coincidence, this has to be connected to your . . . troubles.'

There was an irritating little pause before he actually said the last word, and Jake's dark eyes narrowed with annoyance.

'I worked that out for myself. It makes no sense, though. My wife chose to disappear and – '

'We don't exactly know that she *chose* anything,' the inspector corrected. 'Once again we come to reasons. People disappear every day, but there's always a reason. They either wish to make themselves scarce for reasons of their own or they are abducted . . .'

'Or murdered,' Jake filled in angrily.

'There's that. It's been five months with no sign of her and no word from her. Unless you've heard, Mr Trelawny?'

'I have not!' Jake snapped. 'Believe me, if I had, you would have been the first to know.'

'Yes, it's upset your life,' the inspector muttered thoughtfully. 'Did you get on well with her?'

'You know damned well that I didn't,' Jake snarled. 'You've already questioned all the people I know. We've been through this often enough.'

'Hmm.' The inspector screwed up his lips further and continued to rock back and forth in his usual annoying manner.

'Do you want a drink?' Jake asked vaguely.

'On duty,' Harrison muttered with equal vagueness. 'I've been thinking a lot about you,' he added, and Jake gave a harsh bark of laughter.

'I can believe it. I expect I'm being followed? Every action noted?'

'S'matter of fact, you're not being followed. Not by us at any rate. We haven't the manpower to have someone dogging your footsteps day and night.'

'You mean you've given up?' Jake stared at him in astonishment, and what just might have been a smile touched Inspector Harrison's face.

'No. Your wife is missing, Mr Trelawny. Foul play has to be suspected. You must realize that yourself. We don't just give up.'

'So what about this episode tonight?' Jake asked frustratedly. 'Who do you think it was? Gillian shinning up the fire escape?'

'Unlikely.' The half-smile appeared again. 'She doesn't seem to be the type.'

'A Rolls would be her method of approach,' Jake said sourly.

'You don't like her much, do you?'

'She tore my life apart, even when she was there. She's done worse since she disappeared. All the same . . .'

'All the same, you wish she would come back?'

Jake gave him an irritated glance.

'I don't want her back. I just want to know she's all right.'

'To get you off the hook?'

'Dammit man, she's a human being!'

'Aren't we all?' the inspector muttered, turning to leave.

'Only some of us!' Jake snarled.

Inspector Harrison actually laughed, but his going left Jake with the uneasy feeling that tonight's episode had brought back an unrelenting blood-hound to his own particular trail.

CHAPTER 5

Kathryn was on the settee with her legs up when the phone rang. She had been rather dreamily considering whether or not to venture out and have her hair cut. Ralph had mentioned that it was getting too long. Not that it was any of his business, but he enjoyed interfering with other people's lives.

'Have it cut short,' he had suggested. 'Hair like that would curl up tightly like mine.'

Kathryn was not at all sure that she wanted her hair to look like Ralph's, and she was just considering what she would look like with a curly mop of red hair when the phone rang.

It was Betsy Greene, her editor.

'Smashing,' she pronounced vigorously. 'That's the second Bertie Beetle book. I think we should have three – a trilogy.'

'I'm getting fed up with beetles,' Kathryn grumbled. 'I was thinking of taking time off to do a landscape.

'You can't afford time off,' Betsy assured her briskly. 'Three Bertie Beetles and then choose another insect. You're in demand now. Never fail your readers.'

Kathryn knew it made sense but she hated being pushed around. Anyway, it would mean that she had to go out into the country again and she was just enjoying her home environment. It might mean a trip to the Lakes or somewhere.

'Get back down to Cornwall and start the new book immediately,' Betsy ordered, and Kathryn sat up and frowned at the telephone.

'That's absolutely out of the question!'

It was. In the first place she refused to make demands on her aunt's hospitality again after such a short time away, and secondly there was Jake Trelawny. She couldn't seem to get him out of her mind, and the fact that he was here, somewhere in town, didn't make a lot of difference. London was a big place. The chance of running into him accidentally was about one in a million and it had already happened, so it couldn't happen again.

If she went to Cornwall she would be in his environment. In her mind, the whole area where she had stayed was Jake's home territory, his hunting ground – a realm he prowled like a lean, powerful tiger. She would be expecting to see him at any minute. In London she would never see him. In Cornwall he would be living practically on her doorstep.

'Of course it's not out of the question,' Betsy insisted vehemently. 'You have a public, children who adore your books, and mothers who have lots of money in their purses. Cornwall it is, then.'

'No,' Kathryn said stubbornly.

'Come to lunch tomorrow. Twelve-thirty at the office. See you then.'

Betsy put the phone down, and when Kathryn rang her back at once the answering machine was on. Kathryn's lips tightened in annoyance. Betsy was the most irritating person. She was like a stone wall.

For the rest of the day Betsy was pronounced to be out of the office each time Kathryn rang, and Kathryn had no alternative but to resign herself to a trip out for lunch the following day. She would *not*, however, go back to Cornwall.

Jake Trelawny was too powerful an influence. She had even been scared to go out to dinner with him. And it had not been because she feared a physical assault. The thing that bothered her was what he was doing to her mind. He was filling her head like the mist that rolled in from the sea. Like the mist he was secret, silent, and he didn't even have to be there.

She was strangely attracted to him and she knew nothing about him really. All she knew for certain was not promising. Even her aunt, who defended him stoically, had said he was dangerous, especially to women. His wife might have found that out in the worst possible way.

Kathryn felt trapped by her own thoughts. She wanted to get out of the flat; going out tonight would be a good thing because she was unsettled, restless. She had an invitation for this evening too. She had not wanted to go but now she decided that it would be a good idea to mix with other people, to bring a bit of fresh air to things.

Kathryn got up and found the large gilt-edged card that had come through the post a few days ago. It was a showing at a gallery in the West End, very prestigious. Contemporary art by Vanessa Stokes. Ralph would have received an invitation too, they could go together. He was good company. He would make her laugh.

When she went down to make the arrangements she found Ralph in a foul temper.

'I'm not going,' he snapped when Kathryn mentioned the showing. 'You know what La Stokes is like. One minute she's after me as if I'm some sort of smouldering Romeo and the next she's making spiteful digs at my work.'

Kathryn thought of Vanessa Stokes and smiled. Vanessa had come in to college when they had been there and had acted as a part-time tutor. That had been before her own work had taken off and become the thing to buy. It was true that she had taken quite a shine to Ralph and embarrassed him enormously.

It had been obvious to everyone else that Vanessa had been inviting an affair. She was older than Ralph and very experienced. Ralph had been horrified. He had had his eye on another girl of his own age, a sweet girl called Rosie. Vanessa had taken it out on him in the class with various pointed and extremely catty remarks.

'The place will be packed,' Kathryn said coaxingly. 'Vanessa will never even notice us. She'll be drifting around all gauzy and artistic.'

'She'll be creeping around all sadistic and vampirish,' Ralph corrected sharply. 'I'm not going, and that's that. When I have my showing she'll not come – the ego being shattered.'

'All right, I'll go alone,' Kathryn said soothingly, 'although I think you're wrong. Nothing could shatter her ego. She'll come to your showing and make remarks in a loud voice.'

'I'll handle that. It will be on my territory. I might even drift around and be sadistic myself.'

Kathryn went back to her flat feeling very amused. She was going to the showing whether Ralph accompanied her or not. It would get her out and clear away a few of the idiotic thoughts that came seeping into her mind nowadays.

Her amusement about Vanessa was still there as she got ready and the word 'vampire' had stuck. Kathryn decided to wear black. In any case, it suited her with her red hair, and she had just the thing for tonight. Not that she stood any chance of outshining Vanessa Stokes. Vanessa was now quite secure in the art world and her paintings fetched a small fortune.

Kathryn took a taxi, and as it deposited her at the gallery she noted how many expensive cars were there. It was the thing of the moment to buy a Stokes original, and she knew she would have to listen to a good deal of boring conversation and even more unenlightened assessment of the future value of the 'works'. Vanessa would be in her element. Ralph had been right to avoid the show.

Half an hour later, when Kathryn had spoken to all the people she knew and sipped champagne dutifully, she was becoming even more sure that Ralph had a good deal more sense than she'd ever given him credit for. She was bored to tears, waiting for the opportunity to slip away unnoticed.

In the meantime she was studying one of the paintings and giving some deep consideration to tying a brush to Snowy's tail and letting him have a go. If the prices being spoken of here tonight were anything to go by she could pull in a small fortune and buy herself a Bentley.

'Don't even consider it,' a dark, harsh voice advised. 'It's over-praised and over-priced.'

A tremor ran over Kathryn from her head to her toes. She had forced herself to come here tonight to get Jake Trelawny out of her mind and he was standing right behind her. She was surprised she hadn't known it even before he spoke. He gave off vibes like electricity, and right at that moment they were sparking all over her skin.

She turned slowly, bracing herself for the possibility that she might just be imagining this, but he was there, darker than ever in black tie and dinner jacket. There was something about him that was even more worrying than usual and she had the distinct impression that he was annoyed to see her there, was filled with angry disapproval.

'Mr Trelawny,' she managed, feeling a little breathless.

'Miss Holden.' He looked down at her mockingly. He glanced round the room and then looked back at her with a rather cruel, taunting slant to his mouth. 'I'm really surprised to see you here. Surely you're out of your depth?'

'I have an invitation,' Kathryn assured him tersely, quite certain that the mockery was because she painted children's pictures and should surely be out of place in the world of real artists.

'Of course. You're not exactly the type to gatecrash something like this, are you?' he murmured sardonically.

'Definitely not! I'm ineffectual and dull, timid and pitiful. Obviously you noticed.'

Jake got a flashing burst from the green eyes, and he watched her, enthralled by her face and the witch-green eyes. His desire to goad faded. In fact, he had been standing looking at her for a good while before he had approached her. Once again she had simply appeared, just as she always did. She was in black too, something he had never associated with her, but as usual she made the dress into something entirely different from the maker's original idea.

It swirled down to her ankles – another gauzy creation. It was sleeveless, showing her creamy skin off to perfection and he had been standing looking at her flawless back where the dress was cut away almost down to the waist. She was wearing flat gold shoes and he had been puzzling as to how it was that she managed to look so innocent and wide-eyed in a dress like that. Other women would have teamed it up with high heels, jewellery and an altogether different look on their faces. Kathryn Holden made black look virginal.

He took her arm, and before she could protest led her to another part of the room where there were not so many people. Once there he manoeuvred her so that she was against a tall potted plant and his size was shielding her.

'Are you here alone?' he asked, looking at her intently.

'Ralph had an invitation too but he refused to come. Vanessa annoys him.'

'You know her?' It surprised him, shocked him. She was too delicately innocent to know anyone like Vanessa. What the hell was she doing here anyway? This was not her scene, this loud, sophisticated gathering where the ill-informed made firm pronouncements and other sycophantic idiots agreed at great length.

Besides, she shouldn't know people like Vanessa. If she did then the innocence was an illusion. He knew Vanessa Stokes himself.

'She was a part-time lecturer at art school,' Kathryn said, watching his expression a trifle warily. 'That was before she really got going. She fancied Ralph and it used to embarrass him. That's why he refused to come with me. Also she has rather catty remarks to make about his work.'

'Are the remarks justified?' Jake asked quietly, fascinated by her face and the dark red hair, by the way she stood like a changing shadow against the wall, trapped by the huge plant and by his own lean, powerful frame.

'No. Ralph is good.' She glanced round the room at the various paintings on view. 'I mean, really good. His works will be hanging in galleries when Vanessa's paintings are in somebody's attic gathering dust, but, as I said, she's got going now.'

'Oh, she got going a long time ago,' Jake murmured ironically, and Kathryn's face flushed. She recognized innuendo when she heard it and her mind went back to her Aunt Clare's remarks about all the girls running after Jake Trelawny. Vanessa wasn't exactly a girl, though, and obviously Jake Trelawny hadn't changed much.

'So you came to see Vanessa and not to worship art?' Kathryn said tartly, her eyes on his face with a touch of disdain that annoyed him.

'You think I'm too rough to be in a place like this?' he asked harshly, his anger flaring. 'You think of me as a sort of wild man with no place in polite society?'

His hair was too long but it suited him. Even in a dinner jacket he managed to look wild and free, not quite part of his environment. She looked up at him seriously for a minute and then shook her head.

'A tiger, I think, only partly tamed.'

'I'll take care not to put my paw in the champagne,' Jake growled angrily. 'Now I can understand your reluctance to have dinner with me. I'm a great beast who might just start licking my plate.'

'It wasn't that and you know it,' Kathryn protested, flushing softly. When he was angry those incredibly dark eyes gave off a glow that threatened to burn her.

'Of course not. You suspect me of worse things than being a partly tamed tiger, don't you?'

'I don't suspect you of anything because I never think about you,' Kathryn lied. 'I don't know you.'

'You do,' Jake grated. 'You knew me on sight, feared me on sight. I'm a villain of the worst order, under suspicion. You think I'm hunting you for diabolical reasons of my own.'

Kathryn went even more pale, and there was a rather frantic look in her eyes that filled him with a mixture of rage and compassion. He was just about to rein in his unpredictable temper and apologize when a hand came to his arm.

'Jake, darling! What on earth are you doing hiding in the bushes?' It was Vanessa and Jake turned to face her, struggling with rage and a sort of helpless frustration.

She noticed Kathryn and the coal-black eyes spun over her swiftly.

'Why, hello, Kathryn,' Vanessa purred. 'I really must introduce you to Jake properly one of these days. What a nice little dress, dear.' She turned back to Jake, dismissing Kathryn totally. 'Darling, come and see the latest thing I painted. I know you're bored but I really won't be long, then we can go off for the evening together.'

Jake looked down at her. She was utterly without morals as he knew perfectly well. She had dismissed Kathryn smoothly and he wondered if it was because she knew that she could never look like that. Vanessa was in black too, but it made her look glossy and slinky, the dress too tight, the jewellery over-done.

He looked at Kathryn, his glance shooting over her. She looked pure, ethereal, an angel in black chiffon, the lights behind her giving her red hair a hazy aura that made her almost unreal. But those witch-eyes were knowingly alert, sceptical, disdainful. She had instantly classed him with Vanessa, judged him and written him off. He had a sudden desire to hurt her.

'Lead the way,' he murmured, smiling down at Vanessa. 'I can wait if you can.' He nodded coolly to Kathryn, 'Goodnight, Miss Holden. Don't stay too late. It's dark outside.'

'I'm not staying at all, Mr Trelawny. I've seen all I wanted to see, thank you.'

He glared at her. She was right; they hardly knew each other – but they understood each other with no effort at all and she had left him neatly in a trap of his own making. He turned and walked away but her face lingered in his mind. Why the devil had he wanted to hurt her? Because she had said he was like an untamed creature? It was true anyway. And he had certainly thrown her to the wolves. He turned back but she was gone already. She always went. She disappeared. If he raced outside she wouldn't be there.

'Come along, Jake, darling,' Vanessa purred. 'I really won't be long.'

'Take as long as you like,' Jake advised coldly. 'I'm leaving now but don't let it worry you. Your time was up about five years ago if you recall?'

'You're a bastard!' she hissed, her cheeks colouring angrily.

'Agreed,' he said smoothly. 'But then, that's no surprise is it? You knew that already.'

He walked out of the gallery, trying not to hurry, some vague hope that Kathryn would still be there urging him on. She wasn't, of course, and he walked to his car in a deep, black mood, his mind seeing two faces. One of them belonged to Vanessa, with her dark glittering eyes and long black hair all styled for effect. But Kathryn's face was radiant, haunting him.

It seemed to him that the women he had known had always been like Vanessa Stokes. Gillian had been like that — hard, glossy, over-sophisticated. Perhaps she had not been as obvious as Vanessa but they were of a kind, the only kind he seemed to have known. Kathryn was outside his experience. He didn't know how to deal with her. She was frustrating, like a beautiful elf, and he could never quite get her out of his mind.

Had he but known it, Kathryn had managed to get a taxi and move off just before he came out of the gallery. She was not feeling as haughty as she had looked inside. Seeing Jake had shocked her in the first place. She had never expected him to be there. One of the reasons she had gone was to try and forget about him

His harshly taunting manner had upset her too, hurt her, in fact, and she asked herself angrily why. She didn't know him, didn't want to. He was dangerous, cold, and if she never saw him again it would be too soon. All the same he seemed to have encouraged Vanessa to behave as she had done – and he clearly knew Vanessa well. Very well. They were going to spend the evening together and, knowing Vanessa Stokes' reputation, Kathryn knew what would happened after that.

Ralph was right. The woman was a sort of female vampire and most men seemed to be willing to let her prey on them. Jake Trelawny did not come into that weak category, though. He was hard, sceptical, and not about to fall for any female tricks. He had, therefore, simply wanted to go with that woman.

Kathryn knew he had wished to hurt her. She had seen it in his eyes, a sort of restless, prowling anger. Well, he would never know he had succeeded because she would take care never to see him again. Cornwall was now definitely off the agenda permanently, no longer a place she would visit. She was very fond of her aunt but Aunt Clare could come up here to see her and stay with her in the flat. They could rush around London and enjoy themselves. She would sleep on one of the settees and Clare could have her room. Kathryn began a sort of frantic planning, just to get Jake out of her thoughts.

When she got back, Kathryn went up in the lift, and as she passed Ralph's flat there was the most astonishing din. She stood looking down at his door as the lift took her up. If she hadn't known better she would have said that Ralph was having a party. It was nothing to do with her. By now she felt thoroughly miserable and extremely annoyed with Jake Trelawny. He had no right to behave like that – like a keeper. And he had no right to think he could punish her!

She let herself into the flat and threw down her bag, too annoyed at the moment to think of either getting ready for bed or settling to do anything. In any case, the noise from down below was deafening – but it made her feel strangely safe. Jake scared her.

The noise suddenly stopped, and a few minutes later she heard the lift coming up. Then Ralph was pounding on the door and it appeared that the noise had transferred itself to her landing.

'Surprise!' Ralph shouted when she opened the door.

'Shock,' Kathryn corrected as she looked at the mass of grinning faces. Her landing was packed with people by the look of it. At least two trips on the lift must have been necessary, although she had only heard the one.

'Er – what . . .? she began, but they were too boisterous to be held in check.

'Party!' one yelled, and whether she liked it or not Kathryn found her flat filling with laughing, noisy people who carried their own drinks, nuts, crisps and tasty nibbles. Bottles were deposited in the kitchen, bowls of things on her polished tables and the party simply re-established itself one floor up.

'Ralph?' she shouted wildly, trying to get to him across the room.

'They all came round to wish me well for my showing,' he yelled back. He shrugged helplessly.

'It sort of developed. Couldn't leave you out. Anyway, you know nearly everyone.'

Now that she was getting a grip on things, Kathryn realized that she did know most of the revellers. They were old acquaintances from art school days. Apparently Ralph hadn't grown out of that time, and as her eyes fell on one pretty, plump blonde Kathryn knew why. Rosie Cummings was here. She had been the apple of Ralph's eye at one time. By the look of it, she still was. And she had thought she knew him. When it came down to it, one didn't really know anyone deeply.

Kathryn gave one resigned glance round and then joined in. She was pretty fed up in any case. A party seemed to be just the thing, especially one like this, spontaneous and fun-filled. After a time at Vanessa's showing, Kathryn felt in need of a breath of spontaneity.

The whole noisy scene was still progressing two hours later, and she gave a silent prayer of thanks that there were no neighbours. The market had closed hours ago. It was almost ten. Nobody as yet had spilled drinks on her upholstery, or left sticky rings on her tables. The party nibbles had overflowed in a few places, but all in all it was not too bad. Snowy had gone to earth in his usual hiding place.

When the doorbell rang she felt a little nervous, anxiety from her student days flowing back into her head. She gave herself a small mental shake. There were no neighbours to complain and no landlord. This was her own flat. She owned it. And Ralph owned the one below so nobody had any reason to bother them. It was probably a latecomer. She hoped it was only one.

Before she could quite get to the door, Rosie, laughing and chattering with Ralph, opened it. She didn't even look to see who was there. She just flung the door open and turned away to Ralph with further giggles, and Kathryn was left about three feet from the open door looking into the amazed eyes of Jake Trelawny.

Kathryn didn't know how she felt at that moment – scared, annoyed or embarrassed. His dark eyes found hers; the black, winged brows rose in disbelief. She was feeling pretty much like that herself. What was he doing here? Why had he come? His little sojourn with Vanessa must have ended quite early. She was silent for a minute, and then her natural spirit reasserted itself.

'Come in, Mr Trelawny,' she invited gaily. 'Join the party.'

He stepped into the room but he looked very wary, and Kathryn had to walk round him to close the door.

'I thought you would be alone,' he said gruffly.

'Now why should you think that, Mr Trelawny?' she taunted. 'I have plenty of friends, as you can see.'

For some reason he looked thunderous, and also slightly out of his depth, and Kathryn felt the sweetness of revenge flowering inside. So he'd thought she was coming back to a lonely, empty flat while he sauntered off with Vanessa Stokes? He could not have come at a better moment.

Even more amusing was the fact that nobody took one bit of notice of him. He was so attractive, so striking, that the fact that he seemed to be invisible to everyone else there must have been a great blow to his ego. Normally heads would turn as he walked by. The heads here were fairly full of wine. The music was loud. Everyone was talking at full volume. Just the thing to irritate someone like Jake Trelawny.

One of the men walked past and put a glass of wine in Jake's hand, and Kathryn raised her own glass and looked straight into his eyes.

'Here's to parties, loud noise and old friends,' she said brightly. 'I'm so glad you didn't think to bring Vanessa. There must be about thirty people crowded into here at the moment, and at a guess I would say that at least twenty-nine of them despise her.'

'Dance, Kathie,' somebody said as the music started up again. He made a grab for her hand and she was going to go, but Jake grabbed first.

'My turn,' he said sharply.

'You're not entitled to a turn, Mr Trelawny,' Kathryn pointed out sharply. 'You're a gate-crasher. But then, maybe you are the type to crash a party?'

He put his glass down, took her glass and put that down too and almost pulled her to the side of the room, turning her against the wall and towering over her.

'What the devil are you doing in this chaos?' he demanded angrily.

'I live here!' She waved vaguely round the room as he glared at her. 'It's often like this. I'm a party-goer par excellence.'

'The hell you are!' Jake snapped. 'You're quiet, shy, ethereal.'

'You mean I'm an idiot, a poor little thing who limps?'

'I didn't mean that and you bloody well know it!' Jake took hold of her slender shoulders and seemed to be about to shake her. It infuriated Kathryn. He had no right to be here. Who did he think he was anyway?

'I live a life you know nothing about,' she said in a dignified voice. 'Kindly remove your hands from my person.'

'You've had too much to drink!' he rasped. 'You don't belong in this sort of noise and you don't belong in a drunken stupor.'

'I belong wherever I like,' Kathryn stated firmly. In fact she had only had one glass of wine. The thing that had gone to her head was seeing Jake here. She had no idea why he had come, but even though she was reeling from the unexpectedness of it she still had enough sense to know that he was pursuing her again. He had accused her of thinking that he was hunting her. What did he expect her to think?

'I can't talk to you in this pandemonium,' he muttered frustratedly. 'Come outside with me.' He was holding her wrist, and when Kathryn tried to free herself he simply tightened his grip. She was out on the small landing before she could react. Jake closed the flat door and backed her against the wall, his attitude menacing.

'There's nothing to talk about,' she said breathlessly.

'You know damned well there is!' He glared down at her. 'I have to tell you about tonight, about Vanessa.'

'You don't have to tell me anything, Mr Trelawny!'

'Stop calling me that,' he snapped. 'You're hiding behind formality.'

'I gave up hiding a long time ago.' Kathryn looked up at him firmly. 'I don't know you well enough to bother about hiding from you in any way at all. And I wouldn't lie to you because, quite frankly, you're not important enough to warrant the effort of lying.'

She tried to turn away but he grasped her shoulders, refusing to let her move. Kathryn stared up at him. She wasn't frightened at all. It was almost awesome to know that they were quarrelling. She was quarrelling with a stranger – and yet Jake was not that. She knew him. She somehow knew him deep inside. She could almost hear his thoughts. She went on staring up at him, her own bewilderment at her natural reaction to him showing clearly in her eyes.

'Kathryn,' he muttered raggedly. 'I don't know what to do about you.'

'Nothing. Just – just leave me alone. I promise I'll never come down to Cornwall again. I don't want to know you. I don't want to even catch a glimpse of you ever.'

The words were coming out in a whisper, secretly as if it was terribly important to keep this to themselves, and his eyes narrowed on her face as one hard hand tilted her chin.

'You're snarling up my life, complicating my days,' he accused tautly.

'That's not fair!' Green eyes looked wildly into his. 'I would never have known you at all if you hadn't stopped me on the cliff. I've never tried to be in your uncomplicated life. You followed me here tonight. How was that my fault?'

'I had to come.'

'No, you didn't. You – you're persecuting me.'

'For God's sake, Kathryn! I just want to be with you for a while.'

'Why?' She looked up at him with those clear, green eyes and he felt weighed down with frustration. Why was she so complex, so perplexing when she looked so innocent and unworldly, so naïve?

'I don't know,' he said roughly. 'Maybe you're my next victim.'

He could see the instant shock on her face. She pulled free and made a dive for the door before he could stop her. It opened and she was breathlessly glad that the latch had not caught as they had gone out. But she was not entirely free. Jake grasped her wrist again.

'Kathryn!' he commanded harshly – an order to stop even though no order had been given.

'Leave me alone!'

She snatched her hand free and moved off, mixing with the crowd, ignoring the glittering anger and frustration in his eyes. When she looked round again, he was gone.

He could hear all the noise as he went down in the lift and his anger grew with every second. Why had he said that to her? He had scared her deliberately and he didn't want to scare her. She just made him do things like that.

He hated the way she made him feel, the restless, unmotivated manner he was going about his days, unable to force his mind into any set channel. It wasn't only the mystery, it was Kathryn.

And he hated to think of her being up there in that unruly crowd. They were all drinking. They would probably end the night sleeping on her floor, sleeping with each other. Who would Kathryn sleep with?

He went back to his flat and prowled around for a long time, only stopping when he realized he was behaving exactly in the way she had described him, like a caged beast. He must be careful not to see her again. She had walked into his life right out of the blue and now she was haunting him. He was much better when he was completely alone. He had always been better alone. The feelings he had when he saw her would just have to stop.

Jake sat on the edge of Bob Carter's desk and leafed through the last of the research. It looked good, and even a slight glimpse of it suggested a brilliant ending to the book – if ever he got down to it.

'You know, I never got around to telling you this,' Bob Carter said into the silence that had grown between them, 'but your small fire rang a loud bell with me. Soon after I started on this last batch of research, somebody broke into the office.'

'Here?' Jake looked up at once, a frown on his face. 'Did they take anything?'

'That's the funny thing. They must have been looking through about every paper in the place. It was chaos when I got in the next morning, but nothing was taken. There's plenty of equipment here but it was untouched. They just messed up the papers. It would have been tragic, taken ages to sort out, but I had everything on disk at home. I just burned the lot and reprinted. That's what modern technology is all about.'

He grinned up at Jake but failed to get an answering smile.

'Was anything of mine here?' Jake asked quietly . . .

'Nothing. I hadn't started writing these things down. Complete mystery. Whoever tried to set fire to your Persian rug was about as competent as the person who broke into here.'

'Did you report it to the police?'

'Nah! Nothing was lost. Saw no point in wasting their time and mine. As I said, I simply reprinted – and changed the locks.'

'Life is full of mysteries,' Jake muttered. He picked up the papers and put them into his briefcase. 'Let me know how much I owe you, Bob. I'll probably have to pay by instalments.'

'That would be news,' Bob laughed. 'Jake Trelawny down on his luck.'

He wasn't down on his luck, Jake mused as he went out to try and get a taxi back to his flat. He was just being pulled in several directions all at the same time.

There was Gillian and her disappearance. There was the fire attack – if that was what it had been meant to be. He also had an absolute conviction, with no good reason, that the break-in at Bob's office concerned him too. There was the definite feeling that things were closing in on him. It was like fighting in the dark because he had no idea who to hit out at.

And there was Kathryn, who constantly strayed into his thoughts, wispy, unreal, haunting, like a brightly coloured leaf drifting down the lonely stream of his mind. No wonder the book was being pushed into the background.

And why had he behaved so abominably last night at the gallery? Why had he wanted to hurt her? Why had he so stupidly gone to her flat? She frustrated him, angered him, and she would not stay in one place long enough for him to settle his mind about her.

He had wanted to apologize, but seeing that wild party had shocked him utterly. She wasn't a dream after all; she was real. She had parties, friends, and she had cut him down to size with no effort at all. He would not try to see her again.

He looked up and there she was, standing across the road, looking impatiently about, obviously needing a taxi, and Jake felt as if he had imagined her, as usual. He had to be very stern with himself because his immediate impulse had been to call out to her and that was a pretty pointless thing. They didn't know each other really and she didn't want to have anything to do with him. After their meeting at the gallery, and later at her flat, she would want to know him even less. He had behaved badly and he had the definite feeling that somehow she had made him like that.

He told himself firmly that he didn't want to have anything to do with her either, that he would walk off and ignore her, but he couldn't seem to stop looking at her. And right at that moment she looked across and saw him.

For a moment they just stared at each other, and once again, as their eyes met, Jake felt that surge of feeling. It was like a deep, deep breath, an almost painful expanding inside. Those green eyes seemed to get bigger every time he saw her and she had that unusual hair, deep, vibrant red, like something from an old painting. It was glittering in the sunlight. He was almost turning her into a legend and he knew it, but he couldn't seem to stop.

She started to move, and he knew instinctively that she was coming across the road to him. How she expected to get across the traffic with that limp, he didn't know. She would be knocked down, injured even more. He had to stop her. The thought of her being injured was like a biting pain inside him. All that fragile beauty torn, wasted.

'Stay where you are!'

He called out, leaping into action as he called, and it was only as the words had left his mouth that he saw she had not been coming across to him. She had been going for a taxi that was even now pulling up for her. He was out in the road himself by then, though, and he kept on going. He felt like an idiot, a schoolboy. He had been sure she was going to cross the road to him, he had *known* it, and now it was obvious that she had had no such intention.

Kathryn nervously waved the taxi on, ignoring the driver's caustic comments, and watched uneasily as Jake made his way across to her. She felt jumpy inside, butterflies churning round. They had started when she had seen him and they appeared to be determined to make her feel ill. It was a sort of excitement, as if she were on a fast lift, going down.

When she had met those dark eyes the sounds of the street had seemed to grow dim. For a tiny second nobody else had been there. She forgot about her anger and hurt of the previous night, all she could see was the lean, powerful frame, the black, glittering eyes. She felt almost sick with nervousness.

'I thought you were going to step out into the road,' Jake accused sharply as soon as he was standing by her on the opposite pavement. He glared down at her as if he had every right to do so and she just shook her head, saying nothing. 'What are you doing here?' he asked in that harsh voice, and Kathryn pointed to the building behind her.

'My publisher's. I had to have lunch with my editor and she dropped me back here to get a taxi.' She wanted to look away, to escape, but his eyes held her fast. 'It's funny, seeing you here.' she added shakily.

Spooky, Jake thought. Every time the thought of her came into his mind, she popped up like a pixie. He was beginning to think he deliberately made her appear. Some peculiar power he didn't know he had. He felt as if he owned her, as if he could snap his fingers and produce her from thin air like a magician. Last night she had angered him by stepping out of the slot he had allocated for her in his mind. Today she was back to being a nymph from the woods, lost in all the traffic, vulnerable. His very own responsibility.

'My researcher, Bob Carter, has his office right over there.' Jake pointed across the road, tearing himself away from the green-eyed inspection, and Kathryn looked across and then glanced up at him.

'Isn't it strange? We must have been standing one on each side of the road at the same time in the past and we never noticed each other.'

'We didn't know each other then,' Jake pointed out. He stared down at her in amazement. He never had this sort of mad conversation with anyone but Kathryn. He didn't have time for idle chatter and mystic musings. He was hard, businesslike, an ex-newshound. She was almost reducing him to the status of fortune-teller, and anyway, she should be shouting at him after the way they had parted last night.

'We don't know each other now,' Kathryn said quietly.

'Do you think twenty years will be enough time for a slight acquaintance?' Jake asked drily, and she laughed, glancing up at him with dancing green eyes. 'Have dinner with me tonight,' he ordered sternly, unable to stop himself from saying it.

Somehow this seemed like the last chance and she just kept on smiling, ignoring his authoritarian tone.

'All right.'

CHAPTER 6

Jake could hardly believe his ears. He was stunned at the way she had just given in. He could hardly believe he had asked anyway. Usually one rebuff was enough for him, and after last night he should have known better. He took a deep breath and looked round for a taxi, and as he glanced across the road a face in the crowd caught his eye.

It was years since he had seen that face, and even then never actually in the flesh. But he knew the pale hair, blond to the point of being almost white. He knew the arrogant chin, the straight, aquiline nose. He just stared, his mind working like a well-oiled machine.

'I – I have to get a taxi . . .' Kathryn began, and he snatched his mind back to her, suddenly aware that he had not spoken to her for a few seconds as the past had blotted out the present.

'No. I have to walk down here for a minute. Come with me,' he ordered.

She just stared up at him rather anxiously and he pulled himself back to the present more firmly, back from years ago, from the memory of that face, that hair.

'Now that I've actually captured you I don't want to lose you,' he said quietly. 'Walk with me for a minute and then we'll get a taxi.'

She hesitated for a second and then nodded her head.

'All right.' What could happen when there were so many people around anyway? She felt she ought to be scared but she wasn't really. There was just this funny feeling about being with him. It was almost choking her.

'Will you be all right with that leg?' Jake asked quietly, and once again she astonished him.

'Much better than I would be without it. Lead on. I'm willing to chance it if you are.'

Jake suddenly realized that he wanted to hug her. She was so different, so fresh and alive – no sophistication. He had had enough of that to last him a lifetime and beyond. For the first time since he had seen the man across the street he relaxed.

He took her arm, foolishly pleased with himself when she made no move to pull away and walk alone. He was with someone who was completely outside the world he knew. His eyes were on the man across the road but his mind was on Kathryn. For the first time in a long time he felt as if he belonged somewhere. She was another complication but it didn't seem to matter much.

When his quarry hailed a taxi, Jake gave up. He knew where he could find the man if he needed to.

What was important was the mental jolt the sight of the man had given him. Now all he had to do was hang onto Kathryn until it was time for dinner. If he let her go she would simply disappear again.

He hailed a taxi too, and ushered her into it before she could change her mind.

'This is going in the wrong direction for me,' she protested, and Jake sat back and felt as if he had won a strategically difficult battle with lightning speed.

'I have to drop something off at my flat. Then I'll take you to your place and later we can go out to dinner.'

He knew it would be a false move to let her out of his sight. He hadn't the slightest excuse for calling on her at her flat if she walked out on him now. He had to sort her out, settle his mind on the subject. She was one mystery too many. Besides, she was beginning to fragment his mind, tear him into two parts.

'I only just had lunch,' Kathryn pointed out, and he could see that he was pushing her again. It was only three o'clock.

'We could go to a film or a show first,' he suggested, desperately wanting to keep her now that he had her. He couldn't sort her out in his mind if she was constantly disappearing. She would always linger there, haunting him.

'All right. I haven't been out in the evening for ages – until last night.'

Jake let his breath out slowly. For some obscure reason he seemed to have won that round too. His reasons for wanting to win were equally obscure to him at the moment. She would turn out to be a nuisance. He was sure of that. He had no dark designs on her either. That was something to do with the fact that she wasn't quite real. Beautiful, intriguing, but not real. It was all new ground for him. Last night when she had been real he had been furious about it. The thought reminded him of his behaviour.

'I'm sorry about last night,' he said quietly. 'I don't know why I behaved like that at the gallery.'

'You wanted to hurt me,' she pointed out softly. 'We wanted to hurt each other.'

'Why?'

'I don't know. It doesn't matter anyway, does it? I expect you had a good night in the end.'

'I went immediately,' Jake grated. 'I left directly after you and I left alone.'

'But I thought . . . Vanessa said . . .'

'You told me you knew her,' Jake rasped. 'If you do then her motives should not be all that obscure. I knew her a long time ago.'

'You mean that last night you just walked out on her?'

'Why should that amaze you?' He turned and looked at her steadily. 'Like you, I got an invitation. I was bored so I went to the gallery. I did not go there to meet Vanessa Stokes.'

'It's none of my business,' Kathryn reminded him quickly, and he gave her one of those black scowls that he constantly showed.

'Then stop asking about her!'

135

His voice was sharp and she cringed just a little. Jake gave a great sigh and looked away, staring out of the window.

'I'm putting my paw in the porridge again, aren't I?'

'With consummate ease. You seem to have a flair for it.'

Jake glanced at her sharply but she was looking out of the other window. She was also smiling to herself.

'I'm sorry,' he said quietly.

'That's all right. I'm beginning to expect it.'

'So why did you come with me?'

She glanced across at him and then looked away quickly.

'I don't know.'

Jake watched her for a minute. For some reason she had let him off the hook. He was beginning to feel like that big, partially tamed tiger. Maybe she had taken pity on him because of her fascination with wildlife.

'I walked about after I left the gallery,' he confessed softly. 'I came to your flat to apologize. I treated you badly.'

'You were worse at the flat,' Kathryn reminded him. She didn't asked why he had behaved badly, or why he thought he had the right to.

'I didn't expect to find you having a party. It flipped me.'

'Why?' She turned her head and looked at him strangely. 'You don't know anything about my life.'

He went grimly silent. No, he didn't. He had

simply imagined it, put her into a scenario of his own that suited him. The noisy party hadn't suited him at all.

'It was Ralph's party actually,' she said, when he sat looking very uptight. 'He simply brought it up one floor after I got back in.'

He didn't speak, and Kathryn glanced at him out of her eye-corners. He scared her a bit and she had to admit it. And she was not altogether comfortable with the racy feeling of excitement she felt when she saw him. She was twenty-four, nearly twenty-five, and she had never quite felt like that before.

She assumed it was because she was playing with fire for the first time in her life and actually liking it. He just might have murdered his wife. She didn't really know after all. Just because Aunt Clare stated that he was innocent there was no good reason to trust him. And yet she did trust him – in a way. He had had plenty of opportunities to attack her if he was a crazy murderer and he had only helped her every time.

She gave a little sigh and her mind turned reluctantly to Betsy Greene. The woman could manoeuvre anyone into anything. Kathryn had agreed to do a third Bertie Beetle book. But she had been adamant about not going to Cornwall. There was no way that she was going back there for a good while yet.

The taxi stopped in a very prestigious place and Jake started to get out.

'We've arrived,' he stated, when Kathryn hesitated about following him.

'I could wait here and then you could just nip in and back out again. Or I could take this taxi and go to my flat.' She stayed where she was, looking worriedly up at the huge building

'You're scared.' Jake looked at her steadily, and the quiet certainty of his conclusion made the green eyes flash with annoyance.

'I am not!'

He knew she was lying; she could see that. The dark eyes were sardonic and very penetrating.

'Then what are you waiting for? Come along.'

He seemed to be looking slightly contemptuous, and that irritated Kathryn. In any case, she didn't have much alternative but to obey. The taxi driver was watching her knowingly, as if Jake had picked her up in the street. Which was exactly what he had done, if you put it that way.

Kathryn's cheeks went pink and she got out fast, keeping her eyes turned well away as Jake paid off the taxi. She felt at a decided disadvantage. The butterflies were threatening to choke her. How many men's flats had she been in so far in her life? Ralph's and Colin's – but she knew them very well and she had been about to be engaged to Colin.

Nothing had happened on any occasion anyway, because she had scrupulously kept Colin at arm's length, or almost so. She did not sleep around. Colin had said that he found it touching, but now she knew that she had just not had the proper feelings for him.

It was funny, but nowadays she hardly thought of Colin at all. He had disappeared out of her life. And since she had met Jake Trelawny Colin was fast disappearing from her mind too. The dark, smouldering masculinity that surrounded Jake like a cloud tended to drive the thought of anyone else right away.

This was very much outside her experience though. She quickly thought back to how long she had known Jake Trelawny and asked herself what she had felt each time she had met him. The answer she came up with was disturbance, trouble and fear. And now she was going to his flat because she was too embarrassed to walk off and leave him, too embarrassed to face the knowing eyes of a taxi driver she would probably never see again.

The doorman looked interested but Jake ignored him. He set his pace to Kathryn's and led her to the lift. Something was teasing away at the back of his mind and he was not quite sure what it was. Something Bob had said. He had not had time to think about it before because almost immediately he had seen Kathryn, and she tended to chase other things out of his head.

He had her captured now, though – temporarily – and he felt able to breathe again. For some reason that he couldn't quite fathom she was constantly at the back of his mind. It was more comfortable to have her right beside him.

He went over the conversation with Bob about the break-in. Nothing of his work had been in the office, no notes that could explain anything. In any case, offices were being broken into regularly, so why he should have this conviction that it was anything to do with him was odd.

He ran it through his mind as the lift took them upwards. Nothing written down. He straightened up as a thought struck him. Maybe they hadn't just messed up papers. Bob had an answering machine in the office and a dictating machine. Bob kept messages on the former for ages, until he could bring himself to get around to them. Jake's mind went back to the message he had left on it at the beginning of all this, a few weeks before Gillian had vanished.

'Dig me up anything you can about Giles Renfrew. Go back a long way and get as much detail as you can. Money's no object. I want the whole works. He'll make a good peg to hang a book on.'

Had Bob left that message simply sitting there? Was it an omen that he had seen Giles Renfrew not more than twenty minutes ago, followed him through the street on the opposite side of the road? Was this what it was all about?

As the lift stopped Jake dived out into the passage, his keys in his hand. He clamped one hand round Kathryn's wrist and almost dragged her across to his door.

'In here,' he ordered. He flung the door open and almost forced her inside, and Kathryn was immediately on the very edge of panic. There was real danger now, not something she could push aside as being imagination.

It was quiet up here. One would have thought that nobody else lived in the whole building. It was one of those luxurious places where a hush settled that was permanent. He had propelled her in through the door – and playing with fire didn't seem to be so exciting any more. She was scared out of her wits, and his words at her flat came back to her. 'Maybe you're my next victim.'

Jake ignored her. He grunted at her to shut the door but she wasn't that stupid. She stayed where she was, ready to run and scream. He didn't even look at her, though. He threw his jacket down and went quickly into a room that looked like his sitting room. There was a bureau there and Kathryn watched with fast-beating heart and wide open eyes as Jake fell to his knees and stated pulling open drawers.

The floor was soon covered with files and papers, and he gave a mutter of satisfaction when he pulled out what seemed to be an old scrapbook.

She closed the door and advanced warily, but Jake seemed to have forgotten she was there. He was hunting. He even looked like a hunter. And as she watched he turned to the place he had been searching for and read rapidly. They were old newspaper cuttings, and a slow, savage grin spread across his face as he looked at them.

'Got you. You bastard!' he grated. 'Now we know what it's all about.'

Kathryn walked forward into the room and stood looking down at Jake. He seemed to have dismissed her from his mind. He got up and moved to a chair, taking the book of cuttings with him, and as he moved, he suddenly seemed to remember that he was not alone.

He did not apologize, however. Instead he grunted, 'Want to make some tea?'

Kathryn instantly found it hilarious. It might have been due to the fact that until a moment ago she had feared for her life. Perhaps hysteria threatened, but his unpredictable behaviour reminded her of the way he had casually lifted her onto the huge horse, the way he had come to her flat as if he had every right to act as he wished.

He seemed to have been alarming her since she had first met him. But in spite of his powerful appearance, with his jet-black hair and equally dark eyes, in spite of the look about him that spoke of a ruthless hunter, she found him amusing.

'What's so funny?' he growled when she stood there laughing.

'You are, I suppose. You dragged me into this place and I thought I was going to be attacked . . .'

'Hell! I'm sorry. I never considered what it would look like from your point of view.'

'You then kneel down and mess up a lot of papers and a good deal of your sitting room. Then you tell me to make tea, as if I know you really well and have nothing better to do with my time than allow you to order me about.'

Jake put the book down and looked up at her ruefully.

'I suppose I'm like that.' He gave the side of his forehead a funny little rub, as if he was puzzled. 'The thing is, I've sort of got you painted into my background.'

'What is that supposed to mean?' Kathryn raised her eyebrows and looked at him in amazement.

'Damned if I know. It's got to be your fault. Even when you look normal you never are. You're standing there in a perfectly ordinary dress and yet . . .'

'There's nothing wrong with this dress,' Kathryn protested crossly, looking down at the dark blue dress with white polka dots that fitted smoothly to her slender frame and flared out round her calves. 'I went out to lunch with my editor in this dress. It's very smart and the colour suits me. It's not just any old dress. I bought this in Bond Street for a special occasion.'

'It's very nice,' Jake assured her hastily. 'I like the dress. It's just that I never expect to see you in anything normal.' The way she was prepared to bite back when bitten had surprised him ever since he had first seen her. She just didn't look capable of it and yet she so obviously was.

'Ah! The dress I wore in your woods.' The smile came back to Kathryn's eyes.

'Did you make it yourself?'

'I did not!' Kathryn's eyes flashed green sparks again. 'It was made by a friend from art college. She was doing fashion design. I modelled for her a couple of times and she gave me the dress.'

Jake pulled a wry face and ventured an unwise comment. 'She's not going to make it in the big time.'

'Wrong again. She already is making it. She had clothes in a show in Paris last week. Some of the big names were there. And that dress is an original.'

She glared at him crossly and Jake wondered how he had got into this conversation and how he was going to get out of it. All he wanted at the moment was peace. He didn't want to talk to her. He was much too interested in what he had found. He didn't even want to go out now. He just wanted her wandering around where he could hear her.

He had not exactly been joking when he had said that she was painted into his background, and he had to find out exactly what that meant – but not now. He tried for the simple approach. He didn't have enough knowledge to argue about fashion.

'Want to make that tea?'

Kathryn frowned down at him for a second and then grinned.

'I expect so. I'll look out of the window while you do whatever it is you're doing. The view looks interesting.'

'Does it?' Jake muttered vaguely, his eyes back on the cuttings.

When he heard her pottering around in the kitchen he sighed and relaxed, giving all his mind to the old yellowed bits of newsprint he had hoarded for years.

As a background, Kathryn was perfect. He was by himself but he was not lonely. He had never liked sharing this flat when he was married to Gillian. He didn't particularly like having people around him. But it gave him a strange sense of calm hearing

Kathryn in the background. The silence was not hurting his ears any more.

Reading the cuttings took him back in time with a rush, right back to the days when he had left university and had been a very green newcomer to the world of the Press. He might have been a cub reporter but he'd had big ideas. Jake was a born hunter, and what he liked to hunt for were facts.

His antennae had come up fast one day, when he was in the office by himself over lunchtime and a man had come in with a story about smuggling. It had not been the usual and expected thing that was being smuggled, nothing about drugs or currency. The man had had a broken arm and a badly beaten face. He had been out for revenge.

The goods being smuggled had been furniture, medical supplies and vehicles, all belonging to the British forces in Germany. They were being brought back to this country, the vehicles resprayed, the supplies repackaged and the furniture stripped down and polished.

Jake had looked at the hefty man sitting in front of him and had instantly put him down as being one of the villains. He had been quite right about that, as the man had readily admitted. According to him, though, he was an ex-villain. The mastermind had been called Renfrew – Captain Giles Renfrew. And the irritated ex-villain had been savagely beaten up when he had tried to go into business for himself.

Jake's editor wouldn't touch the story. He'd said there wasn't a shred of proof and had refused to let

Jake follow it up. New reporters obeyed their editors, but Jake had looked into it in his spare time and made notes.

The name had always stuck in his mind, because whoever was running such a risky operation had to be good. Jake got into the habit of scouring the papers every day for news of it. Nobody was ever caught. It looked as if the whole thing was a hoax.

Then one day, years later, the name seemed to leap at him from the page of a well-known daily. Giles Renfrew. There was no rank now, just the name, but Jake had read the piece with mounting interest. Now Renfrew was wealthy, an industrialist, interested in politics and rapidly climbing the social ladder.

It was not a particularly common name and Jake had made a cynical guess as to where the original wealth had come from. Giles Renfrew was a man with a murky past.

After that, merely from interest, Jake watched the man's progress to captain of industry from a captain who stole army goods.

Jake was no longer an eager reporter. He was becoming well known as a writer. His political novels were intriguing, based as they were on years of being a good political journalist. Apart from his dismal mistake in marrying Gillian there had been no trouble at all in Jake's life until he had decided to write a novel based on the life and progress of a villain who had finally made it to the top. A senior minister with a past that had to remain hidden. And Giles Renfrew had come into his mind as a perfect example.

Jake reached out vaguely and took a sip of his tea. It was cold.

'What did you expect?' Kathryn asked when he pulled a face and put the cup down. 'I made it half an hour ago. You've never touched it.'

He looked up and she was standing by the window watching him. The late sunlight was turning her hair to deep fire. She hadn't made a sound. In fact he had forgotten that she was there. He had just known it at the back of his mind and, oddly enough, it had helped him to concentrate.

She could argue and contradict but she had the ability to melt into things. If serenity had a personality it would be like Kathryn. It must be something to do with the way she could sit so still for long periods of time while she painted.

'Do you want me to make another cup?' she asked when he just went on looking at her without speaking.

Jake shook his head and glanced at his watch.

'No thanks. We're a bit late for a show,' he confessed.

'Never mind. We can go another day.'

'Will you come?' He looked at her intently and she smiled.

'Why not? I've been watching you. I've decided that you're quite safe – studious, even. Aunt Clare was right. You wouldn't harm a woman – unless she got on your nerves,' Kathryn added with a little grin.

'Gillian certainly got on my nerves,' Jake growled, getting to his feet and beginning to gather the papers and files that were still strewn around. 'She was like a glittering top. She never stopped spinning and her trajectory usually brought problems – more often than not for me.'

'Then why are you bothering with me?' Kathryn asked astutely. 'I'm all manner of a nuisance. I fight back when oppressed, I like my own company best, I spill paint, I get myself into car accidents and I own a ferocious cat.'

Jake was kneeling at the bureau again, his back to her, and he grinned to himself.

'I told you. You're painted into my background.'

'That's not very complimentary. It sounds sort of washed out, like an old bit of rag.'

He stood up and turned round.

'It is complimentary. I'm not too fond of people. More often than not they irritate me. You have a habit of blending into things. You're soothing.'

Kathryn pulled a face and began to collect the tea things.

'Well, I'm not going to say thank you for that, Mr Trelawny. You could get soothed by buying a fish tank and stocking it with tropical fish.'

'I don't like fish either,' Jake muttered. 'Tropical or otherwise. At the moment I just seem to like you, and I have to confess that the fact puzzles me and annoys me more than somewhat.'

She gave a soft little laugh as she turned to the kitchen and he added more loudly, 'The name is Jake, by the way.'

'All right,' she said over her shoulder. 'I can live with that. I've heard worse names.'

Jake laughed quietly. If he'd had any female relatives he would have wanted at least one of them to be exactly like Kathryn. She was unbelievable. She was soothing, mischievous and always sure of her own mind. She was also, at the moment, quite delicate, but he had the feeling that she would be a good ally in times of trouble.

The odd wave of feeling washed over him again. He found himself wanting to protect her. Not that she would allow it. She knew exactly where she was going and he was lucky that she had consented to let him into her life for a while.

He scowled at the bureau and kicked the bottom drawer shut. Why the hell did he want to be in her life? He had no desire to scoop her up into his arms unless she happened to be about to walk under a bus or fall off a cliff. He had no wish to ravish her. When she got better she would be a damned nuisance and he knew that quite well. All the same, he felt as grateful as a boy that she had agreed to see him.

'Are we ready?' She came back into the room and fixed him with a slight frown. 'I have to put on a different dress if we're going out to dinner.'

'How do you know I haven't changed my mind?' Jake asked, filled with the need to goad her and see those green eyes flash again.

'Because if you *have* changed your mind you will have wasted the better part of my day and I turn nasty very easily. Besides, I have to feed Snowy.'

'I thought he was slimming?'

'He is, but he's not actually being starved. Ralph is out today. The Westlake Gallery is showing some of his paintings in a couple of days and he has to go and arrange things, otherwise he would have fed Snowy for me.'

She walked towards the door and Jake found himself glaring again, the peaceful feeling gone. Ralph seemed to be a fixed part of her life, the ever-present, jovial companion.

'I thought *Ralph* had a flat of his own. He seems to live in yours.'

'Only part-time,' Kathryn said flippantly. 'Even Colin didn't share my flat. I value my privacy.'

'Who the hell is Colin?' Jake snapped, catching her at the door and opening it for her.

'He was almost my fiancé.'

'So what happened?' Jake escorted her to the lift and tried to keep the black scowl from his face. He had more or less pushed himself into her life and fooled himself into thinking that she had no past. It was, after all, none of his business.

'He met someone else while I was very ill in hospital. One of those things.'

'He's a bastard!' Jake grated, making it his business instantly, but she gave him an intrigued glance and shook her head.

'No, he's not,' she assured him softly. 'He's weak, selfish and a little bit lost. I have no hard feelings.'

Jake looked at her closely as the lift took them down. There was something absolutely serene about her. In spite of her peculiarities, the serenity was deep down and remained constant.

'You're not shattered by it?'

'No. Not now. I think I was at the time, but I'm not even sure of that. I was too ill to really take stock of my feelings. Surviving was the most important thing then. Now I've changed. I've changed a lot over the past months, what with one thing and another.'

Her voice trailed away and Jake didn't pry. He was just heartily glad that Colin, whoever he was, was out of the picture. He had a strong desire to punch Colin's nose, and he had an equally strong feeling that Kathryn would fly at him if he did. He wasn't quite sure what he would do then.

At Kathryn's flat, Snowy greeted them deliriously. He leapt on Kathryn's shoulder, making her stagger, and when Jake lifted him off and put him firmly on the ground the cat simply wound itself round Jake's legs and purred. It was more like a tiger growling but it was definitely friendly.

'It's amazing!' Kathryn pronounced as she watched Snowy's antics. 'Ralph once did that, lifted Snowy off my shoulder, and Snowy bit him quite deeply.'

'Poor Ralph,' Jake murmured, feeling enormously smug and gazing down at the cat with approval.

Kathryn went to get the cat food and Jake sat on the settee and beamed at the cat when it jumped up on the arm beside him.

'Between us, we could get rid of Ralph,' he suggested in a low voice. 'As a team we would be unbeatable.'

'Are you talking to yourself?' Kathryn called out, and Jake gave a wry grin.

'I was addressing the cat.'

'Well, speak up. I have to answer for him. His education is limited.'

'Too late. The moment has passed,' Jake said more loudly. 'We understood each other, though.'

The trouble was, Jake mused, he didn't understand himself. Kathryn's relationship with Ralph was none of his business and he had no intention of making it his business. She was just the odd pixie, the passing nymph who had wandered into his life. Her undoubted beauty did not stir his masculine urges. He just appreciated it quietly. Kathryn, he decided, was a good thing. She could have whatever relationship she wanted with Ralph.

Over dinner she had the same air of tranquillity, and when she found him watching her intently she merely raised her eyebrows in polite enquiry.

'You're definitely good for the digestion,' Jake assured her. 'I used to bring Gillian here, before she demanded bigger and better things. She spent all her time looking round.'

'Well, I'm doing that,' Kathryn pointed out, and he shook his head.

'Not the same. You're merely interested. Gillian was trying to make everyone notice her.'

'What an alarming thought,' Kathryn murmured. 'I would probably get under the table if they all noticed me.'

Privately she thought that Gillian sounded awful, and she had a definite aversion to hearing about her. All the same she asked, 'What did she look like?'

Jake sat there studying her quietly for a minute and then he shrugged, as if he had little interest in the subject of Gillian's looks.

'Beautiful, immaculate, very blonde, very plastic. There was nothing real about Gillian.' He frowned when he realized that he was speaking of her as if she were dead.

'Why wasn't she real?' Kathryn persisted.

'Because she was never herself. I didn't know what she was like. I was married to her for three years and in all that time she stayed exactly as she had been before I knew her – beautiful, immaculate and plastic. Like someone on the front of a magazine.'

'I always fancied being like that,' Kathryn mused dreamily. 'Smiling, with gleaming teeth and bright red lips.'

'You've got beautiful teeth.'

'They don't gleam at people. It's not the same.'

'You wouldn't look right on a magazine,' Jake assured her with a frown. 'You would make a good illustration for an old book.'

'Drab and forbidding? You certainly know how to flatter a girl.' Kathryn's green eyes filled with laughter and Jake looked rueful.

'I didn't mean that and you know it. What I meant was that you're more of the legendary beauty. Knights and things,' he finished lamely. 'You're not modern.'

'I'm definitely modern, absolutely normal and well able to take care of myself. I'm not a weepy, weak female. I don't really need anyone. Certainly I don't need a knight.'

'What about Ralph?' Jake looked at her intently and she looked straight back, making herself face his unwavering stare. He often did that, as if he were seeing into her mind.

'Ralph is my friend.'

'What am I?' Jake asked quietly, and she looked amused.

'You're my mystery. And I'm not even sure how I came to collect you.'

'You didn't. I collected you.' The night-black eyes held hers easily, and Kathryn had to look away because she was on that lift again, going down fast, sounds dying away.

'I can't think why you would want to collect me,' she murmured a little shakily.

'I'm saving you until I need you,' Jake told her softly, and he suddenly knew it was true. He had put her into a carefully protected pigeonhole in his mind and he didn't want her to get out of there. His thoughts were racing around and had been racing around for months.

There was the mystery of Gillian, the danger of it. Now the danger seemed to be even more real than it had been when he had felt himself to be on the verge of being arrested. His book was going to be a veiled exposé of Giles Renfrew, and even though it would be fiction – 'the characters bearing no relation to anyone, living or dead' – any reader who'd had any dealings with Giles Renfrew would know at once who it was.

Somehow they had got wind of it. He knew without doubt that he would have to watch his step. He could not afford to be involved with anyone. But he had somehow scooped Kathryn into his life and he didn't want her out of it. She had to stay in her pigeonhole, though, because he had no time to get her out and think about her. Besides, she would be safer in there, and he was just a little afraid of what he would find if he thought about her too much.

'I rather think you're scaring me,' Kathryn said quietly as he continued to watch her unswervingly.

'You're quite safe. You said yourself that I would only attack people who got on my nerves.'

'That doesn't seem like much of a joke right now.'

'Look at it this way. Your cat trusts me.' Jake gave her a slow, tantalizing smile and the atmosphere changed again.

For those few minutes Kathryn had felt as if her heart was going to stop. She knew that he was not actually bantering. A lot of thoughts had been running around behind those dark eyes – and something else too.

Since she had been in his flat earlier, Jake had changed in some subtle manner. He had gone into some alert mode, ready to do battle. She was glad he was on her side. At least, she thought he was.

'When you were looking at those papers in your flat,' she said quietly, 'who was it you were speaking about?'

'I was simply reading.' Jake's face closed up again, his expression like stone, unyielding. But she persisted.

'You said, "Got you. You bastard!" I heard you quite clearly. Who was it?'

'You don't want to know, nymph,' he assured her softly.

Kathryn looked startled.

'I am most certainly not a nymph, whatever that means.'

'Let's just say that's how I think of you – a water nymph painted into my background.'

'I don't like that.'

'Why not? You're extremely safe there – a backwash to my life.'

'I don't want to be in your life,' Kathryn stated sharply, her anxiety growing again. Suddenly he looked more powerful than ever. She had begun to think that she knew him. She had begun to feel comfortable with him. But now he was different – alarming, a prowling stranger. Besides, he was married, had been married for three years. She was sure that Gillian would turn up. She refused to believe he had in any way harmed her.

'Too late, Kathryn. You already are. You wandered into my orbit and I collected you, like a planet circling the sun. You should never have come into my woods. You should never have walked on my land. But you did both of those things and now you have to slowly revolve until I have you sorted out.'

'That's not very funny. I don't want you to talk like that,' she said urgently, but he just went on looking at her.

'Why not? Don't you like the truth?'

She hoped it was not the truth. She hoped he was joking in some obscure way. But he didn't look amused. He looked serious. She regretted coming out with him. She had known she would never be able to cope and she had been right. Last night he had deliberately hurt her and now he was frightening her very quietly

Jake took her back to her flat and left immediately, as if he could not wait to get back to something else, and by now Kathryn was uneasy. She was not at all sure that she wanted to have anything more to do with him. She liked her life exactly as it was, and now that she had managed to push her accident and Colin right to the back of her mind she was finding things much more comfortable.

There was nothing comfortable about Jake. There was something very dangerous about him – and she couldn't think why she had ever agreed to have dinner with him when she had been so determined not to.

Looking back, she realized that in some odd way he had became, or was fast becoming, inevitable. He had seen her when she had hurt her leg and had been in trouble and he had pursued her to her flat, insisting upon helping. She asked herself if she had been in any way responsible for that and the answer was definitely no. And she had flatly refused to have dinner with him then.

Today, when she had looked up and found him watching her from across the road as she had waited for a taxi, she had most certainly felt peculiar inside. If she had been in her right mind she would have leapt into the taxi and gone. She had the feeling that he would not have followed her if she had done that.

But she had stood there as if she was waiting for fate. Jake had shouted, 'Stay where you are.' And she had obeyed as if she was mesmerized. What had followed had been both alarming and intriguing, especially his odd remark that he had collected her and would keep her in his orbit . . .

Something important was happening in his life, something important and dangerous. She had seen it on his face as he had studied those papers. She had seen the satisfied look of a hunter who had spotted his prey. Jake Trelawny lived in a different world and Kathryn had the feeling that it would be an uncomfortable world.

Painted into his background. It sounded possessive, alarming and terribly final. 'Stay there.' 'Wait there.' 'Make some tea.' What sort of idiot did he think she was? She had a perfectly good life of her own and she had no intention of being part of somebody's background.

She couldn't think why he wanted her there anyway. He had never looked at her as a man looked when he was interested in a woman. Apart from those intent, dark-eyed looks that left her feeling shaky, he just seemed to want to move along with her in tow.

No way! The next time he got in touch with her she would be unavailable. Besides, she had to get out to somewhere in the country for this third Bertie book. It would be a good way of slipping the leash.

'What am I thinking?' She glared at Snowy, quite angry with herself. 'I am not on a leash. I know next to nothing about Jake Trelawny and I don't want to know anything about him either.' Snowy glared back at her and she pointed an accusing finger at him. 'If you've been conspiring with him, you can forget it. And don't let it slip your mind that you're on a diet.'

CHAPTER 7

Ralph walked in, using the key he had kept since she was in Cornwall.

'No wonder that cat's antisocial,' he said, giving her an odd look. 'He already thinks he's people and now here you are having an argument with him. Let me know his point of view – or does he send you written rejoinders?'

'You can give me my key back,' Kathryn ordered, going red-faced as she wondered just how much he had heard. 'I'm not having you sneaking in here at any time you please. Just because you happen to have a key it does not stop you ringing the bell or knocking on the door. This is my own place.'

'If I thought you meant that I'd take the cat and go, you ungrateful wretch. As I'm sure you don't mean it, the question arises – what's up?'

'Nothing,' Kathryn muttered uncomfortably. 'Well, it's just somebody.' She felt embarrassed and uneasy, and most assuredly the wretch he had called her.

'Could it be the well-dressed caveman who was at your flat a couple of weeks ago and again tonight?'

160

'I didn't know you'd seen him.' Kathryn felt quite startled. She had been under the impression that somehow Jake was a secret. They seemed to live in a world of their own, where other people were merely a background.

'On each occasion I was waiting to come up in the lift as he was going down. Both times I was treated to a glance of intense dislike. It was a bit like being hit with a black laser beam. Are you sure you can handle him, my friend? He looks tough and dangerous.'

'Oh, it's nothing like that,' Kathryn assured him, trying to sound airy.

'What is it like, then?'

'You pry too much, Ralph.'

'Possibly. But life has to be made interesting. So what is it like?'

Kathryn handed him his coffee and then sat down on the settee facing him, her legs tucked under her.

'I don't know what he wants with me,' she confessed with a frown. 'Every time I look up he's there – at least, it's getting to feel like that.'

'Why, he's after you, you poor, silly creature.'

'He's not, Ralph,' Kathryn assured him seriously, not even managing to raise a slight smile. 'He just seems to keep appearing.' She bit her lip thoughtfully. 'He says I'm painted into his background. He says he's collected me.'

Ralph burst into laughter.

'As I said, even without those terribly good clues, he's after you. What will convince you? Are you waiting for him to grab your hair and take a club to you?'

'It's not like that!' Kathryn snapped. 'You don't understand. He doesn't look at me like that, as if – as if . . .'

'As if he wants you in bed? Maybe he's playing a waiting game.'

'Honestly, Ralph, he might be dangerous.'

'Why?' Ralph looked serious at last but Kathryn could not bring herself to tell him about Jake's wife. It seemed like treachery, as if she would be letting Jake down.

'I don't know,' she confessed lamely.

'So I'll keep the key and get ready to burst in on you the next time he comes.'

Kathryn grinned at him. She wasn't sure at all if Jake would come back. He had simply gone away and said nothing, as if he had totally lost interest.

'You'd better keep it,' she said. 'I'll be wanting your services again. I'm going back to Cornwall. Another Bertie Beetle book,' she added with a wry face as he looked startled. 'Editor's orders.'

Until that moment she had been quite adamant that she was not going anywhere near Cornwall, but talking about Jake to Ralph had made her mind up for her. Jake was here and she really ought to get away. It seemed to make good sense.

Of course, she could go somewhere else entirely, but she wanted to know more about Jake and where better to find out about him than in Cornwall? She wanted to go back in the woods too, and as Jake was in London she might just be able to go up to the house and peer in through the windows.

It was in Cornwall that Gillian had disappeared. At least, that had been the last time she had been seen, according to Aunt Clare. Kathryn needed to find out because she didn't know whether to be afraid of Jake or fascinated by him. She was never going to find out when he was there. The effect he had on her was too alarming.

She rang Aunt Clare the next morning and asked if she could come back, and there was no doubt at all about her aunt's enthusiasm.

'Of course you can, Kathryn. You're feeling ill in London, aren't you? Well, I did tell you, dear. I'm glad you've come to your senses.'

'I'm much better, actually,' Kathryn said firmly. 'I feel very well. The thing is, my editor is insisting on another book in the series and I feel it should be drawn where the others were drawn. How is the weather?'

'Oh, perfect. It usually is in September, and September is almost upon us so you can more or less guarantee fine weather for a month. Just right for you to do your book.'

There seemed to be nothing to stop the trip and no real reason to put it off. As Aunt Clare had pointed out not too long ago, there was everything she needed in Cornwall by way of physiotherapists. Kathryn would go down by train – she had no intention of driving all that way – but her aunt had a car and she would be able to use that.

'By the way,' Clare said in the excited way she reserved for gossip, 'Jake Trelawny went away again, soon after you left, and he hasn't come back.' Kathryn was relieved to hear it, but she did not like the next bit of news.

'There have been people round Pengarron Manor, snooping around the outside, or so Mrs Pengelly says. I can't quite see from here, although I've been keeping a good watch.'

'What sort of people?' Kathryn asked with a fresh burst of anxiety. 'Was it the police?'

'We haven't been able to find out. I really think that if it was the police they should have questioned some of us. They're not going to solve anything without help as far as I can see. After all, we know the place. We live here.'

Kathryn murmured her agreement but her mind was not really on it. Was she doing a stupid thing by going back there? She could hardly go snooping round Pengarron Manor if the police were watching it. Why would they be watching it if Jake was not under suspicion still?

It didn't seem to bother him overmuch. He had seemed to be merely irritated by the whole affair until he had pounced on those papers and cuttings at his flat.

Thinking about him brought back a fact that she had vaguely noticed and then dismissed from her mind. When they had been having dinner he had spoken of Gillian as if she were dead. He had spoken as if he knew for sure she was dead. So had she, for

164

that matter. She could remember saying, 'What did she look like?' Supposing he already knew for sure that Gillian was dead? It could have been a slip of the tongue.

Kathryn dismissed it. She didn't want to believe it. Jake might be subtly alarming but it was only something she had seen in his face, something she'd sensed. She was more inclined than ever to agree with her aunt. He would never hurt a woman. Hadn't he rescued her at least twice? Hadn't he gone out of his way to see that she was safe, even when he had thought she was going to limp across a busy road? Hadn't he painted her into his background?

When he had said that she might be his next victim he had been saying it because he was angry, hurt for some reason, like a wild creature with a thorn in its foot who lashed out in pain. It had frightened her at the time but now she was not really scared at all. She was wary, though, she had to admit that.

One thing was for sure; she had to find out the truth. It was either exonerate him completely or keep out of his way permanently, and she wasn't sure that she wanted to do that. Life had gone a little flat since she had last seen him. The days seemed to be dull without his smouldering presence, and she also had the odd conviction that he needed her.

Kathryn was almost ready to leave a couple of days later. She was standing in her flat, contemplating whether or not she had everything she needed, when the telephone rang.

Her heart gave a little lurch as she thought it might be Jake. He hadn't been in touch with her, and although she had told herself that it was better that way it did not stop her from feeling disappointed and slightly lost.

It was not Jake, and her heart went from excited pounding to a swift embarrassed fall when Colin's voice sounded in her ear.

'Kath, it's wonderful to hear your voice,' he said when she answered. 'I've missed you, love.'

Kathryn frowned at the phone.

'So I noticed,' she murmured. 'I can hardly get out of the flat without falling over you.'

As soon as the words had left her mouth she felt like kicking herself. This was just playing into his hands, as usual. She could just picture his face, just see the glowing satisfaction when he thought she was missing him. She was not missing him. She suddenly realized that she had never felt so clear-minded, so free in her whole life.

'I would have come sooner,' Colin vowed. 'It was awkward, though, Kath. In the hospital you sort of dismissed me.'

'Do you know, I can't quite remember that.' Kathryn said ironically. 'I think it was something to do with being semi-conscious at the time. I do seem to remember, though, that there was some talk of another woman. Just one of those things, as I recall. Of course I may have been delirious, but it will keep coming back into my mind.'

'I was letting you off, in case you were angry with me and felt worried about saying it. There was nobody else, Kath. You must know that.'

'In a pig's ear!' Kathryn muttered to herself. She was glad to hear his voice because it brought home to her as nothing else would have done that she felt nothing at all. Even the self-pity had gone. She felt like someone about to go on a mission. There was excitement in her life, intrigue, mystery, a sort of elation. Knowing Jake had shaken her out of her usual apathy.

While she stood there thinking and didn't reply, Colin pressed home the advantage he seemed to think he had,

'I'll come round to see you,' he declared earnestly, and it sounded for all the world as if he thought he was doing her a favour.

'Sorry, I'm leaving right now,' Kathryn told him firmly. She heard Ralph coming in through the door to get his orders about Snowy, the plants and the flat. 'I'm going away and I don't exactly know when I'll be back,' she added for good measure.

'I'll keep ringing,' Colin promised in a sickening voice. 'Take care, love. As soon as you get back we'll get together again.'

Kathryn grimaced at the phone as she put it down and turned to find Ralph watching her intently.

'Who?' he pried.

'Colin. He's wanting to get together again.'

'And?' He looked at her steadily and she scowled at him.

'Honestly, Ralph! Do I look that stupid?'

'It's not so much the stupidity as the kindness of the heart. Anyway, I'm glad you're showing some sense. The caveman wouldn't like it.'

'If you mean Jake Trelawny, then what I do is nothing to do with him at all. And he's not a caveman,' she added crossly.'

'He's big as a house-end and his heart's as black as the ace of spades. Nobody but you could ever contemplate collecting a caveman as if he were a pet poodle.'

'I did not collect him and he is not black as the ace of spades. He merely has dark hair and dark eyes.'

'Like coal. So where is he, then?'

'How do I know?' Kathryn asked peevishly. 'I'm not his keeper. I hardly know him. Do get that imagination under control, Ralph.'

'It's the mouth. It keeps on asking questions even though I order it to stop. Where did you meet him, by the way?'

'Cornwall,' Kathryn stated briefly and grumpily.

'And you're going back there. I see.'

Kathryn straightened up from fastening her last piece of luggage and glared at him.

'You don't see anything at all. I'm going back to Aunt Clare's because Betsy wants another Bertie book. Obviously they all have to have the same sort of background. Anyway, Jake is in London as you know very well.'

'What does a beetle care where it lives?' Ralph mused. 'One piece of grass is pretty much like another. You could have done it in Hyde Park and nobody would have been any the wiser, not with your talent.'

'It's the atmosphere.'

'Beetles crave atmosphere? Every day I learn more. Is this Trelawny chap going back down to Cornwall?'

'He is not. He has too much to do here in town. He's working on a new book, I believe. I don't suppose you've heard of him, but . . .'

'I have,' Ralph assured her quietly. 'I've even read a couple of his books.'

Kathryn looked up sharply.

'Have you? What are they like?'

'Political, complicated and intriguing. A few of them have been filmed, I think.'

'I didn't know that,' Kathryn said slowly, and Ralph gave her one of his superior looks.

'You don't know much about him, do you? Watch your step, my girl. He's big guns. He even looks like big guns. I wouldn't really like to take him on so look after yourself.'

'Luggage to the lift, Ralph,' Kathryn ordered. 'I don't need a nanny. Don't get Snowy fat and water the plants regularly. If by any chance Colin calls, tell him I've gone to live in the Far East.'

'What do I say if Jake Trelawny calls?' Ralph asked as he put her things in the lift and stepped in with her.

'He won't.'

'But if he does?'

'Then obviously I'm out.'

'Are you in Cornwall?'

'No.'

'Understood,' Ralph murmured in an approving voice. 'With you there and him here, nothing can go wrong.'

Kathryn hoped not. She was not at all sure that what she was about to do was wise. Jake was so obviously clever. If he wrote complicated novels it would not have been too difficult for him to kill Gillian and hide her away somewhere. She wasn't sure how he would have managed his alibi, but he was so intelligent that it almost glittered from his eyes.

She had to know because she had the shaky feeling that he had become part of her life. What he wanted out of it was a mystery, but he didn't look like the sort of person who would waste his time saying things he did not mean.

He had collected her. It was frightening and thrilling all at the same time. Jake made ordinary life seem terribly dull. Perhaps she would end up wishing frantically for an ordinary life. She reminded herself that if Gillian was alive, then Jake was married. It didn't seem to make a lot of difference to her state of mind. She was locked into this, unable to stop.

Kathryn took one last wistful look at the brightly lit market as the taxi arrived for her. Bert waved, the other men waved, Ralph waved – and she nearly got out then and there and changed her plans. She did not, though. There was a bubbling excitement inside her and she knew she was going to see this through, wherever it led.

Since she had met Jake her lingering depression had gone and she hadn't even noticed its passing. Life seemed to be bright again, colourful, and she knew that while her fingers were busy drawing for this new book her mind would not go skimming to Colin. He wasn't even real now. If her mind went skimming anywhere, it would skim to Jake.

Kathryn started work on the cliff top, admitting as she did so that she had no desire to work there at all. The natural progression would have been to work in the wood. In fact she *had* to work in the wood for this last book of the three. That was where she had left things, and it would look strange to go back to the cliff and start from there again.

In reality, she was a little too nervous to venture into the woods around Pengarron Manor. It had been well enough to make the decision when she was in London, with safety around her, but now that she was back in Cornwall the silence and the mystery of the old house seemed to be a real force that seeped into her head.

Clare was very busy. Kathryn's unexpected arrival had rather messed up her arrangements, and although she had said nothing about her appointments on the telephone when Kathryn had asked to come there were things she could not put off; several jumble sales, a trip to Plymouth with her friends and one whole week when she would be in hospital.

'Why?' Kathryn had asked worriedly. 'You never told me that anything was wrong with you.' She'd felt a great flare of anxiety. Clare was very dear to her, the last of her family.

'There isn't anything wrong with me,' Clare had stated firmly. 'It's that old fusspot, Gordon Phelps. I went in for a check-up, as I do every two years, and he says he heard something.'

'What did he hear?' Kathryn could see the way her aunt was going slightly pink and knew at once that she was going to try evasion.

'A heart murmur, if you really must know. It's utterly ridiculous but he insists.'

Kathryn had met Dr Phelps on several occasions, namely when her Aunt Clare had dragged him in to have a close look when she had been here before and Clare had been worried. She knew he would not take action for any foolish reason.

'Why a whole week?' Kathryn asked cautiously.

'Observation. I really can't spare the time, and with you here alone . . .'

'I'm alone in London for most of the time,' Kathryn pointed out. 'I can cope here quite easily, unless you want me to go back to my flat.'

'I most certainly do not!' Clare insisted sharply. 'It's perfect, actually. You can see to things here – when I go in and don't even consider visiting. It's too far for you to drive with that leg and there's absolutely nothing wrong with me. Jean Pengelly will visit, so will some of the other girls. Anyway, it's not for a couple of weeks.'

Well, it was tomorrow, Kathryn reminded herself now as she sat and looked at the sea. The couple of weeks had passed. Basically she was doing nothing here. The story was in the woods and there was no way she could work up the correct atmosphere by sitting out on the cliff top and sketching small creatures. There would be a good deal more of them in the quiet of the woodland.

She turned her head and looked across towards Jake's house. With the leaves still lush and green the house was almost hidden from here when she was in her little hollow. She could only see a part of the front and the tall chimneys that stood out clearly against the rising ground at the other side.

She nibbled at her lip. There was no need to go to the house. She could just set up in the wood where she had been before. If the police were indeed watching the house they wouldn't even notice her. In any case, since she had arrived at her aunt's cottage Kathryn had done a good deal of watching herself, and in spite of Mrs Pengelly's certainty, Kathryn had seen no sign of anyone. The only person who seemed to be interested in Pengarron Manor was her.

It was getting late, and she gathered her things and started back, but when she came to the part of the path that led to Jake's house and land curiosity got the better of her. She had to go into the wood and take a look, even if only for a minute.

The woodland was still filled with light, but Kathryn knew that within the next hour or so the light that glowed on the sea and the cliff top would be muted here. The trees would cast longer shadows, the colour would fade, the birds would be silent and the only sound would be the quiet running of the stream that led through the woods into the wider creek that meandered to the sea.

Kathryn went as silently as she could. She had no wish to find herself explaining her actions to the police, and although she had seen no sign of them since she had come back to Cornwall she knew that Mrs Pengelly had seen something, no matter what it was. Her aunt's friends were gossipy but they were not idiots.

She went to the place she had been before, the place where she had caught and sketched the field mouse, but she was not searching for any creature this time. From here she had seen the house when Jake had pointed it out to her and she went forward cautiously and stood at the very edge of the wood, looking into the wide sweep of the garden.

The garden was overgrown, beautiful bushes and plants that had once been tended with pride now struggling for a place amongst weeds. In some parts the weeds themselves were knee-high. It was somehow sad and showed Jake's utter indifference to his home. He was wealthy enough to hire a small army of gardeners to put this place right but he stayed in his luxurious London flat and ignored his birthright.

He had brought his wife here, though. Gillian, who was beautiful, perfect and plastic, according to Jake. His wife had liked good things. What had she thought of Pengarron? Even from this distance it was easy to see that the old manor house was neglected. It was silent, dark. Its front windows faced the sea, and although the light was catching the panes the place had an air of melancholy about it.

Kathryn glanced at the sky. The light would be fading soon. If she wanted to see anything now was the time, because she had no intention of being here after dark. Her courage didn't stretch that far. She glanced behind her into the wood. There were paths that had long since become overgrown, and a few small clearings such as the one where she had worked, but beyond these there was darkness – a darkness that would soon become more pronounced. If she was to explore it had to be now.

She started forward cautiously, expecting at any minute to be challenged by either the police or some person who had been left to look after the estate. Surely Jake had cleaners, workers to tidy the house and the parts of the garden that were close to the house?

As she went nearer Kathryn could see that he had not bothered with that either, and nobody came to ask her business there. Before she had half realized it she was up to the house, standing by the stone steps that led to a terrace – a terrace which faced the sea – and still she was alone.

She looked up and the house seemed to be standing aloof and bitter, ignoring her presence, its tall chimneys looking as if they had never seen the smoke from cheerful fires. What should have been beautiful was stiff, chill and she felt that if she laid a hand on the old stone of the house it would surely shrink away.

In an odd way it reminded her of Jake. He had been unhappy here, lonely, she was suddenly sure of that, and into this lonely, forbidding house he had brought a woman he had probably grown to hate. And Gillian had disappeared. Kathryn had never attempted to get any more of the story from her aunt and now she regretted it.

As she made a deliberate move to approach the house more closely, walking up the steps to the terrace that stretched along its whole front, Kathryn made up her mind to steadily grill her aunt on the subject once she was back in Jasmine Cottage. If she left it any longer her aunt would be in hospital, and at this moment Kathryn felt she had to know everything and know it now.

Jake seemed to linger in her mind all the time, and if she was to get him out of her mind she knew she had to get to the bottom of this and make decisions based on her own knowledge. When she had done that she would be able to make her mind up as to whether she was frightened of Jake or fascinated by him.

The sound of her own footsteps sounded far too loud. They seemed to be echoing all around her. If anyone was there, Kathryn knew they would hear her and come out to see who was trespassing. If by any chance it was Jake she could make up some ready excuse, although she was almost certain that he was still in London.

If any stranger appeared she wasn't quite sure what she would say. She could say she was an artist and interested in painting the house. She made a note to add that her friends were still in the wood, with her equipment, because she was suddenly doubly aware of the isolation here. This might not be an inner city area where dreadful things could happen at any time, but it was a place that had for a time at least attained notoriety. A woman had disappeared from this house and it seemed to be miles from anywhere.

Kathryn walked to the nearest window and could not resist peering in. The light from the sinking sun was still lighting up the panes and she had to put her face close to the glass and cup her hands to see anything at all.

She was looking into a sitting room of some sort. There were deep chairs, settees, an old ornate desk and old oil paintings on the walls. The whole place had a neglected air, though that did not take her by surprise. She was seeing more or less what she had expected to see; a place abandoned, overlooked, spurned. Somehow this place explained Jake's strange attitude, and she was more sure than ever that he had been unhappy here, probably always.

Kathryn drew back with a sigh. This was getting her nowhere. She was prying without any real idea of what she was searching for. There would be nothing at this house. If there had been, surely the police would have found it. She stepped back, and as she did so she had an uncanny feeling of being watched.

It frightened her at once. The hairs on the backs of her hands stood up, and a cold feeling ran over her that was as old as time itself, a primeval signal of danger. Kathryn turned her head quickly, looking to the corner of the house. There was nobody there, but there was the faint lingering of a presence that told her quite clearly she had not been mistaken.

If it had been anyone with the right to be here she would have been challenged. Whoever it had been had withdrawn instead, had hidden, was probably at this minute hiding round the side of the house. She stepped away carefully, her eyes still on the place where she knew someone had been standing, and then she turned to the terrace and ran for the woods.

I'm running! The words came into her head and she tried to ignore them in case the very knowledge made it impossible for her to continue. But the thought drummed in her mind as she saw the edge of the woods getting closer. Without even realizing it, she was getting better. Ordinarily she would have been overjoyed, but at the moment all she could think of was getting to safety.

She almost flew into the trees, was disorientated for a second and then righted herself. Her things were where she had left them. She scooped up the basket, ignoring its weight, and waded through the stream with no thought at all of the fact that she was getting wet. All she wanted was to be back in the lane close to the cottage. She wanted to be out of the now darkening wood because she could feel danger behind her. One glance assured her that she was not being followed but her imagination was now wild and running as fast as she was moving.

The wood that had intrigued and delighted her now seemed to be menacing. She thought of someone racing through the trees out of her sight, keeping pace with her, placing themselves where they could catch her before she reached safety, but she was too scared to stop and listen. All the time in her head she was thinking with a sort of wonder, I can run!

It wouldn't last long; she was sure of that. Already her leg was hurting badly, her breath gasping in her throat. Soon she would have to walk, she might even have to stop altogether. She burst out of the wood and was in the low, narrow lane that led to her aunt's cottage. That was when her leg gave out, and from then on Kathryn was almost in a state of collapse.

She had pushed herself more than had seemed possible. She had run for the first time in almost nine months. She was shaking from head to foot, both from the great effort and from fear. Because now that she was reasonably safe the adrenaline had deserted her, and she knew she had to make one last effort to get to the cottage.

She also had to pull herself together before her aunt came in from her visit to the church jumble sale. Clare was looking for any excuse to put off her hospital trip and this would be the only one she needed. Whatever happened, her aunt must be at that hospital tomorrow, and Kathryn took a deep, shuddering breath and limped along the lane, looking behind her frequently.

There was nobody there but she knew she had not imagined it. She was an artist, her imagination finely tuned, but this had not been imagination. It had been instinct and she had always respected her instinct. She had ignored it just the once, when she had got into the car with Colin on that fated night. She would never ignore her instincts again.

Who had been there? Kathryn felt quite cold when the idea came to her that it might perhaps have been Gillian. The thought of the woman hiding, hanging around the empty house waiting for Jake to be arrested in connection with her disappearance was terrible.

One thing was quite certain: Gillian could not do that alone. Somebody else had to be helping her. Food would be needed, some form of communication. Perhaps that other person had been there too, hiding round the side of the house, watching, and, from what she'd learned of Gillian, her companion would no doubt be a man. The idea frightened Kathryn even more.

Before Clare came home, Kathryn was able to get a bath and soothe her leg. She had managed to calm herself and she felt very annoyed that her realization of getting better should have come when she was under such pressure to move fast. It would not have done the leg a bit of good. Still, it had held out, and if it could do it once it would work better soon – even if she was housebound tomorrow.

At the moment, being housebound did not seem to be too bad an idea. She glanced surreptitiously through the curtains as she drew them against the dusk. There was no light at Pengarron Manor. Whoever had been watching her had not been Jake. And she had been glad to close the curtains tonight. She had needed no bidding from Clare. The thought of someone peering in at them as she had peered into Jake's house was not a very pleasant thought.

Kathryn pulled herself up smartly. Such thoughts were useless and probably erroneous. She told herself it might all have been imagination, but deep inside she knew it was no such thing. And the watcher had not been a policeman. The police did not lurk about. She would have been stopped and faced with explaining herself.

'You never actually finished telling me about Jake Trelawny,' she murmured carelessly to her aunt as they ate their evening meal.

'You didn't seem terribly interested, dear,' Clare pointed out, and Kathryn had to concede silently that she had not been too interested, not at first. She hadn't known then, of course, that Jake would become some recurring part of her life. She had not known that he would collect her, paint her into his background. Now she was almost hungry for details about him.

She shrugged nonchalantly, taking care to seem merely interested for the sake of something to pass the evening.

'It's just that I saw the house today. The whole thing came back into my mind.'

'Yes, well it would,' Clare murmured thoughtfully. 'That house is so neglected. Of course, none

181

of us have been near, but even from the distance you can tell. According to Jean Pengelly it used to be the grandest house in the area, one of the best in the county. Apparently there were parties that went on for days. Great comings and goings. But after his parents died, Jake shunned it.'

'Why?' Kathryn asked softly, noting that her instincts about the house had been right. It made her more sure than ever that her other instincts were right too. Someone had been watching her and it had not been Jake. What would have happened if she had not run?

'They say Jake was never happy. They also say that he was neglected. I don't mean undernourished and badly dressed, that sort of thing, but according to Jean the servants took care of him most of the time. She had it from the servants years ago that Jake's parents had never wanted children. They were totally wrapped up in each other. Everyone suspected that they only had Jake to make sure things were passed on – the house, the money, the land.'

Clare sighed and got on with her meal. 'As it turned out he never needed the money. He's probably never touched it. He makes enough of his own. And the way he just scorned Pengarron Manor and went off shows how he hated it there. I can't see him having bothered with the money either. It's a shame, though. It could still be a lovely place to live, but if he was unhappy . . .'

'But he brought his wife there,' Kathryn prompted, and Clare looked thoughtful.

'I've thought about that and often wondered why. I saw her once in the village. Of course I didn't know who she was, but the man at the post office did. Such a beauty. She must have been a perfect foil for Jake's hard dark looks. She was fair as a lily. The hair looked natural too,' she mused. 'I wonder if she really is dead. If she was alive, surely someone would have spotted her by now. She was so beautiful – quite noticeable.'

Kathryn suddenly wished she had never started this. Jake spoke of Gillian with such hard indifference and yet he must have loved her at one time. Even Jake had said she was beautiful. Kathryn didn't want to know. She frowned and got on with her meal. What was she doing, prying into things that did not concern her, letting herself accept that she was 'painted into his background', bothering about whether he had been happy as a child?

'I kept the papers at the time.' Clare looked up and offered this information. 'There in the bottom of the bureau. I never got around to throwing them out. If you're interested you could read through them when I'm in hospital.'

Kathryn smiled and nodded but she was perfectly sure that she would do no such thing. She was going to keep out of this, forget all about Jake Trelawny. As it was, however, she crept downstairs when her aunt was asleep and read them there and then.

There was a picture of Jake on the front cover of the first paper she opened. She didn't know where they had dug it up from because it was so unusual for

Jake. He was laughing, and the sight of him hit Kathryn like an actual blow. She just sat there on the floor in her nightie, the papers strewn around her, and for a long time she just looked at Jake's picture. It was only when she realized that she was smiling at him and not getting on at all that she firmly ignored the picture and looked at the actual newsprint.

There was a lot of fact about Jake's writing and Ralph had been quite right; he had had two books filmed. It then went on to say that his wife had disappeared under unusual circumstances while they had been staying at Pengarron Manor. On the centre spread there was more, but the thing that held Kathryn's eyes was a picture of Gillian Trelawny.

She was beautiful, more beautiful than Kathryn had imagined, and seeing her name written down – Gillian Trelawny – brought home to her as nothing else could have done that Jake had a wife. He was not free to paint anyone into his background unless he already knew that Gillian was dead.

Kathryn couldn't read any more. She wished she had not read any of the papers at all because she had not found out one thing. How could she have expected to find anything when the police had not? The Press, as usual, were simply speculating. He had come down here with his wife and she had disappeared, but by then he had been back in London, seen with other people. And Gillian had been seen here after that.

Jake could not have killed her – unless he had come back secretly, unless he had left some sort of trap. He was clever, with a mind that invented complicated plots. He could easily have invented one for himself. He had told her that Gillian had got on his nerves.

Kathryn folded the papers up and crept back to bed wishing she had never started this, wishing she had never seen Jake at all. She would stay here with her aunt and keep out of London for a while. If he came here she would go back fast. She knew he had been pursuing her. He had even done it as if he had every right to pursue her. He knew where she lived.

Kathryn turned over fretfully and frowned into the darkness. She would go and live somewhere else. As she found herself thinking that she frowned even more. She would do no such thing! She liked her artist's lair. She liked Ralph and Bert Lewis at the market. She liked young Teddy and the other men who whistled the day away and greeted her cheerfully. She was not giving that up because of Jake Trelawny.

Kathryn began to drift off to sleep. She was tired after her day, especially after that rather wild run. But her leg was getting better. She smiled drowsily into her pillow, quite shocked when she found herself musing that Jake would be surprised to see her walking normally.

She had to stop thinking about him like that, but even as she fell asleep she could hear her aunt's voice saying that he had been neglected, unhappy, and she could hear Jake's voice too. 'Look at it this way, your cat trusts me.' Painted into his background. She had let it happen but, thinking it over drowsily, she could not see any way she could have prevented it.

'What the hell did you think you were doing?' Giles Renfrew strode across the deep luxurious carpet that covered the drawing room of his London penthouse and felt his temper soar almost out of control as he looked at the woman who lounged gracefully on the huge curved settee.

'I was trying to help, darling.' Gillian pouted, a thing she did beautifully, but he was too angry to fall for it this time.

'Helping? You could have blown the whole thing! Suppose somebody recognized you? You're not exactly invisible.' His eyes slid over the long legs, the way she had arranged herself like a slinky cat against the covers, the fair hair and beautiful face. 'Not many months ago you were splashed on the front page of every paper. Everybody in the whole damned country was searching for you. Do you realize what the outcome would be if they discovered you've been here with me the whole time, sitting pretty and waiting for your husband to be arrested for your murder?'

His eyes narrowed on her sharply. She was more of a liability than an asset as things had turned out. He sometimes wondered if she had made up the whole story about the book based on his own life. It would not be beyond her to worm her way in like that. Trelawny had money but he himself had a damned sight more, and he had not one single doubt that if Gillian found a better offer she would take it.

'I was well disguised,' Gillian snapped. 'I had a black wig and dark glasses. Anyway, I had peculiar clothes. Nobody noticed me and nobody even *saw* me at Pengarron Manor.'

Giles Renfrew gritted his teeth. Peculiar clothes. God help them! He often thought she had the brains of a gnat.

'This girl damned near saw you,' he snapped.

'She didn't see me. She was too scared. She took off like a rocket.'

'She's lame,' Giles pointed out menacingly. 'She couldn't take off like anything. She saw you, didn't she?'

'No, she didn't! Why can't you believe me? Lame or not, she was running. It gave me the chance to search the place again. You know Jake was down there not too long ago and he never moves without his damned work. He's just stupid enough to have left things there.'

'He's not stupid at all,' Renfrew muttered, throwing himself down on the far end of the settee. 'He's clever – highly intelligent. I can't dismiss him at all. His books are too well researched.'

'Well, if he mentions you, sue him,' Gillian said in a flare of annoyance. She had been expecting praise after her little adventure. Instead, Giles was angry. She was cautious enough to know that anger and Giles were a bad mixture. There was a lot in his past that she could only guess at.

'Oh, brilliant,' he sneered. 'Sue him! Point out to all and sundry that there's fire behind the smoke. I would be dropped like a hot potato – and just when I'm ready to move into the political field.' He turned pale angry eyes on her. 'You stay in here until this is over. You can have anything you want but you stay undercover, and that means in this place until I've dealt with Trelawny and his damned notes.'

Gillian tossed up her chin. 'I might just walk off and leave you,' she threatened defiantly.

'You wouldn't get far. You came to me, my dear. You were the one who discovered Trelawny's next project. But now you know a little too much and your sudden reappearance would be very embarrassing.'

Gillian felt a cold shiver pass over her skin. She didn't know a lot about Giles's past but Jake did; she was sure of that. This had all turned out to be bigger than she had expected and it wasn't much fun anymore. Hiding until the police arrested Jake had seemed to be a good idea, with the promise of plenty of rewards afterwards. She was expecting Giles to marry her when she was free. Now she was seeing that she had stepped into a situation that would be difficult to get out of.

She thought about Jake. He was like a big, bad-tempered bear – no social polish in spite of his high beginnings and his private education. He wasn't an ex-crook, though, and he *did* have money.

'Don't even let the idea enter your mind,' Giles murmured, reaching across for her and pulling her into his arms.

'I don't know what you mean.' She snuggled up to him at once, and his smile was lost on her as he tucked her against his shoulder.

'Very good,' he said softly. 'I'm really glad.'

Gillian bit her lip and said nothing. He sometimes sounded quite sinister. She gave a sigh and relaxed. She knew how to take care of herself, and anyway, if they could stop this book of Jake's, Giles would be very generous.

Jake took extra precautions. He always guarded his work carefully, but now he went to great lengths to make sure that nothing was stolen or destroyed. Normally he worked with two word processors. He worked on one and the other was used for his research. Even so, the main bulk of the research was always on paper. He was used to handling it that way.

Now he asked for copies of all the work on disk that Bob Carter had. In doing so, he was pretty much obliged to tell Bob everything about his suspicions. In all fairness, he had to keep Bob in the picture too because now Bob knew almost as much about Giles Renfrew as he did himself, and Jake was convinced the man would stop at nothing to suppress his book.

Perhaps Renfrew was expecting to be actually named in the book? Maybe he thought it would do him more damage than he could cope with? Renfrew was going to enter the government; there was no doubt about that. He had bought himself into favour in high places. A safe seat would be assured.

Plenty of Members of Parliament had faced scandal in the past. It was possible to dig into history and find more than a few villains who had served in public places. Nowadays, though, they had more news coverage than they wanted, and Giles Renfrew had a very murky past.

But how had he known about the proposed book? How had he even known about Bob Carter? There was only one answer to that; Gillian. Jake did not know who her lovers had been but it was more than likely that she had homed in on Renfrew. He had wealth and social status.

After some deep consideration Jake decided to keep a copy of everything in his security box at the bank and, though it was somewhat of a nuisance, every few days he took along the work he had done and deposited that too.

There was very little else he could do to safeguard his work. Had it not been for Gillian's disappearance he might well have ignored the fire attack and the break-in at Bob's office. As it was, he was taking everything seriously.

Giles Renfrew had been working his way up for a long time. It was rumoured that at the next general election he would be put up for a safe seat and it was obvious that he would not be some lowly member of parliament for long. He had his eye on big things and he could not afford to have anyone pointing a finger at him either in suspicion or amusement.

Renfrew and his associates had found out about the book some time ago, that much was obvious, and it was unlikely that Gillian's disappearance was a coincidence so in some way she was involved too.

At least Kathryn was out of it. It was nearly three weeks since Jake had seen her, and he stifled the urge every time he felt like ringing her or calling round at her flat. He worked on doggedly, pushing her out of the way whenever the thought of her crept into his mind. He wanted to see her even though he denied it forcefully. He wanted to look at her and hear her soft voice. She was constantly in his mind but he could do nothing about it. In any case, at the moment he was not safe to be with, not safe to be seen with. The break-in at Bob's office had made him realize that.

The phone rang when he was taping some notes and he answered with only half his mind on it. It was just half past nine in the morning and Jake felt as if he had been up for hours.

'Jake? I've been firebombed.' It was Bob, sounding remarkably cool under the circumstances, and Jake felt a wave of icy cold wash over him.

'Are you hurt?'

'No. There was nobody here at the time. When I got to the office the police were there and the fire brigade. They're putting it down to one of the never-ending assaults on property and not too important at that, because they had a warning call that there was a fire at my place and they were there just as it was really starting to take hold. You might say it was all a waste of time, but after what you told me . . .'

'Anything of value destroyed?'

'Papers – papers again. Same old process; reprint from the disk. Obviously the modern burglar is not high-tech. One word processor gone, one answering machine. Both insured. You might say it's no more than nuisance value, although the place is a bloody mess – it'll take us a couple of days to clean it up.' He paused for a moment and then added, 'They might have thought that some of your stuff was still here, Jake. Nobody knows but you and I how fast we work.'

They had worked fast this time, Jake mused. In fact, most of his own extra work had been done by Bob at home after that first break-in.

'I'm too busy to come with my brushes and mops,' Jake said laconically. 'Take care, Bob.'

'No need to tell me that. I feel like somebody in a spy story. Nail the bastard, Jake.'

'With a bit of luck,' Jake promised.

He walked round the flat for a long time, thinking. Who knew what? They knew where Bob was and hadn't fathomed yet that Bob's involvement was over, unless the attack on Bob's office had been another warning.

They knew where he was too; the fiery rags had been proof of that. Did they know about Kathryn? How carefully was he being watched? How long had they been watching him – if they were. And, if they were, he had brought Kathryn here and then led them straight back to her place.

CHAPTER 8

He picked up the phone and did what he had been wanting to do since he had seen her last; he dialled her number – a number she had not given him. He had taken it off the phone in her place when she was in the kitchen. Another despicable act. It didn't matter; he would deal with her temper when he knew she was safe.

The phone just kept on ringing and Kathryn did not have an answering machine. She wasn't there. After trying her number several times more, he decided to risk a visit. If he didn't he would be up all night, and arriving at her flat at about two in the morning would look odd. Kathryn would throw him out.

Jake changed taxi's three times, feeling idiotic and overly dramatic. It was hard to believe that this sort of thing was happening, hard not to simply shrug it off, but the proof was there. Renfrew knew about the forthcoming book and he intended to stop it.

Jake frowned at the road as the last taxi brought him closer to the funny little market and Kathryn's flat. If he had been arrested over Gillian's disappearance, his book might never have been written. Even if he had been acquitted, his credibility would have been stretched. His publisher might have disowned him, and so might his readers. It all had to tie in to Gillian. It had started a good while ago. It also meant that they, whoever they were, knew about Pengarron.

'Miss Katie's gone away,' Teddy announced as Jake walked into the market.

'Where?' Jake snapped, and Teddy looked at him warily.

'Dunno. Maybe Ralph knows. He's in now. You could go up.'

Jake was not waiting for permission. He was already on his way to the lift. As it stopped at the place where he had twice seen Kathryn's 'friend' Jake got out and hammered on the door. At the best of times his patience was limited. Now it was quite gone.

'Where's Kathryn?' Jake bit out as soon as Ralph opened his door.

'She's out,' Ralph announced, sticking to Kathryn's words exactly – although it didn't seem such a good idea with Jake looking like a black-haired demon with glowing black eyes.

'Out where?' Jake rasped, and Ralph managed a shrug that he felt quite proud of under the circumstances.

'Who knows? I don't keep track of her.' Snowy came to investigate and began to purr as soon as he saw Jake. He strutted through the door and wound himself round Jake's legs. Jake picked him up and eyed Ralph coldly.

'She leaves the cat when she's away for a long time. You water her plants, feed the cat and generally house-sit. So where is Kathryn?' There was a dangerous pause and then he added, 'Or would you like me to shove Snowy down your shirt-front?'

Ralph's nonchalance fled.

'I'm not supposed to tell you – or anyone,' he added with speed when Jake's eyes narrowed alarmingly. 'She's gone to do another Bertie thing.'

'What Bertie thing?' Jake rasped, looking more violent than ever.

'Beetle,' Ralph said quickly. 'Bertie Beetle. She went to Cornwall. She went about two weeks ago – nearly three, actually.'

Jake felt as if he had been hit in the midriff with a heavy weight. Cornwall! He knew her ways. She would be around Pengarron Manor, walking in the woods or sitting on that damned cliff top with not a soul around for miles.

He pushed Snowy into Ralph's arms and had the satisfaction of seeing the claws come out. Snowy did not care for Ralph. 'You and me both, you white monster,' Jake muttered to himself, but by that time he was going down in the lift and he knew where he was going next. Pengarron!

By the time he was able to get off it was almost afternoon, and it was only as he was well on his way

195

that Jake realized he had completely missed lunch. It seemed to be some sort of lull time in the day because the roads were not crowded, and when he saw the sign for a motorway service station he pulled off to get a drink and any sort of sandwich he could find. He didn't stay long. He was too anxious to make sure that Kathryn was safe.

As he went back to the car park a man was just straightening up from leaning over Jake's car.

Instantly Jake's suspicions were aroused, but the man made no move to hurry off when it became apparent he had been spotted.

'Just admiring the Jag,' he told Jake with a winning smile. 'Beautiful machine.'

'It goes,' Jake murmured warily.

'That must be this year's understatement,' the man laughed. 'I wouldn't mind being at the wheel of that.'

Jake relaxed. It was easy enough to see villains under every bush. He was miles away from both London and Cornwall at the moment. He had stopped almost on impulse. He was glaring at a stranger who was doing his best to be sociable.

'Why don't you get some firm to let you test-drive one?'

He got a wry grin in answer.

'You maybe,' he said, glancing at Jake's clothes and wealthy appearance. 'They'd have me followed by a police car.'

Jake smiled and got into the car. The man had himself pegged as unacceptable but he looked all right. Ex-army probably, by his bearing, maybe even ex-commando. He looked tough enough, but respectable all the same.

Jake drove off feeling slightly more relaxed. Maybe this was all his imagination. Why should Renfrew bother after all? The man might be a scoundrel but he had friends in high places. Why should he bother about a work of fiction?

A few miles later, Jake had to brake sharply on a corner. He had left the motorway and was into the steep lanes of Devon, a route he knew from his younger days that would cut off miles from the journey. The car was unexpectedly slow in stopping – or more likely, he himself had been paying less than his usual attention. He hit a gate at the side of the road and was almost blinded by a hard thump on the head as his head snapped forward and connected with the windscreen.

Kathryn rushed around helping Clare to pack for her week in hospital. Her aunt had been so determined that it was not going to happen anyway that she had left everything to the last minute. The flurry of activity only stopped when Mrs Pengelly arrived in her small red car to escort Clare away.

'Now, no visiting,' Clare ordered as she got into the passenger seat. 'You can use my car, Kathryn, for trips to the village but no further. That leg looks bad today. You rest it. And eat properly,' she shouted as Mrs Pengelly skimmed her away with remarkable speed.

Kathryn smiled and waved them off, Jean Pengelly driving the car like a hot-rod. Her aunt was a quite remarkable woman and so were her friends apparently. As to the leg, she really was feeling the effects of yesterday's enforced exercise. It hurt.

Kathryn went back into the cottage and slipped the latch on the door. With the sun shining her fears of the evening before seemed to be a little ridiculous, but she was not falling for that line. She would be cautious.

Anyway, there were her exercises, and today she would have to massage her leg with oil. It was time-consuming but it had to be done. So had the book, she mused as she got on with the task of her leg. She had to face that wood whether she liked it or not. It was either that or go back to London and head out to find another wood.

She glared down at her leg. She did not want to find another wood. Somehow or other Jake's wood had become hers, and she resented being frightened out of it. She glanced through the window and took heart from the bright, sunny day. If she didn't get back to the wood soon she would never go again because the fear would simply grow, and she knew all about fear; she had learned about it many months ago.

It might just have been her imagination, and she had sworn never again to be afraid of anything, never again to allow anyone to talk her into something she did not want to do. What was the difference really? She was in danger of letting something stop her when in actual fact she might well have been imagining everything.

She packed her things methodically, ignoring the drawer where the newspapers were, putting the whole thing out of her mind. The problem of Bertie Beetle was enough to be going on with. Jake's problems were his own and they were pushing all inventive thought out of her head. It was time she began to behave sensibly.

Kathryn walked out of the cottage, locked the door and started determinedly down the little lane. No more cliff top. She was going to the wood but not under any circumstances was she about to approach Pengarron Manor. Nobody would know that she was in the wood. She ignored the fact that Jake had found her there with no effort at all. She also ignored the fact that today she would not be able to run as well, should the need arise.

There was no instinctive feeling of any other presence as Kathryn entered the wood. From time to time she stopped and listened but there was no alien sound. The birds sang, the little stream gurgled along and the trees made their usual soft swishing as the slight breeze touched their uppermost branches.

It was safe, she felt it, and she would rely on her feelings. Whoever had been around yesterday was not there now. She settled down to work and after a time the thought of danger left her mind as the sketches grew beneath her fingers and the story grew in her imagination.

By the late afternoon, Kathryn had worked so fast that much of the time she had lost since she had arrived in Cornwall had been made up. She stopped and stretched. Tonight she would have to make her own meal and she looked forward to it. Her days of never feeling hungry were gone.

There was a faint loss of light in the wood by now. The full glare of brightness had gone out of the day. She looked round and began to gather her things together, ready for the walk back, and just as she had her basket filled she heard a noise from the direction of the house. It echoed across the silence and it was not her imagination.

In spite of her determined thoughts of earlier, her first thought was flight. But there had been nothing surreptitious about the noise and she stood and walked cautiously to the edge of the wood that faced the garden. There was nothing to see. The house looked exactly as it had done yesterday – empty, neglected and forlorn.

Kathryn bit at her lip, trying to make up her mind about her next action. She had come here to find out all she could about Jake and so far she had done nothing. The choices were very simple. She could go away, ignore the house and make quite sure that Jake Trelawny stayed out of her life. Or she could face the possibility of danger in finding out the truth.

Her hands clenched by her sides as she admitted that she did not really want Jake out of her life. When she thought of him, when she saw him, her feelings ranged from fright to excitement until she could barely sort out one from the other. She didn't really know how she felt about Jake. Even so, he had made such an impact on her mind that it was not easy to contemplate forcing him away entirely, never seeing him again.

She rarely thought of Colin now, and when she did think of him it was with some astonishment that she should have been so stupid as to let him dictate anything to her at all. She had a weakness that she readily admitted and that was to feel sorry for people. That was how she had felt about Colin, protective, motherly, because she'd known perfectly well inside that he was not able to cope alone. Colin had made use of that weakness. He had used it to control her when she had thought that she was in perfect control of her own life.

She did not feel protective towards Jake. Her feelings about Jake had been set from the first, long before she had known that he had been a lonely and probably unloved child. Nobody would think of offering comfort and protection to a man like Jake. He was a fortress of strength and he kept behind his own wall of power, his dark eyes hiding any feeling.

If she did not show some courage she would never be sure about him, never really know what had happened in this lovely but forsaken place. And it would haunt her; she knew that. It would spoil everything for her because she would always find herself thinking of the beautiful Gillian Trelawny.

Kathryn picked up her sketchpad from the basket, collected a pencil and then, straightening her shoulders, moved back to the edge of the wood and stepped out into the garden. If anyone saw her, she was about to sketch the house. If they ordered her away she would go, of course, but not before she had managed to engage anyone who approached her in some sort of conversation.

Apart from going to the village and encouraging people to talk she would get nowhere at all without some action, and it had to be now. If there had been anything to learn in the village, her aunt would have already told her.

Whatever the noise had been it had now stopped, and as she came close to the house Kathryn saw no more sign of anyone than she had done the day before. Nothing seemed to have changed. But as she went to the steps leading to the long stone terrace she stopped for a second in surprise. The huge, glass door leading into the house was open.

Kathryn let her mind absorb the shock waves. She was not about to race off to the shelter of the trees this time. If someone was here and had opened the door they must have keys, and that sounded very official. She would ask permission to draw the house and then try to get them to talk. She pushed the thought of danger right out of her mind. She could not afford to be anxious.

With a fixed smile on her face she went up the steps, but even when she was on the terrace, her footsteps loud enough to be heard, nobody appeared to ask her why she was there. She assumed what she hoped was a pleasant, nonchalant look and walked closer to the open door. This was the best chance she had had and it might never come again.

She knocked and stood there for a minute, but it was quite clear that whoever was in the house was not hearing her at all so she stepped firmly inside, her heart beating like a hammer as she hastily tried to work out what she would say when someone told her she was trespassing.

What could she get away with?

Oh, I thought Jake was home. That sounded reasonable, and a good excuse for stepping inside. She decided to elaborate on that theme by calling out 'Jake! Are you here?' She did not, however, call too loudly, because now that she was in the house her nervous anxiety was threatening to take over again, her mind turning more and more to the shelter of the wood.

It was gloomy in the house, as gloomy as she had surmised yesterday. Through a door that was open at the far side of the room she could see a wide, dark staircase, and she knew right then that she would never have the courage to go as far as that.

The low, afternoon sun flooded into this room, but all it seemed to do was illuminate the stark nature of the place. When the sunlight faded the house would once more return to its austere neglect, its aloof coldness. She certainly didn't want to be here then.

She thought of calling out again, but the atmosphere of the place was really clutching at her by now and she felt stifled, trapped, the desire to find out more about Jake Trelawny pushed aside by her more primitive desire to flee.

A sudden shadow partly blocked out the sun and she turned quickly, a sharp cry of fear escaping from her throat as she saw that her escape route was blocked by the figure of a man. He stood tall and intimidating in the doorway, the sunlight behind him making all but his massive outline too dark to see.

Kathryn clutched her sketchpad close to her chest, her eyes wild with the need to escape. She took a step backwards, ready to run round the long settee and dodge away from the danger, but she never actually got that far.

'What the *hell* are you doing here?' Jake's harsh voice snapped out at her from the open doorway and she stood trembling and scared as he advanced into the room.

'Well?' he grated as he came steadily forward, and Kathryn swallowed hard, trying to get control of her racing heart. She still couldn't see him clearly, the sun behind him was too strong, but she knew it was Jake. His size and his temper were unmistakable, and so was the gravelly darkness of his voice.

'I – I heard a noise when I was in the wood and . . .' Kathryn suddenly felt the very last of her courage ooze away and she dropped her pad and flew at him, hurling herself into his arms. 'Oh, Jake! I'm so glad it's you. I was scared out of my wits.'

'What wits?' he growled, but all the same his arms came round her, strong and reassuring, and she didn't particularly care if he was furious – which she was more or less certain he would be.

He only held her for a second, and then he let her go and stepped back slightly, glowering down at her.

'You came up here alone because you thought you heard a noise?' he reminded her icily, and Kathryn intervened quickly before he could really take hold of the subject. She had the definite feeling that if she didn't sidetrack him he would fly into a real rage.

'Well, obviously it was you I heard, because when I got up here the door was open,' she pointed out firmly. 'It was quite different from yesterday. The door wasn't open yesterday but there was somebody here all the same. I never actually saw them, you understand, but I could feel somebody watching me and . . .'

Jake seized her shoulders and gave her a very sharp shake.

'You've spent your time wandering around Pengarron alone?' he rasped. 'You little fool! You were in enough danger in the wood or on the top of the cliff without coming anywhere near the house.' He spun her round and propelled her towards the door. 'Out!' he snapped. 'I'm taking you home and I'm about to give that aunt of yours a piece of my mind. If she has you down here she's responsible for you. She just lets you wander about wherever you like.'

He pushed her out to the terrace and turned to lock the door, and that was all the time Kathryn needed to gather her breath.

'How dare you?' she shouted, glaring at his back. 'Nobody is responsible for me. I'm grown up, self-supporting. I'll do as I damned well like!'

'Not when I'm around, you won't,' Jake snarled as he turned round. 'You'll keep away from here and you'll keep away from me. You are not allowed near my house, in my wood or anywhere on my land. Is that clear?'

Any words of defiance Kathryn had been about to hurl at him died in her throat as she saw his face clearly for the first time. He was in khaki trousers with a matching shirt, its sleeves rolled up, and down his right forearm was a long jagged cut. Her green eyes raced over it and then went back to his face. There was a great bruise on his forehead and his normally impassive face was tight and strained.

He just stared at her, holding her eyes, and she looked back in horror, his harsh commands forgotten.

'Jake! You're hurt.'

'I'm all right,' he assured her tightly, but she knew he was lying.

'You're not. You've been hurt.' Her hand came up to touch the bruise on his forehead but he moved his head away sharply as soon as her fingers touched his skin.

'Leave it,' he ordered icily. He looked round and then stepped back to the house, unlocking the door again. 'Your sketchbook,' he rasped. 'I'll get it. You stay put.'

Kathryn bit at her lip and did as she was told, watching him warily as he went back and collected her sketchpad. She had forgotten all about it and right now it did not seem at all important, even though her day's work was there.

Jake was hurt, no matter what he said. He did not look too good but he was also adamant that she should stay away from him. Considering the way he had pursued her in London, it was curious to say the least.

One thing was very clear. He did not want her anywhere near Pengarron Manor. Her presence in his house had shocked him considerably and she did not dare to think what the implications of that were, or what he had expected her to find. Gillian was still missing after all. Did he keep coming back here because he was afraid someone would find his wife, or did he suspect she was hiding here? Was he trying to find Gillian himself? And if he did, what would he do?

He came back out and handed Kathryn the sketch-pad, then glared at her again. 'Where's your damned basket?'

'It's in the wood,' Kathryn offered quietly. She couldn't seem to make her mind up about Jake. She should be scared of him, and in a way she was. She should be furious with him, and there was that too, but her overall feeling was one of anxiety about his state of health. He did not look ill in any way but he had obviously been hurt, and to her mind he was in pain; it showed in the strained lines on his face.

'We'll get the basket,' he muttered, turning impatiently away from her wide-eyed inspection. 'You'd better come too. I'm not leaving you here alone.'

'I'm not about to break into your house,' she said stiffly. 'I have good hearing. You've ordered me off your property and off your land. I heard you. Though why you should object to my presence when you more or less charged into my life in London, following me around and –'

'Shut up, Kathryn!' he snarled, marching out towards the woods at the end of the garden and expecting her to follow.

She did, keeping up with him easily, and after a second he slanted her a dark-eyed look that swept from her haughtily held head to her feet.

'You're walking better,' he muttered.

'Yes,' Kathryn answered coldly, determined to say no more than was absolutely necessary. Hadn't she been admitting to herself that she easily felt sorry for people? Hadn't she been thinking that very thing not more than half an hour ago? And hadn't she decided that Jake Trelawny needed no sympathy at all? He was not about to get any. If he fell down she would step over him.

'Damn it, Kathryn,' he growled suddenly. 'Why can't you behave as you look? Why can't you be delicate and dreamy? Why aren't you wearing that peculiar dress and sitting on one of your settees with that monster of a cat you own? That's how I think of you, and you could never survive in this sort of environment. Why do you constantly behave like a half-wit?'

'Look!' she shouted, turning on him furiously. 'I don't know you. I never wanted to know you – and I can survive anywhere. I survived an accident, pneumonia and I survived meeting you. You've behaved like a lunatic since I first saw you, lifting me up onto that wretched horse, following me home in a taxi, dragging me forcibly into your flat . . .'

'You saw everything from the wrong angle,' he muttered, but she was not letting him get away with that.

'You mean the viewpoint of a sane person gazing at a mad man? Yes, I can quite agree with that. It's obvious when you come to consider it.'

'As you're determined that you don't know me,' Jake replied angrily, 'that little speech comes under the heading of impertinence.'

'Children are impertinent,' Kathryn shot back at him. 'Grown-ups are rude. I'm rude and I admit it. I'm not one bit sorry either.'

'One of these days I'll have time to get around to you,' Jake breathed warningly, and Kathryn tightened her lips and stopped talking. One good thing had come out of this. She wasn't a bit scared now. Jake had infuriated her. He saw her basket and scooped it up, turning her back towards the house as he did so, all in one smoothly co-ordinated movement.

'I'll walk through the wood,' Kathryn informed him coldly, but Jake's grip tightened on her arm and he held the basket out of her reach.

'You'll stay securely in my sight until I get you back to that cottage and your aunt. I'll let you go when you're safely in her care – after I've told her what I think and pointed out that your trespassing days are over.'

Kathryn held her tongue and walked back with him to the house. He stopped holding her arm, evidently quite sure that if she made a run for it he could catch her. In any case, he had all her things in the basket. She was not about to abandon those.

She was well aware that from time to time his night-black gaze swept over her, but she ignored him, and she was determined to keep quiet about the fact that her aunt would not be available for taking orders.

His car was round at the side of the house, and as soon as Kathryn saw it her temper faded again and her anxiety for him came rushing back. The near-side wing of the car was badly dented. Apart from that there wasn't a scratch on the gleamingly new Jaguar.

Jake had been in an accident and he had not received any medical care as far as she could see. The jagged cut on his arm had stopped bleeding but it had not been cleaned. She wondered if he was up to date with his tetanus jabs. She wondered how she could see to him in his present savage mood without being savaged herself.

He put her basket on the back seat and then bowed her sardonically into the passenger seat. Kathryn got in silently and he shut the door and went round to the driver's side. He had given her a very scathing look as she got into the car and she nibbled at her lip worriedly. He needed help but he was not about to confess to that weakness. He would snarl at anyone who even suggested helping him.

She wondered rather uneasily what he would say when he found out that she was living alone at the cottage. By then, of course, he might have changed his mind and decided to leave matters as they were, secure in the knowledge that she would never again trespass in any of the places he owned – house, wood or cliff top.

And she certainly would not. If her aunt had not been in hospital she would have left Cornwall then and there and gone to some other place. The Lakes would be a lot safer and they were a long way from either Cornwall or London. A long way from Jake Trelawny. The trouble was she loved it here and she had already started the book. She needed the atmosphere. Damn Jake! She had never asked him to come into her life, to paint her into his background or to take any interest in her at all.

'You have no business to be in my life. I didn't invite you into it. I don't even like you,' she said loudly and angrily, and Jake grunted in annoyance.

'Fine. Right now I haven't time to put that to the test,' he snapped. 'I have things to do – important things that do not include you. When I've solved my present problems we'll take you out and look at you. Then we'll see how much you like or dislike me. Until then, I've put you on hold.'

'You've what? Why, you – you arrogant, infuriating . . .' Kathryn paused, momentarily lost for words, and then she turned in her seat to glare at him furiously. 'What do you mean, you've put me on hold? You have nothing to do with me at all!'

'At this moment I wish that were true,' he said softly. 'I wish I could put the clock back and get everything sorted out before I found a nymph in my wood. As it is I can do nothing but tuck you away, put you on hold and hope for the best.'

He stopped the car at Jasmine Cottage but Kathryn just sat there staring at him, and he looked steadily back at her until her cheeks flushed.

'You're as bad as my aunt,' she finally managed uneasily. 'I rarely know what she's talking about either.'

Jake reached out and lifted up a few strands of her hair, letting it slip like fire through his fingers, and then his dark eyes came back to hers.

'You know what I'm talking about, Kathryn,' he assured her quietly. 'You always know what I'm talking about. I can't do with you in my life for the time being so tucking you away is necessary. If you had never known me it would have been different. As it is, you do know me. You wandered into my life at the wrong time.' He tilted her astonished face. 'You're in danger, Kathryn.'

CHAPTER 9

She just went on looking into his eyes, lost in the blackness, and then she took a deep breath because she had unknowingly been holding her breath for the past few minutes.

'In danger from you?' she whispered.

Jake opened the door to get out of the car and gave her a wry look.

'It would be better if I could leave you thinking that,' he said drily. 'Unfortunately it wouldn't help in the present situation. No, Kathryn, you are not in danger from me. You're in danger because you know me, and I have to figure out a way to keep you safe. So far I haven't managed to do that, because you wander about mysteriously, turning up where I least expect you to be. Until I can fathom a way of making sure that you're safe, you keep in your pigeonhole and keep quiet – and so does your aunt.'

He reached into the back of the car and got her basket and Kathryn decided it was time to confess. Quite clearly he had not changed his mind about Aunt Clare. He intended to lay down the law and it

213

really was a good thing that Clare was out of the way. Kathryn was not at all sure how her aunt would take to Jake's threatened tyranny.

She stood at the side of the car and looked at him levelly.

'My aunt is not here,' she informed him.

Jake's dark eyebrows rose. 'Lying will not get you out of this,' he said. 'I intend to speak to her.' He indicated the door of the cottage. 'After you, Miss Holden.'

'I'm not lying,' Kathryn assured him. 'It would be childish.'

'And quite in character. I haven't all day, Kathryn.'

'She's in hospital. She went today. She has to be there for a week to have a check-up. Her heart.'

Jake looked at her with narrowed dark eyes, his mouth set in very disapproving lines.

'Let's get this straight. Your aunt is in hospital and you're here all alone?'

'Obviously.'

'There's nothing obvious about it,' Jake growled. 'Ralph is your constant shadow, and then, of course, there's Colin. For all I know you might have brought reinforcements.'

'Well, I haven't,' Kathryn snapped, irritated with herself when her face began to flood with colour. 'I'm quite self-sufficient.'

'Hmm,' Jake grunted. 'We'll see. Open the door and let's get inside.'

'I can't allow you to . . . Really it wouldn't look too good if . . . They gossip here and . . .'

'For God's sake, Kathryn,' Jake snapped, 'I'm just about ready to keel over. Make me a cup of tea and stop babbling about your reputation. I've got some thinking to do and I'm not about to do it while standing here at the side of the road. Besides,' he added irritably, 'I've got a headache the size of boulder.'

'Oh, yes. I see. I'm sorry . . .' Kathryn began, looking at him anxiously.

'Don't overdo it,' Jake growled. 'You get to make the tea. That's all.'

Once inside, Jake looked round swiftly, his eyes guarded. Apparently he was still not sure that Kathryn was telling the truth and she looked at him with some exasperation.

'Aunt Clare is not hiding under the stairs,' she pointed out sharply. 'I'm alone here – except for you. If you'd like to sit down, I'll make that tea.'

He just nodded and took no further notice of her. He was staring out of the window at the sea and Kathryn gave another great sigh of annoyance and went into the kitchen. He was utterly impossible, she decided. He was behaving as if he was her keeper, as if he had rights, and come to think of it he had done that pretty much since he had first seen her.

He was arrogant, forceful and very, very secretive. For instance, he had assured her that she was in danger but not in danger from himself. He had not, however, made one single attempt to tell her what the danger was.

'Why am I in danger?' she called out from the kitchen.

'Because you know me.' It seemed that he was not about to elaborate on that, and Kathryn frowned at the teapot and pressed the matter further.

'How could knowing you put me in any danger?' she persisted, with what she thought was a great deal of patience, and he came to stand in the doorway of the kitchen, his dark eyes on her bent head, her glowing red hair.

'I think I've inadvertently led you into trouble,' he said quietly, when she turned from making the tea and found him watching her. 'If I'd known what I know now when I first saw you I would have ignored you and left you alone.' He grimaced to himself and turned back into the small, comfortable sitting room. 'Hindsight, as they say, gives one twenty-twenty vision. Before I knew what was going on you were most definitely compromised, or so I am assuming.'

'Compromised is not a good choice of word,' Kathryn pointed out primly as she set the tray on the coffee-table. 'It has – er – unpleasant connotations.'

She looked up severely and found Jake looking at her with wry amusement.

'Slip of the tongue,' he agreed. 'I'll be more explicit. They know about you. Or at least I think they do.'

Kathryn poured tea and looked across at him as he sat in a facing armchair.

'You're going to explain, of course?'

'I don't have a lot of choice, do I? If I thought you would simply take orders and obey them I might just keep quiet, but you're not very co-operative, so you'd better know the truth.'

He told her about Giles Renfrew, right from the beginning, and Kathryn forgot all about her tea. It just sat there going cold as Jake talked.

'So you think he got wind of your book, the fact that it was going to be based roughly on his life, and decided to silence you?'

'It looks that way,' Jake agreed. She had taken the story very calmly but now she was thinking, putting things together. He knew she had a very sharp mind and he was watching for her final reaction and waiting for the thing he knew would come. She thought for a moment and then looked straight at him.

'Did they, whoever they are, have anything to do with your wife's disappearance? It seems to me to be too much of a coincidence.'

'I think so too,' he said quietly. 'Either she was part of it willingly, or they took her to assure themselves I would stop the book, or they killed her. I've thought about it for a good while. If they were holding her to make me drop the whole thing they would already have made demands. I don't think she's a prisoner.'

'Then she's either with them willingly or she's dead,' Kathryn stated solemnly, and Jake simply nodded in agreement.

'Why are we saying "they" instead of him? He's only one man.'

'He's achieved his present dubious success by being an organizer. I assume he still has some part of his organization around him – or at least is able to call on it when the need arises. His past is well hidden. Inadvertently I stirred up the ashes. I never intended to expose him. It was just an idea for a book and his life seemed to be running along the same lines. I thought a few examples of his handiwork would add colour. I had no intention of naming him. But I'd lost track of him over the past few years, so I asked Bob to look up some facts.'

'So do you think this – Bob Carter let it slip about you?'

'Definitely not. He works for several writers. Discretion and confidentiality are essential. No, they found out some other way and probably trailed me to Bob's place.'

'Are you going to work at it like that still? Just using the odd bit of Renfrew's life for colour?' Kathryn asked quietly, and his face hardened over at once.

'No,' he snapped. 'I'm going to really point at him without actually naming him. I'm going to get the bastard.'

She was silent for a minute and then nodded, got up and lifted the tray, making for the kitchen.

'Come in here and sit down,' she ordered. 'I'll see to your wounds. It might be a good idea to tell me where you got them too.'

'I had a car accident.' He did not tell her that he had been coming to find her so hurriedly that for the first time in his life he had been careless. To his astonishment he had braked too late.

'I figured that out for myself,' Kathryn pointed out tartly. 'One bent Jaguar was the only clue I needed. Come and let me see to those wounds.'

'They're not wounds and they don't need seeing to. If they did,' he added firmly when she turned on him, 'I could see to them myself.'

'Oh, don't be stupid!' Kathryn snapped with sudden anger. 'I really hate that idiotic, stiff-faced male attitude.'

'Is Colin a stiff-faced male?' Jake enquired, sitting obediently at the table, feeling somewhat chastened by her swift attack. At the moment she was anything but dreamy. She was an efficient female who was not going to stand for any nonsense.

'No. I'm speaking generally. Unfortunately Colin is a coward,' Kathryn told him mildly, her quick flash of temper dying. 'That, however, is neither here nor there and comes under the heading of none of your business. Let me see that arm first.'

Jake sat quietly as she dealt with his arm. She was gentle but definitely firm. It stung quite a lot but he stuck it out silently, keeping up the stiff-faced male attitude. He found his lips quirking in spite of the fix he seemed to be in and the night-black eyes softened as he looked down at her shining head, every silken strand of hair glowing like fire.

She looked up at his forehead and went to work on that too, and it gave him the chance to see the serious expression in her wide, fascinating green eyes. The

Lady of the Lake. He was beginning to understand why he followed her about, and the more real she became the more alarmed he felt about her.

'I'll make a meal now,' Kathryn announced, standing and beginning to put away her aunt's well-thought-out first aid box. 'You'd better eat here with me.'

'I can see to myself,' Jake began, getting to his feet, and she looked at him with mounting exasperation.

'Don't start all that again, for heaven's sake. It's quite obvious that you've had a nasty bump and a good deal of shock. You really are like a caged beast, thrashing about angrily even when nobody is attacking you. I have to cook for myself and it's no trouble to cook extra. Go back in there and sit down or something, then I can get on. I'm starving and I'm not about to die of hunger to satisfy your little quirks.'

'What about these gossipy neighbours?' Jake enquired, trying not to laugh. 'When we arrived here your thoughts on that subject were very anxious, as I recall.'

'I have other anxieties now,' Kathryn muttered, turning away to put the cooker on. 'I seem to be part of one of your books. In view of possible attack, nosy neighbours might just come in useful.'

Jake's lips twisted in amusement and he went back to sit down as ordered. He certainly needed it and he was glad of Kathryn's level-headed thinking. Unfortunately, in reality any neighbours were a good distance away, and any observing they did would have to be with binoculars. He was not about to point that out to her.

'I think you'd better stay here tonight,' Kathryn stated vigorously as they ate their meal, and Jake put down his knife and fork to stare at her in astonishment.

'Just say that again, because I'm not altogether sure what I heard. It's probably confusion from the bump on the head.' His dark eyes narrowed on her face but Kathryn was not at all embarrassed.

'I said that you should stay here tonight,' she repeated staunchly.

'Alone with you? Isn't that rather putting the neighbours to the final test?' Jake enquired, feeling stunned and disorientated at finding her saying anything like that. She was supposed to be scared of him. He had always been quite sure that she was. Her invitation left him wallowing in a sea of turbulent emotions. Why should she trust him? Hardly anyone else did.

Kathryn shrugged.

'I can't see that it really matters, and in any case the damage is done as far as neighbours are concerned. If you're alone at that great big house you'll be vulnerable. If I'm alone here I'll be vulnerable also. It's better to be together. We can fight them if we need to.'

Jake's dark eyes softened. 'I can't stay here, Kathryn. I'm much too big to sleep on that settee and I'm too tired to sit up all night, guarding us both.'

Kathryn thought he might just be looking amused, and that was annoying. He was watching her in a peculiar, kindly manner too, as if she were some sort of soft, woolly toy. It was rather condescending. After all, he had been the one to sharply warn her of the danger.

'I've thought about that,' Kathryn assured him, making her point strongly by jabbing her fork in the air in his general direction. 'You can sleep in my bed.'

Jake looked speechless. He just stared at her and she went on seriously, 'It wouldn't really be right, if you slept in Aunt Clare's bed, would it? I could wash the bedding afterwards but it would all be done without her permission. I feel it would be greatly intruding on her privacy. Besides, we don't really know how long you'll have to sleep here with me, do we?' She frowned thoughtfully. 'That could be another problem. So I'll sleep in Aunt Clare's bed and you can sleep in mine.'

She looked across at him expectantly and Jake looked back quite blankly. He wasn't thinking straight. He was losing the thread of things again. She did that to him frequently. It sometimes seemed as if she lived slightly on the edge of the world, or even above it instead of being in it. She was inviting him to stay the night with her, even though in separate rooms, and she was doing it with all the vigour of a general planning a campaign.

He opened his mouth to speak and then closed it again. Why not? He could protect her a lot better here than he could if they were in separate houses. He hadn't even unpacked his things. They were still in the car. She was so innocently trusting that he was beginning to worry when she was out of his sight. She was headstrong too. She'd probably inherited that from her Aunt Clare, from what he remembered of that lady.

'You don't really know me, Kathryn,' he began, but she waved her fork in the air again and nodded, eating away rapidly with more gusto than he would have imagined possible. The thrill of the chase. She probably thought this was just exciting. Her innocence astonished him. Didn't she realize he was suspected of killing his wife? Didn't she understand that he was mixed up with people who might do anything? The man who had originally told him about Giles Renfrew had been killed in a hit and run accident not long afterwards. It might have been just bad luck, but Jake had never thought so.

'I've got you figured out,' she said, swallowing her food and jabbing her fork towards him again. 'You're the victim of a terrible plot. We'll stand together in this. As they're probably after me too, there's little choice. However,' she added sternly as she got to her feet and began to clear the table, 'it has all come about because you meddled in other people's affairs.'

'He's a villain, Kathryn,' Jake stated, looking up at her from his seat at the table and wondering how he had got into this sort of situation with her and why it was amusing him so much when he had plenty to worry about.

'Obviously he's a villain, and I expect you'll finally get him fixed, but in the meantime we have ourselves a problem, don't we?'

'Kathryn . . .' he began, about to point out to her that all she had to do was hide, that the problem was his. He never got the words out.

'I'll make you some tea now,' she said as she went to the kitchen. 'You can't have coffee with a head like that.'

He found himself shaking his head in disbelief but stopped when the pain hit him again. He couldn't stop grinning, though. Kathryn had the bit between her teeth. He would have to think of a way to use that trait to keep her safe – like sending her to Scotland or somewhere to look for imaginary clues. She was ethereal to look at, living in some world of her own making. She was also very satisfyingly crazy.

He wondered what the mysterious Colin had done to have her classifying him as a coward? Kathryn would never say anything like that without just cause. He frowned and stopped right there. He was in danger of putting her on a pedestal. All he had to do was keep her safe, because it was his fault that she had been dragged into this mess.

Besides, he often had the strong desire to beat her soundly. She was big on imagination and short of common sense. All the same, staying here tonight made very good sense. It was a pity, though, that there was nowhere to leave his car other than outside the cottage. It proclaimed his presence like a homing beacon.

Before she went to bed Kathryn stood in the doorway and looked at him solemnly.

'I suppose I'd better tell you my thoughts,' she murmured worriedly. 'I know that nothing happened to me when I had to race out of the wood yesterday, when I thought someone was watching me, but I'm sure someone was there. I rely on my instincts. Most women do. And I couldn't help thinking about your wife. What if it was her? What if she's hiding somewhere and just letting you be under suspicion?'

'If she's alive then that's exactly what she's doing,' Jake said quietly, his dark eyes on her anxious face. His blood ran cold at the thought of her having to run from possible danger. He didn't know how she'd managed it. The limp was much better, but to run must have been a terrible ordeal.

'Suppose, though, that she's never really gone away?' Kathryn persisted quietly. 'Suppose she's still somewhere round Pengarron just – just waiting?'

'I looked for her, Kathryn. I looked for her for a long time. If Gillian *is* at Pengarron, or anywhere near it, then she didn't just stay there. She's come back.'

Ghosts came into Kathryn's mind and she gave him a weak smile and went to bed as fast as she could. Perhaps, like her first impression of Jake, Gillian Trelawny had come in on the mists from the sea, waiting to haunt him. The trouble was, Gillian Trelawny was haunting her too. She was always thinking about her and reminding herself that Jake

225

was married. All the same, he was here with her now. Gillian was not.

In the night Kathryn heard a noise. She had been oddly restless with Jake in the house. She was feeling safe but uneasy all at the same time, very much aware that he was there, under the same roof. He had brought so much excitement into her life that her days of depression seemed to have been nothing but a dream.

It had not taken much to waken her, and as she lay in bed listening she heard the noise again. It was stealthy. Somebody was in the house, creeping about. 'They' had come, just as Jake had feared, and he wasn't in any state to tackle anyone. He had looked quite pale when he had gone to bed.

Kathryn knew she would have to cope with this alone. Jake could not do with another blow to his head. She should have fussed over him more, made sure he was all right. He might be unconscious even now for all she knew. Nobody had ever cared about him and she had not seen to him properly either.

She threw the bed-clothes back and slid her feet to the floor, taking care not to make a sound. Floorboards creaked in this old cottage but she had the advantage there. She knew where every single creaking floorboard was because they irritated her and she always stepped over them. She was quite sure she could move silently.

She was a bit disorientated in her aunt's bedroom, but she had left the curtains open and the bright moonlight made seeing easy. It would not do to blunder into anything and alert the intruder. The thought that there might be more than one worried her. She had quickly got used to thinking of Jake's enemy as 'they', but really, even when she had been discussing it with Jake, she had really only seen one man in her mind – this Giles Renfrew. If he was in her aunt's kitchen by himself, well and good. If he had brought others with him it was not so good. She would have to play it by ear, think on her feet.

She crept to the door of the bedroom and peered out into the little passage. Even there it was light enough because there was a small window and it was getting the full flood of moonlight. The moonlight also fell in an illuminating shaft on the tall antique box that stood at the top of the stairs. It was about three feet high and had long since lost its lid. Her aunt kept odds and ends in there – a couple of walking sticks, assorted useless objects and one very old umbrella.

Kathryn had noted the umbrella with amusement when she had been here before, but since then she had more or less taken it for granted. If anything could be disgustingly old it was that umbrella. It was big, black and decrepit, like an ancient crow who had fought a lot of battles, but it had a really wicked-looking metal ferrule.

As far as she knew its sharp, gleaming end was actually made of steel. Certainly it had been made to last, because it had outlasted the umbrella with a sort of vicious glory of its own. What a weapon! It was a club and a sword all rolled into one. Kathryn slid it carefully from the tall box and grasped it firmly. She might even be able to deal with two people before she had to scream for Jake.

She crept down the stairs, carefully avoiding the places where the wood creaked, and felt doubly annoyed when she saw that the light was on in the kitchen. What a damned cheek! They felt so secure that they were not even bothering to stay in darkness. They would not be feeling so smug in another second.

When she peered cautiously into the kitchen there was not a soul to be seen and for a split second she relaxed, wondering if she had imagined the noise, wondering if she had left the light on herself. She had been the last up. Jake had been glad to get to bed because he was obviously dropping from exhaustion,

Kathryn stood irresolute for a moment, almost ready to switch off the light and go back to bed. And then it came to her. If she couldn't see anyone then there could only be one person in this small kitchen and he must be behind the door. That was why she could not see him. She had watched that happen on television plenty of times and always wondered why the hero was so stupid that the obvious never occurred to him. Now she had nearly fallen for the trick herself.

One person she could deal with easily. She had the advantage of surprise. She was also very annoyed. She grasped her weapon in both hands and launched herself into the kitchen, lashing out wildly, aiming for the villain behind the door and not much caring if she injured him seriously.

There was a startled oath, a crash as crockery hit the floor and then Kathryn felt something scalding hot on her foot. She went on furiously, aiming again and again, but her weapon was wrenched from her hands and her blind frenzy came to a startled halt as Jake roared at her.

She had been so worked up, so battle-ready, that it took a second or two to sink in that she had been attacking Jake. He was looking at her as if she was insane and he was not at all pleased by his observations.

'What the hell are you doing?' he roared. 'Do you realize how many times I've needed to say those words to you? Now you go utterly berserk in the middle of the night, but I expect you've got some idiotic explanation – or are you just stark raving mad anyway?'

'I – I thought it was them,' Kathryn explained shakily. 'I heard a noise, and you looked so ill when you went to bed that I . . .'

'That you got up to defend me with that!' Jake raged, pointing at the discarded umbrella that now lay in a pool of hot coffee.

Kathryn stood on one leg and lifted her burning foot into her hand. His remarks had drawn her attention to the smashed crockery and she looked at the pieces of the cup worriedly.

'Oh, dear. That's one of Aunt Clare's best cups. It will take some explaining,' she murmured, gazing down at it.

'I'll buy her a new set,' Jake snarled. 'I'll buy her a new cottage – anything she wants if she can just get control of you!'

'It's vulgar to make a big display of wealth,' Kathryn pointed out shakily. 'You couldn't replace that anyway. They stopped making it thirty years ago.'

'Will you stop talking in that lunatic way?' Jake shouted. He looked as if he was giving some consideration to strangling her, and then he noticed her peculiar stance and saw her wince as she moved her foot.

'Now you're burned, on top of everything else you are,' he snapped

'It's all right,' she muttered, but he suddenly reached for her, his powerful hands spanning her waist, and Kathryn found herself being carried without ceremony to the sink at the other side of the room. Jake sat her on the draining board and turned on the cold tap.

'What are you doing?' she yelped anxiously.

'What I should be doing is filling the sink and making some move to drown you,' Jake grated. 'As that would perhaps be illegal, I'm about to take care of your foot.' He grasped her ankle and thrust the scalded foot under the icy fall of water from the cold tap.

'It's cold!' Kathryn shrieked, trying to wriggle free, but the hand on her ankle stayed firm.

'I've read about it,' Jake assured her caustically. 'It takes the heat out of the cells of the skin. As it's all for your own good, you'll just have to put up with it.' He looked as if he was enjoying her discomfort, and Kathryn glared at him but decided that he was too strong to struggle against.

'I can see to myself.'

'Really?' he murmured sarcastically. 'One set of rules for me and a different set for you? You gave me a short lecture on the stiff-faced male attitude.'

'Why were you in the kitchen?' Kathryn asked quickly to get him off the subject.

'I had a headache that woke me up. I came down to see if your aunt had any painkillers. I made myself some coffee and then you ran amok. You may just remember the latter.'

'Coffee is not good when you've got a bad head,' Kathryn began, but two dark eyes looked at her from beneath winged black brows and she changed her mind about a further lecture. Instead she said, 'My foot is numb. I think it's frozen. If you give my leg a sharp rap the foot will probably crack and fall off.'

Jake's face was quite close to hers. He looked at her for a moment and then asked quietly, 'Why do you say extravagant things like that?'

She gave a delicate little shrug.

'That's how my mind works. I feel my foot freezing and then the natural progression of ideas takes hold. It's not surprising, really.'

'Perhaps not – for you.'

'My foot is cold enough to hurt,' she told him with complete seriousness, and his dark gaze flashed over her face before he turned off the tap and brought her

231

foot back to a more normal position. He began to dry it carefully with the towel by the sink and it was only then that Kathryn realized how terribly undressed she was. Until that moment she hadn't given it a thought.

She had come down to do battle with no thought in her head but fighting, and now she suddenly found herself sitting up on the draining board in her aunt's kitchen with a man drying her foot and her person covered in a short cotton nightie. She felt her cheeks begin to flush and she wondered how she was going to make a dignified exit.

'What's wrong?' Jake asked quietly, as if he was busy reading her mind.

'Er – nothing. Did you find the painkillers?' She sounded breathless and Jake's gaze flashed to her face, his eyes intent.

'No.' His midnight-dark eyes were holding hers and Kathryn forgot how cold her foot was. His hand closed round it warmly. 'The cold will go when the blood starts getting back into the skin.'

Kathryn's tongue ran along the edge of her bottom lip and her teeth bit down on the moistened skin as she felt his hand move from her foot to slide over her ankle and wander gently to the back of her leg. His eyes didn't leave hers and she gazed back at him with fascinated anxiety.

'Thank you for getting up to defend me,' he said softly. He moved forward until her legs were pressed against him, and just as she was thinking her breath would actually stop his other hand cupped the back of her neck beneath the tousled fall of her hair and he brought her mouth to his.

Kathryn was frightened, startled, because she hadn't been expecting it. Jake had never looked at her like that, never led her to believe that this sort of thing could happen. Now he was kissing her gently, firmly, and the lift inside her started going down fast again, too fast, as if everything was melting and out of control.

She took a small gasping breath, her lips opening as she murmured, and Jake's reaction to that was swift. His lips began to move over hers more firmly, searching, questing, and his hand moved on her leg in long, caressing strokes. Nobody had ever kissed her quite like this and Kathryn felt herself sinking into it, her hands rising to touch him, to rest lightly on his chest.

He urged her forward gently, until he was standing between her legs, and his hand began to stroke her back, making her sink against him even more. She wanted to wind her legs round him because she was so lost in the feelings that she had almost forgotten where she was. Only by resisting strongly did she stop herself from letting her legs cling round his waist, and the effort to resist made a soft moan leave her throat.

It was only as Jake heard it and felt the tentative touch of her fingers on his face that he came to his senses. He had been stepping deeper and deeper into desire, desire that had hit him right out of the blue – for *Kathryn*! His hand had wandered from her rounded calf to the silky skin of her thigh and he didn't want to move it away.

It didn't happen like that. When he wanted a woman he knew the moment he set eyes on her, and he had never felt that for Kathryn. All the same, his heart was pounding and he could feel heat racing through his body, deepening with each second. He didn't want to move and his lips seemed to have a mind of their own, lingering at the corner of her mouth to the very last second. He could feel her soft body close and he felt that she was wanting to be closer still. She was warm, eager. It was madness.

He stepped back and lifted her to the floor without a word, ignoring her wide open green eyes. God, they were beautiful eyes, huge, tilted, glistening like warm emeralds. At this moment he wanted to sink into them. His hands started to lift to touch her face but he stopped them.

'Go to bed, Kathryn,' he said harshly, and she looked at him in that startled way of hers, trying to sort out what had happened. He felt like a villain.

'I'll show you where the painkillers are,' she offered in a shaken voice, and he was going to tell her not to bother until he saw how much she was trembling. It would give her something to do, give her a way to extricate herself from this. He had placed her in a diabolical situation. With any other woman he would instantly have taken advantage of it but not with her.

She stepped carefully round the broken cup, glancing down at it as if she had forgotten all about it.

'I'll have to see to that,' she said in the same shaken way.

'No. I'll do it. I'll get it mended. I'm sure there's someone in London with that sort of skill.'

'That would be nice,' Kathryn agreed tremulously, moving to the bank of cupboards. 'It will have to be washed carefully, though, or the coffee will stain it and then the stain will show through the cracks.'

She stopped as if she realized she was simply babbling on nervously and Jake said nothing. He was watching her, looking at that glorious hair, thinking about the beautiful eyes. He wondered if she realized that her nightie was hardly covering her. When she stood on her toes to reach up into the cupboard he could see a long length of slender leg. He never thought about that limp now. He had simply built it into the way he saw her. In any case, she was too beautiful and unusual for it to matter.

He clenched his hands. He could still feel her leg under his fingers, the silken warmth of her skin, the softness of her body. He looked away abruptly. He wanted to pull that nightie over her head and toss it down to the floor. He wanted to kiss her fiercely all over. It didn't happen like this. He had told himself many times that he didn't want Kathryn, that he was only interested in her because she had strange habits and needed to be watched carefully.

'Here they are.' She found the tablets and turned to him, still looking at him in that odd way, partly puzzled, partly scared, partly excited. The flush on her face had faded now and there was no knowing how she really felt.

'Thank you,' Jake said quietly. He looked across at her. 'I'm sorry, Kathryn.'

She shook her head, for once avoiding his eyes, and then she stepped carefully once more round the broken cup and went out of the kitchen. He could hear her going up the stairs and he wondered if he had frightened her so much that she would be unable to sleep. It bothered him enormously.

'Kathryn.' He went to the door and stood at the bottom of the stairs looking up at her. 'You're quite safe. I never meant . . . You can sleep without being afraid of me.'

'I know,' she assured him quietly, stopping and looking down at him over her shoulder. 'If I hadn't known that I would never have invited you to stay here. It was just that – well – I got a bit worked up when – when I ran amok.'

She was gone before it dawned on him that she was taking the blame for his actions in the kitchen. He nearly went up after her to argue about it but he knew it would not have been a good idea. He was by no means back to normal. He still wanted to touch her. He wanted to lift her out of bed and take her to his room. The feeling was like an ache in his gut. But this was Kathryn and she was special.

He went back to the kitchen and surveyed the chaos she had caused. He had to wash the pieces of that cup so that the coffee didn't leave stains; that was what she had said. He did it methodically. It was a good, safe occupation for now. He had about as much chance of sleeping as flying to the moon.

Kathryn huddled up in bed. She wanted to get as far into the mattress as she could, anything to escape the feelings that washed over her like small tidal waves. Jake's unexpected actions had left her vulnerable, defenceless, utterly shaken. She had been kissed before but not like that. She thought about Colin kissing her, went over the mechanics of it in her mind, something she had never considered before.

She had never asked herself if Colin had been experienced, sensuous, exciting. He had just been Colin and he had kissed her. Now she knew that she had been the one in the wrong. She had never reacted at all to Colin. She could quite easily have patted him on the head and said, 'There, there now,' as if he were a child.

It had not been like that with Jake. He had kissed her slowly, his lips probing hers as if he was searching for something inside her – and he had almost found it, brought it out. She'd known when he stopped that she didn't want him to stop at all. The odd excitement she usually felt when she saw him had erupted inside like a storm. It had scared her. It had not been Jake she was scared of; it had been her own growing emotions, her own susceptibility. She had wanted him to go on and on and she was not a fool at all. She'd known exactly where the kisses were leading.

Jake had stopped because he had felt her reaction to him. Kathryn buried her head in the pillows and gave a tiny little groan. What must he think of her? And she had been racing around in her nightie! No wonder he thought she was mad. In the morning she would have to face him and it would not be easy, especially if these sensations were still drowning her. She did not expect to sleep at all.

CHAPTER 10

When Kathryn woke up the next morning she looked around her aunt's room and wondered if she could stay there all day and hide. She was astonished that she had not had any trouble at all sleeping. Tiredness had simply washed over her. And now she had to face Jake.

She could hear someone down in the kitchen and she assumed he was up and getting ready to leave. He would not want to linger here after last night. If it wasn't Jake downstairs she was not about to do anything at all. There would be no further charging about like an idiot. Kathryn dressed quickly and went down to join him. It was no use putting this off. He had to be faced sooner or later.

When she walked into the kitchen he was standing with a hot drink and he did not turn immediately. He was looking out of the window. She saw that he had cleaned the floor where she had made such a mess last night, and the broken cup was on the work-top, each piece washed. It made her feel worse than ever.

239

When he turned to face her she chewed at her lip and then looked straight at him.

'I'm sorry about last night,' she said quietly.

'Apart from the cup there seems to be no damage,' Jake murmured.

'I wasn't meaning that. I was talking about – afterwards. I know I must have surprised you. It's just that I got all excited with the thought that someone had broken into the cottage and then there was my foot and I . . .'

Jake put his cup on the table and walked slowly towards her. She had to be very firm with herself about backing away but she managed to hold her ground until he was almost close.

'Do you always take the blame for other people's folly?' he asked softly.

'It was my fault and I . . .'

'Did you take the blame for everything that Colin did?'

'No.' She shook her head vigorously and then gave a little smile. 'I really don't think I could have kept up with that. He had quite a few follies.'

'So have I,' Jake said tightly, 'and one of them was kissing you last night. I had no right to do that. I'm hoping you'll forget it – put it down to lack of sleep and the blow to my head.'

She looked flustered and he went to pour her some tea, pulling a chair out for her so that she could sit at the table. He then sat opposite and looked at her seriously.

'I want you to go back to London, Kathryn. I want you to go back to your flat, or whatever you call it.

Your artist's lair. I came down here to take you back and I want you to agree to go with me. You have to go now. You must.'

'I can't. My aunt's in hospital and . . .'

'It's not safe here. You're a sitting target. We both are. I may be over-dramatizing this situation but it's better to think like that than sit around carelessly and walk into any trap.'

'Surely they'll not bother with me,' Kathryn protested, but the dark eyes held hers fast and he looked even more serious.

'Gillian disappeared,' he reminded her. 'You saw the probable connection yourself. I don't want anything to happen to you. Please agree to go back to London.'

'My aunt more or less left me to look after things. If I go, the cottage will be empty for when she comes back. I know it's not as if she's having an operation but she didn't want to go.'

'If you hadn't come here she would have been alone,' Jake persisted. 'Surely she has friends?'

'There's Mrs Pengelly. I don't know her other friends.'

'Look, Kathryn,' he said softly 'If being with me is putting you in danger, then staying with your aunt puts her in danger too. We have to leave here. We'll pack our things, take the key to Mrs Pengelly and get started for London right away. When you get back you can write to your aunt. There's no need for her to be anxious about you. You can tell her that something unexpected turned up.'

241

'It did,' Kathryn muttered thoughtlessly, and then blushed bright red. The thought of last night had been driven out by Jake's urgent demands that she should go back to London but now the feelings came flooding back.

'Kathryn!' Jake's hands covered hers on the table. 'Try to stop blaming yourself for last night. I had no right to act as I did.'

'Oh, I brought it on,' she said earnestly, looking up at him. 'I do bring things on, you know. I can never quite be bothered to behave like other people do and then things happen. I know you never really wanted to kiss me. I expect it was because I went wild like that.'

'Why wouldn't I want to kiss you?' Jake asked sharply, vaguely annoyed that she was making excuses for him. 'You're beautiful, talented, brave.'

'You – you mean you actually *did* want to – to kiss me?'

She was watching him with those huge green eyes and Jake turned away angrily and stood up when he felt his body clench in a way he didn't want at all, heat pooling into him. Annoyance was as good a way as anything to stop it.

'No,' he said flatly. 'I did not want to kiss you. It just happened. Put it down to my accident but stop being a martyr. I was to blame entirely.'

He heard her sigh with a sort of dubious resignation.

'Well,' she murmured, 'I expect it was no big deal anyway.'

Jake felt like turning on her and giving her a good shaking. It was a bigger deal than he cared to contemplate. But right at this moment there must be no complications in his life at all. His days were complicated enough already, without adding more problems. Kathryn was unpredictable and often utterly scatterbrained. He already knew that she simply charged into situations without much thought – last night had really proved that beyond doubt.

He stayed firm and quiet, and over breakfast Kathryn mulled over the problems. She wasn't quite sure in her mind if she had any problems. The attacks on Jake and his friend Bob Carter had not in any way included her. All she had, after all, was her vague feeling of being watched that day and then the two scares she had had since. Both times it had been Jake who had scared her.

Even so, she was not too happy about staying here alone if Jake went back, and after last night it was obvious that he could not go on staying here. He would be embarrassed.

She went upstairs and changed the beds but she knew that Jake would not wait around while she did any washing. She would have to ask Mrs Pengelly to do the sheets. It was all going to take a lot of explaining. It would be awkward.

It was. Jake brought her things down and got them into his car and they set off along the road to the cottage where her aunt's friend lived. It wasn't far away along the flat road and Kathryn was doing a lot of rapid rehearsing.

It didn't do a lot of good. As soon as she found herself facing bright-eyed interest Kathryn felt flustered, and Jean Pengelly didn't help at all with her outspoken ways.

'Of course I'll keep an eye on things if you have to go back,' she said in a kindly voice. 'We thought you were staying, but as your boyfriend has come for you . . .'

'He isn't my boyfriend,' Kathryn stated quickly. Jake got out of the car to help, but it was the last thing he should have done.

'Oh! Why, it's Jake Trelawny!' Jean Pengelly's eyes opened wide. 'I had no idea you knew each other so well.'

As far as Kathryn could see she'd had no idea they knew each other at all, but Jake stepped round the car and gave one of his icy smiles.

'I'm taking her back to London,' he stated coldly. 'I don't really want her staying alone at Jasmine Cottage. I'll be happier in my mind if she's back in London with her friends. You'll be around if her aunt needs any assistance?'

'Er – yes,' Mrs Pengelly said, obviously not believing a word of it.

Kathryn could see her stashing the information away for when her aunt came back. In fact it was such powerful news that there was no doubt it would have to be told well before then. Her aunt would be getting a visit at the hospital today.

'It would have been better if you had stayed hidden in the car,' Kathryn remonstrated as they finally

244

managed to leave and drive off. 'We've left a lot of gossip behind us now, and, after all, my aunt has to live here.'

'You seemed to be having a slight problem getting clear of her.'

'It was merely a problem of getting her off the scent, leading her away from the truth.'

'What truth?' Jake enquired coldly. 'That the notorious Jake Trelawny is your latest boyfriend?'

'I was just setting her right on that point,' Kathryn snapped as she felt her face begin to flush. She had hoped he hadn't heard that bit of the conversation. 'And you're not notorious either.'

'I'll be notorious until Gillian is found,' Jake grated. 'And even then, she's got to be found alive.'

'Are they looking for her?'

'I don't give a damn,' Jake snapped, but she knew he did. Unless his wife was found he would always have people looking at him with suspicion. If Gillian was found and she was dead, then things would be worse.

'What do your friends think?' she ventured quietly.

'Friends? Now what are they, I wonder? According to popular myth, a friend is someone who sticks by you through thick and thin, who never doubts you. I seem to have very few friends.'

'What about this Bob Carter?'

'A business associate, in a manner of speaking. Before this happened we never spoke of anything of great moment or of a personal nature. I told him because I had to, as he seemed to be taking risks. I don't really know him. I don't even know if he's married.'

Kathryn went silent. It seemed so sad. She had no friends either, really, not close friends. When she had been ill there had only been Ralph and her aunt. Jake didn't seem to have even that. There were the men at the market, though. She supposed she could call them friends. Thinking it over, there were quite a few people she could count on, Ralph especially, and Rosie was nice. She wasn't in the sort of cold, friendless world that Jake seemed to occupy.

Jake braked at a bend in the road but nothing much happened and she heard his sharply indrawn breath.

'What's wrong?' she asked quickly, and he stared ahead, concentrating deeply on the road.

'Brakes,' he told her sharply. 'I hardly seem to have any. If we come to a hill we're going to go down like a snowball into hell.'

Kathryn froze up inside. It seemed that she had been here before. There had been nothing wrong with Colin's brakes, but she had been injured all the same. It was going to happen again. Her mouth was too dry to swallow and she gripped the seat with both hands. Even that reminded her.

The road was fairly flat for now, and Jake slowly eased on the handbrake. There was not a lot of help there, and out of her eye corner she saw him pumping the brake pedal. They slowed just a little, and as the bank at the side of the road became higher Jake ran the car at it, on and off, like a crazy film.

That helped too, and as they rounded a bend she saw a short gravelled turn-off, an emergency stopping place. The car dived into it as Jake veered suddenly off the road. He switched off the engine and in a few yards the car ploughed to a halt and they were stationary and silent.

Kathryn jumped out and leaned back against the car door, her breathing not in any way normal, but Jake ignored her after one quick look at her pale face. He had the bonnet of the car up when she looked again and she heard him mutter to himself at what he found.

'Brake fluid,' he told her when she went unsteadily round to him. 'There's about a teaspoonful left. It explains a lot of things. Maybe if we'd stayed any longer at your aunt's cottage we would have had no brakes at all.'

He had a portable phone and he called the nearest services on that. Then he came round to Kathryn.

'You took that well,' he said softly. 'You're a brave little thing, aren't you?'

'Not really. My legs are shaking. I thought history was about to repeat itself, although I don't suppose you would have walked off and left me.'

'Is that what happened?' Jake asked quietly, tilting her downcast face, and all she could do for a moment was nod her head frantically. He pulled her close, settling her against him, holding her until the trembling stopped. When she looked up anxiously he was staring down at her, his face like ice again.

'Colin?' he asked, and she nodded, still very upset.

'I expect he felt – felt shaken,' she ventured on Colin's behalf.

'That's not at all what he should have felt,' Jake assured her in a threatening voice, and she was very glad that he would never meet Colin. He pulled her back close to him, his hand stroking her hair, and it was so wonderfully soothing that she could have closed her eyes and gone to sleep.

Jake suddenly put her from him, though, and started to walk around impatiently. She knew why. He was remembering last night and regretting it deeply. The feelings of guilt and humiliation at her own actions came back very strongly.

She was also feeling guilty about abandoning her aunt. Not that Clare really needed her. She was the most self-sufficient person that Kathryn knew. All the same, she should have been there when her aunt came home. Instead she was running off with Jake.

'I really should have waited for Aunt Clare,' she said, worried, as Jake came near her on his impatient walk-about. 'I know it was only for tests, but she's been in hospital after all, and here I am running off with you instead of waiting to see that she's comfortable.'

'You are not "running off" with me,' Jake corrected irascibly. 'You are running for cover. What did you want us to do? Stay there and put your aunt in the firing line?'

'No!' Kathryn looked horrified and his face softened as he realized he was almost deliberately frightening her. All the same, he had to do something to make her take care. At Pengarron she could have been attacked with impunity, and he had the feeling she would even have gone back again if he had not shown up.

'It will all work out,' he said soothingly, and Kathryn looked at him glumly.

'I expect it will,' she muttered. '*How* it will work out is what's bothering me. The righteous don't always triumph, you know.'

Jake knew that. She had an uncanny knack of pointing out things he was just at that moment contemplating. A soul mate. He glanced at her and as quickly looked away. He needed all his wits about him. There was no time to consider his feelings for Kathryn.

Later, Kathryn found herself sitting high up in the cab of the recovery vehicle, Jake between her and the driver as the car was towed off to the nearest garage. It was a long way off, but a very efficient-looking man inspected it.

'Nipples from the brake pipe fully open,' the man at the garage informed Jake with an odd look at him. He had the car up on the ramp and Jake walked round to look at the problem. 'Pressure has blown off the dust caps. After that the fluid would leak every time you braked.'

'To what extent?' Jake looked icily angry, but his voice showed no more emotion than it had done about his accident, and much less emotion than he had shown when he had found Kathryn in Pengarron Manor all alone.

'Depends on how much you brake and how hard you brake. Fifty percent the first time you brake hard, seventy the next, then goodbye brakes. This has been a very professional – mistake. You've lost the fluid in bits with the pressure. It's neat, fool – proof – because nobody could ever prove when a thing like this happened.'

The man squinted up at Jake and saw Jake's violent expression.

'What more can I say?' He stood and wiped his hands on an oily rag. 'Can't get it done now. I'll have it done by about ten tomorrow.'

'Okay,' Jake muttered thoughtfully. 'We'll stay at that hotel I saw as we came into the village.' He collected their luggage out of the Jaguar and then turned again to the garage man. 'I want the car put out of sight. Preferably under lock and key.'

'Will do.' They seemed to understand each other without further discussion, and Kathryn was still feeling too shattered to take a lot of notice.

She came to the present with a bang when they walked into the small hotel at the end of the village street and Jake booked a room – just one.

'Double or twin beds?' the woman at the reception desk enquired with a smile.

'Twin,' Jake murmured, as if his mind was on something else entirely, and before Kathryn could intervene they were being escorted up a narrow flight of stairs into a room that overlooked the village street.

'No *ensuite* bathroom, I'm afraid,' the woman said with an apologetic glance at Jake's obviously wealthy appearance.

'No problem,' he assured her with one of his tight smiles. He manoeuvred her out through the door and then locked it securely.

'The problem,' Kathryn pointed out with an astonished look at him, 'is the not the lack of *ensuite* facilities but the lack of another room. I know you were a bit stunned when the brakes failed, and I know you've been under stress and had that bang on your head, but you never even mentioned two rooms. They're obviously not full just now. You should go and . . .'

'We want one room,' Jake assured her with the same tight look about him. 'We have twin beds but I wouldn't have been bothered with one double bed. You're the only one who's going to be in it. I'm going to sit up and watch.'

'What are you watching for?' Kathryn looked at him in amazement. 'In a few miles we'll be on the motorway. Nobody knows where we are.'

'Unless they've been following, waiting for an accident,' Jake growled, walking to the window and looking down into the street as he pulled the lace curtains carefully aside.

'But how could anyone possibly know that your brakes were going to fail?' Kathryn protested wildly.

'Oh, easily enough,' Jake snapped. 'They've been tampered with. It was just a matter of time. You heard what the man at the garage said – a professional mistake.'

Kathryn sat down on the bed abruptly.

'You mean that last night while we were asleep . . .?'

'No,' Jake said grimly. 'This was done before then. I don't exactly know when, but I can guess. On the way down here. I stopped to eat. When I came back to the car there was a man admiring it. He had probably just finished sabotaging it. I know now why I got the bump on the head. I thought I was being careless, braking too late. I thought it was because I was rushing to get to you with my mind on other things. I wasn't rushing anywhere this morning and the same thing happened. This time, though, it was that much worse. A few miles further on and there would have been no braking at all. You heard the man, surely? Neat, fool-proof and impossible to prove when it happened.'

'It's unbelievable,' Kathryn muttered. She put her hands to her face and shook her head. 'I have to be dreaming this.'

'You're not dreaming anything,' Jake assured her. He came away from the window and stood looking down at her. 'I know this sounds overly dramatic, but I could not let you stay in one room with me in another. I honestly don't know where anyone involved is. To know where my car would be on the way down here they had to be following. I don't know how far they're prepared to go to stop my book so we take precautions, no matter how foolish you think they are.'

'I think tampering with your brakes is going pretty far,' Kathryn stated, looking up at him seriously. 'If you were killed in an accident it would be perfect, wouldn't it?'

'It would.' Jake turned away and sat down in the only chair the room possessed. 'Until the book is finished, and safely with the publisher, they have a chance to stop it.'

'But who would go so far? It's a very serious business, injuring someone.'

'This is a serious business to Renfrew,' Jake stated flatly. 'He's got wealth now, more than he needs. The only thing he has *not* got is power. Get him in a safe seat, into parliament, and he'll shoot up like a rocket. He's an organizer, a planner. He's left the past behind. All he wants now is the future. It's got to be him. I don't have this sort of enemy. Mostly people avoid me. It's got to be Renfrew, and with his wealth the sky's the limit.'

'Oh, my goodness! A future Prime Minister,' Kathryn mused anxiously. 'And you're the only one who could stop him.'

'I'm writing fiction,' Jake grated.

'Based on fact,' she corrected firmly. 'Ralph has read some of your books. He says they're gripping and intricate, and even Ralph learned a lot about things from reading them.'

Jake scowled at her. He did not feel particularly flattered. The last thing he wanted was to further Ralph's education.

'I don't give a damn what your *friend* Ralph thinks,' Jake snapped, and Kathryn looked surprised and cross.

'That was unnecessary and uncalled for! Don't you dare start on about Ralph. You don't even know him.

I *do* pay attention when my friends speak and I expect you do too.'

'I only seem to have one friend at the moment,' Jake muttered. 'And as she has a habit of speaking first and thinking much later I don't always pay much attention to her either.'

Kathryn was shocked at the feeling of annoyance that came over her at the idea of Jake having a woman for his only friend. Her mind went instantly to beautiful, sophisticated women, and she knew quite well how ordinary she was herself.

'Maybe you should listen to her,' she said frostily. 'You're lucky to have a friend who has stood by you when the others have gone.'

'I know,' Jake told her wearily, getting up to peer out of the window again. 'She's remarkable.'

Kathryn felt quite downcast that Jake should have such a high opinion of a woman she didn't know. He was becoming such a part of her life that she felt stunned at the idea of some secret friend – probably more than just a friend.

'Who is she?' she found herself asking, much against her will, trying to put a face to this women.

'You,' Jake muttered, still staring out of the window. He turned to the door before she could fully take in what he had just admitted. 'Let's stroll through the village until it's time for lunch. I'm damned if we're going to skulk in here in broad daylight.'

Later they had their evening meal and Jake said very little. He had said very little since they arrived. He was alert, watchful, but as far as Kathryn could see there was no sign of anything suspicious. They had more or less sauntered through the village earlier and seen nothing of note.

Kathryn had looked in the windows of a few shops and they had both bought books. They had inspected the village pond with bored resignation and she had pondered on the latest turn of events. Had it not been for the fact that the car was now locked in a garage she would have thought she was imagining everything.

Looking back to her experiences at Pengarron, there had been just that one time when she had sensed someone else there. All her other frightening encounters had been with Jake himself. Nothing extraordinary had happened to her unless Jake had been there. Apart from the car it could all have been imagination – and Jake.

She was also very uneasy about bedtime. Now that she had got over the shock of the failing brakes, one room only seemed to her to be going too far, way over the top, and as the evening progressed she began to feel that she was being deliberately frightened – or worse. Suppose Jake had killed his wife after all? Was she letting her attraction to him blind her to the truth?

'I don't like the idea of one room,' she advised Jake as they sat in the small dining room of the hotel.

In spite of the good weather and the fairly close proximity to the sea there seemed to be few other guests, and even small facts like that were starting suspicious and unlikely thoughts in Kathryn's mind.

'Last night we slept in one cottage,' Jake pointed out irritably. 'As it turned out, the only danger was to me. You went quite noisily mad, if you recall.'

'Exactly!' Kathryn pounced on the fact with satisfaction. 'Nothing happened. *That's* the whole point. Nobody broke into the cottage and the only real problem was my fear and suspicion. All for nothing, as it turned out. It's going to be the same thing tonight. There'll be all the embarrassment of being in the same room and it will all be to no avail.'

'I don't intend to feel embarrassed,' Jake growled, glancing up at her as he got on with his meal. 'Let it go, Kathryn. The arrangements have been made. We'll be off tomorrow as soon as the car is ready.'

She let the matter drop but it had not left her mind by any means. It was already getting late. They had neither of them had much sleep the night before and as they left the dining room, Jake nodded towards a small lounge area.

'I'll stay there until you're ready for bed,' he said coolly. 'I'll give you fifteen minutes.'

Kathryn went off, managing a bright smile of sorts, but she was really beginning to feel oppressed, surrounded. She grumbled about it in her head as she went up to the room. Jake had upset her life, turned her small, safe world on its head.

She had come to terms with her accident, her illness was a thing of the past and she rarely thought of Colin now. But she had been doing that quite nicely long before she saw Jake Trelawny. What did she know about him anyway? Only the things he had told her himself and the rather scrappy information her aunt had volunteered, all of it prejudiced in Jake's favour.

Her own thoughts were prejudiced in Jake's favour too for most of the time, and all because he made her feel excited. It just would not do. She got ready quickly, putting on her nightie and dressing gown, her mind teasing away at the subject of Jake all the time.

Before the fifteen minutes were up she had made up her mind. She could not, would not sleep in here with Jake in the same room. It was unnerving to think of him watching her in the night. He might be dangerous. It wouldn't be the first time that a dangerous man had excited a woman.

He only had one bag. She put it outside and locked the door. Then she waited for trouble to arrive.

It did not take long. Jake banged on the door impatiently.

'Kathryn. Open the door,' he ordered, in what she thought was a reasonably quiet but somewhat menacing voice.

'I'm sorry but I really can't do that.' She knelt down and spoke through the keyhole, and she was able to hear his grunt of exasperation and annoyance.

'You realize that this is merely drawing attention to us?' he grated. 'If I sit outside the door all night, somebody is going to notice me.'

'Oh! I never meant you to do that,' Kathryn assured him earnestly. 'That would be dreadful. You must be tired. You can go and get another room. I put your bag out there.'

'That fact did not escape my notice. Asking for another room is going to draw attention to us also,' he rasped.

'They'll simply think we've had a quarrel.' She paused but he said nothing and she added more firmly, 'I really can't do with you in my life. I've decided that and I'm quite adamant about it. You're upsetting everything. Besides, I think I'm scared.'

He didn't answer and she could hear no sound at all now. Kathryn took the key out of the lock and peered through the keyhole, but there was nothing to see except the opposite wall of the passage. Jake had gone away without any further argument. It was a relief but she was quite annoyed with herself at feeling uneasy about it. She might have hurt his feelings.

There was no reason to feel uneasy, she told herself firmly. She had done the sensible and proper thing. The closer she was to Jake the more she would be in danger – if he was telling the truth. If he was lying and if he was responsible for his wife's disappearance then she had to get completely away from him. And sleeping in the same room as him would be utter madness.

Kathryn was well pleased with her reasoning and her actions. She finished her preparations for bed and then remembered that she had not been to the bathroom. Having no *ensuite* facilities suddenly proved to be a great problem.

She went over the soft carpet and listened at the door, but there was no sound at all. She decided that if she was going to get to the bathroom and back, now was the time to go. He would probably be down at Reception, trying to explain why he suddenly wanted another room.

She unlocked the door, looked into the passage and then rushed along as fast as she could. The bathroom was just two doors away. She would be back long before Jake had sorted anything out downstairs. In the morning she would be quite aloof with him and make it very clear that his problems were nothing to do with her at all.

Kathryn had a nasty shock when she came back. She had rushed out and left the door ajar. She had been too agitated to be methodical. Luckily, the passage was still deserted, and she slipped into the room and locked the door behind her with a sigh of relief. When she turned round her relief turned to astonishment tinged with fear.

Jake was in the room. He had taken off his jacket and tie, dropped his bag by one of the beds and was just in the process of taking off his shoes.

'No more nonsense!' he rapped out when she opened her mouth to shout at him. 'Put off the main light and get into bed. I can see the one you've chosen by the amount of things strewn over it. Clear up, get into bed and go to sleep. Meanwhile, I'll recover my temper and settle down in this chair.'

It posed a problem with no solution. She could not throw him out and she was really unwilling to create a scene. Letting Jake go down to face Reception was one thing; doing it herself and demanding another room was not what she had had in mind at all. It would be embarrassing, something she was not prepared to face herself. She decided to let matters stay as they were.

'This is terribly improper,' she pointed out angrily, but Jake took very little notice of her remonstration.

'Last night you insisted that I stay the night with you,' he reminded her. 'You tended my wounds, fed me, became quite firm about my staying with you and then you got up in the night to defend me.'

'That was different,' Kathryn stated frostily. 'We were quite alone, almost isolated. It made good sense. Tonight we're in a hotel with other people around. Besides,' she added, looking at him suspiciously, 'nothing happened.'

'Except that you tried to kill me,' Jake prompted irascibly.

That reminded her of the unexpected kiss, and her cheeks flushed immediately.

'That was merely because I felt we were in danger. We are not in danger now.'

'Of course not,' Jake murmured sarcastically. 'We escaped a crash after they tampered with the brakes. Quite clearly it was all our imagination.'

'Your imagination,' Kathryn countered sharply. 'Nobody has done anything to me at all. The only person to frighten me has been you, and as to the brakes – it might have been a fluke, a weakness. I only have your word for it.'

She wished she had not said any of those things, because Jake just sat and looked up at her bleakly. His eyes like black ice, cold and scary.

'So you don't trust me at all, Kathryn,' he enquired softly. 'You think I may have killed Gillian and I'm making everything else up to cover my tracks. You're afraid of me.'

'I'm not!' Kathryn shot back angrily. She threw her dressing gown off and climbed into the single bed furthest away from him, pulling the sheets up to her neck. 'If I was afraid of you I would be screaming. I would be rushing to the door and out into the passage.'

'If you could move that fast,' he said quietly. 'I could catch you and silence you before you were halfway there.'

She stared at him, trying not to look anxious but not succeeding at all, and Jake stared back in that intent way he had and then turned away in disgust.

'Oh, go to sleep,' he rasped. 'I have enough problems with professional lunatics. I can manage without the amateur variety.'

Kathryn stayed quiet, but she knew she was not going to go to sleep. She was too mixed up and it was all his fault. Why had he pursued her all this time? Why had he rushed down to Cornwall when he knew she was there? Why had he kissed her anyway? She could have done without Jake Trelawny in her life. And there was still the third Bertie Beetle book. How was she going to get that finished now?

She turned restlessly on her side, risking a quick glance at him through her lashes. He was reading, still sitting in the chair. And that was another thing. The light from the lamp was shining in her eyes. She turned the other way and resolved not to move again until morning, even if she got up as stiff as a board. She would keep taking a quick look at him all night, just to be sure. It was really odd that he had said she was his friend. She hadn't done a thing to prove it and he never paid any attention at all to her advice.

The car was going fantastically fast. Colin was laughing and shouting, looking at her instead of the road, and when she asked him to be careful he just went faster. It was raining ice, the hard drops piercing her skin because there was no roof on the car. When she tried to get away from the small jabs of pain she unbalanced everything and the car turned over and over, taking them both with it. Colin was screaming at her, blaming her, and she could see him setting fire to the engine with a huge, long match.

'Don't! Don't, Colin!' she screamed, but he shouted at her and told her it was all her fault. He jumped out and left her screaming.

'Kathryn! Kathryn!' She fought off the hands that clutched at her, struggling to get free. 'Wake up!' She was shaken, lifted up in bed, and when her eyes managed to open Kathryn found Jake holding her, calling to her. He seemed to be looking at her through flames and she opened her mouth to scream, pushed at him to get free.

'I'll die! I'll die in the fire and the ice.' She fought him, and then the flames faded and she knew it was not Colin.

'Jake?' Kathryn stared at him, her mind still not quite her own, and Jake lowered her back to the pillows, watching her warily.

'You were dreaming, having a nightmare. It was a particularly good one by the sound of it,' he told her quietly. 'If you're all right, I'll get you a cup of tea.'

Kathryn glanced at her watch and tried to pull herself round. 'It's almost four o'clock in the morning. The staff will all be asleep.'

'We may not have *ensuite* facilities but we have tea-making equipment,' Jake grunted as he turned away, and then she could see the kettle and the teapot and cups. She had been too agitated since they had come to this room to notice before. Jake didn't ask if she wanted one. He just switched on the kettle and put teabags into the pot.

Her breathing returned to normal as she watched him. She had never intended to go to sleep but she had all the same. It was the nightmare again. It was back with a vengeance. It had been weeks since she had been bothered with that.

'I haven't had that nightmare for ages,' she murmured quietly. 'It happened a lot after the car crash but I eventually got over it.'

'The failed brakes today probably brought it all back,' Jake surmised. 'Maybe you'll have to get over it again. It's unfortunate, but then, so is all this.'

He carried the tea over and put her cup down on the cabinet. It seemed to Kathryn that he was avoiding her eyes.

'I'm sorry,' she said quickly, before he could go away.

'No problem. I was awake.'

'I don't mean that. I couldn't help the dream so I'm not going to apologize for it. I'm sorry about how I behaved earlier. I talked myself into a panic.'

'Forget it,' Jake said coldly, turning away. She clutched at his sleeve, forcing him to stop.

'Forgetting it is not on the agenda. I was quite cruel. I can behave really badly sometimes, you know.'

'I would never have known it,' Jake murmured sardonically. 'Drink your tea and go back to sleep.'

She sipped at her tea, watching him when he went back to reading. He looked tired and it made her feel more guilty than ever. He had a long drive ahead of him in the morning. Once again he had been good to her, and he hadn't killed her in the night either.

'Please come to bed, Jake,' she muttered fretfully, and Jake's head shot up, his expression startled.

'Is this another example of you behaving badly, Miss Holden?' he enquired, and she blushed furiously even though she was greatly relieved to see his lips quirking.

'There's a perfectly good bed going to waste here,' she stated firmly. 'You've got a long drive ahead of you tomorrow and I won't be able to help. I find it painful to drive long distances now. Anyway,' she added, 'it's a Jaguar.'

'I don't see what that has to do with it,' Jake murmured. He got up and stretched and then came to throw himself down on the other bed. 'It's only a car – nothing special.'

Colin had thought his car to be very special. She thought about it and then said it aloud. 'Colin wouldn't let anyone drive his car. He said it was a collector's item.'

Jake lay with his hands behind his head and turned to glance at her.

'What happened to it?'

'It was smashed up in the crash. I don't know what happened then because I've not seen it since, of course. By the time I was better, Colin had disappeared off the map.'

'Do you miss him?' Jake asked, and she shook her head, yawning and turning to face him.

'No, not now. I was pretty devastated after the accident, but I was too ill to really dwell on things. After that I was a bit lost for a while, depressed, but I expect that was the illness. In any case, by then he had someone else.'

Jake was silent for a minute and then he said. 'Was there a fire when the car crashed?'

'No, but I expected one. I was trapped, lying on ice, and the car was sort of hovering over me. The lights were still on and there was a very strong smell of petrol. Colin was thrown clear but I couldn't move.'

'Did he get you free before he left you?'

'No. As I said, he was probably shaken. He – he went to get help. Later someone else drove up and called the police and the ambulance.' She was not about to tell Jake the whole sorry story. She closed her eyes. End of discussion. When she opened them again, Jake was not asleep. He was staring at the ceiling. She was glad she had not mentioned Colin ringing her up.

CHAPTER 11

Jake's mind was not sufficiently easy for sleep. He was thinking about the brakes and when some-one could have got to them. He was certain it was when he had stopped for a meal on the way. The sabotage must have been effected then. In all probability it had been the man he had spoken to. That would mean that he was being followed, though. Were they still following? What would they do next?

Kathryn's story about her car accident was in his mind too. He could see her lying there with a car almost on top of her, the risk of fire. The swine had gone off and left her by herself. How could anyone do that? How could anyone risk Kathryn being hurt, killed? She needed looking after, even if she didn't know it herself.

He had a terrible desire to pull her onto the bed with him and hold her protectively close. It would scare her, though. He knew she didn't entirely trust him in spite of her constant efforts to defend him. He gave a wry smile. She thought he was an untamed beast of some sort, and yet she seemed to spend a lot of time attempting to shield him. He slanted a look at her as she lay sleeping, her clouds of red hair spread across the pillow. An unlikely champion. His smile faded as he felt again the hot pooling of desire inside him. What a predicament! If only he had never seen her.

Kathryn didn't know whether Jake slept or not, because he was up and ready when she awoke next morning – in fact he woke her up.

'Are we ready for off?' Kathryn opened her eyes and peered at him over the sheets. She was very comfortable and she felt extremely safe. The fact surprised her.

'I rang the garage. The car will be ready in about two hours.'

'Good. I can sleep longer.' Kathryn closed her eyes and snuggled down. It was strange being so comfortable, so secure when she was in the same room as Jake. Why wasn't she worried? Why wasn't she shy and embarrassed? She smiled to herself, feeling drowsily secure.

'Hit the deck!' Jake shook the covers and she opened her eyes again, giving him a startled look.

'Where did you get such an expression?'

'I write coarse books.'

'What a lie,' Kathryn muttered, struggling to sit up. 'I told you, Ralph reads your books. He would have told me if they were anything other than respectable. I should warn you that he's not at all sure I should know you as it is.'

'Brotherly or jealous?' Jake enquired sardonically.

'Friend! He's a friend,' Kathryn flashed an indignant look at him, until she saw his lips twisting in amusement. 'And I can do without having fun poked at me first thing in the morning, thank you.'

'I wouldn't make fun of you, Kathryn,' he assured her silkily. 'I'm your friend too, aren't I?'

She didn't say anything to that, and she could hardly get up until he left the room, even though she had flounced into bed in a rage the night before. She was still feeling a little guilty at the cruel way she had treated him the night before too, but he seemed to have let that drop.

'Well, am I?' he asked softly, coming to the bed and tilting her defiant chin.

'Are you what?' She was not going to be drawn into any arguments today. They would be off soon and then she would be back at her own place, making her own decisions. She knew she was particularly good at saying the wrong thing and she wanted no trouble at all.

'Your friend?' Jake stood looking down at her, his hand still tilting her face, and she tried to look away.

'I don't know. You're the only one who knows that. You have to decide for yourself.

'Then I think I probably am,' he stated quietly. 'Even though you have the biggest, most green eyes in the world and the damnedest hair.' He walked out of the room and Kathryn sprang up and rushed to the mirror.

Her hair was tousled somewhat but there was nothing really wrong with it. Was it the damnedest

269

hair? She wondered if she should follow Ralph's advice and have it cut short. Maybe Jake thought it looked a mess?

She brought this up in a vague sort of way as they travelled fast along the motorway later.

'I might get my hair cut really short,' she muttered. 'Ralph thinks I should.'

Jake shot her an annoyed glance and then looked back at the road.

'Don't,' he snapped. 'Your hair is perfect as it is. If you follow Ralph's advice in any way at all, I'll strangle him with the cat.'

Kathryn couldn't stop laughing. It was so bizarre and out of character. In a moment or two she looked at him and found him smiling. He glanced across at her again, a lightning glance like black fire.

'I would never harm you, Kathryn,' he told her softly. 'You have a vivid imagination but don't imagine me into being a villain. I only want you to be safe.'

Kathryn returned his smile and nodded, but she wondered about it. She had worked out that she knew exactly nothing at all. That was why she had gone to Cornwall again. Well, she still knew nothing, other than the story Jake had told her. And he had swiftly plucked her out of Cornwall. She wasn't going to find out anything now. She just didn't know what to believe. She didn't even know if she was safe with Jake. She just seemed to let him get away with anything.

After several necessary breaks they arrived in London well after seven in the evening. They had made one stop for dinner and all Kathryn could think about was getting back and going to bed. She would not even bother to collect Snowy tonight.

When Jake stopped by the market it was still well lit and appeared to be going strong and he sat for a few seconds and watched the bustle inside.

'Don't they ever close?'

'Not until about nine,' Kathryn assured him. 'They work hard, and whilever there's trade they keep going.' She glanced across at him. He seemed to be deeply interested in the market and she couldn't think why. She wanted to go to bed.

'Bert or Teddy will help me to the lift with my luggage,' she said when he just went on staring at the market. 'Of course I'll have to stand a bit of teasing. It's not long since I went away. They'll be wondering why I'm back so soon.'

'You were away too long,' Jake muttered, shooting her one of his lightning glances. 'You don't need Bert or anyone else, because I'm coming up with you to see that everything is all right.'

'Why shouldn't it be? Nobody can get into my flat. Ralph has the only other key and, in any case, Bert would want to know where they were going if any stranger came to use the lift. There are no stairs, you know, apart from the fire escape. The lift is the only way up.'

'Good,' Jake said tightly. 'All the same, I want to see you safely in. After all,' he added tauntingly, 'I'm classed as the boyfriend in your aunt's immediate circle. Seeing you home is expected.'

Kathryn glared at him.

'I set her right on that particular point, so if you think you can keep throwing it at me . . .'

Jake just grinned to himself and she got out of the car in a huff, grabbing one of her cases before he could even move. He was beside her quickly and took it from her hand without a word, and when he had collected the other case they entered the market together.

Nobody teased her at all. Jake's presence seemed to have robbed them of speech. They just smiled and waved at her. It was annoying. Once again she felt as if Jake was surrounding her. It was oppression. She was sure of that. She stood grimly in the lift and didn't speak to him.

Ralph must be out, because as the lift passed his door he didn't come to see who it was. Kathryn was glad. After the things Jake had muttered about Ralph she was not at all anxious to have them meeting. She went into her flat and moved aside as Jake walked in with the luggage.

He didn't move far in immediately. He stood and looked round the place as if he was all set to buy it.

'You don't have to inspect it,' Kathryn pointed out irritably. 'It's not for sale.'

'Don't be petulant,' Jake advised mildly, his eyes still roaming round the place. He walked over to the window and looked down. 'I'm merely checking on your safety. The market has to close at some time and then your unpaid bodyguards will all go home.'

To her annoyance he walked into her bedroom and looked round there too.

'What do you think you're doing?' She stormed after him and looked at him angrily. 'I refuse to have you invading my privacy.'

All she got was one of his slight, enigmatic smiles.

'How can you say that, Kathryn?' he taunted. 'For the last two nights we've slept together.'

'We have not!' Kathryn went red and looked outraged but he simply took her by the shoulders and put her aside so that he could get out of the room.

'Not a soul would believe you,' he murmured, going to the kitchen to complete his inspection. When he came out she was standing in the main room, staring at him angrily, but his desire to torment her had evidently faded. He looked at her seriously.

'From now on, you keep away from me – ' he started, but she opened her mouth to put him right on that.

'It has never been my intention to be anywhere near you in any case, and . . .'

'Stop threatening to fight me,' he said quietly, walking towards her and looking down into her angry face. 'I'm trying to extricate you from this, to get you out of my life as far as any interested party is concerned. I'll ring you every day but I won't come near you. I want them to forget you, or at the very least dismiss you as an unimportant part of things.'

'There's really no need to ring me at all,' Kathryn stated, beginning to feel subdued again.

'I have to know how you are,' Jake said firmly. 'In any case, I want to ring you.'

'Why?' She looked up at him with wide green eyes and he stared at her for a second before she got that twisted smile again.

'Why, you're my friend, Kathryn. I told you that.' He wrote quickly on a card from his pocket and put it into her hand. 'This is my number. Ring me if you're at all worried – day or night.'

He walked to the door and she stood staring after him, only coming to life when she knew he was about to go. It suddenly struck her that she didn't want him to go. Everything would be dull and dreary if he left and never came again. They had gone into a little world of their own and now he was walking out of it.

'What am I going to do about my book?' she asked. 'You made me come back but I've still got to finish it.'

'Can't you do it from memory?' Jake turned to look at her and she thought for a minute, biting at her lip.

'I suppose so, at a push. The woods at Pengarron seem to linger in my mind even when I'm not there. I don't know how it will come out, though. I wouldn't want it to be any less real than the others. It would seem like cheating.'

'You like Pengarron, don't you?' Jake walked back towards her and spoke quietly, and she looked up at him a little wistfully.

'Yes. It's a lovely, dreamy place. It's such a pity it's been neglected. Of course, it's none of my business.' She bit her lip again and Jake tilted her face up.

'You've never worried about interfering before. Don't let this lapse bother you.' His eyes ran slowly over her face and fastened on her lips. 'Don't do that,' he ordered softly. 'When you nibble away at your lip you look just too vulnerable and I get this terrible urge to stay.'

Kathryn tried to look away but he would not let her, and she found herself looking up into dark eyes that were almost hypnotic. The butterflies were back inside her and that lift was going down again fast. She wondered if he was going to kiss her, and her face began to flush when she realized that she was hoping he would.

'This is crazy,' Jake murmured, but his arms came round her and when she just went on looking at him his head bent to hers and he captured her mouth in a fierce kiss that seemed to be as dark as his eyes.

This time she wasn't startled. It had not taken her by surprise and she welcomed it, standing on her toes when he pulled her even closer. His hand cradled her head as the kiss deepened and deepened, and after a second Kathryn wound her arms round his neck and just gave up.

If it was her fault this time she would face that later. At the moment there was too much magic to miss, too much excitement to turn from. She sighed against his mouth. It was like spinning in space, wonderful.

Jake lifted his head and looked down at her, and when she went on clinging to him, with her face still turned up for his kisses, Jake ran his tongue gently across her lips until she opened them and let him inside.

The shock of the more intimate contact seemed to hit them both at the same time. Their arms tightened and Jake's lips became demanding as his tongue explored the inside of her mouth in secret little movements that made her press herself against him. Her fingers clutched in his black hair, and when his body hardened against her she moved into him softly and eagerly.

Jake lifted his head and put his face against her hair, his arm still holding her fast. His hand was moving imperatively over her back, over her slender flanks, his fingers flexing like a hungry tiger's claws, and she let her lips trail over his throat.

'You're supposed to be ethereal, to drift out of reach and haunt me,' he told her in a low voice, clutching her more tightly when he felt her small caress. 'You have this astonishing way of surprising me, Kathryn. Now I don't want to go at all.'

'I – I could make some coffee,' she offered tremulously, but he eased the pressure of his arms and looked down at her, the old enigmatic smile back on his lips.

'Not a good idea. I'm trying to protect you, and you once told me that "compromised" was not a good choice of word.'

Kathryn swallowed uneasily and his hand trailed over her face.

'Don't start trying to take the blame again,' he warned softly. 'It was all my idea this time too. At this moment I really don't know if it was one of my better ideas or not.' He let her go and walked back to the door before turning to look at her seriously. 'I don't really like to say this,' he confessed, 'but I have the decided feeling that Ralph should know at least part of the story.'

'It might put him at risk,' Kathryn pointed out solemnly, and he nodded in agreement.

'It might, just possibly, but I'm thinking of you. If he knows how things stand, he'll be on the alert for strangers. He'll be less inclined to be careless with that key he has.' He suddenly looked hard at her, the old black frown surfacing. 'Does he *have* to have a key now that you're back?'

'We help each other. I have a key to Ralph's place too.'

Jake's scowl deepened.

'That doesn't fill me with great glee.' He suddenly smiled at her, the frown vanishing. 'Lock the door and don't go wandering out in the dark,' he ordered quietly. 'And don't lose my phone number – that's an order.'

Kathryn was so bemused that she let him walk out without saying another word. There were questions racing around in her mind. So many that they collided with each other. But at the moment she was too bewildered to ask herself anything.

The kisses lingered on her stinging lips. Her hand came up to touch them as she locked the door behind Jake. For the few minutes he had held her and kissed her she had been deep in a dream world, a place she had never ventured into before, and it was hard to look around her flat and face any sort of reality.

She made herself a drink and curled up on the settee, simply staring into space. She was still trembling inside but it was a sort of magical feeling. She didn't want the trembling to stop. Whatever Jake was, he was not a friend. He was a lot more than that. She wanted to tell somebody, anybody, even Snowy, but there was nobody to tell – and, in any case, at the moment it felt as if she had a wonderful secret that she must hug to herself.

She was still in the same dreamy state when she went to bed. Deep inside, caution sat uneasily, nudging at her mind. What did she know of him after all? Had her first sight of him when she had felt fear been another example of her instincts? Was she letting the unusual glamour of being with someone like Jake take over and drown her common sense? She didn't know. That was the trouble.

Ralph arrived the next day with Snowy sitting irritably in his arms.

'Back already?' he enquired as she opened the door only wide enough to peer at him.

'Come in quickly,' Kathryn urged, glancing outside furtively and then almost dragging him into her flat. She took Snowy from him and dumped the cat unceremoniously on the floor. 'There's something I have to tell you. Sit there. I'll make you a coffee and we'll talk.'

Ralph was instantly intrigued, but she flatly refused to say another word until they were both sitting with a drink.

'Jake suggested that I tell you this,' she began earnestly. 'I'm not sure I should. It might put you in some danger but that's how Jake wants it.'

'He wants me in danger,' Ralph mused drily. 'Yes. I can follow his line of reasoning.'

'I didn't mean that,' Kathryn protested seriously, and he nodded at her, giving her a wry look.

'I'm sure you didn't. Let's get down to it.'

She told him about Jake's enemy, about the book, the problems Jake had had and her own involvement, and as she talked Ralph's face became more and more grim.

'You believe all this?' he asked sharply. 'Let's face it, most of this could have been lies. The brakes failing was real enough, but if mine failed I wouldn't go looking for an assassin, I'd be round to the garage with a threatening look on my face. I've been reading old papers about Trelawny while you were away. He might very well have murdered his wife. He was under suspicion.'

'I know.' Kathryn chewed at her lip and thought it over. Ralph was right, of course, and he was the outsider now, the cool voice of reason. She was no longer being sensible because she wanted it all to be true. If it wasn't then Jake was lying to her, and if he was lying there could only be one explanation; he wanted to hide the facts about Gillian's disappearance.

'All the same,' Ralph muttered thoughtfully, 'there's always the off-chance that he's not lying, and if he isn't then you could be in considerable danger. We'd better watch carefully. Don't go out.'

'You're not serious?' Kathryn exclaimed. 'What am I supposed to do? Hide here for a while? It may be for ever the way things are going. I have a book to do and, besides that, I have a life to live. I'm not skulking here.'

'All right,' Ralph agreed reluctantly. 'But watch your step. If anything happens to you he'll take it out on me, and, quite frankly, he scares me to death just by looking at me.'

'I know what you mean,' Kathryn murmured. 'Sometimes he scares me too.'

'But all the same, you constantly go off with him,' Ralph pointed out as he made for the door. 'Has he grabbed your hair and taken that club to you yet?' he added as she let him out.

'No!' Kathryn told him forcefully, glaring at him as her cheeks flushed. He went and she locked the door. 'Not exactly,' she reminded herself quietly when she was alone. He had not needed any caveman tactics. He had simply reached for her and she had been more than willing.

Staying indoors was not an option as far as Kathryn was concerned. Apart from shopping there were several things she had to do, and in any case she refused to hide behind locked doors. For a couple of days she tried to work at her book, working from memory, trying to get the atmosphere, but it was not the same. She could imagine herself in the woods but her work seemed to her to be stilted and not altogether real.

She was staring at it in a disgruntled manner one afternoon when the doorbell rang. The leap her heart gave told its own story, but she knew that Jake would not come. He had phoned her briefly each day, his voice very businesslike. It was impossible to imagine from the tone of his voice that he had ever held her and kissed her.

It would be Ralph. She got up and went to answer the door and then stood back in shock when she saw her visitor. Colin! It was the last person she had expected to see. She rarely thought of him now. Jake had changed her whole life. In fact she was not even the same person.

'Hello, Kath,' he said rather sheepishly. 'I've been trying to get in touch with you but you never answer your phone.'

'I've been away.' Kathryn looked at him in a dazed way, wondering what he wanted, why he had decided to come here. She just didn't want to see him at all. 'I told you I was going away when you rang.'

'I know. I was hoping you would be back sooner, though. I came here. The men downstairs told me you were still away.'

'They never mentioned it,' Kathryn murmured, still keeping him at the door, and he shrugged, the easy way he'd used to, the way she had always thought to be attractive. Now it seemed to be a rather foolish gesture, not at all natural to him, as if he had read about it somewhere and decided to adopt it.

'I expect they forgot,' he said. He looked rather nonplussed. 'Are you going to invite me in?'

'Oh, sorry.' Kathryn stepped aside, trying to pull herself out of a daze. It was like talking to a complete stranger. Almost ten months and she hadn't seen him at all. Now, out of the blue, he was here. Her heart sank. Surely he wasn't here to ask her to begin again? Surely he hadn't meant that when he phoned?

'How's your leg?' When Kathryn moved away from the door, his eyes fastened on the way she moved.

'Almost better. It's going to take some time yet but I'm improving.'

He looked ashamed of himself. It was all very awkward and Kathryn couldn't imagine why she had ever gone out with him at all. She walked towards the kitchen,

'I'll make you some coffee.'

'I thought you might like to go out.' He looked at her with that little boy expression he used when he wanted his own way, charming and contrite. It didn't work now. All she could think of was how to get rid of him without being unkind.

'I'm very busy, Colin,' she pointed out, indicating her work that still lay around the room.

'It's good,' he muttered. 'You should be working at something more grand, though, like a real artist.'

Kathryn turned to look at him. She remembered

when she had praised Ralph to Jake, saying what a good artist Ralph was. Jake had not denigrated her work. He had been somewhat disgruntled. He had pointed out that she was also a good artist.

How different they were. Colin was good-looking, she supposed. It was something she had never really thought of before and that in itself was strange. He had just been Colin, someone she knew and cared about. His hair was brown, waving pleasantly enough, and his blue eyes were smiling most of the time, unless he was annoyed and grumbling, trying to control her.

A picture of Jake came into her mind readily. He was vivid, from the way he moved to the blackness of his hair, the dark, secret depths of his eyes. Jake didn't smile so much, and then never like Colin. When Jake smiled it was from deep inside, something that grew right from the depths of his being. He lost his temper, got very angry, but it was all real. He didn't grumble and whinge. Jake roared at her like a lion if she annoyed him. At the side of Jake, Colin seemed pitiful.

Suddenly she couldn't wait to get him out of her flat, to see the back of him. Why had he come here anyway? She really didn't want to know. She just wanted him to go and he was obviously intent on staying.

'I've changed my mind,' she said with a bright smile. 'Let's go out. I haven't been out for ages. We can get a coffee in town. I have some shopping to do in any case. You can help me.'

He was delighted. It gave her a guilty pang but she stuck to the decision. Once outside she could go along with him pleasantly and then get rid of him. If they stayed in the flat he would get all cloying and then morbid. The thought made her shudder.

It was sunny anyway, and Kathryn ignored the surprised looks she got from Bert and the others. They had seen her with Jake and she knew they were doing a bit of quick comparing. When Jake went through the market he drew all eyes with his dark, vibrant presence. She hurried Colin out into the street and looked round rather frantically for a taxi.

'I've got my car here,' he pointed out, and only then did Kathryn realize how she was behaving, how nervous she felt. She just had this feeling that Jake would suddenly appear and react like thunder. For the time being she had forgotten completely about any danger. Jake was danger enough at the moment. She almost rushed to Colin's car. He was pleased at that and settled her comfortably for the drive into town.

'Thought you might not come out with me,' he confessed with a rather smug smile. 'It's good to see that you're eager.'

He didn't know how eager she was, and it was nothing to do with seeing him. The thought of Jake seemed to be almost choking her, as if he was breathing down her neck, ready to pounce.

When the car was moving she came to her senses. Jake did not have any authority at all. She should be thinking about the men who were after him – after her too, if Jake's surmising was correct. She should not be worrying about Jake's reaction to her trip out.

'It's a new car,' she managed pleasantly, and that pleased Colin at once.

'It's a beauty. Goes like a bomb.'

Kathryn hoped not. If he started to do any speeding he would find that she was a different person. And, actually, his childish obsession with cars was quite nauseating. Jake had looked amazed when she had made remarks about his new Jaguar. He had told her it was only a car, and that was what this was – only a car. But once again Colin was enthralled with it. She didn't ask about his previous 'collector's item'. She didn't care what had happened to that.

They had coffee in a little bistro and then she resolutely did her shopping, only half listening to Colin as he talked on and on. She was planning to take a taxi back to her flat and get rid of Colin first, thereby killing two birds with one stone. She would have her shopping done with a safe companion and she would be rid of him without the need to hurt his feelings by telling him to go. He was even carrying most of her parcels and she didn't feel at all guilty. He owed her that much.

They were walking out of a shop later when the thunder hit them hard. Jake appeared without warning, looming up before them, a black, threatening cloud, and before she could stop him he had one hand round Colin's throat like a steel gauntlet.

'What do you want with her?' he grated, and when Colin was too stunned to answer the hand tightened dangerously.

'Jake!' Kathryn clutched his arm, trying to break the powerful grip, but he seemed to be deaf. There was just a murderous ferocity about him. It was the first time she had ever seen blind rage. She noticed vaguely that his black hair was even longer. Was he never going to get it cut?

'Jake! Let him go!' she shouted desperately. 'It's Colin.'

She became aware then that they were the centre of a good deal of interest from other shoppers. For one thing they were blocking the doorway, and for another Jake was not a man to ignore – especially in his present mood.

'Jake! *Please!*' Kathryn tugged at his arm as she watched Colin's face slowly redden with the need to breathe. Jake did not relax his grip but he turned his head to look at her furiously.

'Are you sure?' he rasped.

'Of course I'm sure! He came to visit me. I – I'm shopping. He's helping me.' She indicated the parcels that Colin was still clutching and Jake slowly loosened his grip, his expression still so threatening that she was unsure if this was over.

'You're not supposed to be out,' he reminded her angrily, and Kathryn felt so frustrated that she actually stamped her foot.

'Jake! I refuse to hide all day and every day. I had shopping to do. Colin came and it was a good chance to get out. I was perfectly safe.'

'Were you safe with him before?' Jake asked, glaring at her.

'That was different,' she pointed out sharply.

'Was it? How safe would you have been if his assailant hadn't been me? Would he have thrown him to the ground, protected you, stopped all comers? As you see, I'm still standing.'

'You took him by surprise,' Kathryn accused angrily.

'You imagine they would have issued warnings?' Jake shouted at the top of his voice. 'Everything will be a surprise, you little fool!' He took her arm in a tight grip. 'My car's round the corner. I'm taking you home.'

Kathryn was only too pleased. Jake's roaring was very embarrassing now that the shock was over.

'She's staying with me,' Colin said in a choking voice, suddenly finding courage as his breath came back. 'And while you're still here I'd better warn you that I'm going to report this assault.'

'Go ahead!' Jake snarled, turning on him ferociously. 'Better get your witnesses before they fade away.'

They were fading away fast. Once Jake had released his victim the whole thing had become a mortifying quarrel in public – not acceptable to the English mind. Their audience had dispersed rapidly.

'I don't need them,' Colin spluttered angrily. 'There's Kath.'

'She's coming with me and she's staying with me,' Jake pointed out. He deftly removed the parcels from Colin's arms and pulled her away. 'And her name,' he added icily, giving Colin one last glare, 'is Kathryn.'

She just had time to give Colin one glance on her own behalf, apologetic, before Jake whisked her round the corner and out of sight. By the time Colin had gathered his wits, Jake's car was moving and it was so much history. Rather violent history.

'You had no right . . .' Kathryn began, but he glanced at her furiously.

'Not one word,' he warned blackly. 'I'm almost ready to explode with rage. Just one whisper would be enough to tip me right over the edge.'

Kathryn decided to keep quiet, and after a moment, when her legs had stopped shaking and she was far enough away from the shock and embarrassment to see it as an onlooker, she found it amusing, crazy. She seemed to have stepped into a different world with Jake. He said *she* was mad. At the moment he didn't seem too well balanced himself.

She started to laugh and just couldn't keep it quiet. She could see Colin's astonished face, his growing fear, and it seemed like a sort of belated rough justice. Anyway, he wouldn't call again. His nerve was somewhat stretched at the best of times.

Her amusement didn't seem to be pleasing Jake but she ignored him. She didn't care. She was still grinning as he drew up in front of the market and marched her inside. Bert and his cronies watched with interest. She had gone out with one man and she was returning with another. They nodded at Jake pleasantly and he unbent far enough to nod back. Then Kathryn was in the lift, going up to her flat with a big, silent man beside her who still looked ferocious.

She let them into the flat and then took the parcels from him without a word. Snowy watched warily. Cats, of course, had very good instincts, and he was not about to get drawn into this sort of thing. The thought amused her even more and she put the shopping on the worktops in the kitchen, unable to stop the amusement that bubbled up inside. She bent over laughing.

She was still laughing when Jake came in silently and spun her round. For a second he glared down into her laughing face and then he clasped her head in his hands and caught her mouth with his fiercely. She didn't know whether he was being violent or not. She was just glad, and her arms wound round his neck instantly.

It surprised him, because he raised his head to look down at her and then his arm came round her waist and his hand cradled her head more gently.

'You little nuisance,' he breathed against her lips, 'You're upsetting my well-planned life. When I first saw you I knew you were crazy. I should have turned round and ignored you.'

'Why didn't you?' Kathryn murmured softly, thrilled by this whispered conversation, excited by the way his thumb probed the corner of her mouth.

'It was too late. I was worried about you,' he whispered. 'I'm worried about you now. I'm always worried about you.'

'I'm safe, Jake.' She let the tip of her tongue touch his lips and his reaction delighted her. His muscles seemed to tighten and contract as if he found it unbearably pleasing.

'You're not safe,' he muttered thickly, 'You were not safe this afternoon with that idiot and you're not safe now, not the way I feel at this moment.' His mouth opened over hers and Kathryn let herself sink into him. It was like being devoured, and every other thought left her head at the pleasure and excitement of it all.

She clung to him with her arms tightly around his neck. There was no necessity for him to hold her and his hands were free to explore her body. She was so soft, smooth, rounded, and Jake's hands made a slow, lingering exploration as his lips probed hers deeply. This was what she had wanted. She knew it and so did he.

When his hands slowly rose to cup her breasts, Kathryn moaned against his lips and he swung her up into his arms with a feeling of urgency growing inside him that at that moment he made no move to control. She was feather-light, almost unreal, a nymph again.

He buried his lips in the slender column of her neck as he made his way into the bedroom. He promised himself one minute with her, one small time to relish her complete surrender to him, and then he would go. There was no doubt about her surrender. She was almost dazed as he looked down at her, tiny sounds of pleasure leaving her throat.

Nobody else had ever reacted to him like this, not even in the very act of lovemaking, and her excited, bewildered compliance told him as nothing else could that she was untouched. The knowledge raced through his blood, hardened his body even more, and he put her on the bed and came down with her, taking her back into his arms fiercely.

'You should be afraid of me,' he warned thickly, but she looked straight into his eyes, her gaze as green and pure as emeralds.

'I know,' she whispered, 'but I can't seem to keep up any defence against you. I just don't want to believe anything bad about you. When I think about it at all, my mind always argues in your favour so I don't quarrel with it. I go by my instincts and they lead me to you.'

A strange look came over his face and his dark eyes roamed over her, half closed and secret. He pulled her towards him and his hand stroked back her hair. Even without his lips on hers she was so obviously entranced. His gaze moved over her pure face, her soft lips and the slender length of her body.

'You belong at Pengarron,' he said deeply. 'Every other place is wrong for you. You're the red-haired nymph from the woods and the house needs you. Nothing else will bring it back to life.'

CHAPTER 12

His lips came back to hers gently and firmly and she lay entranced as he explored the warm, dark interior of her mouth. When his hands began to make their own exploration of her body she sighed and moved restlessly. This was what she had been waiting for all her life; she could see that now. There could be nothing wrong when it was Jake.

He kissed the length of her neck and the softly rounded contours of her breasts and Kathryn grieved that they hadn't done this before. It was so much magic. She lay there letting him do anything he wished, trusting him as she had never before trusted anyone.

When he paused she moved towards him, eagerly asking for more with no sound at all except a low, thrilling moan, and his head bent to rest between her breasts.

'Kathryn, I have to stop,' he said raggedly.

'Why? Oh, please, don't.' She gave a pained little cry and he groaned aloud before moving to take her breast into the warmth of his mouth, his tongue wetting the thin material of her dress. He lifted his head to look down at her and then his hands went slowly to the buttons, his fingers opening them with a fine delicacy, one at a time.

She could feel the cooler air on her skin and saw Jake's eyes were riveted to his task, his breathing heavy and deep, his eyes half closed. When he finally exposed her naked flesh he gasped and allowed his hand to trail slowly over her, gently lingering on the rose-pink bud at the centre, staying to tease it to life as he watched, and then with a loud moan he bent his head to touch it with his tongue and draw her breast into his mouth hungrily.

Kathryn felt as if she were flying off the edge of the world. She arched against him, crying out, her arms flung wide and then curling into him, pressing herself closer and threading her fingers through his black hair.

'Jake!' she whimpered, 'Jake!'

'Shh. I know,' he whispered. He pulled her closely against him, tightening his arms and kissing the smooth length of her neck. He wanted her. It was driving him mad. But this was not the time, not the place.

He ran his hands over her body, torturing himself further. Every move she made, every response to his touch told him she was willing to give him everything and for no reason at all.

Kathryn wanted no riches, no jewels, no furs or fine clothes. She was fiercely proud of a peculiar dress made by a friend, proud of her monstrous cat, loyal to her friendship with Ralph but she was willing to give herself to *him*.

He lifted her, cradling her in his arms, looking down into her face.

'I want you,' he said huskily. 'Would you let me take you?'

'Yes.' She looked up at him with wide green eyes, her enchantment clear as the water of a mountain stream.

'Knowing what you do about me, knowing what people suspect, would you still come to me, sleep with me, stay with me?'

'Yes.' Her hands touched his face and he saw tears in her eyes. They shocked him. She never cried, not even with pain. One tear rolled down her cheek and he bent to take it in his lips.

'Don't, Kathryn,' he begged thickly. 'Don't cry. You never cry. I don't think I could bear it.'

She blinked the tears away and smiled at him wistfully.

'You're going to go, aren't you? You're going to be all noble and strong. You're going to walk out and leave me.'

'Yes.' He gave her that long, crooked smile. 'I don't want to.'

'But you'll do it all the same.'

'I have to. You're into my life too deeply as it is.'

'So I may as well drown in it.'

He looked down at her, his eyes moving to the beautiful shape of her bared breast.

'I'm the one drowning,' he told her unevenly.

He suddenly pulled her tightly to him and held her fast, his heart beating madly. He knew what the rush of feeling was that had come over him whenever he had seen her and he was filled with a sort of blind joy. Kathryn wanted nothing; she just wanted to give and she had chosen him.

He rocked her in his arms. She made him feel almost humble. His parents had wanted an heir. His wife had wanted wealth. Kathryn just wanted him.

He eased her away and began to fasten the buttons methodically, trying to keep his mind away from the beauty and pleasure he was resolutely hiding from his own eyes. She didn't protest. The tears had stopped and when he lifted her to her feet and held her safely for a minute she took a deep breath and smiled up at him.

'I'm not going to feel guilty because I'm not at all sorry,' she said firmly. 'If you don't want to . . .'

'I want to.' He tilted her face and looked at her seriously and she smiled, suddenly shy again.

'I'll make some tea,' she offered, so much like a demure hostess that Jake found himself grinning.

'Actually,' she pointed out severely, 'nothing is exactly funny.'

'That's how I felt when you tittered all the way back in the car and went into the kitchen to giggle,' Jake remarked, following her into the kitchen now, admiring the way she had pulled herself back to normality when he was still churning up inside.

'But it was hilarious.' She was busily putting on the kettle and getting the cups. 'You just appeared like a devil and grabbed Colin's throat. I don't think he's had such a fright in his life.'

'Why did you go out with him?' Jake asked harshly, the lingering passion dying from his face as the old black scowl surfaced.

Kathryn didn't even turn round.

'He came. I wanted him out but I didn't want to be so cruel as to simply tell him to go. I took him shopping. I thought it was a rather bright idea.'

'You can be as cruel to him as you like,' Jake muttered crossly. He could not resist going behind her, though, spanning her slender waist and pulling her back against him, and his heart took off like a hammer when she leaned softly into him, willing and eager at once.

'No.' He let her go and walked away, putting a safe distance between them.

'It was your idea,' Kathryn murmured, glancing at him over her shoulder.

'Your madness is obviously contagious,' Jake growled. He sat down in the main room and waited for the tea, and when she brought it in he was grateful that she went to sit opposite.

'Did he ask you to take up where you left off?' Jake murmured, looking up at her from beneath dark brows as he drank his tea

'No. He never got around to it. I had him out on the street before he had the chance.

'Would he have got around to it?'

'I expect so.'

'And if he had?'

She looked at him in the old level way, clear-eyed and courageous.

'Would you like me to curl at your feet so that you can put your foot on me?' she asked, and Jake was shocked into sitting up straight and staring at her.

'Am I treating you like that?'

'A little. But don't let it bother you. You'll not get away with it.'

He smiled ruefully. Her sweet compliance to his ardour had made him forget that she was a woman with a mind of her own and not just some enchanted creature who was willing to be in his arms. It made her surrender more poignant. She was beautiful, talented and she wanted him. He felt that peculiar rush of feeling again, swelling inside him.

'Did you mention our problem to Ralph?' he asked, managing to keep the desire out of his voice. She looked away and simply nodded, and he felt a stab of cold premonition. He knew what Ralph would have said. Under the circumstances he would have said the same thing himself.

'What did he say?' He wanted to hear her tell him, to watch her expression.

'He said it might all be lies,' she told him, with no attempt at subterfuge. 'He said that the only concrete thing was the brakes and if it had happened to him he would be blaming his own garage. Ralph thinks I should be careful, though, just in case it's all true.'

They just sat looking at each other and Jake felt his heart constrict.

'Do you think I'm lying, Kathryn?'

'I don't know, do I?' she said honestly. 'I only know that I'm on your side because I can't help it.'

'Do you think I'm dangerous?'

'Yes.' She looked down and then glanced back up, meeting his eyes. 'You're a dangerous sort of person.'

'Then why do you put up with me?' He felt as if he were about to choke.

The green eyes kept looking into his and she said, 'Because I want to, because you're part of my dream, because I feel safe with you.'

'Even though I'm dangerous.'

'You're not dangerous to me.' She just drank her tea in that precise, demure manner and all his tension ebbed away like breath leaving his body.

'You're crazy, Kathryn,' he told her huskily, and she nodded, smiling at him cheerfully.

'I know. It's something to do with my genes, I expect. My grandmother and grandfather were very down-to-earth people, though.' She put her head on one side and gave it some consideration. 'Aunt Clare isn't exactly crazy,' she mused, 'but she's getting there, I think.'

He wanted to get up and take her in his arms, to make love to her until she couldn't breathe.

'Are you still my friend?' he asked unevenly, and she gave him a surprised look.

'I expect so. Although Ralph is my friend too, and he doesn't behave like you at all.'

'He'd better not,' Jake snapped, and she just sat grinning at him until he laughed, quite shaken by her clear-eyed, sensuous stare. If he didn't get out of there he knew where they would end up. She was putting a spell on him and he was more than willing to accept it.

Jake didn't come back again. She wanted him to but he was determined to stay away. He phoned her regularly and he was back to normal: dark, secret and matter-of-fact. Kathryn began to feel as if she had imagined it all, imagined the lovemaking, the things they had said so openly to each other.

She was restless without him, cooped up inside unless Ralph offered to take her out. When he did, his behaviour was so startling that she was sure he would draw attention to them without effort. He behaved like a secret service agent who was guarding an important person. All he needed was his hand inside his jacket on a gun.

She told him sharply to be normal, but he seemed to think he was being very normal and inconspicuous under the circumstances.

'Under the circumstances?' Kathryn repeated. 'What circumstances? You as good as said that Jake was lying to me.'

'Well, I've been thinking it over. The police would have been on to him by now. In fact, they would have been following him round, harassing him. They'll have searched the house, searched the area. They would have come up with something if there had been anything to come up with. No, I think he's telling the truth.'

'Bless you, Ralph,' Kathryn murmured, slipping her arm into his.

'You're mad about him, aren't you?' he said, and she smiled to herself.

'Does it show?' she asked quietly.

Ralph shook his head and assured her in a taunting voice, 'Only when you speak about him or think about him.'

He let the matter drop and then he was back to glancing suspiciously around, fixing perfectly respectable people with his narrow-eyed stare. Kathryn began to suspect he was enjoying this. And at least it got her out of the house and took her mind off Jake for some of the time.

Each night she locked up carefully, and even though she was on the top storey she drew the curtains. She was still nervous about someone looking in the window at her although she knew it was absolutely impossible. She urged Ralph to do the same and he assured her he was being particularly careful, even though he was just on the fringe of this.

Kathryn began to feel even more that he was actually enjoying the scare, but she was not enjoying it. She wanted things to be normal, back to peace. She wanted to go to Pengarron and draw in the glittering tranquillity of the woods. She wanted Jake to be there with her.

Aunt Clare phoned and told her she was home at last.

'How are you?' Kathryn asked anxiously, and she got the old annoyed snort that her aunt had perfected years ago.

'Fit as a fiddle! Didn't I tell you that Gordon Phelps was an old fusspot? I'm more concerned with how you are, though. I hear you were spirited away by Jake Trelawny.'

'Er – I know him,' Kathryn managed rather lamely.

'Well, I expect you do, dear. Jean Pengelly said he was most possessive with you.'

'I – I met him in London, after I'd been down with you the first time. He – he's a friend.'

'Jean assured me he was your boyfriend. I suppose he is. You're a beautiful girl and you'll be all right with Jake. He knows how to take care of his own.'

Kathryn did not protest. In the first place she knew it would do no good. Her aunt had already made up her mind on the subject and would not be moved until something momentous made her change her mind. It was how she functioned.

In any case, what was *she* to Jake? She just didn't know. He watched over her, worried about her, was willing to keep away so that she could be safe. He wanted her too, but she didn't know if that had merely been the heat of the moment. All she could do was wait and see.

'Have there been any new developments at Pengarron Manor?' she asked her aunt.

'Not that we've seen, dear. We took it in turns to watch, Jean and I, but nothing happened so we dropped it. One day we'll know the truth. I bet that woman just ran off with somebody else. As if Jake hasn't had enough unhappiness in his life without that sort of thing.'

And Gillian was very beautiful, Kathryn mused as her aunt finally put the phone down. Did he miss her? Was he just being self-protective when he said he had hated her? Secretly, did he still love his wife?

The thought brought on a great attack of depression for Kathryn, and for the next few days she ignored safety and went out, even when Ralph was not with her. She went to art galleries, gazed in shop windows, walked aimlessly around all the big stores and managed to get herself so tired that at night she could sleep without worry or misery.

Jake heard it in her voice. He let it go on for a few days and then took up the subject.

'What's the matter, Kathryn? Are you very frightened?'

'I'm not frightened at all,' she assured him. 'I'm just tired. I – I've been busy.'

'Is the book getting on well, then?'

'No.' She didn't want to say any more and she was glad that this conversation was on the telephone and he could not see her face.

'What is it?' he persisted, and she thought he sounded gentle. She was probably wrong. He was not often gentle but he sounded like that now.

'Aunt Clare was on the phone the other day,' she blurted out. 'Nothing's happening at Pengarron.'

'You must not go back there, Kathryn!' he said sharply, and she hung her head.

'I wasn't going to.' There was silence for a minute and then she whispered, 'Was she very beautiful, Jake?'

'Gillian? Yes, she was very beautiful,' he said softly. 'I told you that. Have you ever seen a picture of her? There were plenty of her in the papers at the time.'

'I saw one. It called her Gillian Trelawny.'

'That was her name. I married her, Kathryn.' There was a long pause and then he said heavily, 'I'm still married to her.'

'If she's alive,' Kathryn whispered. 'Is that why — why you . . .?'

'Why I stopped making love to you? Why I left you? No! I left you for your own safety. The state of matrimony does not impress me. My mother and father were married. They made me miserable. I was married to Gillian. I hated her.'

Kathryn was silent and after a while he said, 'I've made you unhappy too, Kathryn, haven't I? You were breezing along, getting better, drawing, writing, and I brought you into my life and made you unhappy. I'm better alone, where nothing can touch me and I can't bring trouble down on anyone.'

'No, Jake!' She heard the anger in his voice, the self-disgust, but she was too late. He put the phone down and she had the terrible feeling that her jealous prying had driven him away for ever. She dared not ring him back and she dared not go to see him. It would all have to be left to Jake. For once in her life she indulged in a good cry.

The next day Colin rang, and he did not wait for her to begin a conversation.

'You must be out of your mind!' he stated angrily. 'I was too stunned to do anything when that madman attacked me but I noticed how you willingly went off with him. I thought his face seemed familiar and it came to me right after you left. That's Jake Trelawny, the writer, isn't it?

'It is,' Kathryn stated firmly, already annoyed at his tone. 'He's my friend.'

'Another friend? I expect he's another one like Ralph Preston. Don't think you ever fooled me about that. While you were being all coy with me, hardly letting me touch you, I knew you were sleeping in that flat below for most of the time. Now you've got another one. He's not like Ralph, though, is he? Now you're sleeping with someone who murdered his wife.'

'He did not!' Kathryn shouted down the phone. 'If Jake hears you say that he'll either sue you or take you to pieces.'

'I'm glad you know he's capable of violence,' Colin sneered. 'Haven't you got a single brain cell working? If he didn't murder his wife then he's married, isn't he? I never thought you'd sink to going out with a married man. And if she's dead then the person likely to be taken to pieces is you.'

He slammed the phone down and Kathryn realized she was shaking. Nobody had ever spoken to her like that in her life. She knew that Colin had been getting his own back in the most despicable way. She knew he would now be feeling good again, secure in the knowledge that he had reasserted himself. He must have had a very bruised ego after his encounter with Jake. Knowing it didn't make it any the less upsetting, though.

She rushed down to Ralph's flat to tell him and Ralph's reaction was predictable.

'The little worm,' he said angrily. 'What's his address? I'll go round and beat him up.'

'He's bigger than you, Ralph,' Kathryn pointed out glumly.

'Then you've got two choices. Ignore him or send your precious Jake round.'

'Jake would kill him!' Kathryn said with real alarm. 'In no way must this be mentioned to Jake.'

'Don't look at me in horror,' Ralph advised. 'Trelawny doesn't speak to me. The only time he's ever actually spoken to me was when he threatened to shove Snowy down my shirt-front.'

'Did he?' Kathryn asked in amazement. 'What had you done?'

'There, you see!' Ralph exclaimed indignantly. 'Everybody can take the blame except Jake Trelawny. What I did was refuse to tell him where you were. I was only following your orders anyway. I had to tell him in the end. I'm not violent.'

'So he came to find me? He actually came to Cornwall to look for me?' Kathryn said dreamily. 'I didn't really believe him. I thought it was just chance.'

'With a man like that, nothing is just chance,' Ralph stated firmly. 'Which brings us back to the slimy Colin. If Trelawny isn't allowed to batter him you're left with one choice only; ignore him.'

'I was going to do that anyway,' Kathryn murmured.

'Then stop bothering me. In any case you have a wicked tongue, Kathryn. You should have given him a piece of your mind.'

'He was saying nasty things about Jake. I was shocked that anyone could be so despicable.'

'Plenty of people are saying nasty things about your precious Jake,' Ralph muttered. 'You can't fight them all, even if I help you. Now, if you don't mind, I have a masterpiece to complete. Either make some coffee or go, and I would prefer the latter, even though you are my bosom pal, because Rosie is about due here.'

Kathryn came back home one evening with Ralph. Jake had not phoned for a whole week and she had more or less thrown caution to the winds. She was so miserable that she didn't *care* if she met his villains. She'd gone to the cinema with Ralph and ignored the fact that it was late and the market would be closed when they got back.

It was only as they made it to the lift across the darkened market that she realized Ralph was rather nervous.

'This is ridiculous,' he muttered as the lift took them up to their flats. 'I know why you're doing this, Kathryn. You've quarrelled with Trelawny, or something, and you just don't care. You're probably trying to make him worried.'

'I am not!' Kathryn snapped. 'I would never do anything like that.'

'Well, you're making me worried,' Ralph assured her. 'No more evening jaunts.'

She had to agree that it had been stupid, and not at all fair to Ralph. She told him so and he was somewhat mollified.

'I'll make you some supper to show how sorry I am,' she offered, so they went straight up to her flat together.

When she opened the door, Kathryn just stopped. For a second she couldn't even move. Her face changed colour, she felt sick, her legs threatened to let her down. She managed to step aside, to ease herself to the side of the door and lean against the wall so that Ralph could get in.

'What –?' he began, and then he too stopped. '*Christ*!' He stood there as stunned as Kathryn, his gaze sweeping round an utterly devastated room. It wasn't just the one room either. The door to the kitchen was open and that too was devastated, torn apart.

In the main room the settees and chairs were ripped asunder, the fillings spread around the room, even the soft-coloured scatter cushions were torn open. The cherished pictures were all over the floor, the canvas cut from the frames. Nothing had escaped the attention of whoever had come into the flat while they were out.

The kitchen floor was strewn with pans, cooking utensils, flour, sugar – everything. And as Ralph walked around he could see into Kathryn's bedroom. It was the same in there. All her clothes were scattered around. The bed had been stripped, the mattress cut open. There was nothing he could say. He was too stunned.

Kathryn hadn't left the wall. She was standing there staring and she was not even staring at anything in particular. She worried him. The shock on her face was frightening.

'Kathryn,' he said quietly, walking towards her, and she stared at him blankly for a second and then rushed forward.

'Jake,' she muttered. 'I've got to tell Jake.'

She couldn't find the phone. It seemed to have been swamped by the filling from the chairs and settees. There was hardly an inch of floor-space clear. She found the line and followed it, muttering to herself, moving along on her hands and knees with the telephone cable in her hand until she came to the phone itself.

Nothing happened when she dialled and she looked up at Ralph in a panic.

'It won't work! I can't get to Jake!'

'You pulled it out of the wall,' he told her quietly, walking forward to reconnect it. He surely hoped Jake Trelawny was in when she rang. Kathryn looked as if she was about to collapse and he wasn't surprised. He would have liked to give her a comforting hug but he suspected that she would scream. Her mind was solely on Trelawny. It was obvious that nobody else would do.

When she had finished with the phone, Ralph intended to call the police. This had gone on long enough. Kathryn should not be involved in anything like this. He walked into the kitchen and he could see where they had got in. The fire escape.

Kathryn was on her knees with the phone when he went back and Trelawny's line was ringing, apparently, because she was listening like someone waiting for a guardian angel to appear. Trelawny didn't look a bit like that to him. He watched her face and saw the pain on it. They had ruined her whole flat, wiped out all the time she had been here. For the first time in his life, Ralph felt murderous.

'Jake? Jake they came!' Kathryn spoke into the phone almost hysterically. She burst into tears and sobbed out the next words. 'Jake. I *need* you.'

'Is he coming?' Ralph asked when she put down the phone and she nodded, still crying.

'I must stop this,' she managed shakily. 'Jake will be shocked. I never cry. He – he said that the last time he was – was here.'

'You've got a good excuse,' Ralph said gruffly, but she shook her head and got to her feet, obviously trying to pull herself together and be ready to face the man who would be storming in here soon. Ralph assumed he would be storming. He couldn't think of Jake Trelawny in any other manner.

'Suppose they've been in your flat too?' Kathryn suddenly said. 'You have to go and look, Ralph.'

'When he gets here,' Ralph muttered. 'I'm not leaving you until then.'

In fact he was hoping to keep her mind off things for a while longer. He had noticed something that she

309

had not. There was no sign of Snowy. If they had killed that cat she would just about collapse entirely. It might be all manner of a freak but Kathryn doted on it, she even consulted it about things as far as he had been able to make out. He found himself anxious to have Trelawny here as soon as possible. The man looked as if he could cope with anything.

They were still standing about in the room, not able even to sit down, when they heard the lift coming up. In seconds Jake was in the doorway, his eyes skimming across the devastation and then going straight to Kathryn.

'Look what they did, Jake,' she whispered, and he just held out his arms for her. The way she flew into them was enough to tell Ralph anything he wanted to know and the look on Jake's face was enough to assure him that Kathryn was safe.

She buried her head against Jake's shoulder and his arms tightened round her as he rocked her gently, his hand on her hair.

'I'll go down and see if they've done anything to my place,' Ralph muttered uncomfortably. He wasn't quite sure if he was needed here at all. He had the feeling of being locked outside their tight little world.

To his surprise, Jake said, 'Come back when you can.'

He nodded and went out and Jake looked around. There was no place where she could even sit down. Fury was growing inside him like a raging fire. This was her home, her place, her artist's lair. He only had to see the wreckage to know why it had happened.

This was no warning. Whoever had been here, and there had been more than one person, had been looking for his notes, his manuscript. They were getting desperate. His lips tightened. They were not as desperate as they would be.

'Better now?' He looked down at her and Kathryn nodded. The tears had stopped a good while ago, before he came, but there were still signs of them on her face. He touched her cheek. 'Let's have a good look at the damage,' he suggested quietly.

Inside he was battling with mixed emotions. He blamed himself for the way her life had been disrupted, for the danger she had been in, was still in. He should never have known her at all.

But he could hear her voice too, the way she had cried out to him when she rang. 'Jake. I *need* you.' It had broken through a wall of ice he had built up and the rush of feeling inside had almost overwhelmed him. She was his own and nothing like that had ever happened to him before. Even after a week when he had stubbornly left her alone she had called out to him when she was afraid. Ralph had been here with her but she had wanted *him*.

He tightened his arms round her again and kissed the top of her head as his eyes scanned the room again. They had not just violated the place and destroyed her things, they had wiped out part of her life. Fury raced through him like red flame but he held it in check. Open rage would not help Kathryn now.

'Care to show me around?' he asked drily, and she looked up at him and then, to his relief, she laughed.

'Of course. How remiss of me. I'll give you a conducted tour of a once desirable residence.'

Jake let her go and she led the way first into the bedroom, where the destruction was almost total. The mattress had been pulled from the bed, ripped open and then tossed aside. Her clothes were strewn across the floor – skirts, blouses and sweaters mixed with delicate undies – and Jake's fury grew at the thought that they had dared to touch her things, things she had worn next to her skin, intimate personal garments that belonged to Kathryn.

He saw her slight shudder and he knew she was thinking about that too. He started collecting coat hangers, handing them to her one by one, not saying a word and she started picking up her clothes and hanging them in the empty wardrobe.

'I'll have to have them cleaned,' she whispered. 'I could never . . .'

'We can simply throw them out,' Jake suggested tightly. 'In the morning we can replace everything.'

'No!' Kathryn snapped, glancing up with flashing eyes. 'These are my things. I wouldn't have got them if I hadn't liked them. I'll get them cleaned. Until then I'll wear what I'm standing up in. They can't drive me out. I'll not be frightened off.'

'They were looking for the manuscript,' Jake said quietly. 'They won't be back here again.' He turned away and looked into the main room. 'I'll replace all this, Kathryn. I know it won't be exactly the same but we can get things as close as possible. We can get the pictures fixed too. They cut them out of the frames. It should be possible to have that seen to – like your aunt's cup.'

She nodded, too tired really to think straight. Jake had had the cup repaired and sent back to her aunt with his apologies. Aunt Clare had told her. She had said it made her feel important.

Jake was picking up pans in the kitchen and Kathryn was still sorting out her clothes when Ralph came back into the flat.

'Well?' Jake asked, and Ralph shook his head.

'Not a thing touched in my place.'

'Then obviously you're out of it,' Jake muttered. He found the kettle, filled it and put it to boil. 'They got in through the fire escape door. How did they manage that without being heard?'

'We were out,' Ralph confessed warily. 'Kathryn was fed up, so we went to the cinema. She's been a bit miserable this week.'

'My fault,' Jake murmured. 'Perhaps it's a good thing you were out. I expect they waited for the market to close. It does mean, though, that they were watching you.'

'Don't remind me,' Ralph begged. He looked round as if a thought had just occurred to him. 'We really shouldn't be touching anything here until we've had the police. Did you call them?'

'No.'

'Well, I did,' Ralph stated emphatically. 'This has gone on long enough.'

'We don't need the police. They could never catch the people who did this,' Jake said darkly.

'So they're going to get away with it?' Ralph asked in annoyance, and Jake shot him a look that spoke volumes.

'Oh, no. It's Tuesday today –' he glanced at his watch '– almost Wednesday. By the weekend they'll be silenced.'

'What are you going to do?' Ralph looked at him in awe and it dawned on him that he was actually having a talk with this tall, dark, powerful man who scared him half to death.

'I'm going to use my influence,' Jake informed him grimly. Ralph asked nothing more. It sounded too alarming, right outside his sphere.

'Snowy seems to have disappeared,' he said in a low voice, making sure that Kathryn could not hear, and Jake spun round and looked at him, his face showing the first signs of normality that Ralph had seen.

'It will devastate Kathryn,' he said, with a glance at the bedroom. 'Have you looked?'

'I didn't dare,' Ralph muttered. 'So far she's been too shattered to notice. I thought she could do without the added grief.'

They went out onto the fire escape. The door had been prised open and almost taken from its hinges. It had not been a silent entry by any means and it proved that the watching villains had known they had nothing to fear. The market had been closed and they must have seen Kathryn leave with Ralph. Jake was white with anger but the cat had to be found. He was dreading that they would find it dead.

They went down into the yard at the back but there was no sign of it, and as they came back up Jake felt a sort of peculiar kinship with Ralph. They were both worried about the effect it would have on Kathryn.

She was just walking into the kitchen with Snowy in her arms when they came back through the door and they both stopped and stared at her.

'Where was he?' Jake asked blankly.

'We thought they'd taken him from sheer spite, or killed him,' Ralph blurted out.

To their joint astonishment, Kathryn laughed and put her face against the cat's white fur.

'Taken him?' she laughed. 'Would they dare? Would you? This is not your run-of-the-mill pussy cat. Snowy *thinks*! You can ask Jake. Jake makes plots with him.' Her laughing green-eyes looked into Jake's and he wanted to walk forward and crush her against him, to lift her up in his arms and shout for joy. This was his own, crazy girl. She laughed when the whole of her little world was in ruins.

She dropped the cat to the floor and Snowy looked more annoyed than usual.

'He was under the bath,' she told them. 'That's the good thing about having a Victorian bath with legs. I knew where to look. He always goes there when he's in a bad grump. He'll be back there again in a minute. He doesn't like mess.' She smiled gleefully. 'There was a bit of blood on the bathroom floor. I think they

315

tried to get him out. Idiots! They obviously know nothing about cats.'

Kathryn walked forward and switched off the kettle. She started to make coffee and Ralph went to pat her on the shoulder.

'I'm proud of you, kid.' he said affectionately, even if Jake didn't like it.

Jake didn't seem to mind. He just took his cup and looked deeply into Kathryn's eyes. She smiled back. They didn't say a word.

As they drank their coffee and looked round at the ruins of the room where Kathryn worked Ralph brought up the immediate problem.

'You can't stay here tonight, Kathryn. I could sleep on the settee in my place and . . .'

'No need,' Jake intervened. 'She'll come with me. If you could keep the cat until we have things sorted out?'

'Sure.' Ralph nodded, avoiding Kathryn's eyes. She was flushed as a wild rose, happy. Anyone would have thought that this debacle was nothing to do with her at all. He had been right after all. She was crazy about Jake Trelawny. And after tonight, Ralph was not at all opposed to him. Anyone would get to Kathryn over Jake's dead body. That much was obvious. Somehow he couldn't see Jake flat on his face. It would take a small army.

When the police came they were much more interested than they seemed to have been when Jake had had his fire attack at his own flat. It was under-standable. Kathryn's place was a scene of utter devastation. They took names and rang in for the experts.

'We may get lucky,' one of them muttered to Ralph. 'There may be fingerprints.'

Jake kept quiet. It had not escaped his attention that the two policemen were ignoring him since they had learned his name. His face was impassive but he was burning with fury inside. Notoriety. This was what it meant: The men were too well trained to make any remarks but he could see the thoughts on their faces. What can you expect with Trelawny involved?

He'd expected to see his own particular bloodhound and he was not disappointed. Inspector Harrison walked in, quite animated for him. His eyebrows rose at the sight of the chaos. It was more emotion than he had shown in all the time that Jake had had dealings with him.

He walked around looking, saying nothing. Ralph watched him with every sign of expectation, as if he thought the inspector might snap his fingers and start to reel off names for the policemen present to jot down in their notebooks. Jake knew his tormentor better.

'You're well acquainted with Miss Holden?' he asked finally, pinning Jake with his mournful eyes.

'Obviously. I'm here.'

Kathryn glanced across at Jake when she heard the tight tone of his voice. His expression hadn't altered but everything inside her was alerted. He was dark, brooding, his face stiff, as if he was ready for a battle with no hope of winning.

'I expect you were both out when this happened?'

'No, we sat here and helped them!' Jake snarled.

'That attitude is no sort of help . . .' the inspector began, and Ralph stepped in hastily.

'Kathryn – er – Miss Holden was out with me,' he volunteered. 'I live downstairs – the flat below this.'

'And where were you, Mr Trelawny?' The inspector stood rocking on his heels in his usual manner and Jake tried to hold onto his growing rage.

'In my flat.'

'Alone?'

Hostility rolled off Jake in almost tangible waves and Kathryn stepped forward, facing Inspector Harrison close up.

'Just a minute,' she snapped. 'What are you suggesting exactly? That Mr Trelawny did this, created this havoc?'

'I'm not suggesting anything, Miss Holden. I just want the truth.'

'You can see the truth,' Kathryn pointed out hotly. 'Someone broke into my flat and vandalized it. I was out. Mr Trelawny was at the other side of London. While you're *baiting* him the perpetrators are getting clean away. I expect you're a detective. Well, detect! Otherwise just go and leave me to sort this mess out.'

'Now then, Miss Holden, things are not always what they seem. I can understand you being upset.'

'Don't you patronize me,' Kathryn raged. 'This is breaking and entering followed by vandalism. Are you going to make some attempt to catch them or are you going to let it ride – like you did when Jake had burning rags thrown into his flat or when his researcher was firebombed?'

'Hey, now, Kathryn,' Ralph muttered worriedly.

'Oh, shut up, Ralph!' Kathryn snapped. 'What do you think he's going to do? Arrest me for insubordination? If he does I'll tell them he's incompetent.'

Jake walked forward and put his arm round her shoulders. She was stiff with annoyance.

'Enough, sweetheart,' he said softly. 'Let the poor man start his detecting.'

There was laughter in his voice and a light in his eyes that had never been there before in his life. Nobody had ever flown to his defence before but Kathryn, who was tucked under his shoulder, small, delicate as porcelain, was quivering with rage on his behalf.

CHAPTER 13

The working had stopped while everyone sat back on their heels and watched the battle. If there were any fingerprints no one was getting them at the moment. Inspector Harrison turned baleful eyes on them and work began again. The two policemen who had first arrived were studying their notebooks and obviously trying not to laugh.

'You should try to control that temper, Miss Holden,' the inspector began, and she was straining at the leash immediately.

'Why?' she asked aggressively.

'Let it go, Kathryn,' Jake ordered softly, tightening his arm around her shoulders. 'I really think you've made your point.'

'I can understand why you have that cat now,' Ralph murmured as the inspector turned away. 'And there was I, scared that somebody would attack us when we were out in the dark.'

'He had no business to go on at Jake,' Kathryn said in a low and angry voice, and Jake took her face between his hands, looking down at her intently.

'Make us some more coffee,' he said quietly. She stared into his eyes for a minute and all her anger drained away. Dark, brooding, intensely male, he looked capable of anything, but she had felt the need to go to his defence. Desire stirred unbidden and she looked quickly away. If Jake was backed into a corner she would fight for him and with him. It was instinctive.

Jake had seen the look on her face before she hid it from him. He kissed the top of her silky head and then let her go. He watched her walk away, muttering to herself that she would definitely not make coffee for Inspector Harrison. His little tiger. He made a silent vow to have this place back to normal as soon as possible.

Nobody was going to drive her out of her lair, make her leave her own private place. Tomorrow they would start a list and he would take her mind off all the horror by shopping for her home again. His manuscript could wait. He already knew what he was going to do about that.

'Collect what you need for now,' he said later, when everyone had gone. 'It's late. I think we could say that you've had a busy day.'

Kathryn went to get her things. Now that she had finished battling the horror of it was back again, and she felt exhausted.

Jake looked at Ralph.

'Thanks,' he said quietly. 'I know why she values your friendship.'

'We're old buddies,' Ralph assured him. 'Kathryn and I go way back.' He looked squarely at Jake and took his courage into both hands. 'She needs you,' he said firmly. 'One jerk in a lifetime is more than enough for anyone.'

'Colin?' Jake asked drily. 'I met him.'

'She told me.' Ralph grinned and then got up to try and coax the cat out from under the bath again, although it seemed more like a job for Kathryn to him. Jake came and did it and Ralph was not one bit jealous. The cat scared him almost as much as Jake Trelawny – more, now that he was getting to know Kathryn's hero. She was pretty ferocious herself anyway.

When they left Kathryn took just one small bag with her. She had been loath to take anything at all, but she had to have night attire and her make-up. Tomorrow she would collect all her clothes and take then to the cleaners. She could do her washing and then she would have something to wear. Until then she would have to manage.

As to the flat, she just tried not to think about it. Jake had said he would fix it and she would leave it at that until morning. It was almost two o'clock. She was exhausted. She lay back in the seat at the side of Jake as he drove them through the streets to his flat and in a few minutes she fell asleep, tired and worn out by events.

There was an underground car park that belonged to the whole block. It was big, and the lift to each floor was waiting at the side, ready and open. Jake woke her up and took her arm, guiding her to the lift and pressing the button for his floor. She leaned against the panelled wall of the lift, her eyes partly closed, and Jake watched her.

She looked like an exhausted child with her dark red hair falling partly across her face, her mouth drooping with sleep. She was too tired to talk, too tired to really care where she was going.

He wondered if she would have come with him so readily if she had been fully awake and not so shattered by events. He smiled to himself. She would have come. She had flown into his arms as soon as she had seen him tonight. She had run into his arms when he had scared her at Pengarron. She had come to him willingly and sweetly when he had made love to her. She had raged like a tiger to defend him. She was his – his very own.

He put his arm round her as the lift stopped at his floor and guided her forward until he had the door open. Then he lifted her up and took her inside. She just wound her arms round his neck and closed her eyes.

When he took her into the bedroom and stood her down she looked round drowsily.

'Is this it?' she asked sleepily.

'This is where you're sleeping tonight,' he told her quietly. 'This is your room.'

Kathryn just nodded and made no move at all. She was literally swaying on her feet, and when Jake began to undress her she made no protest. She just held up her arms as he slid the nightie over her head and he even had to guide her arms through the correct holes. He lifted her into bed and she was asleep immediately.

She trusted him. He stood looking down at her and then he leaned forward and kissed her forehead before going out and closing the door. She was safe. He would kill anyone who touched her. Thank God she hadn't been in her flat when they came to search. His opinion of the ever-faithful Ralph had done a complete turnabout.

Why hadn't they raided this flat? Possibly because it was not so easy to get into or possibly because they suspected him of some diabolical craftiness – like piling all the risk on Kathryn.

He checked the door and then went to his own room to get ready for bed. He had a lot to do tomorrow.

He knew deep down exactly how Renfrew thought. Renfrew thought he would have left a copy of his work with Kathryn. It was just the sort of thing that Renfrew would have done himself, putting a woman at risk. He was beginning to see into the man's mind. He was beginning to see how to strike back.

What had happened to Gillian? Jake lay in the dark and thought about her. She had come from that time in his life when he had allowed himself to be dragged into glamorous places, when he had tried to live up to the image his publishers were pushing on him with book signings, cocktail parties – things he hated and shunned. The filming of his first book had made matters worse and for a time he had gone along with it.

Gillian had latched onto him like a homing pigeon with a taste for good things and he had fallen for it.

He'd been lonely, out of his depth, and she had been there, waiting and willing, smoothing things over for him with her sophistication.

His strength and his 'go to the devil' attitude had been with him since childhood. It had been his defence then and it had become his character. With Gillian he had been able to keep safely in that character. She had done all the talking, all the glittering. He had been able to stand at one side and watch.

By the time he had come to his senses it had been too late. He was married to her. His lips twisted sardonically in the darkness. She had wanted a child too. He remembered that with bitter amusement. With a child she would have had a grip on him to last a lifetime of misery. But he had already lived one part of his life in misery and by then he'd discovered what Gillian was. He knew all about the men, the social 'friendships'.

Jake turned over to go to sleep and his mind went winging across the passage to his slender, trusting guest. His tight mouth softened and his body suddenly surged with desire. He wanted Kathryn to have his child. He wanted to see her pregnant, laughing, the red hair falling over her shoulders. He wanted to know that a part of him was growing inside her. He wanted her to stay with him, live with him. He wondered if she would.

When Jake came out of the shower the next morning he could hear Kathryn singing softly in the kitchen.

He quickly pulled on jeans and a sweater and went to see what she was up to.

She was making tea, and his mind went back to the time when he had first brought her here and ordered her to make tea while he read his notes on Renfrew. Then, though, she had been wearing a dark blue dress with white spots on it. Now she was in her nightie with a silky robe over it. She looked silky herself, soft and desirable.

He walked into the kitchen quietly and pulled her back against him, taking her by surprise.

'Jake!' She leaned her head back and looked up at him with laughing green eyes. 'You made me jump,' she complained.

'Good morning, Kathryn,' he said quietly.

He could feel her softness in his arms. The way she just stayed against him. He wanted her now. If he held her close for another moment she would know, because it was becoming very obvious.

He had things to do, important things that could not wait, and besides, it was too soon. He had to give her time. Last night must have been a shattering blow to her. At the moment she was more or less homeless. If she wanted to walk out on him she had nowhere to go other than to Ralph.

Oddly enough, the thought did not make him jealous. He knew very well that if she ran from him she would not be sharing a bed with her friend.

He released her and reached for his tea

'I should be dressed.' There was a slight flush on her cheeks when they sat with their tea, facing each other across the table in the kitchen.

'There's only one shower,' Jake pointed out in a matter-of-fact voice. 'I was in it. You can have it all to yourself when you've had your tea. I have some phoning to do then we'll get out to the shops and set about putting your flat to rights.'

'I can't afford to have it done all at one time,' she protested quietly. 'It will have to be done bit by bit. The way I did it at first.'

'I can afford it,' Jake stated firmly, his eyes holding hers. 'This is my fault, Kathryn. I want that flat back to normal before next week is out.'

She just stared at him.

'It's Wednesday already.'

'Okay. Before half of next week is out, then.'

'Jake, you can't!' she laughed. 'I would feel bad about it.'

'Let me,' he asked softly. His hand covered hers on the table-top. 'A man has to be able to do *something* for his woodland nymph.'

'Am I?' she asked, her cheeks flushing again.

'Will you be?' Jake's eyes were burning into hers and she saw desire like a banked-down fire in his gaze. She nibbled at her lip, her old habit, and Jake's eyes fastened on the softness at once. His hand tightened on hers and she gave a soft little moan that made sparks flash in front of his eyes.

'Kathryn?' he said thickly, and she just went on looking at him until he was sinking into the glowing green of her eyes.

He got up and walked round the table to her, his eyes never leaving hers. There was a taut expression on his face that would have frightened her if she had not known what it was. She felt the same inside too, and when he drew her to her feet she stood and lifted her face for the kiss she knew was coming.

He held her close, kissing her deeply, enjoying the luxury of her soft body, the way she just came to him. It was torture but he would not make love to her now. He had made a promise to her even though she had not heard it.

'No, no, no,' he murmured against her lips, punctuating the husky words with kisses. 'We have other things to do and at the moment you're at my mercy.'

'I always am,' she whispered, going onto her toes to kiss the edge of his jaw. Her breasts were swelling against him. He could feel them like ripe fruit. If he lifted her up now she would come willingly. He would have her tied fast to him for always because he knew her. Once she belonged to him she would never leave. That was how Kathryn was. His loneliness would be a thing of the past. He put her from him and pointed at the door.

'Shower,' he ordered sternly. 'Today I'm going to take care of you, spoil you, and feed you as you've never been fed before.'

Kathryn gave him one laughing, reproachful look and then she went out of the room. He didn't know where he had found the strength to let her go. He was almost dazed with desire and damned uncomfortable. He swallowed the rest of his tea and then went into the sitting room. Today he was going to strike back.

He dialled, and when the phone was picked up at

the other end he asked for Jimmy Warrender. Then he waited for the terse, clipped tones of the man he had known for a long time.

'Warrender.'

Jake smiled grimly to himself. The voice had not changed. There was still the hard tone of the cynical newsman in the one word. This was his man.

'Jake Trelawny,' Jake announced, and waited for the outburst that usually followed.

The profanities were short and to the point, and then, 'A whole bloody year, Jake! I tried to get in touch with you but you were constantly not available. You knew I would have stood by you. As it was I had to slant my column in your favour without any facts from the horse's mouth.'

'Do you want a story?' Jake asked, cutting through the rest in his usual incisive manner. 'The horse's mouth?'

'Is this for book publicity, Jake? I don't waste my column on things like that.'

'This is for a lot of things,' Jake stated grimly. 'This is for self-protection, revenge and to issue a warning. If you're interested I'll hand it all over to you. You can decide what you want to do about it.'

'Come on in,' Jimmy Warrender ordered. 'I'll get it all down and then we'll see. I haven't done my weekend column yet.'

'I've got important things to do today. I'll fax it direct to you,' Jake stated firmly. 'I can still pen a line. You can read it and rewrite it then. If you decide to use it you're going to need more than a column.'

'Any legal repercussions?'

'It depends how you write it,' Jake murmured drily. 'In any case, I doubt it. I'll photocopy old clippings too.

'Right! I'll sit here and wait. I don't suppose I'm going to get anything else out of you over the phone – like what it's all about?'

'Oh, I'll tell you that right now. You're going to flush out a snake.'

'Thanks. You always were a bastard.'

Jake put the phone down with a satisfied smile on his face and then went into the room he kept as a study. When Kathryn came past on her way from the shower, Jake's fingers were flying over the keys of a word processor. There was the steady hum of a fax machine at the ready and Jake had that look on his face again – the hunter.

She went past and didn't disturb him. She knew somehow that however long he was she would have to keep out of the way. She wondered if she would ever understand him, if she would ever get the chance even to begin. He was, in many ways, the man she had first seen on the cliff top, dark, mysterious and aloof. The only real change had been the change in herself. She wanted to be part of his strange life.

Lunchtime approached. Kathryn looked round at the things in the kitchen, made sandwiches and coffee and quietly took some in to Jake. She put them on his desk without a word and he never even looked up. He just grunted at her, which might have meant anything.

He was terribly intent on what he was doing. There was the old book of clippings on a table at his side. Some of the pages had been neatly torn out and she glanced at them as she left. It was Giles Renfrew, but not as he was now, because the papers were yellowed. He must be older. He was a handsome man. It seemed unreal that he should be doing these things. He had a look of importance about him, as if he would never stoop to anything underhand. A man to have confidence in. If he got into Parliament he would go all the way to the top. The thought was frightening.

She did not linger. Jake was unaware that she had even come in. He had gone into some world of his own and she understood it. She was like that herself when she was working. But she would never have Jake's superb self-control, his ability to switch off any feelings.

He had wanted her badly earlier but it had not fitted in with his plans. How could he be like that? It made her feel curiously saddened and she started to get ready to leave. She couldn't simply stay here. Last night had been an emergency. She packed her small bag and took it out into the sitting room.

Kathryn was wondering how she was going to communicate with Jake without interrupting him when he walked out of his study.

'Running out on me, Miss Holden?' he asked quizzically, looking down at her intently, and she felt very much an intruder in his life, unsure of what to say.

'You were busy. I didn't exactly know what to do,' she began, and he said nothing at all. He simply picked up her bag and took it back into the bedroom.

'Jake! I can't just stay here. Last night was different, but today I . . .'

'Today you feel guilty,' he surmised astutely. 'You're wondering if I'm about to get on with things and ignore you.' He came back to her and took her slender shoulders in his hands. 'What I've been doing had to be done now – immediately. The sort of thing that happened to you last night cannot be allowed to continue. I imagine that by the end of the week we'll have some reaction.'

'What have you done?' She looked up at him worriedly and got the old, crooked grin. He held her loosely in the circle of his arms.

'I've thrown Renfrew to the wolves of the Press. If I'm wrong and this has nothing to do with him then at least I can console myself with the thought that he deserves it. If I'm right, and I think I am, then the reaction should be interesting. Watch this space.'

'You've told some newspaper all about him?' Kathryn asked anxiously. 'Won't that infuriate him?'

'More than likely,' Jake said in an unconcerned voice. 'On the other hand, his hands will be well and truly tied. For instance, questions would be asked if anything happened to me or mine. He couldn't afford that. Like all creatures who work in the dark, the light is threatening.'

Kathryn's heart lifted when he said 'me and mine'. Did he mean her? She hoped so, because she knew she could never forget Jake and simply go away as she had done with Colin.

'But what about your book? If you've given the story away . . .'

'Only part of the story,' Jake assured her with a wry smile. 'Enough to frighten Renfrew and whet the appetite of the reading public. I wanted to wait a while longer because the book is still unfinished, but last night brought matters to a head. Now I'll have to get down to some hard work. I expect the book will sell out as soon as it hits the shelves.'

'You're quite wicked,' Kathryn accused, giving him a wary look.

'I thought you knew that already? Let's get out to the shops now.'

'Did you enjoy the sandwiches?' Kathryn asked.

'Very nice.'

As she passed the door of the study she glanced in. The sandwiches sat there unnoticed, forlornly untouched. If that was how Jake worked she would have to keep an eye on him.

She quickly avoided his eyes. She was thinking like a wife, imagining that this would simply go on and on. Jake would never stay with her. He was a loner, a man with no trust in anyone. He had been hurt and ignored as a child and cheated by his wife. Why should he place any faith in her?

She was new to his life, so very different from him. Jake was a giant in every way, untamed and aloof. She was ordinary. She wasn't even glamorous, like Gillian Trelawny. The name saddened her even more. Jake was married. She often forgot about that. It was easy to forget things when you had no wish to remember.

They spent the next few hours going round shops, trying to find things to replace everything Kathryn had lost. At first she was uneasy about it, but after a while she just gave in and succumbed to Jake's determination. Long before the shops closed they had ordered settees, cushions and a mattress. Everything else could be salvaged. The people who had entered Kathryn's flat and wrecked it had not been on some mission merely to vandalize. They had not even scratched the tables. They had been searching for Jake's manuscript.

Jake took her back to the flat to collect her clothes for cleaning and washing and while she was doing that he gathered the pictures.

'These are not so bad,' he muttered, eyeing them critically. 'Most of them will repair.

'I hope so. They're important to me. They added the final touch to this place. Made it into a home. When I get them back up I'll feel secure again.'

Jake's lips tightened but he said nothing. It had just dawned on him that he was, in fact, standing in Kathryn's home, a place she wanted to be. He had never felt as if he had a home. He had a place to sleep, a place to eat, somewhere to hang his clothes. That was all.

Would she be willing to leave all this to come with him? Did he have the right to ask her? He was married, still under suspicion, and she was so bright, so fresh, so innocent.

Ralph came up and had coffee with them and the subject of the cat came up.

'Can you keep him for now?' Jake asked before Kathryn could speak. 'No pets allowed where we are at the moment.' He glanced at the cat thoughtfully when Ralph agreed. 'What you need, Snowy,' he muttered, 'is a home in the country.'

'If you imagine for one minute that I'm giving Snowy away . . .' Kathryn began indignantly, and Jake looked up at her in surprise. She looked hurt.

'Did I suggest it?' He gave her a quizzical glance. 'I can see where the cat gets his bad temper,' he murmured drily.

Kathryn felt duly chastened. Her burst of annoyance had been because the mention of a home in the country had brought her thoughts to Pengarron. She would have to stop thinking like that.

Her relationship with Jake could never be permanent. His world was so different. And besides, he was married. What did she have with Jake? They had a shared passion, but there must have been other women in his life both before and after Gillian, women from a glittering world.

As Ralph left she turned to Jake seriously. 'I can't go on relying on your good nature,' she pointed out.

'Why? Do you think it's going to fade away?'

He was looking at her with sardonic amusement and Kathryn felt insecure, hurting inside.

'If I hadn't known you I would have managed anyhow. I would have slept on Ralph's settee and started cleaning up this place first thing this morning.'

'But you do know me,' Jake said quietly. 'Staying with me is not so bad, is it?'

Kathryn shook her head, defeated again, and he walked to the door and opened it.

'Bring your washing. There are laundry facilities at my flat. You can't hang around here doing it when there's not even a place to sit down. Besides which, I would not allow it.'

'You can't order me about,' Kathryn muttered with a faint trace of mutiny.

'Somebody has to and obviously it must be me. Nobody else would dare, would they?'

Kathryn didn't know what he meant by that. He might be staking a claim on her. On the other hand, he might just be being sarcastic. She went out quietly, realizing that her earlier high spirits, when they were shopping, had totally evaporated. They didn't seem to belong together anymore.

Jake showed her how the washing machine worked when they arrived back at his flat and left her to it. He seemed to have gone as silent as she was herself. But then, silence was nothing to Jake. He was probably happier by himself. He would probably have been happier by himself tonight, alone in this flat, getting on with his book.

He was pacing about the sitting room when she came back in and he turned to her in a very similar manner to someone at bay.

'Do you want anything to drink?' he asked tersely, and Kathryn shook her head. She felt as if she was here on sufferance now, as somebody he owed a favour to. She thought longingly of Ralph's settee. It was terrible to feel that she was relying on Jake because he felt guilty about her.

'Jake,' she began anxiously, 'I know this is messing up your life a lot. I don't want you to feel guilty about things. I mean – to an outsider this would look bad, and you have to think about that. People will see me coming in here with you. With Ralph and I there are just the two flats. I could stay there while I fix things up and nobody would know about it.'

'I would know,' Jake said harshly. He turned away and paced about restlessly before spinning back to face her. 'Do you really want to go, Kathryn? Have I bullied you into being here with me?'

'It's not that.' She turned away from the intense dark eyes and then gave a delicate little shrug. 'I've managed to intrude on your life since that first time when I was trespassing on your land. Somehow or other we seem to have got ourselves into a strange tangle, caught up in each other almost by accident. Now you've more or less got me on your hands.'

'I want you on my hands,' Jake assured her darkly. 'I don't just want you staying here, I want you living here. If you walk out I'll follow you,' he finished angrily.

Kathryn turned and looked at him with wide open green eyes and he came over to her quickly, taking her by the shoulders and looking down into her face.

'Stay with me. Live with me,' he said urgently. He was not ordering. He wasn't even begging. But there was a sort of stark desperation in his voice and

Kathryn's hands came to his chest, resting there like two delicate birds, unsure, ready for flight.

'Will you, Kathryn? Will you live with me? When you called me on the phone you said you needed me. Do you? Do you need me as much as I need you?'

'Oh, yes.'

She just closed her eyes and wound her arms round his neck and Jake brought her fiercely into his arms as his head bent and his lips searched frustratedly for hers. It seemed a long time since he had realized that he wanted her – years. But there was still that faint air of unreality and fragility about her, the slender limbs, the small, fine bones, smooth, tender skin.

He lifted his head and ran his fingers through her hair, the glorious dark red tresses that glittered in the light. She kept her arms round his neck and he moved his hands over her, cupping her breasts, spanning her waist, moving over her slender hips and curving round the tight roundness of her bottom, pulling her into him.

He had never held her like that before, in this possessive, intimate manner, and the way she submitted made him instantly aroused. She wanted him. He had captured a woodland nymph who would allow him to take her, keep her.

His lips opened over hers as he held her fast and Kathryn shuddered with pleasure as his tongue began a long, hot exploration inside her mouth. She was turning to liquid gold, murmuring against his lips, and she arched back with a small unearthly cry when his mouth found the hard peak of her breast where his searching fingers had opened buttons and bared the entrancing fruit to his sight.

She clutched at him, pressing herself closer, and his knee parted her legs possessively. This time he would take her, enjoy her delicate body, the wonder of her, and he would bind her to him so that she could never disappear. He would be able to conjure her up without any mystical powers, without snapping his fingers, because she would be there – his.

'Is it true?' he asked thickly against her lips. 'Is it true that if you take a nymph and possess her she's trapped in the world, clinging to you always, unable to escape?'

'Yes,' she whispered, prepared to play his sensuous game. 'She would never be able to go away.'

He swung her up into his arms, holding her tightly.

'Then I must hurry and capture you. That way I'll know you'll be here in the morning and every other morning, always in my sight.'

She had never been in his bedroom before and even now she did not look around. Her eyes were only for Jake, and he looked deeply into her own eyes as he placed her gently on the bed.

'Be sure, Kathryn,' he warned her unevenly. 'Remember who I am, all the things you've heard about me. Remember your suspicions and fears. I haven't changed into someone else suddenly.'

'I wouldn't want you to change,' Kathryn told him tremulously. 'I feel safe with you. I want to be with you or I would never have come at all.'

'Is that true?' He sat beside her, his hand tracing her face, his fingers running over the silken skin of her neck.

'Yes, Jake,' she whispered. 'I could have stayed with Ralph or gone to some hotel. But you said come and I came. I suppose I would follow you anywhere.'

'Kathryn!' He lifted her into his arms, cradling her against him, grateful that she was his so willingly, this strange, beautiful girl who had faced fear and still instinctively came to him, trusted him. Nothing about them was alike. He was hard, sceptical, with the unyielding, inflexible wall he had built around himself at an early age still intact. But Kathryn had broken through it with no effort. She wanted nothing. She merely wanted him. She was like a dream he had conjured up, misty, unreal, but she was lying beneath him, warm and yielding.

He clasped her face in his hands, covering it with kisses, his body warm with the knowledge of her soft commitment to him.

'You're beautiful,' he whispered, 'My dream. I imagined you and you appeared.'

Her arms curled around his neck, clinging to him urgently, and his hands traced her body with growing desire. The need to see her, all of her, tore over him like a fire and he unfastened her dress more, sweeping it to her waist and then easing it over her hips and tossing it aside.

Kathryn felt his eyes on her but she could not meet his gaze. Her heart was hammering, her cheeks flushed, and when she felt his hands on the clip of her bra she moaned in protest and turned her face against his chest to hide like a wild thing caught in a trap.

'There's so little of you I haven't seen already,' he reminded her huskily. His hands traced her breasts with exquisite care. 'I've seen you here, kissed you here.' He allowed his fingers to move tantalizingly over the length of her legs. 'I've stroked you here before, felt your silken skin beneath my hands, dreamed of it, wondered if I had frightened you and yet still you came back to me. Why are you afraid now, Kathryn?'

'I'm not afraid.' She opened her eyes and drew back to look at him, fearful now that he would stop, leave her as he had done before. 'It's just shyness.'

Jake moved away, and as she watched he pulled his shirt over his head and dropped it to the floor. His dark eyes came back to hers, drowning her, black, compelling as he slowly lowered himself against her until the softly abrasive hair on his chest touched the tender peaks of her breasts.

She gave a startled little cry as his skin touched hers and he smiled that long, slow smile that seemed to come from deep inside him. He kissed her lingeringly and when she relaxed and curled against him his lips trailed a path down her slender neck to her breasts and on to the supple, unresisting contours of her belly.

Heat began to generate between them as his lips caressed and his tongue flicked out to trace a pattern around her navel, making erotic circles that brought moans of pleasure from Kathryn's lips. She showed no signs of fear when his hand gently cupped the mound between her legs. She was relaxed, acquiescent, and when his hand gently removed the last tiny scrap of her covering she merely pressed herself more closely to him, her legs anxious to wind around his own.

'Kathryn, my beautiful girl.' He held her away so that his eyes could discover what his hands had disclosed, and this time she did not try to hide. She watched the wonderful strain on his face, the vivid black shine of his hair, his eyes, the way his thick lashes hid his eyes from her as he looked down at her body.

Her gaze ran over the broad muscles of his chest, the wide shoulders. He was brown, not because of any tan but because he was like that – smooth, brown skin, and muscles in his arms that rippled as he moved. The suppressed strength was both alarming and thrilling and her aunt's words came into her mind; 'wild as a gypsy'. Jake was like that – an educated, successful man who took the world by the throat because he must. But his heart was wild, untamed.

Kathryn touched his face, letting her fingers move over his lips, and his eyes came back to hers, probing, searching her mind.

'Love me, Jake,' she whispered, and the dark eyes flared with desire as his lips came back to capture hers.

He held her fast, kissing her deeply until so much passion threatened to send her mad. He eased away to slide out of the rest of his clothes, but his lips never stopped their heated exploration of her mouth, her face and the tender mounds of her breasts.

When he came back to her they lay for a moment locked together, their breathing heavy, and Kathryn wound her arms tightly around him, astonished at the comfort that one body could give to another. She seemed to have been made for Jake, fashioned for him alone, and she was fiercely glad that no one else had ever touched her or held her like this.

He was sleek, powerful, crushing her against him, the strength of his body alarming her slightly until his hand moved and slid between her thighs with wonderful gentleness. His fingers searched for the warm, moist core of her desire, everything about him telling her without words that he understood her trepidation, that he knew this was the first time she had ever been like this in a man's arms.

Heat seemed to grow from the centre of her being and she moved wildly, the pleasure of his touch thrilling and unexpected. His lips caressed her breasts, his hand still exploring gently inside her.

'Carefully,' he whispered against her skin. 'If I were to hurt you I would never forgive myself. I'm used to thinking of you as delicate, almost unreal. Go wild in my arms like that and I may forget.'

It startled her. She had never thought of hurt, of pain. She could feel the hardened length of his manhood against her thigh. She thought of Jake's strength and power and she opened her eyes wide, searching his face when he lifted his head and looked down at her.

'Now, Jake,' she said breathlessly. 'Now, before I panic.'

She saw the white flash of his teeth as he laughed, saw his dark head bend as he kissed the tip of her nose.

'Crazy girl,' he said softly. 'This isn't some sort of sacrifice you're compelled to make. You won't panic. You'll be desperate.'

A few minutes later she understood. His caressing hands and mouth drove all other thoughts away. The explosion of feeling inside that Jake had provoked before, even that first time in her aunt's cottage, now raged out of control. Kathryn could feel herself going wild, could hear her own cries of frustration with Jake. He had a tight grip on his own control and she wanted him to be as committed as she was herself.

She called his name, her nails digging into his skin as his searching fingers made ripples of pleasure start inside her, and only as her cries became insistent and distressed did she feel the strong, powerful pressure within her as Jake entered her with firm, unshakeable control.

Kathryn felt nothing but wonder, sheer delight. She looked into his eyes, saw the taut restraint and understood.

'Jake,' she whispered, gratitude for his consideration bringing tears to her eyes. She relaxed and let the ripples grow, and as Jake finally allowed himself to enjoy her body and begin to move inside her, she gave a soft, unearthly cry and held him tightly, letting him take them together into a realm of light and drifting colours, a golden explosion of pleasure . . .

Finally they lay spent and complete, but he did not move from her and Kathryn never wanted him to move again. They were joined together, part of each other, and only then did she fully realize how much she loved this dark and unusual man. She ran her hands over his back, feeling the relaxation that had swept through him, knowing that she had been responsible for it. His skin was hot, damp, his breathing still uneven, and when he looked at her there was peace on his face.

He raised himself on his elbows and looked down at her, his hand stroking back her dark red hair. It was curling and damp against her forehead and his eyes followed the movement of his hands and then met her gaze, looked into the glowing green of her eyes.

'Never to escape.' he reminded her huskily. 'Stolen from the woods, possessed and captured.' His eyes roamed over her face. 'You are possessed, Kathryn. I mean to keep you, hold you and never allow you to leave me.'

She smiled tremulously, still shaken by the greatest emotion of her life, and his dark eyes held hers.

'Do I frighten you?' he asked. She shook her head, watching him in bewildered joy, and after concentrating on her for a long time, Jake finally moved.

She cried out as he moved from her, astonished by the ripples of feeling that still flooded through her, and he smiled down at her in a slow, lazy way, his eyes flashing with amusement. He rolled over and got to his feet, pulling her upright and gathering her in his arms.

'Are you mine, Kathryn?' he asked softly. 'Will you try to escape?'

She shook her head. Never. She would never try to escape. Jake was all she would ever want. She was in a magical world.

CHAPTER 14

He carried her out of the bedroom and she roused herself sufficiently to ask, 'Where are we going?'

'To shower. Something I wanted us to do together yesterday, when you went off all silky and warm. I had to stay away from you and suffer. I don't have to suffer now.'

Kathryn felt almost crushed by a new wave of shyness. To be with Jake when he made love to her was different, but to stand naked together as they showered would almost make her faint with embarrassment.

Jake switched on the shower and then lowered her to her feet, beginning to draw her under the warm, swirling water. Kathryn tried to hang back, and when he looked at her in surprise, her cheeks flushed wildly.

'I – I can't!' she gasped. 'It will be so – so cold-blooded.'

Jake gave a great shout of laughter and swept her in beside him and under the water.

'Kathryn, you're crazy,' he laughed. 'What am I to do with you?'

347

Kathryn couldn't answer. The water poured over her, drenching her skin and hair, running down her face, and she was quite out of breath when Jake pulled her forward and stroked her hair out of her eyes. Before she could protest he began to wash her, soaping her skin with sensuous hands until all thoughts of embarrassment left her and she moved forward into his arms, collapsing against him.

'Kathryn,' he murmured, his hands shaping the slick wetness of her skin, 'I think I'm never going to have enough of you. Why did I ever let you leave the woods that first time you came there? I should have been doing this then, capturing you, because at the back of my mind I knew you belonged there always.'

Always. The word rang in her ears as she wound her arms round him. Would it be for always? She would never get over it if Jake finally left her. Somewhere he had a wife, a wife who was beautiful. She gave a soft, sad little cry and he gathered her closer, his body responding to her need instantly, his knee parting her thighs as he realized she was ready for him again, so quickly, so willingly, his mischievous nymph with eyes like emeralds and hair like the midnight sun.

Next day when Kathryn awoke Jake was not there, and her instant feeling of loss told its own story better than any words. She could not believe it was true. She did not expect it to be true. She had been wrapped in magic, transported to another world, but this world was always there, waiting. Her soft mouth drooped and she was lying like that, almost afraid to get up, when Jake walked in.

'What?' he asked when he saw the look on her face.

'Nothing.' She turned her face away, unable to look at him, afraid her feelings would show in her eyes. But it was too late. Jake had already seen how she looked.

'Are you regretting last night?' he asked, with such a sound of controlled despair in his voice that she spun round at once.

'No. Jake, no! I don't regret anything.'

'Then you thought I'd left you,' he surmised correctly. 'You thought I had taken you and now I was ready to discard you. You don't trust me, do you, Kathryn?'

'I do,' she cried, with tears back in her eyes. 'It's just that I can't believe . . . When you're not there I'm afraid. Nothing could be so beautiful and last.'

'Oh, Kathryn.' He lifted her into his arms and held her against him. 'Did you think it was beautiful? I thought so too. Do you imagine I could walk away and leave you? I seem to have been chasing around after you since I first saw you.'

'You're married, Jake,' she reminded him, with a heartfelt sigh that seemed to come from the very depths of her being.

'For now there's nothing I can do about that,' he reminded her quietly. He eased away to look into her face. 'So should I have left you, waited, longed for you and let you go until some far-off time in the future when Gillian may or may not reappear?'

'No,' she said instantly, and he gave her one of his smiles but this time there was just the touch of bitterness.

'I couldn't leave you and wait,' he confessed deeply. 'I've tried that before. When I saw you with that wretch, I thought you were back with him.'

'Colin?' It took her a second to realize what he was talking about. Colin was never in her mind, had hardly been in her mind at all since she had first seen Jake. 'I never even thought of going back to him. I just wanted to get rid of him.'

'At the time, I didn't know it,' he muttered, and she started to laugh, her happiness restored.

'I've never been fought over before. For a time there you were just like Snowy.'

Jake smiled, not at all insulted at the idea. He had felt pretty much like growling himself when he had seen her with another man. He stood up and looked round the room, finding his bathrobe and holding it out for her.

'Come and get your breakfast,' he said. 'Today we have things to do. I have plans.' He walked out and left her and Kathryn slid from the bed and enveloped herself in Jake's robe. It smelled like Jake – talc, aftershave and man. She shivered with pleasure and went to find him.

The paper had decided to print Jake's article. A telephone call from Jimmy Warrender confirmed that as they were having breakfast.

'Saturday's edition,' he confirmed. 'Double-page spread. Luckily my editor is a fan of yours, Jake. I've

350

been given the go-ahead to push it to the limit. No names, just "a certain well-known figure with a possible future in politics". The way we're playing it is that your forthcoming book will be remarkably close to the history of a real-life person – amazing coincidence. The theme will be you. How much does a writer use instinct, or is it fact? We've rooted out other writers of the past who have either hit on truth with astonishing regularity or made uncanny predictions. There'll be a full photograph of you and smaller ones of the other writers.'

'What about legal action?' Jake asked.

'We're a cunning lot here,' Jimmy Warrender stated sarcastically. 'We know how to skate the line. In any case, do you think he would take us to court? Think of the publicity! Our legal people assure us it's tight as a drum.'

'Good,' Jake muttered coldly. Kathryn glanced at him. The hunter was back, with an unholy satisfaction in the depths of his eyes.

'Better crack on with the book,' Jimmy advised. 'When this edition hits the stands your publishers will be thumping the table to get the book out. There'll be queues at the bookshops.'

'Did you hear all that?' Jake asked when he'd put the phone down.

'Most of it. You need time to work, don't you?'

He nodded and took her hand as it lay on the table.

'Yes. I'm torn between just leaving everything to stay close to you and locking myself in to work. I've got to get that manuscript finished, Kathryn.'

'Well, I have to clean my flat and sort everything out. I can't bear to think of it being left in a mess. The men are coming to fix the door today. I have to be there.'

'Can you get a taxi?'

She nodded and smiled, but Jake still held onto her hand.

'I'll come to get you later,' he assured her softly. 'Promise me you'll come back.'

'I will. I'm still bewildered by everything, but I'll come back.'

By the time she was ready to leave, Jake was writing, the door to his study shut fast, and Kathryn took her clothes and called a taxi. She had food at her own place, more or less everything she needed, and there was a lot to do before night time.

The workmen were there when she arrived and the door they were fitting had been ordered by Jake. It was steel, ugly-looking, but definitely secure.

'He doesn't mean to let anyone else get in,' Ralph commented, arriving with Rosie as the men left.

'Nobody else will try, in my opinion. Jake's taken care of it. It will be in the papers on Saturday. He's sure they'll do nothing here again and they don't have a lot of time to do anything anywhere else.'

'And when the paper comes out?'

'I don't know,' Kathryn confessed worriedly. 'We'll have to wait and see.'

She only hoped that Jake was right about all this, because neither of them could get on with their lives until it was all over. And there would still be the problem of Gillian Trelawny even then.

'I'm going to help you to clear up,' Rosie told her when she suddenly went silent. 'Ralph is going to make lunch for us in his place. We could get most of this sorted before nightfall.'

Kathryn did not refuse the offer and Ralph left them to it. He had a pretty good idea of the sort of things that would be chasing round in her head. It was diabolical. Things should have gone smoothly in life for Kathryn but they never had, not since he had known her. He only hoped that Trelawny loved her enough to guard her for the rest of her life.

Rosie's bouncy personality was like a tonic, and Kathryn's spirits were soon restored. It made the work less arduous.

'It's a pity we weren't all here to get them when they broke in,' Rosie muttered as she cleaned up the mess that had been left. 'They wouldn't have got away with this.'

'They wouldn't have tried to get in if we had been here,' Kathryn pointed out. 'These are people who work in the dark, stealthily. Nobody is going to catch them. They didn't leave any prints – in fact they left no clues at all. Inspector Harrison told us that. I suppose we should be grateful that nobody was hurt.'

The thought of Jake being hurt terrified her, and gloom washed over her again. Suppose his plan simply made them more determined to silence him? Suppose Gillian was already dead and the police blamed Jake? Kathryn fell silent again, and even Rosie's chatter could not lift her spirits. Even over lunch she was quiet, a feeling of dread hanging over her.

Jake did not come when she expected him and Kathryn didn't know what to do. She was still so vulnerable, so unsure of her place in Jake's world. It was late, almost ten o'clock, and it seemed she had been watching for him for most of the day. When the clock showed that it was actually ten, she had to decide how much courage she really had. Dared she ring Jake and ask why he hadn't come? Was he still working or had he simply decided to forget her?

She stood by the phone anxiously and then decided to ring. She was being foolish, she told herself. Jake had just not looked at the time. He had probably not even eaten all day. But as the telephone at his flat rang and rang Kathryn began to worry about more than her own place in his life. They had broken into her flat, wrecked it. Suppose they were doing the same to Jake's?

She hurried down to Ralph's place and told him.

'Look. I know how people can be when they're working,' he said, trying to calm her down. 'I'm like that myself. He's probably forgotten.'

'Jake would not forget me,' Kathryn said strongly. She could remember Jake's face when they had made love, remember the things he had said to her, the way he was afraid she would leave him. 'I'm going over there.'

'Aw, Kathryn!' Ralph moaned. 'I've only just got in from taking Rosie back home. You decide to go and I have to go too. For all we know he might be on his way here now. If we cross on the way he'll take it out on me.'

'Stay here,' Kathryn advised. 'If he comes you can tell him where I am.'

She made for the door but Ralph came with her, a resigned look on his face.

'You go, I go,' he stated. 'If I let you go alone, he'll take that out on me too.'

'He is not violent!' Kathryn snapped, turning on Ralph with flashing eyes.

'Not to you. Let me remind you about that creep, Colin, though. You told me about that particular violence yourself.'

He insisted on going with her and got out his car from the parking place round the back of the market. It was quite dark by now but Kathryn was too worried about Jake to give any thought to someone waiting to waylay them. They had finished here and they would not bother to come back. She agreed with Jake about that.

At the block where Jake lived the doorman let them in. He recognized Kathryn and told them that as far as he knew Mr Trelawny had not been out at all.

'I don't always know, though,' he admitted. 'If any of the residents take their cars then they don't come through the foyer. There's a lift from each floor to the garage.'

Kathryn vaguely remembered that, although she had been too tired when Jake had brought her home to really pay much attention. They went up to his flat and the doorman came with them. Jake was not in but Kathryn insisted that he use his key to get inside and have a look. He was not too happy about it but when her mind was made up Kathryn could be very forceful, and her mind was made up now.

She looked round the flat but there was nothing out of place.

'I told you,' Ralph muttered in embarrassment. 'He'll be back at your flat, fuming.'

'Perhaps,' Kathryn said. 'We'll look in the garage all the same.'

'He probably called a taxi,' Ralph said irritably, and she pounced on that at once.

'Then why wasn't he seen going out?'

'There is that, sir,' the doorman intervened worriedly. 'We'd better go down to the garage.

'Could anyone get into the building by using the garage lift?' Kathryn wanted to know, but he shook his head firmly.

'No, miss. The lift will take the residents down but they can't bring it up without the key. They all have one for security. The lift doors stay open down there but if anyone was waiting to try and sneak up it would be a waste of time. No key means no access. All they could do would be to stay in the lift until someone called it up. Then I would have been told about it. There are no new residents. They all know each other by sight. This place is very secure.'

Kathryn thought of the fire that had been pushed through Jake's letter box but she said nothing about it. Jake had thought they had used the fire escape and left in the same way. They were not dealing with amateurs here. Giles Renfrew had his helpers well organized. He always had done.

They saw Jake as soon as they stepped out of the lift. He was lying beside his car. He seemed to be covered with blood, and at first Kathryn thought he was dead. She didn't scream, though. Ralph tried to hold her back but she pushed him aside and ran to Jake, sitting on the hard concrete floor of the garage and lifting his dark head to cradle it on her lap.

'Call an ambulance!' she ordered when the doorman stood there looking stupefied. He went back to the lift and as Ralph came to crouch beside her she rocked Jake against her, murmuring his name in a distracted voice, stroking his hair and ignoring Ralph altogether.

'Don't die, Jake,' she whispered distractedly. 'Don't you dare die on me.' There were tears on her face but her voice was angry, demanding, as if she could will Jake to live whether he wanted to or not.

Jake groaned and Kathryn gave a little cry, cradling him close. Ralph knew better than to speak to her but he was greatly relieved. Jake Trelawny was alive, even though he looked as if he had been badly beaten up.

'They must have been waiting for him, taken him by surprise,' he muttered, because he was absolutely sure that it would have had to be more than one and they would have to have had the element of surprise. Jake was too strong, too ferocious. He wouldn't have liked to tackle Jake himself even with a heavy club, surprise or not.

Jake stirred and half opened his eyes and Kathryn stroked his face gently.

'Jake,' she whispered. 'Oh, Jake.'

'Kathryn? You came for me? Have they managed to get away?'

'There was nobody here, Jake. We came down to see if your car was here and found you like this. What happened to you?'

'I don't really know,' he managed weakly. 'There seemed to be so damned many of them.'

'Never mind for now. Don't talk,' she said, hushing him. 'An ambulance will be here soon.'

He closed his eyes and they thought he was drifting back into unconsciousness, but his hand came up to hold Kathryn's and when she bent to kiss his fingers he even managed a smile.

'Let's go home, Kathryn,' he muttered. 'Let's go back to Pengarron where you belong. It's peaceful there and you'll make it happy.'

'We'll go, Jake,' she promised. 'I'm going to decorate it and clean it until it sparkles. We'll get all that lovely garden back to normal. I'll make it happy. We'll go as soon as you're better.'

He closed his eyes, his fingers tightening on hers.

'That will be tomorrow, then,' he whispered. 'Too many people here. We'll go back even if we have to live with your aunt Clare until Pengarron is ready for you.'

'Yes, Jake,' she agreed fiercely, with tears running down her cheeks. 'We'll go tomorrow.' She loved him so much and he was hurt badly. At that moment she was afraid of nobody at all. She was wild with anger.

'Don't leave me, Kathryn,' he said faintly.

'I won't leave you, Jake. I'll never leave you.'

Jake was to be kept in hospital for a few days, mainly for observation. He was badly bruised and there was some worry about concussion, but basically he was so strong that no real damage had been done. Kathryn went to visit him as soon as she could, expecting that he would instantly return to the subject of Pengarron. As soon as she had known he would be all right, she had been overwhelmed with happiness that he wanted her to go with him to his family home. It was a commitment.

He was propped up with pillows, talking on the phone when she went into his room, and he looked across at her and held out his hand. When his fingers closed round hers, he pulled her to the bed so that she could sit beside him. He still went on listening, his face alive with a sort of furious enjoyment. She knew him. He had trapped his prey.

'The paper's out,' he told her when he'd put the phone down. 'Jimmy is sending me a copy round right away. They've done an extra edition to get the news out early. Apparently the editor couldn't wait for the normal day of Jimmy's column. Before this day is over, Renfrew will know what it's like to be scared. And you'll be safe.'

'And what about you?' Kathryn asked quietly, worried that he would let her go when he knew she was safe.

He held her hand and carried it to his lips.

'I'll be with you – unless you think I'm too repulsive after that beating?'

'No, you look reasonably all right,' Kathryn murmured teasingly, her heart bursting with joy at the look in his eyes. 'For a fairly untamed tiger you might even pass unnoticed.'

She touched his face gently, regret in her eyes at the bruises she saw.

'They hurt you, Jake,' she said softly. 'I could kill them. I *will* if I see them.'

That slow smile grew on his face and he used his grip to pull her closer.

'Are we going to Pengarron, Kathryn?' he asked huskily. 'Will you live with me, let me love you? Will you appear every time I look up? Will you haunt my woods and sleep in my bed?'

'Oh, Jake!' She leaned forward and he pulled her against him, his lips searching urgently for hers. 'Jake! You're hurt,' she protested, afraid that this passionate embrace would injure him more.

'Cure me,' he breathed against her lips. 'Cure me, Kathryn. Nothing is ever going to be right again unless I can hold you.'

His lips closed fiercely over hers and he pulled her down to him, ignoring any pain just to have her close. She was lying in his arms where she belonged and his desire raged at the feel of her next to him.

His hand closed possessively over her breast. He was hungry for her. The moment she had walked through the door his heart had taken off like a machine out of control. He needed her softness, her untutored passion, her willing acceptance of him when everyone else either feared him or suspected him.

'Come into bed with me,' he murmured fiercely against her mouth, and Kathryn's face flushed like a rose when a voice from the doorway said,

'My God, Trelawny! You need locking up. Leave the poor girl alone, you brute.'

Jake reluctantly let her go and Kathryn turned round to see a tall, ugly-looking man grinning at them.

'Thought I was the ward sister, didn't you?' he taunted, winking wickedly at Kathryn.

'Jimmy Warrender,' Jake introduced, pulling himself up in the bed and giving the newcomer a sardonic look.' He's a nasty part of my past.'

'I have to state that I prefer the look of your future,' Jimmy drawled. 'Is she real?'

'Only when I have my hands on her,' Jake said, taking Kathryn's hand and engulfing it in his. 'At other times she's merely an illusion. Where's the paper?' His mocking tone changed and Kathryn instantly felt like an insignificant being on the edge of a powerful force.

'I'll go,' she said quickly, but Jake merely tightened his hold on her.

'No. Jimmy will go as soon as he's told me the news. My interest in him is strictly limited. You're here to cure me.' He turned his dark head and smiled at her. 'We have somewhere to go, don't we? The sooner you cure me, the sooner we can go home.'

They did have somewhere to go – Pengarron – and Jake was calling it home. She smiled into his eyes and relaxed. Whatever happened they would be together. She waited for the news with as much interest as Jake.

'The paper hit the streets first thing,' Jimmy said with cold satisfaction. 'Renfrew's solicitor hit the phone an hour later.'

'And?' Jake asked quietly.

'We expressed astonishment and a great deal of journalistic interest. "Mr Giles Renfrew. Really? Are you saying that there are parallels in this story with his own life? Of course we had no idea. This thriller will be fiction, but if Mr Renfrew can point out similarities between his own life and the story then we would certainly be interested. Would he care to make a statement, do you think?" There was a hasty retreat. He said he would consult his client.'

'Now we wait to see if his nerve holds.' Jake looked at Warrender and smiled that cold smile he had that had at first frightened Kathryn.

'He's not going to be put up for a safe seat when this breaks open. Will he go for cover now or try to brazen it out?'

'Time,' Jake murmured softly, 'will tell. I want my life back under my own control and that's all I want. Renfrew wants power and glory. Maybe he'll have one last throw at things.'

'He could turn exceptionally nasty,' Jimmy Warrender warned, with a quick glance at Kathryn.

'Perhaps, but I've banked on his need for secrecy, his obsession with it. From now on things are out in the open. All he can hope for is to fade quietly away.' He took Kathryn's hand in his again. 'If you're worried about Kathryn, don't bother. From now on we intend to stick very close together.'

'I noticed when I came in,' Jimmy murmured drily. 'I'm not worried about her but the nurses might object. I could send a photographer round if you like. More publicity for your forthcoming book?'

'Go!' Jake said threateningly. 'The news was good but your presence is no longer required.'

Jimmy turned obediently to the door and gave Kathryn one of his wolfish grins.

'You're making a big mistake, my dear. Trelawny is barely one step above the origin of the species.'

'What do you think?' Jake asked as the door closed behind his visitor.

'He's seriously ugly,' Kathryn murmured, with a nervous glance at the closed door.

'I was asking for your opinion about our present predicament with Renfrew,' Jake pointed out, grinning at her.

'Oh!' She gave a little shrug and nibbled at her lip. 'I never even thought about that. I'm always much more interested in trivia.'

Jake gave a shout of laughter and pulled her close.

'Next time I see Warrender I'll sneer at him and point out that he's merely trivia.' Kathryn looked horrified and his dark eyes fastened on her mouth.

'Don't nibble at your lip like that,' he warned seductively. 'It attracts my attention.'

Jake had used a lot of pressure to get the things that Kathryn needed delivered with speed. She spent every spare minute sorting out her flat and very soon it was almost back to normal. Between them, she and Ralph had a good many contacts in the art world and the pictures were well on the way to being restored. A couple of them were already back on the walls.

She went, one afternoon, to Ralph's viewing at the gallery. Evenings were reserved for her visits to Jake, but when she came hurrying home to get ready to go to see him, he was already there, waiting for her. He was sitting on the floor of the mean little landing outside her door and Kathryn was shocked to see him back so soon. She was also quite stunned at the way he simply sat on the floor with his back to the wall. It didn't seem like Jake at all.

'What happened?' When the lift stopped, Kathryn rushed across to him and he got to his feet and smiled down at her.

'I came out of hospital. I was bored and in any case, I have things to do.'

'Come inside,' Kathryn muttered anxiously, inserting her keys and opening the door. 'I'm sure you shouldn't be out yet.'

'I'm fine,' he said vaguely. His eyes were roaming around, inspecting the room. 'It's almost back to normal.'

'When all the pictures are back up,' Kathryn agreed. She went to put the kettle on, almost afraid to look at him closely. Jake had been doing a lot of thinking. She knew without being told.

He came into the kitchen but she did not turn round.

'Will you be prepared to give all this up?'

'The flat? No,' she said quietly. 'I own it after all. Why should I give it up?'

'You said you would come with me to Pengarron.' Jake's voice was almost bitter, and she turned swiftly and caught a look on his face that reminded her of a wounded animal. The half-tamed tiger was hurt, preparing to defend himself.

'You asked me to live with you, to haunt the woods and sleep in the same bed,' she reminded him softly. 'I'm waiting. I don't want to go there without you. Will you give up your flat?'

'No!' Jake looked startled. 'It's my London place.'

'This is *my* London place,' Kathryn pointed out firmly. 'The difference is that I own this place. What a waste of money. I was hoping that this one flat would do. After all, we'll be spending most of our time at Pengarron.'

'Kathryn!' He swept her up into his arms, holding her close, burying his face in her hair. 'I was afraid you might change your mind about Pengarron. I thought you were running out on me, leaving me.'

'How could I?' She wound her arms round his neck and smiled up at him. 'I have some haunting to do and a lot of polishing.'

'Where have you been sleeping while I've been in hospital?' Jake asked when he finally let her go.

'Oh, I've been sleeping with Ralph – in a manner of speaking. He let me have his settee. The bed came today, though, so I'm back to normal.'

When she looked up Jake was grinning at her, and she knew she had reassured him. It was something she would have to do for a long time. Somehow she knew that Jake didn't expect happiness. She would make Pengarron live again, wipe out the past. She would transform it.

Jake went back to his manuscript. Kathryn wanted to finish her flat before they went to Cornwall and he made no demands on her about that. They were both working. When she was with him he worked better, just knowing she was around, and Kathryn showed that she could be a tyrant, insisting that he ate at the proper times and went out for fresh air every day.

It was almost like being married, but always at the back of her mind she saw Gillian. She never mentioned it and neither did Jake. It was a shadow that just stayed there, silent and threatening, as if somewhere that beautiful face was laughing at them.

The papers had followed up Jimmy Warrender's article, delving into their archives to search for clues. The more daring of them even came up with ideas of their own. 'WHO IS THE MYSTERY MAN?' 'WHICH FUTURE MEMBER OF PARLIAMENT HAS A SECRET PAST?' Kathryn was intrigued but Jake was disgruntled.

'Seven-day wonder,' he snapped one day when she pored over the pages. 'It will be old news soon and gone to make way for something else. Today's shock revelation is tomorrow's boring copy. That's how the newspaper business operates.'

'Is Renfrew going to get away with things, then?'

'No!' Jake said savagely. 'Over my dead body!'

It frightened her because it could so nearly have been just that, if Jake had not been so strong. Now was not the time to attempt to change the untamed tiger, though.

Two days later Giles Renfrew came. He came in the evening when Jake was still working and Kathryn was sitting in another room touching up some of her pictures.

Jake seemed to have a sixth sense, because when she got up to answer the door he shot out of his study and ordered her away.

'Stay out of sight,' he said quietly. 'I don't encourage visitors so this isn't a neighbourly call. Don't come out until I know who it is.'

'But supposing it's one of them?' Kathryn whispered anxiously, but he just looked at her severely and pointed to the door of the sitting room.

'Kathryn!' There was a gentle menace in his voice and Kathryn went. She forgave him instantly, even though it was not in her nature to allow bullying. She supposed, though, that any beast would defend his lair. All the same, she looked round for anything that could be used as a weapon and left the door just slightly ajar so that she could peer through the crack.

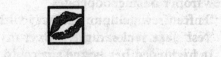

CHAPTER 15

She recognized Giles Renfrew instantly and geared herself up for trouble, thinking with some real longing of the old-fashioned umbrella at Aunt Clare's cottage. There wasn't even a good old-fashioned poker in this modern flat.

'May I come in?'

Knowing what she did of him, Kathryn was astonished by the beautiful, cultured tone. Of course he had been an officer in the army at one time, and now he was trying to get into public life after years as a rich businessman. All the same, his dirty tricks and his connections with lowlife had left with her the impression that he would be somehow coarse and sordid. He was nothing of the sort. He was beautifully dressed. He looked like a gentleman.

'Is this a case of Mohammed coming to the mountain or are you thinking of tackling me single-handed?' Jake asked menacingly.

'We need to talk.'

'I've already talked,' Jake reminded him with icy sarcasm: 'It's all over the papers. You can come in but I'll tell you right now that the only word I want to hear from you is goodbye.'

Renfrew walked into the flat, looking round with interest as Jake closed the door.

'In here?' Renfrew asked smoothly, indicating the sitting room where Kathryn was hiding, and Jake walked forward and opened the door.

'Why not?' he rasped. 'I may as well be comfortable while I listen to your suggestions.'

Kathryn could see Jake's dilemma at once. He could not stand talking in the hall, there was very little room and nowhere at all to sit down, and he would not take Renfrew into his study; the manuscript was there. Apart from the bedrooms and the kitchen there was nowhere else to go. She sat down quickly and assumed a deep interest in a magazine.

Jake came in, glanced at her with approval and led his unwelcome visitor into the room.

'Good evening, Miss Holden,' Renfrew said pleasantly, and Jake's face became savage.

'Don't even look at her or I'll take you apart,' he threatened harshly. 'This battle was always between you and me. Now it's over. The only reason you're allowed in my flat is so that you can tell me your future plans, but take any interest in her and I'll throw you out head-first.'

'I'll give you three million pounds to suppress the book,' Renfrew said straight out, and Kathryn's eyes felt as if they were popping from her head. She knew that Jake earned a lot, she had vaguely thought that he might be a millionaire by now, but hearing that sort of money mentioned quite casually left her almost open-mouthed.

'I earn my money the hard way, the clean way,' Jake bit out. 'No amount of money could buy me off. I want you out of the country and out of my life. I also want to know what happened to my wife.'

'She's with me at the moment. She sought me out. I never went looking for her. A beautiful woman.' He glanced at Kathryn. 'You seem to have a flair for collecting things of beauty.'

'At the moment I'm only interested in collecting a head,' Jake rasped. 'Yours!'

'But you would like your wife back, wouldn't you?'

'You can keep her,' Jake said coldly. 'Take her with you when you go. All I want to know is that she's safe.'

Kathryn felt her face fall. Jake was worried about Gillian. The words he had used hit her hard before she came to her senses. Of course he wanted her to be safe, or his trouble with the police would never end. In any case, he would want to know that Gillian was all right. He was not a cruel man, whatever Gillian had done to him he would not want her to be harmed.

Renfrew watched for a minute, his calculating gaze going from one to the other, then he said quietly, 'You obviously have all you want here.' He nodded towards Kathryn. 'I've heard how you race after her when you think she's in danger. I've also heard how she came wildly to your defence when the police were harassing you.'

'So, you even have informants amongst the police?' Jake noted coldly.

'Money talks,' Renfrew said with a little smile. He glanced back at Kathryn and then looked steadily at Jake. 'Take the three million and settle down happily. I'll arrange for Gillian to reappear with a suitable story. I'll even take her off your hands. You can divorce her and have what you really want. Gillian tells me you've not had a happy life. Get your happiness now.'

'With your help?' Jake asked scornfully. 'We need nothing from you – neither your dirty money nor your blessing.'

Renfrew shrugged, smiling the little smile again.

'I'll live it down.'

'Maybe, if you live it down about a million miles away,' Jake snapped.

'Just as a matter of interest,' Renfrew asked, 'where do you keep your manuscript? I assumed it would not be here. I gave you more credit than that sort of stupidity.'

'Yes. You imagined I would be willing to let Kathryn keep it, to place her in danger!'

'It entered my mind. My people were perhaps a little too enthusiastic, I apologize, Miss Holden.' He then glanced up at Jake, who was still standing, towering over him like a dark threat. 'So where *do* you keep the damned thing, Trelawny?'

'A copy with my bank, another with my solicitor and another with my publisher,' Jake told him with a grim smile. 'They had instructions. If any one of the copies was destroyed or stolen, one of the remaining copies was to be given to the Press immediately.'

'Clever,' Renfrew murmured admiringly.

'Modern technology,' Jake snapped. 'Let's get down to business. I want you out of the country, the sooner the better. I want Gillian with you – openly with you. I have the police to calm. At the moment I'm under suspicion. Gillian stays healthy and happy.'

'Health I can guarantee. Happiness is elusive,' Renfrew murmured, and Jake glared at him blackly.

'Not with her. Just cover her with diamonds and furs. Happiness is then assured.'

'*If* I leave the country,' Renfrew said quietly.

'Oh, you'll leave the country,' Jake promised him. 'I've been expecting you for a few days, Renfrew. I was all ready for you. This conversation is being taped. It was being taped from the moment you stepped through the front door.' He smiled grimly into the startled face before him. 'Modern technology,' he repeated sardonically. 'There are three machines running at this moment. Unless you feel like taking me on and then searching the place, I've got you.'

'All right.' For the first time the suave face showed signs of annoyance. 'There are other places, other governments.'

'If they're sufficiently obscure,' Jake remarked drily. 'My books have worldwide sales. You'll have to find a place with some outlandish language if you want to go into public life. If, on the other hand, you decide to stay here and live life a little more quietly, I'll do another book. This time it will be factual, no holds barred. I'll risk the lawyers' writs.'

'Why the hell did you pick me out for punishment?' Renfrew asked angrily. 'I never knew you. I'd never done anything to you. Why me?'

'I didn't pick you out. I was doing a book and I remembered you. There was to be no mention at all of you, just odd bits I knew about you from my days of being a journalist. It was only to add colour. Nobody would have given you a thought.'

'But Gillian said . . .'

'Ah,' Jake murmured with satisfaction, 'Gillian. I suspected as much. Her way into your life, Renfrew. She has her methods. I fell for them once myself. She was wrong, though. I never went after you until you intruded into my life.' He glanced at Kathryn. 'Your biggest mistake was intruding into *her* life. No arrangements, Renfrew. I've got a place on my wall for your head.'

When Renfrew had gone, Kathryn waited for Jake to come back into the room after locking the door.

'What will he do now?' she asked.

'He will either go away or he will creep back into the woodwork and wait for better times.'

'If he does that, what will you do?' Kathryn wanted to know, and Jake began to pace restlessly about.

'I'm not sure. I want to get on with life. Now that we're together I want to be able to wake up each day and just be with you. I want to go home, wipe out the past, see you working in the woods.'

'Will he let us just get on with life, do you think?'

'There's not a lot he can do about it,' Jake assured her grimly. 'He already has the full attention of the

Press. When my book comes out, attention will be renewed. Anyone interested in him will buy the book and the papers will all be talking about it. I would think that for quite a time television cameras will be following him around. He knows he can't get the manuscript, and now he knows about the taping I did tonight. He may just go quietly.'

All the same Jake looked thoughtful, and Kathryn could see that whatever his further ideas were he was not about to tell her at the moment. Something troubled him. Sooner or later she would know, but for now she would have to wait.

'What about your wife?' she asked quietly, and Jake turned quickly at the sound of her voice. He seemed to know her so well.

'You can call her Gillian,' he said softly. 'She can't hurt you in any way. The moment she comes to the surface you won't need to think of her at all.' He reached for her and wrapped her in his arms, looking down into her eyes. 'You've rarely left my mind since I first saw you,' he whispered. 'If I lost you I wouldn't know what to do.'

'You won't lose me, Jake,' Kathryn assured him gently. 'I'm a very stubborn person. Besides,' she added with a mischievous smile, 'how am I going to get my hands on Pengarron if I leave you?'

Kathryn stood back and looked round the room. The huge glass door was open to the sunshine and the gloom that normally rested on Pengarron Manor was beginning to go. The decorators had almost finished and she had had no opposition from Jake when she had planned the renovations. All he had wanted was to get on with the manuscript that was now finished, to hear her moving around the house, giving orders to the men and being with him every day. He never passed her without stopping to put his arms around her. Every time she saw him, his eyes devoured her possessively. He was happy.

She put a final gloss to the great round table that stood in the middle of the room. She had brought and arranged flowers from the garden and now she lifted the ornate silver bowl back onto the table and looked at everything with satisfaction.

'Almost finished,' she told Aunt Clare with a smile. 'I couldn't have done it without you and your friends.'

'We've loved it,' Clare said enthusiastically. 'To see this house lived in again, to see Jake so happy. It's wonderful.' She took off her apron and handed it to Kathryn. 'Now, the cleaners we organized will be down to see you early tomorrow. They're both good and reliable, both girls from my days at school. See what you make of them, Kathryn, and don't forget that you and Jake are coming to me for dinner tonight.'

She went off briskly and Kathryn stood at the door watching her with a smile on her face. It was a long time since her aunt had been head of the local school. The 'girls' would probably be two fat matrons.

She sighed happily and went back to give one last shine to the hall table. Now she could get back on with her own work, go out into the woods and finish off her book. She was happy too. Loving Jake, being in this house, wandering in the woods around filled her days with joy. Being in his arms at night was heaven. Her old life seemed almost like a dream.

And there was family. Aunt Clare had taken Jake under her wing and he suffered it with a wry grin. Her aunt was always popping in and Kathryn knew that Jake liked it. The danger seemed far away now. They had heard nothing from Renfrew at all.

As she put down the cloth she had been using and turned around to go and find Jake the sunlight was blocked for a moment, just as it had been once before when she had been alone here. But now the outline was not so big, not so familiar. It was altogether more slender and fine. It was a woman.

She moved into the room with complete assurance, and as soon as her eyes adjusted from the brilliant sunlight Kathryn knew who it was. Gillian had come back.

Fear clutched at Kathryn as it had never done before. Jake's wife was here and suddenly her own hold on Jake seemed tenuous, fragile, unable to last. He had married this woman, lived with her, and now she was back to claim him, walking into the house as if she belonged.

'Very nice,' the cool voice said. 'What a change. The last time I was here this place was disgusting. What firm do you work for?'

'I don't work for any firm,' Kathryn told her in a choked voice, and Gillian nodded, having obviously

376

known that already. The remark had been simply a cruel jab that came with a superior attitude.

'Of course not. You're the girl who is living with my husband. I'm really surprised. You look so young. Doesn't living in sin bother you?' She stared at Kathryn with cold blue eyes. 'Maybe not, though. He's very attractive. They all flock after him.'

Kathryn had felt trapped, cornered, but now her temper began to rise at the sheer effrontery of this woman. Jake loved *her*, he proved it every day, and this woman had hurt him – as most people had.

'What do you want?' she asked angrily.

'I want my husband, of course!'

'And what will you do with him when you get him?' a softly menacing voice demanded, and Kathryn turned to see Jake standing in the door-way that led from the inner hall and the stairs. He had come silently, had listened, and now his presence seemed to be all over the room, dominating, dark.

'I've come home,' Gillian said calmly, looking across at him with a thin smile.

'Home? You were here for one brief night, raging and shouting.' His voice dropped lower still. 'And then, as I recall, you *died*, Gillian.'

It was frightening, making Kathryn's blood run cold. She had always known he would defend his lair and now it was endangered.

'Is that a threat?' Gillian asked shrilly. 'Are you threatening to kill me? Because if you are . . .'

'According to popular belief, I already have killed you,' Jake said silkily. 'What is that saying about being hung for a sheep?'

'Jake!' Kathryn looked at him in horror and he walked forward and put his hand on her shoulder.

'Don't worry, nymph,' he said softly. 'I have too much to live for. Go out into the garden. I'll deal with her.'

Kathryn left with some reluctance. She had not liked the look on Jake's face and this woman had put him through hell. Now she was back. What did she want? Had she come to try to claim Jake or was there something else? Something that was still hidden?

She walked down the garden towards the sea, her ears attuned for any noise, any shouting, her heart beating loudly enough to be heard. Gillian was back. It was either the final piece of the puzzle or the beginning of a nightmare.

Inside the house Jake looked at his wife with distaste.

'You expected me to be arrested when you disappeared,' he said flatly.

'Something like that,' she murmured in an amused voice. 'I'd had my eye on Giles for some time. He's so rich and so cultured. Giles thought my disappearance would stop you in your tracks, prevent the book from being published. In any case, you were such a bore, my dear. All that work, all that silence. There were no parties with you, Jake, nothing exciting.' She glanced at him sceptically. 'Your hair's too long. Your skin is too dark. You're almost uncouth.'

'A half-tamed beast – I know. Kathryn thinks that too.'

'Well, there you are, then. You'll have no luck with her either.'

'You're so wrong,' Jake said quietly. 'There's a good deal of difference between Kathryn and some-one like you. She cares about me. If I'm a beast then I'm *her* beast. Kathryn is prepared to fight beside me and for me.'

'Giles said she was beautiful,' Gillian murmured, turning to watch Kathryn walk down towards the sea. 'I heard she was lame.'

'She's quite better now, thank you,' Jake said coldly. 'What do you want? Get down to it or get out.'

'Giles wants me to go overseas with him,' Gillian told him as she started to wander around, looking at things.

Jake kept his eyes on her, watching her closely. He didn't trust her an inch.

'You're lucky. I would have thought he would have ditched you by now, especially after the wrong information you gave him. Of course, you're co-conspirators, though, aren't you? Tied together by crime. It should be interesting.'

'I don't want to go to some godforsaken hole!' Gillian snapped, spinning round to face him. 'If you want that odd girl, divorce me and give me half of everything. I'll not stand in your way.'

'How kind,' Jake murmured wryly. 'Yes. I do want her. You seem to have forgotten something, though. Either you're dead, and I killed you, or you've been living with Renfrew, hiding away and wasting police time. Laying your hands on anything of mine is going to be tricky, especially as I'll fight you to the last breath.'

'Maybe Giles hasn't finished with you yet,' Gillian told him viciously. 'He's a clever man.'

'He's a crook. What can he do? If anything happens to me the book goes out at once. The clues are now so strong that in all probability he'll be arrested.'

'Something might happen to *her*,' Gillian threatened spitefully, indicating Kathryn, who now stood at the end of the garden by the drop to the sea.

Her red hair was blowing in the wind, her dress billowing out behind her. A water sprite watching the tossing waves.

'Then I would kill him,' Jake said harshly, his eyes on Kathryn too. 'She's my life. She is always going to be my life.'

'You're stupid!' Gillian snapped, glaring at him. 'Nobody is going to put up with you indefinitely.'

The telephone in the inner hall rang and Jake gave her a menacing look and went to answer it. Gillian watched Kathryn for a second and then went outside, walking quietly over the grass, her mouth tight with anger.

'So you're going to tame him?' Her voice made Kathryn jump. She hadn't heard Gillian approach and now she was almost behind her, standing close.

'I'm not even going to attempt it,' Kathryn said quietly. 'I love him just as he is.'

'In that case, you're a fool,' Gillian said scathingly. 'Jake is and always was a lost cause. He could have had a terrific life, but he stays inside, working, growling at everyone. People are scared of him. He's almost a recluse, anti-social.'

'Then we suit each other,' Kathryn assured her, watching the sea and smiling. 'And I'm not scared of him. I'm like that too. I like painting in the woods, walking on the cliffs, watching the sea . . .'

'It's a long drop,' Gillian pointed out, and Kathryn heard something in her voice that frightened her. She looked down at the rocks. She was almost at the edge of the cliff, and although the drop was not too far it was too far to survive.

Danger was all around her and she knew it. She could almost hear Gillian's thoughts. She tensed up in readiness.

'Don't touch her!' Jake warned savagely. He too had approached in silence and Gillian turned, fear on her own face.

'I wasn't going to touch her,' she protested, too quickly. She gave him a nasty smile. 'If I had been thinking about it I would have already done it, wouldn't I? It would have been too late then. You could have done nothing about it.'

'I could have picked you up and dropped you down onto the rocks,' Jake said, with such soft certainty that Gillian went pale.

'I'm going.' She turned but Jake caught her arm.

'Not yet,' he corrected quietly. 'I saw you arrive, Gillian. I left you to Kathryn for a few moments at first because I was calling the police. They've just phoned back. They're on their way. You wait for them and you wait where I can keep an eye on you. The police are very interested in you. They want to know exactly where you've been and why. You can pass the time thinking of answers. They'll need some. Go back to the house and don't try to run. I would hunt you down in seconds.' He held out his hand to Kathryn. 'Come here, love,' he said.

She went to him instantly and he took her hand tightly in his. It was the first time he had ever called her that and inside she was glowing with happiness. When Jake said something, he meant it. Gillian stalked off in front of them and Kathryn looked at the house. It did not look cold in the sunlight any more. It was going to be a real home for both of them. The final piece of the jigsaw had slotted into place.

The local police came and, hard on their heels, Inspector Harrison.

'What the hell are you doing down here?' Jake snapped when he saw him.

'Vacation, Mr Trelawny. It's a beautiful part of the world. I'm staying a few miles down the coast. I just happened to be around when your call came in.'

Jake snorted in disbelief. The bloodhound had been on his trail even when he'd thought he was happily free.

'Well, you've got her now,' he pointed out coldly. 'No doubt she's got some story that you're going to believe and no doubt it will all be my fault finally.'

'Oh, I don't think so, Mr Trelawny. We're not as stupid as we look, you know. A car picked your wife up that night after you had gone to London – a very distinctive-looking car, a Rolls. One of the local police spotted it. We asked him to keep quiet. We've had our eye on Giles Renfrew for a number of years but he's never slipped up. We did know his car, though. Of course we didn't know if she was alive and we couldn't face him with it. He's too slippery. Now you seem to have him well and truly hooked, and out pops your wife right on cue.'

'All this time you've let me think –!' Jake began furiously, and the inspector shook his head sadly, the mournful bloodhound expression back on his face.

'It was necessary, Mr Trelawny. This was a very intricate thing and we couldn't risk anything getting out. That man could have been a future Prime Minister. Have you thought of that?'

'Yes, we have,' Kathryn intervened sharply. 'And I agree that it was tricky, but you should have relied on Jake's integrity.'

'He's a loner, Miss Holden. Loners are unpredictable. I was lucky to have the case handed over to me. Interesting to work with Special Branch . . . most interesting.' He turned to walk away and then turned back. 'I really would like a copy of your book when it comes out, Mr Trelawny.'

'Oh, certainly,' Jake snarled. 'Any bookshop. About nineteen pounds.'

'Jake!' Kathryn burst into laughter and grasped his arm. She turned to Inspector Harrison. 'I'll see that

383

you get a copy, Inspector,' she assured him. 'Would you like it signed?'

'That would be nice, Miss Holden, very nice.' He beamed at her and then walked out, nodding pleasantly to Jake. 'My wife will be thrilled,' he murmured as he left.

Jake stared after him in astonishment.

'He actually smiles,' he muttered. 'And he's got a wife. Bloody hell! Poor damned woman.'

Kathryn couldn't stop laughing. She was so happy she thought she might burst with joy.

'I wonder how many people will say that about me?' she asked impishly, and Jake growled at her and swung her up in the air, holding her above him and looking into her laughing green eyes.

'They'll never know,' he said huskily. 'I'm never going to let you out of the house.'

'Oh, Jake, thank you,' she laughed, and he let her slide down into his arms to capture her lips hungrily.

There was a big table on the lawn in front of the house and they were all sitting round it in cane chairs. Kathryn and Jake were entertaining. Aunt Clare had come just before lunch and Ralph had stayed the previous night. Rosie Cummings was with him and they had made a one-night stop before they went on to tour Cornwall. Rosie was looking for a good seascape, something wild, and Ralph intended to paint local fishermen.

'So what finally happened?' Clare wanted to know.

'The police collected Gillian and took her off our hands,' Kathryn said. 'She wasted a lot of police time and resources by disappearing like that. She's in trouble – big trouble.'

'She's not going to be able to get out of it as far as I can see,' Ralph mused. He looked across at Jake. 'What will she do? Plead loss of memory?'

Jake gave him an approving glance,

'It seems to be her only way out. She was muttering about that when they came. If she implicates Renfrew then she's in even more deeply, so I imagine she'll keep quiet. No doubt she's been promised rewards for her silence.'

'He left the country. Did you know?' Aunt Clare cut in eagerly. 'It was on television. I was watching it with Jean Pengelly. He was going through the airport building with a whole horde of TV cameramen trailing him. I wonder where he's gone?'

'Somewhere obscure, no doubt,' Ralph surmised. 'What do you think he will do, Jake? Will he lie low and then come back?'

'Not if he has any sense,' Jake muttered. 'I could still fly into a rage at the thought of him.'

'Please don't,' Kathryn said firmly, her hand coming to his arm. He grinned down at her and covered her hand with his. Kathryn was well on the way to taming him.

Clare looked from one to the other and smiled with satisfaction. Things had worked out very nicely. As she had been saying to Jean Pengelly only the other day, Kathryn was now living close to her and they were both obviously happy. Not that she had Jean's hopes that Pengarron Manor would soon echo to the sound of parties. Jake and Kathryn liked to be quiet and they liked their own company best.

'Where had Gillian been hiding?' Rosie suddenly asked.

'We never found out,' Jake said. 'But Renfrew has plenty of property. It would have been easy enough to tuck her away somewhere. She could have been in his London place all the time for all we know, although it would have been difficult to keep her away from the bright lights.'

'I wonder who it was round the side of the house watching me that day?' Kathryn mused. 'I always had the idea that it was Gillian.'

'It may have been,' Jake said. 'She might have been brought down here to search the house and found you wandering around. She probably had a key. She was always good at picking things up that she might need in the future.'

'It's a creepy thought.' Kathryn gave a little shudder. 'She probably had someone with her and yet they let me get away.'

'Maybe at that time it hadn't dawned on them who you were,' Ralph said. 'In any case, she may have been alone.'

'And you do look just like an artist, dear,' Aunt Clare pointed out comfortably.

'Hmm,' Kathryn muttered. 'I was quick off the mark too.'

'You probably scared them,' Jake pointed out, grinning at her. 'You frequently scare me.'

Snowy walked from the house and advanced in a stately manner across the lawn.

'It's a very big cat,' Rosie mused, watching with awe.

'Well slimmed-down, though,' Ralph stated, with a critical glance at his old lodger. 'Considerably tamed too, but don't try to put that to the test. He likes Kathryn and Jake and there his attempts at being civilized fade out.'

'Well, you've all fitted in very nicely,' Clare murmured with satisfaction. 'What do you plan to do now?'

'Get married – as soon as Gillian is out of the picture,' Jake stated firmly. 'The divorce papers are all drawn up. It's just a matter of time. Meanwhile, we wait here and get on with our lives.'

'As you're settled here, do you want to sell your flat, Kathryn?' Rosie asked, and Jake and Kathryn answered in unison.

'No!'

'It's our London place.' Kathryn said. 'Jake let his place go. It was simply a waste of money to keep that on.'

'She pointed that out to me,' Jake admitted with an amused glance at Kathryn. 'Anyway, we like the market, the men – and our immediate neighbour.'

Ralph gave him a stately bow of acknowledgement and kept quiet. He did not intend to tell either of them that the other day Colin Chalmers had called round in a very contrite manner. Ralph had dispatched him quite fiercely, with a few warnings about Jake Trelawny and the rage that could grow if anyone annoyed Kathryn. For himself, Ralph felt quite smug and satisfied. There was a definite feeling of being befriended by the king of the jungle when he saw Jake.

Later, when dinner was over and everyone had left, Jake and Kathryn stood inside the house and watched the sun setting over the sea. Snowy sat beside them, his eyes on the glorious colours in the evening sky.

'He's settled,' Kathryn said. 'He likes it here.'

'So do I,' Jake agreed, his arm coming round her. 'I can't remember how many times I thought of getting rid of this house, wiping out the past and forgetting all about it. Somehow, though, I never quite got around to it.' He kissed the top of her head. 'And then you appeared, drifting into the scenery, changing it. You always belonged here.'

'Are you happy, Jake?' she asked quietly.

'Happier than I've ever been in my life. I love you.'

'You've never said that before,' Kathryn reminded him, and he pulled her closer.

'You knew, though. You always know. I rarely have to tell you anything.'

'I love you too,' she said softly.

'And I know that,' Jake murmured. 'Everything about us fits together and the house is glad. Don't you feel it?'

'Yes. I always liked this house. I always saw what it could be. I wanted to make it happy for you at last.'

They stood watching the fading colours of the sun and Kathryn said. 'Do you think Gillian was going to push me down the cliff that time?'

'I don't know,' Jake confessed tightly. 'I only know that when I saw her standing so close behind you, my heart almost stopped.'

'Oh, she thought about it,' Kathryn told him.

'How do you know?'

'Instinct. I've told you before. I have very strong instincts. I was ready for her, though. There was no need for you to worry.'

'What do you mean, ready for her?' Jake asked. He turned her to face him and looked down at her intently.

'I think very fast, you know,' Kathryn said seriously. 'I was waiting for her to make a move to touch me, then I would have thrown myself sideways and hooked my foot around her leg as I fell.'

She stood looking up at him seriously with her witch-green eyes, the setting sun turning her hair to fire, and Jake stared down at her in astonishment.

'Sometimes you terrify me,' he told her quietly.

'I've seen it on television several times,' she told him earnestly. 'It always works.'

Jake took her hand and led her away from the window, his face still stunned-looking.

'Let's go to bed,' he urged quietly. 'It's the only place where I know exactly how you're going to behave. At all other times you're quite crazy.'

'I'm clever, talented and brave,' Kathryn insisted huffily. '*You* said that!'

'I know,' Jake murmured. 'I forgot to add, though, that those attributes show to their best advantage when I have my arms around you. At all other times you're merely a nymph from the woods and definitely scary.'

'I'll surprise you yet!' Kathryn threatened crossly, and he swung her up into his arms, desire racing across his dark face.

'You always do, love,' he said softly. 'I'm always bewildered by how much I need you. Come to bed and tame me.'

Kathryn looped her arms around his neck, feeling the strength in him and smiling into his night-black eyes.

'I'll try,' she whispered, 'but it's a big task – an ongoing commitment.'

'We'll work at it,' Jake promised thickly. 'Everything else can wait.'

**THE EXCITING NEW NAME
IN WOMEN'S FICTION!**

PLEASE HELP ME TO HELP YOU!

Dear *Scarlet* Reader,

As Editor of *Scarlet* Books I want to make sure that the books I offer you every month are up to the high standards *Scarlet* readers expect. And to do that I need to know a little more about you and your reading likes and dislikes. So please spare a few minutes to fill in the short questionnaire on the following pages and send it to me.

Looking forward to hearing from you,

Sally Cooper

Editor-in-Chief, *Scarlet*

P.S. Make sure you look at these end pages in your *Scarlet* books each month! We hope to have some exciting news for you very soon.

QUESTIONNAIRE

Please tick the appropriate boxes to indicate your answers

1 Where did you get this Scarlet title?
Bought in supermarket ☐
Bought at my local bookstore ☐ Bought at chain bookstore ☐
Bought at book exchange or used bookstore ☐
Borrowed from a friend ☐
Other (please indicate) _____

2 Did you enjoy reading it?
A lot ☐   A little ☐   Not at all ☐

3 What did you particularly like about this book?
Believable characters ☐   Easy to read ☐
Good value for money ☐   Enjoyable locations ☐
Interesting story ☐   Modern setting ☐
Other _____

4 What did you particularly dislike about this book?
_____

5 Would you buy another Scarlet book?
Yes ☐   No ☐

6 What other kinds of book do you enjoy reading?
Horror ☐   Puzzle books ☐   Historical fiction ☐
General fiction ☐   Crime/Detective ☐   Cookery ☐
Other (please indicate) _____

7 Which magazines do you enjoy reading?
1. _____
2. _____
3. _____

And now a little about you –
8 How old are you?
Under 25 ☐   25–34 ☐   35–44 ☐
45–54 ☐   55–64 ☐   over 65 ☐

cont.

9 What is your marital status?
   Single ☐   Married/living with partner ☐
   Widowed ☐   Separated/divorced ☐

10 What is your current occupation?
   Employed full-time ☐   Employed part-time ☐
   Student ☐   Housewife full-time ☐
   Unemployed ☐   Retired ☐

11 Do you have children? If so, how many and how old are they?
   _____
   _____

12 What is your annual household income?
   under $15,000 ☐   or £10,000   ☐
   $15–25,000   ☐   or £10–20,000   ☐
   $25–35,000   ☐   or £20–30,000   ☐
   $35–50,000   ☐   or £30–40,000   ☐
   over $50,000 ☐   or £40,000   ☐

Miss/Mrs/Ms _____
Address _____
_____
_____

Thank you for completing this questionnaire. Now tear it out – put
it in an envelope and send it before 31 August, 1997, to:

Sally Cooper, Editor-in-Chief

USA/Can. address	*UK address/No stamp required*
SCARLET c/o London Bridge	SCARLET
85 River Rock Drive	FREEPOST LON 3335
Suite 202	LONDON W8 4BR
Buffalo	*Please use block capitals for*
NY 14207	*address*
USA	

DADAN/2/97

Scarlet titles coming next month:

TIME TO TRUST Jill Sheldon

Cord isn't impressed by the female of the species! And he certainly doesn't have 'time to trust' one of them! It's just as well, then, that Emily is equally reluctant to let a man into *her* life – even one as irresistible as Cord. But maybe the decision isn't theirs to make – for someone else has a deadly interest in their relationship!

THE PATH TO LOVE Chrissie Loveday

Kerrien has decided that a new life in Australia is just what she needs. So she takes a job with Dr Ashton Philips and is soon hoping there can be more between them than a working relationship. Then Ashton's sister, Kate, and his glamorous colleague, Martine, decide to announce his forthcoming marriage!

LOVERS AND LIARS Sally Steward

Eliot Kane is Leanne Warner's dream man, and she finds herself falling deeper and deeper in love with him. When Eliot confesses to having memory lapses and, even worse, dreams which feature . . . murder, Leanne begins to wonder if she's involved with a man who could be a very, very dangerous lover indeed.

LOVE BEYOND DESIRE Jessica Marchant

Amy is a thoroughly modern woman. She doesn't want marriage and isn't interested in commitment. Robert seems as happy as she is to keep their relationship casual. And what about Paul – does he want more from Amy than just friendship? Then Amy's safe and secure world is suddenly shrouded in darkness and she has to decide which of these two men she can trust with her heart . . . and her future happiness.